Praise for beloved romance author Betty Neels

"Neels is especially good at painting her scenes with choice words, and this adds to the charm of the story."
—*USATODAY.com's Happy Ever After* blog
on *Tulips for Augusta*

"Betty Neels surpasses herself with an excellent storyline, a hearty conflict and pleasing characters."
—*RT Book Reviews* on *The Right Kind of Girl*

"Once again Betty Neels delights readers with a sweet tale in which love conquers all."
—*RT Book Reviews* on *Fate Takes a Hand*

"One of the first Harlequin authors I remember reading. I was completely enthralled by the exotic locales… Her books will always be some of my favorites to re-read."
—*Goodreads* on *A Valentine for Daisy*

"I just love Betty Neels!… If you like a good old-fashioned romance…you can't go wrong with this author."
—*Goodreads* on *Caroline's Waterloo*

MIX
Paper | Supporting
responsible forestry
FSC® C001695

Published by
Mills & Boon
An imprint of Harlequin Enterprises (Australia) Pty Limited (ABN 47 001 180 918), a subsidiary of HarperCollins Publishers Australia Pty Limited (ABN 36 009 913 517)
Level 19, 201 Elizabeth Street
SYDNEY NSW 2000
AUSTRALIA

Printed and bound in Australia by McPherson's Printing Group

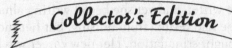

50TH ANNIVERSARY

Collector's Edition

BETTY NEELS

ONCE UPON A DREAM

MILLS & BOON

Romance readers around the world were sad to note the passing of **Betty Neels** in June 2001. Her career spanned thirty years, and she continued to write into her ninetieth year. To her millions of fans, Betty epitomized the romance writer, and yet she began writing almost by accident. She had retired from nursing, but her inquiring mind still sought stimulation. Her new career was born when she heard a lady in her local library bemoaning the lack of good romance novels. Betty's first book, *Sister Peters in Amsterdam*, was published in 1969, and she eventually completed 134 books. Her novels offer a reassuring warmth that was very much a part of her own personality. She was a wonderful writer, and she is greatly missed. Her spirit and genuine talent live on in all her stories.

CONTENTS

The Right Kind Of Girl

Chapter 1

Mrs Smith-Darcy had woken in a bad temper. She reclined, her abundant proportions supported by a number of pillows, in her bed, not bothering to reply to the quiet 'good morning' uttered by the girl who had entered the room; she was not a lady to waste courtesy on those she considered beneath her. Her late husband had left her rich, having made a fortune in pickled onions, and since she had an excellent opinion of herself she found no need to bother with the feelings of anyone whom she considered inferior. And, of course, a paid companion came into that category.

The paid companion crossed the wide expanse of carpet and stood beside the bed, notebook in hand. She looked out of place in the over-furnished, frilly room; a girl of medium height, with pale brown hair smoothed into a French pleat, she had unremarkable features, but her eyes were large, thickly lashed and of a pleasing hazel. She was dressed in a pleated skirt and a white blouse, with a grey cardigan to match the skirt—sober clothes which failed to conceal her pretty figure and elegant legs.

Mrs Smith-Darcy didn't bother to look at her. 'You can go to the bank and cash a cheque—the servants want their wages. Do call in at the butcher's and tell him that I'm not satisfied with the meat he's sending up to the house. When you get back—and don't be all day over a couple of errands—you can make an appointment with my hairdresser and get the invitations written for my luncheon party. The list's on my desk.'

She added pettishly, 'Well, get on with it, then; there's plenty of work waiting for you when you get back.'

The girl went out of the room without a word, closed the door quietly behind her and went downstairs to the kitchen where Cook had a cup of coffee waiting for her.

'Got your orders, Miss Trent? In a mood, is she?'

'I dare say it's this weather, Cook. I have to go to the shops. Is there anything I can bring back for you?'

'Well, now, love, if you could pop into Mr Coffin's and ask him to send up a couple of pounds of sausages with the meat? They'll do us a treat for our dinner.'

Emma Trent, battling on her bike against an icy February wind straight from Dartmoor and driving rain, reflected that there could be worse jobs, only just at that moment she couldn't think of any. It wasn't just the weather—she had lived in Buckfastleigh all her life and found nothing unusual in that; after all, it was only a mile or so from the heart of the moor with its severe winters.

Bad weather she could dismiss easily enough, but Mrs Smith-Darcy was another matter; a selfish lazy woman, uncaring of anyone's feelings but her own, she was Emma's daily trial, but her wages put the butter on the bread of Emma's mother's small pension so she had to be borne. Jobs weren't all that easy to find in a small rural town, and if she went to Plymouth or even Ashburton it would mean living away from home, whereas now they managed very well, although there was never much money over.

Her errands done, and with the sausages crammed into a pocket, since Mr Coffin had said that he wasn't sure if he could deliver the meat before the afternoon, she cycled back to the large house on the other side of the town where her employer lived, parked her bike by the side-door and went into the kitchen. There she handed over the sausages, hung her sopping raincoat to dry and went along to the little cubby-hole where she spent most of her days—making out cheques for the tradesmen, making appointments, writing notes and keeping the household books. When she wasn't doing that, she arranged the flowers, and answered the door if Alice, the housemaid, was busy or having her day off.

'Never a dull moment,' said Emma to her reflection as she tidied her hair and dried the rain from her face. The buzzer Mrs Smith-Darcy used whenever she demanded Emma's presence was clamouring to be answered, and she picked up her notebook and pencil and went unhurriedly upstairs.

Mrs Smith-Darcy had heaved herself out of bed and was sitting before the dressing-table mirror, doing her face. She didn't look up from the task of applying mascara. 'I have been buzzing you for several minutes,' she observed crossly. 'Where have you been? Really, a great, strong girl like you should have done those few errands in twenty minutes...'

Emma said mildly, 'I'm not a great, strong girl, Mrs Smith-Darcy, and cycling into the wind isn't the quickest way of travelling. Besides, I got wet—'

'Don't make childish excuses. Really, Miss Trent, I some-times wonder if you are up to this job. Heaven knows, it's easy enough.'

Emma knew better than to answer that. Instead she asked, 'You wanted me to do something for you, Mrs Smith-Darcy?'

'Tell Cook I want my coffee in half an hour. I shall be out to lunch, and while I'm gone you can fetch Frou-Frou from the vet. I shall need Vickery with the car so I suppose you had better get a taxi—it wouldn't do for Frou-Frou to get wet. You can pay and I'll settle with you later.'

'I haven't brought any money with me.' Emma crossed her fingers behind her back as she spoke, for it was a fib, but on several occasions she had been told to pay for something and that she would be reimbursed later—something which had never happened.

Mrs Smith-Darcy frowned. 'Really, what an incompetent girl you are.' She opened her handbag and found a five-pound note. 'Take this—and I'll expect the correct change.'

'I'll get the driver to write the fare down and sign it,' said Emma quietly, and something in her voice made Mrs Smith-Darcy look at her.

'There's no need for that.'

'It will set your mind at rest,' said Emma sweetly. 'I'll get those invitations written; I can post them on my way home.'

Mrs Smith-Darcy, who liked to have the last word, was for once unable to think of anything to say as Emma left the room.

It was well after five o'clock when Emma got on to her bike and took herself off home—a small, neat house near the abbey where she and her mother had lived since her father had died several years earlier.

He had died suddenly and unexpectedly, and it hadn't been until after his death that Mrs Trent had been told that he had mortgaged the house in order to raise the money to help his younger brother, who had been in financial difficulties, under the impression that he would be repaid within a reasonable time. There hadn't been enough money to pay off the mortgage, so she had sold the house and bought a small terraced house, and, since her brother-in-law had gone abroad without leaving an address, she and Emma now managed on her small pension and Emma's salary. That she herself was underpaid Emma was well aware, but on the other hand her job allowed her to keep an eye on her mother's peptic ulcer...

There was an alley behind the row of houses. She wheeled her bike along its length and into their small back garden, put it in the tumbledown shed outside the kitchen door and went into the house.

The kitchen was small, but its walls were distempered in a cheerful pale yellow and there was room for a small table and two chairs against one wall. She took off her outdoor things, carried them through to the narrow little hall and went into the sitting-room. That was small too, but it was comfortably furnished, although a bit shabby, and there was a cheerful fire burning in the small grate.

Mrs Trent looked up from her sewing. 'Hello, love. Have you had a tiring day? And so wet and cold too. Supper is in the oven but you'd like a cup of tea first...'

'I'll get it.' Emma dropped a kiss on her mother's cheek and went to make the tea and presently carried it back.

'Something smells heavenly,' she observed. 'What have you been cooking?'

'Casserole and dumplings. Did you get a proper lunch?'

Emma assured her that she had, with fleeting regret for most of the sausages she hadn't been given time to eat; Mrs Smith-Darcy had the nasty habit of demanding that some task must be done at once, never mind how inconvenient. She reflected with pleasure that her employer was going away for several days, and although she had been given a list of things to do which would take at least twice that period it would be like having a holiday.

She spent the next day packing Mrs Smith-Darcy's expensive cases with the clothes necessary to make an impression during her stay at Torquay's finest hotel—a stay which, she pointed out to Emma, was vital to her health. This remark reminded her to order the central heating to be turned down while she was absent. 'And I expect an accurate statement of the household expenses.'

Life, after Mrs Smith-Darcy had been driven away by Vickery, the chauffeur, was all of a sudden pleasant.

It was delightful to arrive each morning and get on with her work without having to waste half an hour listening to her employer's querulous voice raised in criticism about something or other, just as it was delightful to go home each evening at five o'clock exactly.

Over and above this, Cook, unhampered by her employer's strictures, allowed her creative skills to run free so that they ate food which was never normally allowed—rich steak and kidney pudding with a drop of stout in the gravy, roasted potatoes—crisply brown, toad-in-the-hole, braised celery, cauliflower smothered in a creamy sauce and all followed by steamed puddings, sticky with treacle or bathed in custard.

Emma, eating her dinners in the kitchen with Cook and Alice, the housemaid, savoured every morsel, dutifully entered the bills in her household ledger and didn't query any of them; she would have to listen to a diatribe about the wicked extravagance of her staff from Mrs Smith-Darcy but it would be worth it, and Cook had given her a cake to take home, declaring that she had made two when one would have done.

On the last day of Mrs Smith-Darcy's absence from home Emma arrived in good time. There were still one or two tasks to do before that lady returned—the flowers to arrange, the last of the post to sort out and have ready for her inspection, a list of the invitations accepted for the luncheon party...

She almost fell off her bike as she shot through the gates into the short drive to the house. The car was before the door and Vickery was taking the cases out of the boot. He cast his eyes up as she jumped off her bike.

'Took bad,' he said. 'During the night. 'Ad the doctor to see 'er—gave her an injection and told 'er it were a bug going round—gastric something or other. Alice is putting 'er to bed, miss. You'd better go up sharp, like.'

'Oh, Vickery, you must have had to get up very early—it's only just nine o'clock.'

'That I did, miss.' He smiled at her. 'I'll see to yer bike.'

'Thank you, Vickery. I'm sure Cook will have breakfast for you.'

She took off her outdoor things and went upstairs. Mrs Smith-Darcy's door was closed but she could hear her voice raised in annoyance. She couldn't be very ill if she could shout like that, thought Emma, opening the door.

'There you are—never where you're wanted, as usual. I'm ill—very ill. That stupid doctor who came to the hotel told me it was some kind of virus. I don't believe him. I'm obviously suffering from some grave internal disorder. Go and phone Dr Treble and tell him to come at once.'

'He'll be taking surgery,' Emma pointed out reasonably. 'I'll ask him to come as soon as he's finished.' She studied

Mrs Smith-Darcy's face. 'Are you in great pain? Did the doctor at Torquay advise you to go to a hospital for emergency treatment?'

'Of course not. If I need anything done I shall go into a private hospital. I am in great pain—agony...' She didn't quite meet Emma's level gaze. 'Do as I tell you; I must be attended to at once.'

She was in bed now, having her pillows arranged just so by the timid Alice. Emma didn't think that she looked in pain; certainly her rather high colour was normal, and if she had been in the agony she described then she wouldn't have been fussing about her pillows and which bed-jacket she would wear. She went downstairs and dialled the surgery.

The receptionist answered. 'Emma—how are you? Your mother's all right? She looked well when I saw her a few days ago.'

'Mother's fine, thanks, Mrs Butts. Mrs Smith-Darcy came back this morning from a few days at Torquay. She wasn't well during the night and the hotel called a doctor who told her it was a bug and that she had better go home—he gave her something—I don't know what. She says she is in great pain and wants Dr Treble to come and see her immediately.'

'The surgery isn't finished—it'll be another half an hour or so, unless she'd like to be brought here in her car.' Mrs Butts chuckled. 'And that's unlikely, isn't it?' She paused. 'Is she really ill, Emma?'

'Her colour is normal; she's very cross...'

'When isn't she very cross? I'll ask Doctor to visit when surgery is over, but, I warn you, if there's anything really urgent he'll have to see to it first.'

Emma went back to Mrs Smith-Darcy and found her sitting up in bed renewing her make-up. 'You're feeling better? Would you like coffee or tea? Or something to eat?'

'Don't be ridiculous, Miss Trent; can you not see how I'm suffering? Is the doctor on his way?'

'He'll come when surgery is finished—about half an hour, Mrs Butts said.'

'Mrs Butts? Do you mean to tell me that you didn't speak to Dr Treble?'

'No, he was busy with a patient.'

'I am a patient,' said Mrs Smith-Darcy in a furious voice.

Emma, as mild as milk and unmoved, said, 'Yes, Mrs Smith-Darcy. I'll be back in a minute; I'm going to open the post while I've the chance.'

There must be easier ways of earning a living, she reflected, going down to the kitchen to ask Cook to make lemonade.

She bore the refreshment upstairs presently, and took it down again as her employer didn't find it sweet enough. When she went back with it she was kept busy closing curtains because the dim light from the February morning was hurting the invalid's eyes, then fetching another blanket to put over her feet, and changing the bed-jacket she had on, which wasn't the right colour...

'Now go and fetch my letters,' said Mrs Smith-Darcy.

Perhaps, thought Emma, nipping smartly downstairs once more, Dr Treble would prescribe something which would soothe the lady and cause her to doze off for long periods. Certainly at the moment Mrs Smith-Darcy had no intention of doing any such thing.

Emma, proffering her post, got the full force of her displeasure.

'Bills,' said Mrs Smith-Darcy. 'Nothing but bills!' And

went on that doubtless, while her back was turned, those whom she employed had eaten her out of house and home, and as for an indigent nephew who had had the effrontery to ask her for a small loan… 'Anyone would think that I was made of money,' she said angrily—which was, in fact, not far wrong.

The richer you are, the meaner you get, reflected Emma, retrieving envelopes and bills scattered over the bed and on the floor.

She was on her knees with her back to the door when it was opened and Alice said, 'The doctor, ma'am,' and something in her voice made Emma turn around. It wasn't Dr Treble but a complete stranger who, from her lowly position, looked enormous.

Indeed, he was a big man; not only very tall but built to match his height, he was also possessed of a handsome face with a high-bridged nose and a firm mouth. Pepper and salt hair, she had time to notice, and on the wrong side of thirty. She was aware of his barely concealed look of amusement as she got to her feet.

'Get up, girl,' said Mrs Smith-Darcy and then added, 'I sent for Dr Treble.' She took a second look at him and altered her tone. 'I don't know you, do I?'

He crossed the room to the bed. 'Dr Wyatt. I have taken over from Dr Treble for a short period. What can I do for you, Mrs Smith-Darcy? I received a message that it was urgent.'

'Oh, Doctor, I have had a shocking experience—' She broke off for a moment. 'Miss Trent, get the doctor a chair.'

But before Emma could move he had picked up a spindly affair and sat on it, seemingly unaware of the alarming creaks; at the same time he had glanced at her again with the ghost of a smile. Nice, thought Emma, making herself as inconspicuous as possible. I hope that he will see through her. At least she won't be able to bully him like she does Dr Treble.

Her hopes were justified. Mrs Smith-Darcy, prepared to discuss her symptoms at some length, found herself answering his questions with no chance of embellishment, although she did her best.

'You dined last evening?' he wanted to know. 'What exactly did you eat and drink?'

'The hotel is noted for its excellent food,' she gushed. 'It's expensive, of course, but one has to pay for the best, does one not?' She waited for him to make some comment and then, when he didn't, added pettishly, 'Well, a drink before I dined, of course, and some of the delightful canapés they serve. I have a small appetite but I managed a little caviare. Then, let me see, a morsel of sole with a mushroom sauce— cooked in cream, of course—and then a simply delicious pheasant with an excellent selection of vegetables.'

'And?' asked Dr Wyatt, his voice as bland as his face.

'Oh, dessert—meringue with a chocolate sauce laced with curaçao—a small portion, I might add.' She laughed. 'A delicious meal—'

'And the reason for your gastric upset. There is nothing seriously wrong, Mrs Smith-Darcy, and it can be easily cured by taking some tablets which you can obtain from the chemist and then keeping to a much plainer diet in future. I'm sure that your daughter—'

'My paid companion,' snapped Mrs Smith-Darcy. 'I am a lonely widow, Doctor, and able to get about very little.'

'I suggest that you take regular exercise each day—a brisk walk, perhaps.'

Mrs Smith-Darcy shuddered. 'I feel that you don't understand my delicate constitution, Doctor; I hope that I shan't need to call you again.'

'I think it unlikely; I can assure you that there is nothing wrong with you, Mrs Smith-Darcy. You will feel better if you get up and dress.'

He bade her goodbye with cool courtesy. 'I will give your companion some instructions and write a prescription for some tablets.'

Emma opened the door for him, but he took the handle from her and ushered her through before closing it gently behind him.

'Is there somewhere we might go?'

'Yes—yes, of course.' She led the way downstairs and into her office.

He looked around him. 'This is where you work at being a companion?'

'Yes. Well, I do the accounts and bills and write the letters here. Most of the time I'm with Mrs Smith-Darcy.'

'But you don't live here?' He had a pleasant, deep voice, quite quiet and soothing, and she answered his questions readily because he sounded so casual.

'No, I live in Buckfastleigh with my mother.'

'A pleasant little town. I prefer the other end, though, nearer the abbey.'

'Oh, so do I; that's where we are...' She stopped there; he wouldn't want to know anything about her—they were strangers, not likely to see each other again. 'Is there anything special I should learn about Mrs Smith-Darcy?'

'No, she is perfectly healthy although very overweight. Next time she overeats try to persuade her to take one of these tablets instead of calling the doctor.' He was writing out a prescription and paused to look at her. 'You're wasted here, you know.'

She blushed. 'I've not had any training—at least, only shorthand and typing and a little bookkeeping—and there aren't many jobs here.'

'You don't wish to leave home?'

'No. I can't do that. Is Dr Treble ill?'

'Yes, he's in hospital. He has had a heart attack and most likely will retire.'

She gave him a thoughtful look. 'I'm very sorry. You don't want me to tell Mrs Smith-Darcy?'

'No. In a little while the practice will be taken over by another doctor.'

'You?'

He smiled. 'No, no. I'm merely filling in until things have been settled.'

He gave her the prescription and closed his bag. The hand he offered was large and very firm and she wanted to keep her hand in his. He was, she reflected, a very nice man—dependable; he would make a splendid friend. It was such an absurd idea that she smiled and he decided that her smile was enchanting.

She went to the door with him and saw the steel-grey Rolls-Royce parked in the drive. 'Is that yours?' she asked.

'Yes.' He sounded amused and she begged his pardon and went pink again and stood, rather prim, in the open door until he got in and drove away.

She turned, and went in and up to the bedroom to find Mrs Smith-Darcy decidedly peevish. 'Really, I don't know what is coming to the medical profession,' she began, the moment Emma opened the door. 'Nothing wrong with me, indeed; I never heard such nonsense. I'm thoroughly upset. Go down and get my coffee and some of those wine biscuits.'

'I have a prescription for you, Mrs Smith-Darcy,' said Emma. 'I'll fetch it while you're getting dressed, shall I?'

'I have no intention of dressing. You can go to the chemist while I'm having my coffee—and don't hang around. There's plenty for you to do here.'

When she got back Mrs Smith-Darcy asked, 'What has happened to Dr Treble? I hope that that man is replacing him for a very short time; I have no wish to see him again.'

To which remark Emma prudently made no answer. Presently she went off to the kitchen to tell Cook that her mistress fancied asparagus soup made with single cream and a touch of parsley, and two lamb cutlets with creamed potatoes and braised celery in a cheese sauce. So much for the new doctor's advice, reflected Emma, ordered down to the cellar to fetch a bottle of Bollinger to tempt the invalid's appetite.

That evening, sitting at supper with her mother, Emma told her of the new doctor. 'He was nice. I expect if you were really ill he would take the greatest care of you.'

'Elderly?' asked Mrs Trent artlessly.

'Something between thirty and thirty-five, I suppose. Pepper and salt hair...'

A not very satisfactory answer from her mother's point of view.

February, tired of being winter, became spring for a couple of days, and Emma, speeding to and fro from Mrs Smith-Darcy's house, had her head full of plans—a day out with her mother on the following Sunday. She could rent a car from Dobbs's garage and drive her mother to Widecombe in the Moor and then on to Bovey Tracey; they could have

lunch there and then go on back home through Ilsington—
no main roads, just a quiet jaunt around the country they
both loved.

She had been saving for a tweed coat and skirt, but she
told herself that since she seldom went anywhere, other than
a rare visit to Exeter or Plymouth, they could wait until autumn. She and her mother both needed a day out...

The weather was kind; Sunday was bright and clear, even
if cold. Emma got up early, fed Queenie, their elderly cat,
took tea to her mother and got the breakfast and, while Mrs
Trent cleared it away, went along to the garage and fetched
the car.

Mr Dobbs had known her father and was always willing to rent her a car, letting her have it at a reduced price
since it was usually the smallest and shabbiest in his garage,
though in good order, as he was always prompt to tell her.
Today she was to have an elderly Fiat, bright red and with
all the basic comforts, but, she was assured, running well.
Emma, casting her eye over it, had a momentary vision of
a sleek Rolls Royce...

They set off in the still, early morning and, since they
had the day before them, Emma drove to Ashburton and
presently took the narrow moor road to Widecombe, where
they stopped for coffee before driving on to Bovey Tracey. It
was too early for lunch, so they drove on then to Lustleigh,
an ancient village deep in the moorland, the hills around it
dotted with granite boulders. But although the houses and
cottages were built of granite there was nothing forbidding
about them—they were charming even on a chilly winter's
day, the thatched roofs gleaming with the last of the previous
night's frost, smoke eddying gently from their chimney-pots.

Scattered around the village were several substantial

houses, tucked cosily between the hills. They were all old—as old as the village—and several of them were prosperous farms while others stood in sheltered grounds.

'I wouldn't mind living here,' said Emma as they passed one particularly handsome house, standing well back from the narrow road, the hills at its back, sheltered by carefully planted trees. 'Shall we go as far as Lustleigh Cleave and take a look at the river?'

After that it was time to find somewhere for lunch. Most of the cafés and restaurants in the little town were closed, since the tourist season was still several months away, but they found a pub where they were served roast beef with all the trimmings and home-made mince tarts to follow.

Watching her mother's pleasure at the simple, well-cooked meal, Emma promised herself that they would do a similar trip before the winter ended, while the villages were quiet and the roads almost empty.

It was still fine weather but the afternoon was already fading, and she had promised to return the car by seven o'clock at the latest. They decided to drive straight home and have tea when they got in, and since it was still a clear afternoon they decided to take a minor road through Ilsington. Emma had turned off the main road on to the small country lane when her mother slumped in her seat without uttering a sound. Emma stopped the car and turned to look at her unconscious parent.

She said, 'Mother—Mother, whatever is the matter...?' And then she pulled herself together—bleating her name wasn't going to help. She undid her safety-belt, took her mother's pulse and called her name again, but Mrs Trent lolled in her seat, her eyes closed. At least Emma could feel her pulse, and her breathing seemed normal.

Emma looked around her. The lane was narrow; she would never be able to turn the car and there was little point in driving on as Ilsington was a small village—too small for a doctor. She pulled a rug from the back seat and wrapped it round her mother and was full of thankful relief when Mrs Trent opened her eyes, but the relief was short-lived. Mrs Trent gave a groan. 'Emma, it's such a pain, I don't think I can bear it...'

There was only one thing to do—to reverse the car back down the lane, return to the main road and race back to Bovey Tracey.

'It's all right, Mother,' said Emma. 'It's not far to Bovey... There's the cottage hospital there; they'll help you.'

She began to reverse, going painfully slowly since the lane curved between high hedges, and it was a good thing she did, for the oncoming car behind her braked smoothly inches from her boot. She got out so fast that she almost tumbled over; here was help! She had no eyes for the other car but rushed to poke her worried face through the window that its driver had just opened.

'It's you!' she exclaimed. 'Oh, you can help. Only, please come quickly.' Dr. Wyatt didn't utter a word but he was beside her before she could draw another breath. 'Mother—it's Mother; she's collapsed and she's in terrible pain. I couldn't turn the car and this lane goes to Ilsington, and it's on the moor miles from anywhere...'

He put a large, steadying hand on her arm. 'Shall I take a look?'

Mrs Trent was a nasty pasty colour and her hand, when he took it, felt cold and clammy. Emma, half-in, half-out of the car on her side, said, 'Mother's got an ulcer—a peptic ulcer; she takes alkaline medicine and small meals and extra milk.'

He was bending over Mrs Trent. 'Will you undo her coat and anything else in the way? I must take a quick look. I'll fetch my bag.'

He straightened up presently. 'Your mother needs to be treated without delay. I'll put her into my car and drive to Exeter. You follow as soon as you can.'

'Yes.' She cast him a bewildered look.

'Problems?' he asked.

'I rented the car from Dobbs's garage; it has to be back by seven o'clock.'

'I'm going to give your mother an injection to take away the pain. Go to my car; there's a phone between the front seats. Phone this Dobbs, tell him what has happened and say that you'll bring the car back as soon as possible.' He turned his back on Mrs Trent, looming over Emma so that she had to crane her neck to see his face. 'I am sure that your mother has a perforated ulcer, which means surgery as soon as possible.'

She stared up at him, pale with shock, unable to think of anything to say. She nodded once and ran back to his car, and by the time she had made her call she had seen him lift her mother gently and carry her to the car. They made her comfortable on the back seat and Emma was thankful to see that her mother appeared to be dozing. 'She'll be all right? You'll hurry, won't you? I'll drive on until I can turn and then I'll come to the hospital—which one?'

'The Royal Devon and Exeter—you know where it is?' He got into his car and began to reverse down the lane. If the circumstances hadn't been so dire, she would have stayed to admire the way he did it—with the same ease as if he were going forwards.

She got into her car, then, and drove on for a mile or more before she came to a rough track leading on to the moor, where she reversed and drove back the way she had come. She was shaking now, in a panic that her mother was in danger of her life and she wouldn't reach the hospital in time, but she forced herself to drive carefully. Once she reached the main road and turned on to the carriageway, it was only thirteen miles to Exeter...

She forced herself to park the car neatly in the hospital forecourt and walk, not run, in through the casualty entrance. There, thank heaven, they knew who she was and why she had come. Sister, a cosy body with a soft Devon voice, came to meet her.

'Miss Trent? Your mother in is Theatre; the professor is operating at the moment. You come and sit down in the waiting-room and a nurse will bring you a cup of tea—you look as though you could do with it. Your mother is in very good hands, and as soon as she is back in her bed you shall go and see her. In a few minutes I should like some details, but you have your tea first.'

Emma nodded; if she had spoken she would have burst into tears; her small world seemed to be tumbling around her ears. She drank her tea, holding the cup in both hands since she was still shaking, and presently, when Sister came back, she gave her the details she needed in a wooden little voice. 'Will it be much longer?' she asked.

Sister glanced at the clock. 'Not long now. I'm sure you'll be told the moment the operation is finished. Will you go back to Buckfastleigh this evening?'

'Could I stay here? I could sit here, couldn't I? I wouldn't get in anyone's way.'

'If you are to stay we'll do better than that, my dear. Do you want to telephone anyone?'

Emma shook her head. 'There's only Mother and me.' She tried to smile and gave a great sniff. 'So sorry, it's all happened so suddenly.'

'You have a nice cry if you want to. I must go and see what's happening. There's been a street-fight and we'll be busy...'

Emma sat still and didn't cry—when she saw her mother she must look cheerful—so that when somebody came at last she turned a rigidly controlled face to hear the news.

Dr Wyatt was crossing the room to her. 'Your mother is going to be all right, Emma.' And then he held her in his arms as she burst into tears.

Chapter 2

Emma didn't cry for long but hiccuped, sniffed, sobbed a bit and drew away from him to blow her nose on the handkerchief he offered her.

'You're sure? Was it a big operation? Were you in the theatre?'

'Well, yes. It was quite a major operation but successful, I'm glad to say. You may see your mother; she will be semi-conscious but she'll know that you are there. She's in Intensive Care just for tonight. Tomorrow she will go to a ward—' He broke off as Sister joined them.

'They're wanting you on Male Surgical, sir—urgently.'

He nodded at Emma and went away.

'Mother's going to get well,' said Emma. She heaved a great sigh. 'What would I have done if Dr Wyatt hadn't been driving down the lane when Mother was taken ill? He works here as well as taking over the practice at home?'

Sister looked surprised and then smiled. 'Indeed he works here; he's our Senior Consultant Surgeon, although he's supposed to be taking a sabbatical, but I hear he's helping out Dr Treble for a week or two.'

'So he's a surgeon, not a GP?'

Sister smiled again. 'Sir Paul Wyatt is a professor of surgery, and much in demand for consultations, lecture-tours and seminars. You were indeed fortunate that he happened to be there when you needed help so urgently.'

'Would Mother have died, Sister?'

'Yes, love.'

'He saved her life...' She would, reflected Emma, do anything—anything at all—to repay him. Sooner or later there would be a chance. Perhaps not for years, but she wouldn't forget.

She was taken to see her mother then, who was lying in a tangle of tubes, surrounded by monitoring screens but blessedly awake. Emma bent to kiss her white face, her own face almost as white. 'Darling, everything's fine; you're going to be all right. I'll be here and come and see you in the morning after you've had a good sleep.'

Her mother frowned. 'Queenie,' she muttered.

'I'll phone Mr Dobbs and ask him to put some food outside the cat-flap.'

'Yes, do that, Emma.' Mrs Trent closed her eyes.

Emma turned at the touch on her arm. 'You're going to stay for the night?' A pretty, young nurse smiled at her. 'There's a rest-room on the ground floor; we'll call you if there's any need but I think your mother will sleep until the morning. You can see her before you go home then.'

Emma nodded. 'Is there a phone?'

'Yes, just by the rest-room, and there's a canteen down the corridor where you can get tea and sandwiches.'

'You're very kind.' Emma took a last look at her mother

and went to the rest-room. There was no one else there and there were comfortable chairs and a table with magazines on it. As she hesitated at the door the sister from Casualty joined her.

'There's a washroom just across the passage. Try and sleep a little, won't you?'

When she had hurried away Emma picked up the phone. Mr Dobbs was sympathetic and very helpful—of course he'd see to Queenie, and Emma wasn't to worry about the car. 'Come back when you feel you can, love,' he told her. 'And you'd better keep the car for a day or two so's you can see your ma as often as possible.'

Mrs Smith-Darcy was an entirely different kettle of fish. 'My luncheon party,' she exclaimed. 'You will have to come back tomorrow morning and see to it; I am not strong enough to cope with it—you know how delicate I am. It is most inconsiderate of you...'

'My mother,' said Emma, between her teeth, 'in case you didn't hear what I have told you, is dangerously ill. I shall stay here with her as long as necessary. And you are not in the least delicate, Mrs Smith-Darcy, only spoilt and lazy and very selfish!'

She hung up, her ear shattered by Mrs Smith-Darcy's furious bellow. Well, she had burnt her boats, cooked her goose and would probably be had up for libel—or was it slander? She didn't care. She had given voice to sentiments she had choked back for more than a year and she didn't care.

She felt better after her outburst, even though she was now out of work. She drank some tea and ate sandwiches from the canteen, resisted a wish to go in search of someone and ask about her mother, washed her face and combed her hair, plaited it and settled in the easiest of the chairs. Underneath her calm front panic and fright bubbled away.

Her mother might have a relapse; she had looked so dreadfully ill. She would need to be looked after for weeks, which was something Emma would do with loving care, but they would be horribly short of money. There was no one around, so she was able to shed a few tears; she was lonely and scared and tired. She mumbled her prayers and fell asleep before she had finished them.

Sir Paul Wyatt, coming to check his patient's condition at two o'clock in the morning and satisfied with it, took himself down to the rest-room. If Emma was awake he would be able to reassure her...

She was curled up in the chair, her knees drawn up under her chin, the half of her face he could see tear-stained, her thick rope of hair hanging over one shoulder. She looked very young and entirely without glamour, and he knew that when she woke in the morning she would have a job uncoiling herself from the tight ball into which she had wound herself.

He went and fetched a blanket from Casualty and laid it carefully over her; she was going to be stiff in the morning—there was no need for her to be cold as well. He put his hand lightly on her hair, touched by the sight of her, and then smiled and frowned at the sentimental gesture and went away again.

Emma woke early, roused by a burst of activity in Casualty, and just as Sir Paul Wyatt had foreseen, discovered that she was stiff and cramped. She got up awkwardly, folding the blanket neatly, and wondered who had been kind during the night. Then she went to wash her face and comb her hair.

Even with powder and lipstick she still looked a mess—not that it mattered, since there was no one to see her. She rubbed her cheeks to get some colour into them and practised a smile in the looking-glass so that her mother would see how cheerful and unworried she was. She would have to drive back to Buckfastleigh after she had visited her and somehow she would come each day to see her, although at the moment she wasn't sure how. Of one thing she was sure—Mrs Smith-Darcy would have dismissed her out-of-hand, so she would have her days free.

She drank tea and polished off some toast in the canteen, then went to find someone who would tell her when she might see her mother. She didn't have far to go—coming towards her along the passage was Sir Paul Wyatt, immaculate in clerical grey and spotless linen, freshly shaved, his shoes brilliantly polished. She wished him a good morning and, without waiting for him to answer, asked, 'Mother—is she all right? May I see her?'

'She had a good night, and of course you may see her.'

He stood looking at her, and the relief at his words was somewhat mitigated by knowing that her scruffy appearance seemed even more scruffy in contrast to his elegance. She rushed into speech to cover her awkwardness. 'They have been very kind to me here...'

He nodded with faint impatience—of course, he was a busy man and hadn't any time to waste. 'I'll go to Mother now,' she told him. 'I'm truly grateful to you for saving Mother. She's going to be quite well again, isn't she?'

'Yes, but you must allow time for her to regain her strength. I'll take you up to the ward on my way.'

She went with him silently, through corridors and then in a lift and finally through swing-doors where he beckoned a nurse, spoke briefly, then turned on his heel with a quick nod, leaving her to follow the nurse into the ward beyond.

Her mother wasn't in the ward but in a small room beyond, sitting up in bed. She looked pale and tired but she was smiling, and Emma had to fight her strong wish to burst into tears at the sight of her. She smiled instead. 'Mother, dear, you look so much better. How do you feel? And how nice that you're in a room by yourself...'

She bent and kissed her parent. 'I've just seen Sir Paul Wyatt and he says everything is most satisfactory.' She pulled up a chair and sat by the bed, taking her mother's hand in hers. 'What a coincidence that he should be here. Sister told me that he's a professor of surgery.'

Her mother smiled. 'Yes, love, and I'm fine. I really am. You're to go home now and not worry.'

'Yes, Mother. I'll phone this evening and I'll be back tomorrow. Do you want me to bring anything? I'll pack nighties and slippers and so on and bring them with me.'

Her mother closed her eyes. 'Yes, you know what to bring...'

Emma bent to kiss her again. 'I'm going now; you're tired. Have a nap, darling.'

It was still early; patients were being washed and tended before the breakfast trolley arrived. Emma was too early for the ward sister but the night staff nurse assured her that she would be told if anything unforeseen occurred. 'But your mother is most satisfactory, Miss Trent. The professor's been to see her already; he came in the night too. He's away for most of the day but his registrar is a splendid man. Ring this evening, if you like. You'll be coming tomorrow?'

Emma nodded. 'Can I come any time?'

'Afternoon or evening is best.'

Emma went down to the car and drove herself back to Buckfastleigh. As she went she planned her day. She would have to go and see Mrs Smith-Darcy and explain that she wouldn't be able to work for her any more. That lady was going to be angry and she supposed that she would have to apologise... She was owed a week's wages too, and she would need it.

Perhaps Mr Dobbs would let her hire the car each day just for the drive to and from the hospital; it would cost more than bus fares but it would be much quicker. She would have to go to the bank too; there wasn't much money there but she was prepared to spend the lot if necessary. It was too early to think about anything but the immediate future.

She took the car back to the garage and was warmed by Mr Dobbs's sympathy and his assurance that if she needed it urgently she had only to say so. 'And no hurry to pay the bill,' he promised her.

She went home then, and fed an anxious Queenie before making coffee. She was hungry, but it was past nine o'clock by now and Mrs Smith-Darcy would have to be faced before anything else. She had a shower, changed into her usual blouse, skirt and cardigan, did her face, brushed her hair into its usual smoothness and got on to her bike.

Alice opened the door to her. 'Oh, miss, whatever's happened? The mistress is in a fine state. Cook says come and have a cup of tea before you go up to her room; you'll need all your strength.'

'How kind of Cook,' said Emma. 'I think I'd rather have it afterwards, if I may.' She ran upstairs and tapped on Mrs Smith-Darcy's door and went in.

Mrs Smith-Darcy wasted no time in expressing her opinion of Emma; she repeated it several times before she ran out of breath, which enabled Emma to say, 'I'm sorry if I was rude to you on the phone, Mrs Smith-Darcy, but you didn't seem to understand that my mother was seriously ill—still is. I shall have to go to the hospital each day until she is well enough to come home, when I shall have to look after her until she is quite recovered—and that will take a considerable time.'

'My luncheon party,' gabbled Mrs Smith-Darcy. 'You wicked girl, leaving me like this. I'm incapable...'

Emma's efforts to behave well melted away. 'Yes, you are incapable,' she agreed. 'You're incapable of sympathy or human kindness. I suggest that you get up, Mrs Smith-Darcy, and see to your luncheon party yourself. I apologised to you just now—that was a mistake. You're everything I said and a lot more beside.'

She went out of the room and closed the door gently behind here. Then she opened it again. 'Will you be good enough to send my wages to my home?' She closed the door again on Mrs Smith-Darcy's enraged gasp.

She was shaking so much that her teeth rattled against the mug of tea Cook offered her.

'Now, don't you mind what she says,' said Cook. 'Nasty old lady she is too. You go on home and have a good sleep, for you're fair worn out. I've put up a pasty and one or two snacks, like; you take them home and if you've no time to cook you just slip round here to the back door—there's always a morsel of something in the fridge.'

The dear soul's kindness was enough to make Emma weep; she sniffed instead, gave Cook a hug and then got on her bike and cycled home, where she did exactly what that lady had told her to do—undressed like lightning and got into bed. She was asleep within minutes.

She woke suddenly to the sound of the door-knocker being thumped.

'Mother,' said Emma, and scrambled out of bed, her heart thumping as loudly as the knocker. Not bothering with slippers, she tugged her dressing-gown on as she flew downstairs. It was already dusk; she had slept for hours—too long—she should have phoned the hospital. She turned the key in the lock and flung the door open.

Professor Sir Paul Wyatt was on the doorstep. He took the door from her and came in and shut it behind him. 'It is most unwise to open your door without putting up the chain or making sure that you know who it is.'

She eyed him through a tangle of hair. 'How can I know if I don't look first, and there isn't a chain?' Her half-awake brain remembered then.

'Mother—what's happened? Why are you here?' She caught at his sleeve. 'She's worse...'

His firm hand covered hers. 'Your mother is doing splendidly; she's an excellent patient. I'm sorry, I should have realised... You were asleep.'

She curled her cold toes on the hall carpet and nodded. 'I didn't mean to sleep for so long; it's getting dark.' She looked up at him. 'Why are you here, then?'

'I'm on my way home, but it has occurred to me that I shall be taking morning surgery here for the next week or two. I'll drive you up to Exeter after my morning visits and bring you back in time for evening surgery here.'

'Oh, would you? Would you really do that? How very kind of you, but won't it be putting you out? Sister said that you were taking a sabbatical, and that means you're on holiday, doesn't it?'

'Hardly a holiday, and I'm free to go in and out as I wish.'

'But you live in Exeter?'

'No, but not far from it; I shall not be in the least inconvenienced.'

She looked at him uncertainly, for he sounded casual and a little annoyed, but before she could speak he went on briskly, 'You'd better go and put some clothes on. Have you food in the house?'

'Yes, thank you. Cook gave me a pasty.' She was suddenly hungry at the thought of it. 'It was kind of you to come. I expect you want to go home—your days are long...'

He smiled. 'I'll make a pot of tea while you dress, and while we are drinking it I can explain exactly what I've done for your mother.'

She flew upstairs and flung on her clothes, washed her face and tied back her hair. Never mind how she looked—he wouldn't notice and he must be wanting to go home, wherever that was.

She perceived that he was a handy man in the kitchen—the tea was made, Queenie had been fed, and he had found a tin of biscuits.

'No milk, I'm afraid,' he said, not looking up from pouring the tea into two mugs. And then, very much to her surprise he asked, 'Have you sufficient money?'

'Yes—yes, thank you, and Mrs Smith-Darcy owes me a week's wages.' Probably in the circumstances she wouldn't get them, but he didn't need to know that.

He nodded, handed her a mug and said, 'Now, as to your mother...'

He explained simply in dry-as-dust words which were

neither threatening nor casual. 'Your mother will stay in hospital for a week—ten days, perhaps—then I propose to send her to a convalescent home—there is a good one at Moretonhampstead, not too far from here—just for a few weeks. When she returns home she should be more or less able to resume her normal way of living, although she will have to keep to some kind of a diet. Time enough for that, however. Will you stay here alone?' He glanced at her. 'Perhaps you have family or a friend who would come...?'

'No family—at least, father had some cousins somewhere in London but they don't—that is, since he died we haven't heard from them. I've friends all over Buckfastleigh, though. If I asked one of them I know they'd come and stay but there's no need. I'm not nervous; besides, I'll try and find some temporary work until Mother comes home.'

'Mrs Smith-Darcy has given you the sack?'

'I'm sure of it. I was very rude to her this morning.' Anxious not to invite his pity, she added, 'There's always part-time work here—the abbey shop or the otter sanctuary.' True enough during the season—some months away!

He put down his mug. 'Good. I'll call for you some time after twelve o'clock tomorrow morning.' His goodbye was brief.

Left alone, she put the pasty to warm in the oven, washed the mugs and laid out a tray. The house was cold—there had never been enough money for central heating, and it was too late to make a fire in the sitting-room. She ate her supper, had a shower and went to bed, reassured by her visitor's calm manner and his certainty that her mother was going to be all right. He was nice, she thought sleepily, and not a bit pompous. She slept on the thought.

* * *

It was raining hard when she woke and there was a vicious wind driving off the moor. She had breakfast and hurried round to Dobbs's garage to use his phone. Her mother had had a good night, she was told, and was looking forward to seeing her later—reassuring news, which sent her back to give the good news to Queenie and then do the housework while she planned all the things she would do before her mother came home.

She had a sandwich and a cup of coffee well before twelve o'clock, anxious not to keep the professor waiting, so that when he arrived a few minutes before that hour she was in her coat, the house secure, Queenie settled in her basket and the bag she had packed for her mother ready in the hall.

He wished her a friendly good morning, remarked upon the bad weather and swept her into the car and drove away without wasting a moment. Conversation, she soon discovered, wasn't going to flourish in the face of his monosyllabic replies to her attempts to make small talk. She decided that he was tired or mulling over his patients and contented herself with watching the bleak landscape around them.

At the hospital he said, 'Will half-past four suit you? Be at the main entrance, will you?' He added kindly, 'I'm sure you'll be pleased with your mother's progress.' He got out of the car and opened her door, waited while she went in and then, contrary to her surmise, drove out of the forecourt and out of the city. Emma, unaware of this, expecting him to be about his own business in the hospital, made her way to her mother's room and forgot him at once.

Her mother was indeed better—pale still, and hung around with various tubes, but her hair had been nicely brushed and when Emma had helped her into her pink bed-jacket she looked very nearly her old self.

'It's a miracle, isn't it?' said Emma, gently embracing her parent. 'I mean, it's only forty-eight or so hours and here you are sitting up in bed.'

Mrs Trent, nicely sedated still, agreed drowsily. 'You brought my knitting? Thank you, dear. Is Queenie all right? And how are you managing to come? It can't be easy—don't come every day; it's such a long way…'

'Professor Wyatt is standing in for Dr Treble, so he brings me here after morning surgery and takes me back in time for his evening surgery.'

'That's nice.' Mrs Trent gave Emma's hand a little squeeze. 'So I'll see you each day; I'm so glad.' She closed her eyes and dropped off and Emma sat holding her hand, making plans.

A job—that was the most important thing to consider; a job she would be able to give up when her mother returned home. She might not be trained for anything much but she could type well enough and she could do simple accounts and housekeep adequately enough; there was sure to be something…

Her mother woke presently and she talked cheerfully about everyday things, not mentioning Mrs Smith-Darcy and, indeed, she didn't intend to do so unless her mother asked.

A nurse came and Emma, watching her skilful handling of tubes and the saline drip, so wished that she could be cool and calm and efficient and—an added bonus—pretty. Probably she worked for the professor—saw him every day, was able to understand him when he gave his orders in strange surgical terms, and received his thanks. He seemed to Emma to be a man of effortless good manners.

Her mother dozed again and didn't rouse as the tea-trolley was wheeled in, which was a good thing since a cup of tea was out of the question, but Emma was given one, with two Petit Beurre biscuits, and since her hurried lunch seemed a long time ago she was grateful.

Her mother was soon awake again, content to lie quietly, not talking much and finally with an eye on the clock, Emma kissed her goodbye. 'I'll be here tomorrow,' she promised, and went down to the main entrance.

She had just reached it when the Rolls came soundlessly to a halt beside her. The professor got out and opened her door, got back in and drove away with nothing more than a murmured greeting, but presently he said, 'Your mother looks better, does she not?'

'Oh, yes. She slept for most of the afternoon but she looks much better than I expected.'

'Of course, she's being sedated, and will be for the next forty-eight hours. After that she will be free of pain and taking an interest in life again. She's had a tiring time...'

It was still raining—a cold rain driven by an icy wind—and the moor looked bleak and forbidding in the early dusk. Emma, who had lived close to it all her life, was untroubled by that; she wondered if the professor felt the same. He had said that he lived near Exeter. She wondered exactly where; perhaps, after a few days of going to and fro, he would be more forthcoming. Certainly he was a very silent man.

The thought struck her that he might find her boring, but on the following day, when she ventured a few remarks of a commonplace nature, he had little to say in reply, although he sounded friendly enough. She decided that silence, unless he began a conversation, was the best policy, so that by the end of a week she was no nearer knowing anything about him than when they had first met. She liked him— she liked him very much—but she had the good sense to know that they inhabited different worlds. He had no wish to get to know her—merely to offer a helping hand, just as he would have done with anyone else in similar circumstances.

Her mother was making good progress and Emma scanned the local paper over the weekend, and checked the advertisements outside the news agents in the hope of finding a job.

Mrs Smith-Darcy had, surprisingly, sent Alice with her wages, and Emma had made a pot of coffee and listened to Alice's outpourings on life with that lady. 'Mad as fire, she was,' Alice had said, with relish. 'You should 'ave 'eard 'er, Miss Trent. And that lunch party—that was a lark and no mistake—'er whingeing away about servants and such like. I didn't 'ear no kind words about you and your poor ma, though. Mean old cat.' She had grinned. 'Can't get another companion for love nor money, either.'

She had drunk most of the coffee and eaten all the biscuits Emma had and then got up to go. 'Almost forgot,' she'd said, suddenly awkward, 'me and Cook thought your ma might like a few chocs now she's better. And there's one of Cook's steak and kidney pies—just wants a warm-up—do for your dinner.'

'How lucky I am to have two such good friends,' Emma had said and meant it.

Going to the hospital on Monday, sitting quietly beside Sir Paul, she noticed him glance down at her lap where the box of chocolates sat.

'I hope that those are not for your mother?'

'Well, yes and no. Cook and Alice—from Mrs Smith-Darcy's house, you know—gave them to me to give her. I don't expect that she can have them, but she'll like to see them and she can give them to her nurses.'

He nodded. 'I examined your mother yesterday evening. I intend to have her transferred to Moretonhampstead within the next day or so. She will remain there for two weeks at least, three if possible, so that when she returns home she will be quite fit.'

'That is good news. Thank you for arranging it,' said Emma gratefully, and wondered how she was going to visit her mother. With a car it would have been easy enough.

She would have to find out how the buses ran—probably along the highway to Exeter and then down the turn-off to Moretonhampstead halfway along it—but the buses might not connect. She had saved as much money as she could and she had her last week's wages; perhaps she could get the car from Mr Dobbs again and visit her mother once a week; it was thirty miles or so, an hour's drive...

She explained this to her mother and was relieved to see that the prospect of going to a convalescent home and starting on a normal life once more had put her in such good spirits that she made no demur when Emma suggested that she might come only once a week to see her.

'It's only for a few weeks, Emma, and I'm sure I shall have plenty to keep me occupied. I've been so well cared for here, and everyone has been so kind. Everything's all right at home? Queenie is well?'

'She's splendid and everything is fine. I'll bring you some more clothes, shall I?' She made a list and observed, 'I'll bring them tomorrow, for the professor didn't say when you were going—when there's a vacancy I expect—he just said a day or two.'

When she got up to go her mother walked part of the way with her, anxious to show how strong she had become. By the lifts they said goodbye, though, 'I'm a slow walker,' said Mrs Trent. 'It won't do to keep him waiting.'

For once, Emma was glad of Sir Paul's silence, for she had a lot to think about. They were almost at Buckfastleigh when he told her that her mother would be transferred on the day after tomorrow.

'So tomorrow will be the last day I go to the hospital?'

'Yes. Talk to Sister when you see her tomorrow; she will give you all the particulars and the phone number. Your mother will go by ambulance. The matron there is a very kind woman, there are plenty of staff and two resident doctors so your mother will be well cared for.'

'I'm sure of that. She's looking foward to going; she feels she's really getting well.'

'It has been a worrying time for you—' his voice was kind '—but I think she will make a complete recovery.'

Indoors she put the pie in the oven, fed an impatient Queenie and sat down to add up the money in her purse—enough to rent a car from Mr Dobbs on the following weekend and not much over. She ate her supper, packed a case with the clothes her mother would need and went to put the dustbin out before she went to bed.

The local paper had been pushed through the letter-box. She took it back to the kitchen and turned to the page where the few advertisements were and there, staring her in the face, was a chance of a job. It stated:

Wanted urgently—a sensible woman to help immediately for two or three weeks while present staff are

ill. Someone able to cope with a small baby as well as
normal household chores and able to cook.

Emma, reading it, thought that the woman wouldn't only
have to be sensible, she would need to be a bundle of energy as well, but it was only for two or three weeks and it
might be exactly what she was looking for. The phone number was a local one too.

Emma went to bed convinced that miracles did happen
and slept soundly.

In the morning she waited with impatience until half-past
eight before going round to use Mr Dobbs's phone. The voice
which answered her was a woman's, shrill and agitated.

'Thank heaven—I'm at my wits' end and there's no one
here. The baby's been crying all night…'

'If you would give me your address. I live in Buckfastleigh.'

'So do I. Picket House—go past the otter sanctuary and
it's at the end of the road down a turning on the left. You've
got a car?'

'No, a bike. I'll come straight away, shall I?'

She listened to a jumble of incoherent thanks and, after
phoning the surgery to cancel her lift with Sir Paul, hurried back to the house. Queenie, having breakfasted, was
preparing to take a nap. Emma left food for her, got into
her coat, tied a scarf over her head and fetched her bike. At
least it wasn't raining as she pedalled briskly from one end
of the little town to the other.

Picket House was a rambling old place, beautifully main-
tained, lying back from the lane, surrounded by a large gar-

den. Emma skidded to the front door and halted, and before she had got off her bike it was opened.

'Come in, come in, do.' The girl wasn't much older than Emma but there the resemblance ended, for she was extremely pretty, with fair, curly hair, big blue eyes and a dainty little nose. She pulled Emma inside and then burst into tears. 'I've had a dreadful night, you have no idea. Cook's ill with flu and so is Elsie, and the nurse who's supposed to come sent a message to say that her mother's ill.'

'There's no one who could come—your mother or a sister?'

'They're in Scotland.' She dismissed them with a wave of the hand. 'And Mike, my husband, he's in America and won't be back for weeks.' She wiped her eyes and smiled a little. 'You will come and help me?'

'Yes—yes, of course. You'll want references...?'

'Yes, yes—but later will do for that. I want a bath and I've not had breakfast. To tell the truth, I'm not much of a cook.'

'The baby?' asked Emma, taking off her coat and scarf and hanging them on the elaborate hat-stand in the hall. 'A boy or a girl?'

'Oh, a boy.'

'Has he had a feed?'

'I gave him one during the night but I'm not sure if I mixed it properly; he was sick afterwards.'

'You don't feed him yourself?'

The pretty face was screwed up in horror. 'No, no, I couldn't possibly—I'm far too sensitive. Could you move in until the nurse can come?'

'I can't live here, but I'll come early in the morning and stay until the baby's last feed, if that would do?'

'I'll be alone during the night...'

'If the baby's had a good feed he should sleep for the night and I'll leave a feed ready for you to warm up.'

'Will you cook and tidy up a bit? I'm hopeless at house-work.'

It seemed to Emma that now would be the time to learn about it, but she didn't say so. 'I don't know your name,' she said.

'Hervey—Doreen Hervey.'

'Emma Trent. Should we take a look at the baby before I get your breakfast?'

'Oh, yes, I suppose so. He's very small, just a month old. You're not a nurse, are you?'

'No, but I took a course in baby care and housewifery when I left school.'

They were going upstairs. 'Would you come for a hundred pounds a week?'

'Yes.' It would be two or three weeks and she could save every penny of it.

They had reached the wide landing, and from somewhere along a passage leading to the back of the house there was a small, wailing noise.

The nursery was perfection—pastel walls, a thick carpet underfoot, pretty curtains drawn back from spotless white net, the right furniture and gloriously warm. The cot was a splendid affair and Mrs Hervey went to lean over it. 'There he is,' she said unnecessarily.

He was a very small baby, with dark hair, screwed up eyes and a wide open mouth. The wails had turned to screams and he was waving miniature fists in a fury of infant rage.

'The lamb,' said Emma. 'He's wet; I'll change him. When did he have his feed? Can you remember the time?'

'I can't possibly remember; I was so tired. I suppose it was about two o'clock.'

'Is his feed in the kitchen?'

'Yes, on the table. I suppose he's hungry?'

Emma suppressed a desire to shake Mrs Hervey. 'Go and have your bath while I change him and feed him. Perhaps you could start breakfast—boil an egg and make toast?'

Mrs Hervey went thankfully away and Emma took the sopping infant from his sopping cot. While she was at it he could be bathed; everything she could possibly need was there...

With the baby tucked under one arm, swathed in his shawl, she went downstairs presently. The tin of baby-milk was on the table in the kind of kitchen every woman dreamt of. She boiled a kettle, mixed a feed and sat down to wait while it cooled. The baby glared at her from under his shawl. Since he looked as if he would cry again at any minute she talked gently to him.

She had fed him, winded him and cuddled him close as he dropped off and there was still no sign of his mother, but presently she came, her make-up immaculate, looking quite lovely.

'Oh, good, he's gone to sleep. I'm so hungry.' She smiled widely, looking like an angel. 'I'm so glad you've come, Emma—may I call you Emma?'

'Please do,' said Emma. She had her reservations about feeling glad as she bore the baby back to his cot.

Chapter 3

By the end of the day Emma realised that she would have her hands full for the next week or two. Mrs Hervey, no doubt a charming and good-natured woman, hadn't the least idea how to be a mother.

Over lunch she had confided to Emma that she had never had to do anything for herself—she had been pampered in succession by a devoted nanny, a doting mother and father, and then an adoring husband with money enough to keep her in the style to which she had been accustomed. 'Everyone's ill,' she had wailed. 'My old nanny ought to be here looking after me while Mike's away, but she's had to go and look after my sister's children—they've got measles. And the mother of this wretched nanny who was supposed to come. Just imagine, Emma, I came home from the nursing home and Cook and Elsie got ill the very next day!'

'You were in the nursing home for several weeks? Were you ill after the baby was born?'

'No, no. Mike arranged that so I could have plenty of time to recover before I had to plunge into normal life again.'

Emma had forborne from telling her that most women plunged back into normal life with no more help than a willing husband. She'd said cautiously, 'While I'm here I'll show you how to look after the baby and how to mix the feeds, so that when Nanny has her days off you'll know what to do.'

'Will you? How sensible you are.'

'Hasn't the baby got a name?'

'We hadn't decided on that when Mike had to go away. We called him "Baby"—I suppose he'll be Bartholemew, after Mike's father, you know. He's very rich.'

It seemed a pity, Emma had reflected, to saddle the baby with such a name for the sake of future money-bags. 'May I call him Bart?' she'd asked.

'Why not?' Mrs Hervey had cast an anxious glance at Emma. 'You're quite happy here? It's a long day...'

As indeed it was.

After the first day, ending well after nine o'clock in the evening, Emma saw that she would have to alter things a bit. A little rearranging was all that was required. Bart needed a six o'clock feed, so she agreed to make it up the evening before for his mother to warm up.

'I'll come in at eight o'clock and get your breakfast, and while you are having it I'll bath Bart and make up his feed for ten o'clock. When he's had his two o'clock feed I'll leave him with you—he'll sleep for several hours and you will be able to rest if you want to.

'I'd like to go home for an hour or two, to do the shopping and so on, but I'll be back in plenty of time to see to his evening feed and get your supper. I'll stay until nine o'clock, so that you can get ready for bed before I go, then all you need to do is feed him at ten o'clock. I'll make up an extra feed in case he wakes at two o'clock.'

Mrs Hervey looked at her with her big blue eyes. 'You're an angel. Of course you must go home—and you will stay until nine o'clock?'

'Yes, of course.'

'You'll have lunch and supper with me, won't you?'

'Thank you, that would be nice. How about shopping? It wouldn't hurt Bart to be taken for an airing in his pram.'

'I'd be scared—all the traffic, and it's so far to the shops. I've always phoned for anything I want.'

'In that case, I'll take him for half an hour in the mornings when the weather's not too bad.'

'Will you? I say, I've just had such a good idea. Couldn't you take him with you in the afternoons?'

Emma had been expecting that. 'Well, no. You see, it's quite a long way and I go on my bike—I haven't anywhere to put the pram. Besides, you are his mum; he wants to be with you.'

'Oh, does he? You see, I'm not sure what to do when he cries...'

'Pick him up and see if he's wet. If he is, change him, and give him a cuddle.'

'It sounds so easy.'

'And it will be very nice if you know how to go on, so that when the nanny comes you can tell her how you want things done.'

Mrs Hervey, much struck with this idea, agreed.

It took a day or two to establish some sort of routine. Mrs Hervey was singularly helpless, not only with her son but about the running of a household; she had always had time to spend on herself and this time was now curtailed. But although she was so helpless, and not very quick to grasp anything, she had a placid nature and was very willing to learn.

The pair of them got on well and Bart, now that his small wants were dealt with promptly, was a contented baby.

Emma phoned her mother during the week and was relieved to hear that she had settled down nicely, and when Emma explained that she had a job, just for a week or two, and might not be able to go and see her, she told her comfortably that she was quite happy and that Emma wasn't to worry.

It was on Saturday that Sir Paul Wyatt, on his way home from a conference in Bristol, decided to visit Mrs Trent. He had seen nothing of Emma in Buckfastleigh, and on the one occasion when he had given way to a wish to visit her the house had been locked up and there had been no sign of her. Staying with friends, probably, he'd decided, and didn't go again.

Mrs Trent was delighted to see him. She was making good progress and seemed happy enough. Indeed, he wondered if she might not be able to return home very shortly. Only her enthusiastic description of Emma's new job made him pause, for, if he sent her home, Emma would have to give it up, at least for a few weeks, and he suspected that the Trent household needed the money.

'Emma has a local job?' he asked kindly.

'Yes. She is able to cycle there every day. It's with a Mrs Hervey; she lives at the other end of Buckfastleigh—a very nice house, Emma says. There is a very new baby and Mrs Hervey's cook and maid are both ill and the nanny she has engaged was unable to come, so Emma's helping out until she turns up and the other two are back.'

'Mrs Hervey is a young woman, presumably?'

'Oh, yes. Her husband is away—in America I believe. Mrs Hervey seems quite lost without him.'

He agreed, that might be so.

'I'm keeping you, Professor,' she went on. 'I'm sure you want to go home to your own family. It was very kind of you to come and see me. I told Emma not to come here; from what she said I rather think that she has very little time to herself and I shall soon be home.'

'Indeed you will, Mrs Trent.'

They shook hands and she added, 'You won't be seeing her, I suppose?'

'If I do I will give her your love,' he assured her.

Fifteen minutes later he stopped the car outside his front door in the heart of Lustleigh village. The house was close to the church, and was a rambling thatched cottage, its roof at various levels, its windows small and diamond-paned. The door was arched and solid and its walls in summer and autumn were a mass of colour from the climbing plants clinging to its irregularities.

He let himself in, to be met in the narrow hall by two dogs—a Jack Russell with an impudent face and a sober golden Labrador. He bent to caress them as a door at the end of the hall was opened and his housekeeper came trotting towards him. She was short and stout with a round, pink-cheeked face, small blue eyes and a smiling mouth.

'There you are, then,' she observed, 'and high time too, if I might say so. There's as nice a dinner waiting for you as you'd find anywhere in the land.'

'Give me ten minutes, Mrs Parfitt, and I'll do it justice.'

'Had a busy day, I reckon. Time you took a bit of a holiday; though it's not my place to say so, dear knows you've earned it.' She gave an indignant snort. 'Supposed to be free of all that operating and hospital work, aren't you, for six months? And look at you, sir, working your fingers off to help out old Dr Treble, going to conferences...'

Sir Paul had taken off his coat, picked up his bag and opened a door. 'I'm rather enjoying it,' he observed mildly, and went into his study.

There was a pile of letters on his desk and the light on the answer-phone was blinking; he ignored them both and sat down at his desk and, lifting the phone's receiver, dialled a number and waited patiently for it to be answered.

Emma had soon discovered that it was impossible to get annoyed or impatient with Mrs Hervey. She had become resigned to the mess she found each morning when she arrived for work—the table in the kitchen left littered with unwashed crockery used by Mrs Hervey for the snack she fancied before she went to bed, the remnants of that snack left to solidify in the frying-pan or saucepan. But at least she had grasped the instructions for Bart's feeds, even though she made no attempt to clean anything once it had been used. She was, however, getting much better at handling her small son, and although she was prone to weep at the slightest set-back she was invariably good-natured.

Towards the end of the week Emma had suggested that it might be a good idea to take Bart to the baby clinic, or find out if there was a health visitor who would check Bart's progress.

'Absolutely not,' Mrs Hervey had said airily. 'They talked about it while I was in the nursing home but of course I said there was no need with a trained nanny already booked.'

'But the nanny isn't here,' Emma had pointed out.

'Well, you are, and she'll come soon—she said she would.'

Mrs Hervey had given her a sunny smile and begged her not to fuss but to come and inspect various baby garments which had just arrived from Harrods.

By the end of the week Emma was tired; her few hours each afternoon were just sufficient for her to look after her house, do the necessary shopping, see to Queenie and do the washing and ironing, and by the time she got home in the evening she was too tired to do more than eat a sandwich and drink a pot of tea before tumbling into bed. She was well aware that she was working for far too many hours, but she told herself it was only for a few weeks and, with the first hundred pounds swelling the woefully meagre sum in their bank account, she went doggedly on.

All the same, on Saturday evening, as nine o'clock approached, she heaved a sigh of relief. Sunday would be a day like any weekday, but perhaps by the end of another week someone—the cook or the housemaid—would be back and then her day's work would be lighter. She had been tempted once or twice to suggest that Mrs Hervey might find someone to come in each day and do some housework, but this had been dismissed with a puzzled, 'But you are managing beautifully, Emma; you're doing all the things I asked for in the advert.'

Emma had said no more—what was the use? She only hoped that Mrs Hervey would never fall on hard times; her cushioned life had hardly prepared her for that.

She was about to put on her coat when Mrs Hervey's agitated voice made her pause. She took off her coat again and went back upstairs to find her bending over Bart's cot. 'He's red in the face,' she cried. 'Look at him; he's going to have a fit, I know it!'

'He needs changing,' said Emma.

'Oh, I'm so glad you're still here.' Mrs Hervey gave her a warm smile and went to answer the phone.

She came back a few moments later. 'A visitor,' she said happily. 'He's on his way. I'll go and get the drinks ready.'

Emma, still coping with Bart's urgent needs, heard the doorbell presently, and voices. Mrs Hervey was laughing a lot; it must be someone she knew very well and was glad to see. She had, so far, refused all invitations from her friends and hadn't invited any of them to come to the house. 'I promised Mike that I'd stay quietly at home and look after Baby,' she had explained to Emma. 'As soon as Nanny is here and settled in then I shall make up for it.' Her eyes had sparkled at the thought.

Bart, now that she had made him comfortable once more, was already half-asleep; Emma was tucking him up when the door was opened and Mrs Hervey came in and, with her, Sir Paul Wyatt.

Emma's heart gave a delighted leap at the sight of him while at the same time she felt a deep annoyance; she looked a fright—even at her best she was nothing to look at, but now, at the end of the day, she wasn't worth a glance. What was he doing here anyway? She gave him a distant look and waited to see who would speak first.

It was Mrs Hervey, bubbling over with pleasure. 'Emma, this is Sir Paul Wyatt; he's a professor or something. He's Mike's oldest friend and he's come to see Bart. He didn't know that I was home—I did say that I would go to Scotland until Mike came home. Just fancy, he's turned into a GP, just for a bit while Dr Treble is away.' She turned a puzzled gaze to him. 'I thought you were a surgeon?'

'I am. This is by way of a change. Emma and I have already met; I operated upon her mother not so long ago.' He smiled at her across the room. 'Good evening, Emma. You are staying here?'

'No, I'm just going home.'

'Rather late, isn't it?'

'Oh, well, that's my fault,' said Mrs Hervey cheerfully. 'Bart went all red and was roaring his head off and Emma hadn't quite gone so she came back. I thought he was ill.'

He lifted an enquiring eyebrow as Emma said in a no-nonsense voice, 'He needed changing.'

He laughed. 'Oh, Doreen, when will you grow up? The sooner Mike gets back the better!' He had gone to lean over the cot and was looking at the sleeping infant. 'The image of his father. He looks healthy enough.' He touched the small cheek with a gentle finger. 'Why do you not have a nanny, and where are the servants?'

Mrs Hervey tugged at his sleeve. 'Come downstairs and have a drink and I'll tell you.'

Emma, longing to go, saw that Bart was already asleep.

'How do you get back?' he enquired of Emma.

'I bike—it's only a short way.' She added, in a convincingly brisk tone, 'I enjoy the exercise.'

He held the door open and she followed Mrs Hervey downstairs, got into her coat once again and heard him telling Mrs Hervey that he could spare ten minutes and no more. She wished them goodnight and then let herself out of the house and pedalled furiously home.

It was already half-past nine and, although she was hungry, she was too tired to do more than put on the kettle for tea. She fed a disgruntled Queenie and poked her head into the fridge and eyed its sparse contents, trying to decide whether a boiled egg and yesterday's loaf would be preferable to a quick bath and a cup of tea in bed.

A brisk tattoo on the door-knocker caused her to withdraw her head smartly and listen. The tattoo was repeated and she went to the door then, suddenly afraid that it was bad news of her mother. She put up the new chain and opened the door a few inches, her view quite blocked by the professor's bulk.

He said testily, 'Yes, it is I, Emma.'

'What do you want?' The door was still on the chain but she looked up into his face, half-hidden in the dark night. 'Mother?' she asked in a sudden panic.

'Your mother is well; I have seen her recently. Now, open the door, there's a good girl.'

She was too tired to argue. She opened it and he crowded into the narrow hall, his arms full.

'Fish and chips,' said Emma, suddenly famished.

'A quick and nourishing meal, but it must be eaten immediately.'

She led the way into the kitchen, took down plates from the small dresser and then paused. 'Oh, you won't want to eat fish and chips...'

'And why not? I have had no dinner this evening and I am extremely hungry.' He was portioning out the food on to the two plates while she laid the cloth and fetched knives and forks.

'I was making tea,' she told him.

'Splendid. You do not mind if I join you?'

Since he was already sitting at the table there seemed no point in objecting, and anyway, she didn't want to!

They sat opposite each other at the small table with Queenie, aroused by the delightful smell, at their feet, and for a few minutes neither of them spoke. Only when the first few mouthfuls had been eaten did Sir Paul ask, 'How long have you been with Doreen Hervey?'

Emma, gobbling chips, told him.

'And what free time do you have? It seems to me that your day is excessively long.'

'I come home each afternoon just for an hour or two…'

'To shop and wash and clean and make your bed? You are too pale, Emma; you need fresh air and a few idle hours.'

'Well, I'll get them in a week or two; the nanny said it would be only a few weeks, and Mrs Hervey told me today that the housemaid is coming back in just over a week.'

'Of course you need the money.'

He said it in such a matter-of-fact way that she said at once, 'Yes, I do, I won't be able to work for a bit when Mother comes home.' She selected a chip and bit into it. She had small very white teeth, and when she smiled and wasn't tired she looked almost pretty.

It was surprising, he reflected, what fish and chips and a pot of tea did for one. He couldn't remember when he had last had such a meal and he was glad to see that Emma's rather pale cheeks had taken on a tinge of colour.

He got up from the table, took their plates to the sink and poured the water from the kettle into the bowl.

'You can't wash up,' said Emma.

'I can and I shall. You may dry the dishes if you wish.'

'Well, really…' muttered Emma and then laughed. 'You're not a bit like a professor of surgery.'

'I am relieved to hear it. I don't spend all day and every day bending over the operating table, you know. I have a social side to my life.'

She felt a pang of regret that she would never know what that was.

As soon as the last knife and fork had been put away he wished her a pleasant good evening and went away. She felt deflated when he had gone. 'Only because,' she explained to Queenie, for lack of any other listener, 'I don't get many people—well, many men.'

Half an hour later Sir Paul let himself into his house, to be greeted as he always was by his dogs and his housekeeper.

'Dear knows, you're a busy man, sir, but it's long past the hour any self-respecting man should be working. You'll be wanting your dinner.'

'I've dined, thank you, Mrs Parfitt. I would have phoned but there was no phone.'

'Dined? With Dr Treble?' She sniffed. 'His housekeeper is a careless one in the kitchen—I doubt you enjoyed your food.'

'Fish and chips, and I enjoyed every mouthful.'

'Not out of newspaper?' Mrs Parfitt's round face was puckered in horror.

'No, no. On a plate in the company of a young lady.'

Mrs Parfitt twinkled at him. 'Ah, I'm glad to hear it, sir. Was she pretty?'

'No.' He smiled at her. 'Don't allow your thoughts to get sentimental, Mrs Parfitt—she needed a meal.'

'Helping another of your lame dogs over the stile, were you? There's a pile of post in your study; I'll bring you a tray of coffee and some of my little biscuits.'

'Excellent. They should dispel any lingering taste of my supper.'

Mrs Parfitt was right; there were a great many letters to

open and read and the answering machine to deal with. He
was occupied until the early hours of the morning, when he
took the dogs for a brisk walk, and saw them to their bas-
kets and finally took himself off to bed. He hadn't thought
of Emma once.

'Fancy you knowing Paul,' said Mrs Hervey, when Emma
arrived in the morning. 'He's a stunner; if Mike hadn't
turned up I could have fallen for him. Not that he gave me
any encouragement.' She sighed. 'You see, he'll pick a suitable wife when he decides he wants one and not a minute
sooner. I don't believe he's ever been in love—oh, he's doz-
ens of girlfriends, of course, but it'll take someone special
to touch his heart.'

Emma nodded. It would have to be someone like Mrs
Hervey, pretty as a picture, amusing and helpless; men,
Emma supposed, would like that. She thought with regret
that she had never had the opportunity to be helpless. And
she would never, she decided, taking a quick look in the unnecessary looking-glass in the nursery, be pretty.

That her eyes were large and thickly lashed and her hair,
confined tidily in a French pleat, was long and silky, and
that her mouth, though too wide, was gentle and her complexion as clear and unblemished as a baby's quite escaped
her attention.

Sir Paul Wyatt, fulfilling his role of general practitioner
in the middle of the following week, allowed his thoughts
to dwell on just those pleasing aspects of Emma's person,
only relinquishing them when the next patients came into
the surgery.

Surgery finished, he went on his rounds; the inhabitants

of Buckfastleigh were, on the whole, a healthy bunch and his visits were few. He drove himself home, ate his lunch, took the dogs for a walk and then got into the Rolls and drove back to Buckfastleigh again.

Emma was at home; her elderly bike was propped against the house wall and the windows were open. He knocked on the door, wondering why he had come.

She answered the door at once, an apron tied round her slender middle, her hair, loosed from its severe plait, tied back with a ribbon.

She stared up at him mutely, and he stared back with a placid face.

'Not Mother?' she said finally, and he shook his head.

'Is Mrs Hervey all right? Bart was asleep when I left.'

He nodded and she asked sharply, 'So why have you come?' She frowned. 'Do you want something?'

He smiled then. 'I am not certain about that... May I come in?'

'Sorry,' said Emma. 'Please do—I was surprised to see you...' She added unnecessarily, 'I was just doing a few chores.'

'When do you have to go back?' He was in the hall, taking up most of the space.

'Just after four o'clock to get Mrs Hervey's tea.'

He glanced at his watch. 'May we have tea here first? I'll go and get something—crumpets—while you do the dusting.'

Emma was surprised, although she agreed readily. Perhaps he had missed his lunch; perhaps surgery was earlier than usual that afternoon. She stood in the doorway and watched him drive away, and then rushed around with the duster and the carpet-sweeper before setting out the tea things. Tea would have to be in the kitchen; there was no fire laid in the sitting-room.

She fed Queenie, filled the kettle and went upstairs to do her face and pin her hair. Studying her reflection, she thought how dull she looked in her tweed skirt, blouse and— that essentially British garment—a cardigan.

She was back downstairs with minutes to spare before he returned.

It wasn't just crumpets he had brought with him—there were scones and doughnuts, a tub of butter and a pot of strawberry jam. He arranged them on a dish while she put the crumpets under the grill and boiled the kettle, all the while carrying on an undemanding conversation about nothing much so that Emma, who had felt suddenly awkward, was soothed into a pleasant feeling of ease.

They had finished the crumpets and were starting on the scones when he asked casually, 'What do you intend doing when you leave Doreen Hervey, Emma?'

'Do? Well, I'll stay at home for a bit, until Mother is quite herself again, and then I'll look for another job.'

He passed her the butter and the jam. 'You might train for something?'

'I can type and do shorthand, though I'm not very good at either, and people always need mother's helps.' She decided that it was time to change the conversation. 'I expect Mother will be on some kind of a diet?'

'Yes—small meals taken frequently, cut out vinegar and pickles and so on.' He sounded impatient. 'She will be given a leaflet when she comes home. The physicians have taken over now.' He frowned. 'Is it easy to get a job here?'

Her red herring hadn't been of much use. 'I think so. My kind of a job anyway.'

'You're wasted—bullied by selfish women and changing babies' nappies.'

'I like babies.' She added tartly, 'It's kind of you to bother, but there is no need—'

'How old are you, Emma?'

'Almost twenty-six.'

He smiled. 'Twenty-five, going on fifteen! I'm forty—do you find that old?'

'Old? Of course not. You're not yet in your prime. And you don't feel like forty, do you?'

'Upon occasion I feel ninety, but at the moment at least I feel thirty at the most!' He smiled at her and she thought what a very nice smile he had—warm and somehow reassuring. 'Have another doughnut?'

She accepted it with the forthright manner of a polite child. She was not, he reflected, in the least coy or self-conscious. He didn't search too deeply into his reasons for worrying about her future, although he admitted to the worry. It was probably because she was so willing to accept what life had to offer her.

He went presently, with a casual goodbye and no mention of seeing her again. Not that she had expected that. She cycled back to Mrs Hervey and Bart, reflecting that she was becoming quite fond of him.

It was the beginning of the third week, with another hundred pounds swelling their bank balance, when Mrs Hervey told her that the new nanny would be with them by the end of the week, and Cook and the housemaid would return in three days' time.

'And about time too,' said Mrs Hervey rather pettishly. 'I mean, three weeks just to get over flu...'

Emma held her tongue and Mrs Hervey went on, 'You'll stay until the end of the week, won't you, Emma? As soon as Cook and that girl are here I shall have a chance to go to the hairdresser. I'm desperate to get to Exeter—I need some clothes and a facial too. You'll only have Bart to look after, and Nanny comes on Friday evening. I dare say she'll want to ask your advice about Bart before you go.'

'I think,' said Emma carefully, 'that she may prefer not to do that. She's professional, you see, and I'm just a temporary help. I'm sure you will be able to tell her everything that she would want to know.'

'Will I? Write it all down for me, Emma, won't you? I never can remember Bart's feeds and what he ought to weigh.'

Certainly, once the cook and housemaid returned, life was much easier for Emma. She devoted the whole of her day to Bart, taking him for long rides in his pram, sitting with him on her lap, cuddling him and singing half-forgotten nursery rhymes while he stared up at her with his blue eyes. Cuddling was something that his mother wasn't very good at. She loved him, Emma was sure of that, but she was awkward with him. Perhaps the new nanny would be able to show Mrs Hervey how to cuddle her small son.

It was on her last day, handing over to a decidedly frosty Nanny, that she heard Sir Paul's voice in the drawing-room. She listened with half an ear to the superior young woman who was to have charge of Bart telling her of all the things she should have done, and wondered if she would see him. It seemed that she wouldn't, for presently Mrs Hervey joined them, remarking that Sir Paul had just called to see if everything was normal again.

'I asked him if he would like to see Bart but he said he

hadn't the time. He was on his way to Plymouth.' She turned to the nanny. 'You've had a talk with Emma? Wasn't it fortunate that she was able to come and help me?' She made a comic little face. 'I'm not much good with babies.'

'I'm accustomed to take sole charge, Mrs Hervey; you need have no further worries about Bart. Tomorrow, perhaps, we might have a little talk and I will explain my duties to you.'

It should surely be the other way round, thought Emma. But Mrs Hervey didn't seem to mind.

'Oh, of course. I'm happy to leave everything to you. You're ready to go, Emma? Say goodbye to Bart; he's got very fond of you...'

A remark which annoyed Nanny, for she said quite sharply that the baby was sleeping and shouldn't be disturbed. So Emma had to content herself with looking at him lying in his cot, profoundly asleep, looking like a very small cherub.

She would miss him.

She bade Nanny a quiet goodbye and went downstairs with Mrs Hervey and got on her bike, warmed by that lady's thanks and the cheque in her pocket. Three hundred pounds would keep them going for quite some time, used sparingly with her mother's pension.

When she got home, she took her bike round to the shed, went indoors and made some supper for Queenie, and boiled an egg for herself. She felt sad that the job was finished, but a good deal of the sadness was because she hadn't seen the professor again.

There was a letter from her mother in the morning, telling her that she would be brought home by ambulance in two days' time. How nice, she wrote, that Emma's job was finished just in time for her return. Emma wondered how she had known that, and then forgot about it as she made plans for the next two days.

It was pleasant to get up the next morning and know that she had the day to herself. It was Sunday, of course, so she wouldn't be able to do any shopping, but there was plenty to do in the house—the bed to make up, wood and coal to be brought in, the whole place to be dusted and aired. And, when that was done, she sat down and made a shopping list.

Bearing in mind what Sir Paul had said about diet, she wrote down what she hoped would be suitable and added flowers and one or two magazines, Earl Grey tea instead of the economical brand they usually drank, extra milk and eggs—the list went on and on, but for once she didn't care. Her mother was coming home and that was a cause for extravagance.

She had the whole of Monday morning in which to shop, and with money in her purse she enjoyed herself, refusing to think about the future, reminding herself that it would soon be the tourist season again and there were always jobs to be found. It didn't matter what she did so long as she could be at home.

Her mother arrived during the afternoon, delighted to be at home again, protesting that she felt marvellous, admiring the flowers and the tea-tray on a small table by the lighted fire in the sitting-room. Emma gave the ambulance driver tea and biscuits, received an envelope with instructions as to her mother's diet and went back to her mother.

Mrs Trent certainly looked well; she drank her weak tea and ate the madeira cake Emma had baked and settled back in her chair. 'Now, tell me all the news, Emma. What was this job like? Were you happy? A nice change looking after a baby?'

Emma recounted her days, making light of the long hours. 'It was a very nice job,' she declared, 'and I earned three hundred pounds, so I can stay at home for as long as you want me to.'

They talked for the rest of that afternoon and evening, with Queenie sitting on Mrs Trent's lap and finally trailing upstairs with her to curl up on her bed.

Emma, taking her some warm milk and making sure that she was comfortable before she went to bed herself, felt a surge of relief at the sight of her mother once more in her own bed. The future was going to be fine, she told herself as she kissed her mother goodnight.

Chapter 4

Emma and her mother settled down into a quiet routine: gentle pottering around the house, short walks in the afternoon, pleasant evenings round the fire at the end of the day. For economy's sake, Emma shared her mother's small, bland meals, and found herself thinking longingly of the fish and chips Sir Paul had brought to the house.

There was no sign of him, of course, and it wasn't likely that she would see him again; the new doctor had come to take over from Dr Treble and the professor had doubtless taken up his normal life again. She speculated a bit about that, imagining him stalking the wards with a bunch of underlings who hung on to any words of wisdom he might choose to utter and watched with awe while he performed some complicated operation. And his private life? Her imagination ran riot over that—married to some beautiful young woman—she would have to be beautiful, he wouldn't look at anyone less—perhaps with children—handsome little boys and pretty little girls. If he wasn't married he would certainly have any number of women-friends and get asked out a great deal—dinner parties and banquets and evenings at the theatre and visits to London.

A waste of time, she told herself time and again—she would forget all about him. But that wasn't easy, because her mother talked about him a great deal although, when pumped by Emma, she was unable to tell her anything about his private life.

Mrs Trent had been home for a week when he came to see her. Emma had seen the Rolls draw up from her mother's bedroom window and had hurried down to open the door, forgetting her unmade-up face and her hair bunched up any-how on top of her head. It was only as she opened the door that she remembered her appearance, so that she met his faintly amused look with a frown and her feelings so plain on her face that he said to her at once, 'I do apologise for coming unexpectedly, but I had half an hour to spare and I wanted to see how your mother was getting on.'

'Hello,' said Emma gruffly, finding her voice and her manners. 'Please come in; she will be glad to see you.'

She led the way into the little sitting-room. 'I was going to make Mother's morning drink and have some coffee. Would you like a cup?' She gave him a brief glance. 'Shall I take your coat?'

'Coffee would be delightful.' He took off his overcoat and flung it over a chair and went to take Mrs Trent's hand, which gave Emma the chance to escape. She galloped up to her room, powdered her nose, pinned up her hair and tore downstairs again to make the coffee and carry it in presently, looking her usual neat self.

Sir Paul, chatting with her mother, looked at her from under his lids and hid a smile, steering the conversation with effortless ease towards trivial matters. It was only when they had finished their coffee that he asked Mrs Trent a few casual questions. He seemed satisfied with her answers and presently took his leave.

As he shook hands with the older woman she asked, 'Are you still working here as a GP? Has the new doctor arrived?'

'Several days ago; he will be calling on you very shortly, I have no doubt.'

'So we shan't see you again? I owe you so much, Sir Paul.'

'It is a great satisfaction to me to see you on your feet again, Mrs Trent. Don't rush things, will you? You're in very capable hands.' He glanced at Emma, who had her gaze fixed on his waistcoat and didn't meet his eye.

When he had driven away Mrs Trent said, 'I'm sorry we shan't see him again. I felt quite safe with him...'

'I expect the new doctor is just as kind as Dr Treble. I'm sure he'll come and see you in a day or two, Mother.'

Which he did—a pleasant, youngish man who asked the same questions that Sir Paul had asked, assured Emma that her mother was making excellent progress and suggested that she might go to the surgery in a month's time for a check-up.

'No need really,' he said cheerfully. 'But I should like to keep an eye on you for a little while.' As Emma saw him to the door he observed, 'I'm sure you're looking after your mother very well; it's fortunate that you are living here with her.' It was a remark which stopped her just in time from asking him when he thought it would be suitable for her to look for a job again.

The days slid past, each one like the previous; Mrs Trent was content to knit and read and go for short walks, and Emma felt a faint prick of unease. Surely by now her mother should be feeling more energetic? She was youngish still—nowadays most people in their fifties were barely middle-aged and still active—but her mother seemed listless, and disinclined to exert herself.

The days lengthened and winter began to give way reluctantly to spring, but Mrs Trent had no inclination to go out and about. Emma got Mr Dobbs to drive them to the surgery, when a month was up, after reminding her mother that it was time she saw the doctor again.

She had already spoken to him on Mr Dobbs's phone, voicing her vague worries and feeling rather silly since there was nothing definite to tell him, but he was kindness itself as he examined Mrs Trent.

He said finally, 'You're doing very well, Mrs Trent—well enough to resume normal life once more. I'll see about some surgical stockings for you—you do have a couple of varicose veins. Recent, are they?'

'Oh, yes, but they don't bother me really. I'm not on my feet all that much.' Mrs Trent laughed. 'I'm getting rather lazy...'

'Well, don't get too lazy; a little more exercise will do you good, I think. The operation was entirely successful and there is no reason why you shouldn't resume your normal way of life.' He gave her an encouraging smile. 'Come and see me in a month's time and do wear those stockings—I'll see you get them.'

'A nice young man,' declared Mrs Trent as they were driven home by Mr Dobbs and Emma agreed, although she had the feeling that he had thought her over-fussy about her mother. Still, he had said that her mother was quite well again, excepting for those veins...

It was several days later, as she was getting their tea, that she heard her mother call out and then the sound of her falling. She flew to the sitting-room and found her mother lying on the floor, and she knew before she picked up her hand that there would be no pulse.

'Mother,' said Emma, and even though it was useless she put a cushion under her head before she tore out of the house to Mr Dobbs and the phone.

An embolism, the doctor said, a pulmonary embolism, sudden and fatal. Emma said, in a voice which didn't sound like hers, 'Varicose veins—it was a blood clot.' She saw his surprised look. 'I've done my First Aid.' She raised anguished eyes to his. 'Couldn't you have known?'

He shook his head. 'No, there were no symptoms and varicose veins are commonplace; one always bears in mind that a clot might get dislodged, but there is usually some warning.'

'She wouldn't have known?'

'No, I'm certain of that.'

There was no one to turn to, no family or very close friends, although the neighbours were kind—cooking her meals she couldn't eat, offering to help. They had liked her mother and they liked her and she was grateful, thanking them in a quiet voice without expression, grief a stone in her chest.

They came to the funeral too, those same neighbors, and the doctor, Cook and Alice from Mrs Smith-Darcy's house, taking no notice of that lady's orders to remain away. Mrs Hervey was there too, and kind Mr Dobbs. The only person Emma wanted to see was absent—Sir Paul Wyatt wasn't there, and she supposed that he had no reason to be there anyway. That he must know she was certain, for the doctor had told her that he had written to him…

There was no money, of course, and no will. She remembered her mother telling her laughingly that when she was sixty she would make one, but in any case there was almost nothing to leave—the house and the furniture and a few trinkets.

Emma, during the next few empty days, pondered her future. She would sell the house if she could find a small flat in Plymouth, and train properly as a shorthand typist and then find a permanent job. She had no real wish to go to Plymouth but if she went to Exeter, a city she knew and loved, she might meet Sir Paul—something, she told herself, she didn't wish to do. Indeed, she didn't want to see him again.

A new life, she decided, and the sooner the better. Thirty wasn't all that far off, and by then she was determined to have built herself a secure future. 'At least I've got Queenie,' she observed to the empty sitting-room as she polished and dusted, quite unnecessarily because the house was clean, but it filled the days. She longed to pack her things and settle her future at once, but there were all the problems of unexpected death to unravel first, so she crammed her days with hard work and cried herself to sleep each night, hugging Queenie for comfort, keeping her sorrow to herself.

People were very kind—calling to see how she was, offering companionship, suggesting small outings—and to all of them she showed a cheerful face and gave the assurance that she was getting along splendidly and making plans for the future, and they went away, relieved that she was coping so well.

'Of course, Emma has always been such a sensible girl,' they told each other, deceived by her calm manner.

Ten days after the funeral, her small affairs not yet settled, she was in the kitchen, making herself an early morning cup of tea and wondering how much longer she would have to wait before she could put the house up for sale. She would keep most of the furniture, she mused, sitting down at the kitchen table, only to be interrupted by a bang on the door-knocker. It must be the postman, earlier than usual, but perhaps there would be something interesting in the post. The unbidden thought that there might be a letter from Sir Paul passed through her mind as she opened the door.

It wasn't a letter from him but he himself in person, looming in the doorway and, before she could speak, inside the house, squashed up against her in the narrow little hall.

At the sight of him she burst into tears, burying her face in the tweed of his jacket without stopping to think what she was doing, only aware of the comfort of his arms around her.

He said gently, 'My poor girl. I didn't know—I've been in America and only got back yesterday evening. I was told what had happened by your doctor. He wrote—but by the time I had read his letter it was too late to come to you. I am so very sorry.'

'There wasn't anyone,' said Emma, between great heaving sobs. 'Everyone was so kind…' It was a muddled remark, which he rightly guessed referred to his absence. He let her cry her fill and presently, when the sobs became snivels, he offered a large white linen handkerchief.

'I'm here now,' he said cheerfully, 'and we'll have breakfast while you tell me what happened.' He gave her an avuncular pat on the back and she drew away from him, feeling ashamed of her outburst but at the same time aware that the hard stone of her grief had softened to a gentle sorrow.

'I'm famished,' said Sir Paul in a matter-of-fact voice which made the day normal again. 'I'll lay the table while you cook.'

'I must look a fright. I'll go and do something to my face...'

He studied her with an impersonal look which she found reassuring. Not a fright, he reflected, but the face far too pale, the lovely eyes with shadows beneath them and the clear skin blotched and pinkened with her tears. 'It looks all right to me,' he told her and knew that, despite the tearstains, she was feeling better.

'As long as you don't mind,' she said rather shyly, and got out the frying-pan. 'Will fried eggs and fried bread do?' she asked. 'I'm afraid there isn't any bacon...'

'Splendidly. Where do you keep the marmalade?'

They sat down eventually, facing each other across the kitchen table and Emma, who had had no appetite for days, discovered that she was hungry. It wasn't until they had topped off the eggs with toast and marmalade that Sir Paul allowed the conversation to become serious.

'What are your plans?' he wanted to know, when he had listened without interruption to her account of her mother's death.

'I'll have to sell this house. I thought I'd find a small flat in Plymouth and take a course in office management and then get a proper job. I've enough furniture and I'll have Queenie.'

'Is there no money other than the proceeds from the house?'

'Well, no, there isn't. Mother's pension won't be paid any more of course.' She added hastily, anxious to let him see that she was able to manage very well, 'I can put the house up for sale just as soon as I'm allowed to. There are still some papers and things. They said they'd let me know.'

'And is that what you would like to do, Emma?'

'Yes, of course.' She caught his eye and added honestly, 'I don't know what else to do.'

He smiled at her across the table. 'Will you marry me, Emma?'

Her mouth dropped open. 'Marry you? You're joking!'

'Er—no, I have never considered marriage a joke.'

'Why do you want to marry me? You don't know anything about me—and I'm plain and not a bit interesting. Besides, you don't—don't love me.'

'I know enough about you to believe that you would make me an admirable wife and, to be truthful, I have never considered you plain. As for loving you, I am perhaps old-fashioned enough to consider that mutual liking and compatibility and the willingness to make a good marriage are excellent foundations for happiness. Since the circumstances are unusual we will marry as soon as possible and get to know each other at our leisure.'

'But your family and your friends...?' She saw his lifted eyebrows and went on awkwardly, 'What I mean is, I don't think I'm used to your kind of life.' She waved a hand round the little kitchen. 'I don't expect it's like this.'

He said evenly, 'I live in a thatched cottage at Lustleigh and I have an elderly housekeeper and two dogs. My mother and father live in the Cotswolds and I have two sisters, both married. I'm a consultant at the Exeter hospitals and I frequently go to London, where I am a consultant at various hospitals. I go abroad fairly frequently, to lecture and operate, but at present I have taken a sabbatical, although I still fulfil one or two appointments.'

'Aren't you too busy to have a wife? I mean—' she frowned, trying to find the right words '—you lead such a busy life.'

'When I come home in the evenings it will be pleasant to find you there, waiting to listen to my grumbles if things haven't gone right with my day, and at the weekends I will have a companion.'

'You don't—that is, you won't mind me not loving you?'

'I think,' he said gently, 'that we might leave love out of it, don't you?' He smiled a tender smile, which warmed her down to the soles of her feet. 'We like each other, don't we? And that's important.'

'You might fall in love with someone...'

She wasn't looking at him, otherwise she would have seen his slow smile.

'So might you—a calculated risk which we must both take.' He smiled again, completely at ease. 'I'll wash up and tidy things away while you go and pack a bag.'

'A bag? What for?'

'You're coming back with me. And while Mrs Parfitt fattens you up and the moor's fresh air brings colour into your cheeks you can decide what you want to do.' When she opened her mouth to speak he raised a hand. 'No, don't argue, Emma. I've no intention of leaving you alone here. Later you can tell me what still has to be settled about the house and furniture and I'll deal with the solicitor. Are the bills paid?'

He was quite matter-of-fact about it and she found herself telling him that there were still a few outstanding. 'But everyone said they'd wait until the house was sold.'

He nodded. 'Leave it to me, if you will. Now, run along and get some things packed. Has Queenie got a basket?'

'Yes, it's beside the dresser.'

She went meekly upstairs, and only as she was packing did she reflect that he was behaving in a high-handed fash-

ion, getting his own way without any effort. That, she reminded herself, was because she was too tired and unhappy
to resist him. She was thankful to leave everything to him,
but once she had pulled herself together she would convince
him that marrying him was quite out of the question.

And, since he didn't say another word about it as he drove
back to Lustleigh, she told herself that he might have made
the suggestion on the spur of the moment and was even
now regretting it.

It was a bright morning and cold, but spring was defi-
nitely upon them. Lustleigh was a pretty village and a pale
sun shone on its cottages. It shone on Sir Paul's home too
and Emma, getting out of the car, fell in love with the house
at first glance.

'Oh, how delightful. It's all nooks and crannies, isn't it?'

He had a hand under her elbow, urging her to the door.
'It has been in the family for a long time, and each generation has added a room or a chimney-pot or another window just as the fancy took it.' He opened the door and Mrs
Parfitt came bustling down the curving staircase at the back
of the hall.

'God bless my soul, so you're back, sir.'

She cast him a reproachful look and he said quickly, 'I
got back late last night and went straight to the hospital
and, since it was already after midnight and I wanted to go
to Buckfastleigh as early as possible, I didn't come home.
They put me up there.' He still had his hand on Emma's
arm. 'Mrs Parfitt, I've brought a guest who will stay with us
for a little while. Miss Trent's mother died recently and she
needs a break. Emma, this is my housekeeper, Mrs Parfitt.'

Emma shook hands, conscious of sharp, elderly eyes looking her over.

'I hope I won't give you too much extra work...'

Mrs Parfitt had approved of what she saw. All in good time, she promised herself, she would discover the whys and wherefores. 'A pleasure to have someone in the house, miss, for Sir Paul is mostly away from home or shut in that study of his—he might just as well be in the middle of the Sahara for all I see of him!'

She chuckled cosily. 'I'll bring coffee into the sitting-room, shall I, sir? And get a room ready for Miss Trent?'

Sir Paul took Emma's coat and opened a door, urging her ahead of him. The room was long and low, with small windows overlooking the narrow street and glass doors opening on to the garden at the far end. He went past her to open them and let in the dogs, who danced around, delighted to see him.

'Come and meet Kate and Willy,' he invited, and Emma crossed the room and offered a balled fist.

'Won't they mind Queenie?' she wanted to know.

'Not in the least, and Mrs Parfitt will be delighted; her cat died some time ago and she is always talking of getting a kitten—Queenie is much more suitable. I'll get her, and they can get used to each other while we have our coffee.'

While he was gone she looked around the room. Its walls were irregular and there were small windows on each side of the inglenook, and a set of heavy oak beams supporting the ceiling. The walls were white but there was no lack of colour in the room—the fine old carpet almost covered the wood floor, its russets and faded blues toning with the velvet curtains. There were bookshelves crammed with books, several easy-chairs, and a vast sofa drawn up to the fire and charming pie-crust tables holding reading lamps—a delightful lived-in room.

She pictured it in mid-winter, when the wind whistled from the moor and snow fell; with the curtains drawn and a fire roaring up the chimney one would feel safe and secure and content. For the first time since her mother's death she felt a small spark of happiness.

Sir Paul, coming in with Queenie under his arm, disturbed her thoughts and saw them reflected in her face. He said casually, 'You like this room? Let us see if Queenie approves of it... No, don't worry about the dogs—they'll not touch her.'

Mrs Parfitt came in to bring the coffee then, and they sat drinking it, watching the dogs, obedient to their master, sitting comfortably while Queenie edged round them and finally, to Emma's surprise, sat down and washed herself.

'The garden is walled—she won't be able to get out; she'll be quite at home in a few days. I've taken your bag upstairs; I expect you would like to unpack before lunch. This afternoon we'll walk round the village so that you can find your way about. I'll take the dogs for a run and see you at lunch.'

Emma, soothed by the room and content to have someone to tell her how to order her day, nodded. It was like being in a dream after the loneliness of the last week or two. It wouldn't last, of course, for she had no intention of marrying Sir Paul. But for the moment she was happy to go on dreaming.

She was led away presently, up the charming little staircase and on to a landing with passages leading from it in all directions.

'A bit of a jumble,' said Mrs Parfitt cheerfully, 'but you'll soon find your way around. I've put you in a nice quiet room overlooking the garden. Down this passage and up these two steps. The door's a bit narrow...'

Which it was—solid oak like the rest of the doors in the cottage and opening into a room with a large circle of windows taking up all of one wall. There was a balcony beyond them with a wrought-iron balustrade and a sloping roof. 'For your little cat,' explained Mrs Parfitt. 'I dare say you like to have her with you at night? I always had my Jenkin—such a comfort he was!'

'How thoughtful of you, Mrs Parfitt. I hope you'll like Queenie; she's really very good.'

'Bless you, miss, I like any cat.' She trotted over to another door by the bed. 'The bathroom's here and mind the step down, and if there's anything you need you just say so. You'll want to hang up your things now. Lunch is at one o'clock, but come downstairs when you're ready and sit by the fire.'

When she had gone Emma looked around her; the room had uneven walls so that the bay window took up the longest of them. There was a small fireplace in the centre of one short wall and the bedhead was against the wall facing the window. That was irregular too, and the fourth wall had a deep-set alcove into which the dressing-table fitted. She ran a finger along its surface, delighting in the golden brown of the wood.

It was a cosy room, despite the awkwardness of its shape, and delightfully furnished in muted pinks and blues. She unpacked her things and laid them away in the tallboy, and hung her dress in the cupboard concealed in one of the walls. She had brought very little with her—her sensible skirt and blouses, her cardigan and this one dress. She tidied away her undies, hung up her dressing-gown and sat down before the dressing-table.

Her reflection wasn't reassuring and that was partly her

fault, for she hadn't bothered much with her appearance during the two weeks since her mother had died—something
she would have to remedy. She did her face and brushed
her hair and pinned it into its neat French pleat and went
downstairs, peering along the various passages as she went.

It was indeed a delightful house, and although Sir Paul
had called it a cottage it was a good deal larger than that.
There was no sign of him when she reached the hall but Mrs
Parfitt popped her head round a door.

'He won't be long, miss. Come into the kitchen if you've
a mind. Your little cat's here, as good as gold, sitting in the
warm. Taken to us like a duck to water, she has.'

Indeed, Queenie looked as though she had lived there all
her life, stretched out before the Aga.

'You don't mind her being here? In your kitchen?'

'Bless you, miss, whatever harm could she do? Just wait
while I give the soup a stir and I'll show you the rest of it...'

She opened a door and led the way down a short passage.
'This bit of the house Sir Paul's grandfather added; you can't
see it from the lane. There's a pantry—' she opened another
door '—and a wash-house opposite and all mod cons—Sir
Paul saw to that. And over here there's what was the still-
room; I use it for bottled fruit and jam and pickles. I make
those myself. Then there's this cubby-hole where the shoes
are cleaned and the dogs' leads and such like are kept. If
ever you should want a good thick coat there's plenty hanging there—boots too.'

She opened the door at the end of the passage. 'The back
garden, miss; leastways, the side of it with a gate into the
path which leads back to the lane.' She gave a chuckle.
'Higgledy-piggledy, as you might say, but you'll soon find
your way around.'

As she spoke the gate opened and Sir Paul and the dogs came through.

'Ready for lunch?' he wanted to know, and swept Emma back with him to the sitting-room. 'A glass of sherry? It will give you an appetite.'

It loosened her tongue too, so that over Mrs Parfitt's delicious lunch she found herself answering his carefully casual questions and even, from time to time, letting slip some of her doubts and fears about the future, until she remembered with a shock that he had offered her a future and here she was talking as though he had said nothing.

He made no comment, but began to talk about the village and the people living in it. It was obvious to her that he was attached to his home, although according to Mrs Parfitt he was away a good deal.

He took her round the house after lunch. There was a small sitting-room at the front of the cottage, with his study behind it. A dining-room was reached through a short passage and, up several steps to one side of the hall, there was a dear little room most comfortably furnished and with rows of bookshelves, filled to overflowing. Emma could imagine sitting there by the fire, reading her fill.

There was a writing-desk under the small window, with blotter, writing-paper and envelopes neatly arranged upon it, and the telephone to one side. One could sit there and write letters in comfort and peace, she thought. Only there was no one for her to write to. Well, there was Mr Dobbs, although he was always so busy he probably wouldn't have time to read a letter, and she hardly thought that Mrs Hervey would be interested. Cook and Alice, of course, but they would prefer postcards...

Sir Paul had been watching her. 'You like this room?'

She nodded. 'I like the whole cottage; it's like home.'

'It is home, Emma.'

She had no answer to that.

She was given no time to brood. During the next few days he walked her over the moor, taking the dogs, bundling her into one of the elderly coats by the back door, marching her along, mile after mile, not talking much, and when they got home Mrs Parfitt had delicious meals waiting for them, so that between the good food and hours in the open air she was blissfully tired at the end of each day, only too willing to accept Sir Paul's suggestion that she should go early to bed—to fall asleep the moment her head touched the pillow.

On Sunday he took her to church. St John's dated from the thirteenth century, old and beautiful, and a mere stone's throw from the cottage. Wearing the dress under her winter coat, and her only hat—a plain felt which did nothing for her—Emma sat beside him in a pew in the front of the church, and watched him read the lesson, surprised that he put on a pair of glasses to do so, but enthralled by his deep, unhurried voice. Afterwards she stood in the church porch while he introduced her to the rector and his wife, and several people who stopped to speak to him.

They were friendly, and if they were curious they were far too well-mannered to show it. They all gave them invitations to come for a drink or to dine, promising to phone and arrange dates, chorusing that they must get to know Emma while she was in Lustleigh.

'We are always glad to see a new face,' declared a talkative middle-aged woman. 'And as for you, Paul, we see you so seldom that you simply must come.'

He replied suitably but, Emma noted, made no promises.

That made sense too; their curiosity would be even greater if she were to return home and never be seen again there. Sir Paul would deal with that without fuss, just as he did everything else. She remained quiet, smiling a little and making vague remarks when she had to.

After Sunday lunch, sitting by the fire, the Sunday papers strewn around, the dogs at Sir Paul's feet and Queenie on her lap, Emma said suddenly, 'You have a great many friends…'

He looked at her over his glasses and then took them off. 'Well, I have lived here for a number of years, and my parents before me, and their parents before them. We aren't exactly cut off from the world but we are a close-knit community.' He added casually, 'I believe you will fit in and settle down very well here.'

His gaze was steady and thoughtful, and after a moment she said, 'I don't understand why you want me to marry you.'

'I have given you my reasons. They are sound and sensible. I am not a young man, to make decisions lightly, Emma.'

'No, I'm sure of that. But it isn't just because you're sorry for me?'

'No, certainly not. That would hardly be a good foundation for a happy marriage.'

He smiled at her and she found herself smiling too. 'We might quarrel…'

'I should be very surprised if we didn't from time to time—which wouldn't matter in the least since we are both sensible enough to make it up afterwards. We are bound to agree to differ about a number of things—life would be dull if we didn't.'

Early the following week he drove her to Buckfastleigh.

'You're having coffee with Doreen Hervey,' he told her. 'Unless you want to come with me to the solicitor and house agent. Will you stay with her until I fetch you?'

'Should I go with you?'

'Not unless you wish to. From what you have told me, everything is settled and you can sell your house. The solicitor has already been in contact with the house agent, hasn't he? It's just a question of tying up the ends. Would you like to go there and see if there's anything you want to keep? There's plenty of room at the cottage.'

'You're talking as though we are going to be married.'

For a moment he covered her clasped hands with one of his. He said quietly, 'Say yes, Emma, and trust me.'

She turned her head to gaze at his calm face. He was not looking at her, but watching the road ahead. Of course she trusted him; he was the nicest person she had ever met, and the kindest.

'I do trust you,' she told him earnestly, 'and I'll marry you and be a good wife.'

He gave her a quick glance—so quick that she hadn't time to puzzle over the look on his face. She dismissed it, suddenly filled quite joyously with quiet content.

Chapter 5

Emma and Paul had a lot to talk about as he drove back later that day. Everything, he assured her, was arranged; it was now only a question of selling the house.

He had settled the few debts, paid the outstanding bills and returned to Doreen Hervey's house, where he found Emma in the nursery, hanging over Bart's cot, heedless of Nanny's disapproval.

Mrs Hervey, sitting meekly in the chair Nanny had offered, had been amused. 'Wait till you've got one of your own,' she had said.

Emma had turned her face away, her cheeks warm, and listened thankfully to his easy, 'One would imagine that you were worn to a thread looking after Bart, Doreen. When will Mike be home?'

He had taken her to her house then, and helped her decide which small keepsakes she wished to have—a few pieces of silver, some precious china, her mother's little Victorian work table, her father's silver tankard, photos in old silver frames.

Standing in the small sitting-room, she had asked diffidently, 'Would you mind if Mr Dobbs and Cook and Alice came and chose something? They were very kind to me and to Mother...'

'Of course. We'll take the car and fetch them now.'

'Mrs Smith-Darcy will never let them come.'

'Leave it to me. You stay here and collect the things you want while I bring them here.'

She didn't know what he had said but they were all there within twenty minutes, and she had left them to choose what they wanted.

'If I could have some of Mrs Trent's clothes?' Alice had whispered. Alice was the eldest of numerous children, whose wages went straight into the family purse. She had gone away delighted, with Cook clutching several pictures she had fancied. As for Mr Dobbs, he had had an eye on the clock in the kitchen for a long time, he had told her.

Sir Paul had taken them all back and mentioned casually on his return that he had arranged to send everything but the furniture to a charity shop. Emma had been dreading packing up her mother's clothes and the contents of the linen cupboard. She had thanked him with gratitude.

He had popped her back into the car then, taken her to Buckland in the Moor and given her lunch at the country hotel there. She had been conscious that her first sharp grief had given way to a gentle sorrow and she had been able to laugh and talk and feel again. She had tried to thank him then. 'I told you that I would never be able to repay you for all you did for Mother, and now I'm doubly in your debt.'

He had smiled his kind smile. 'Shall we cry quits? After all, I'm getting a wife, am I not? And I fancy the debt should be mine.'

That evening, as they sat round the fire, with the dogs and Queenie sprawling at their feet, he suggested that they might go to Exeter on the following day. 'You have plenty of money now,' he reminded her, and when she told him that she had only a few pounds he said, 'You forget your house. Supposing I settle any bills for the present and you pay me when it is sold?'

'I already owe you money for the solicitor and all these debts...'

'You can easily repay those also, but all in good time. I'm sure that the house will sell well enough.'

'Thank you so much, then; I do need some clothes.'

'I have yet to meet a woman who didn't. At the same time we might decide on a date for our wedding. There is no point in waiting, is there? Will you think about it and let me know what you would like to do?'

When she didn't reply he went on quietly, 'Supposing we go along and see the vicar? He can read the banns; that will give you three weeks to decide on a date. It will also give you a breathing-space to think things over.'

'You mean if I should want to back out?'

'Precisely.' He was smiling at her.

'I'll not do that,' said Emma.

She was uncertain what to buy and sat up in bed that night making a list. Good clothes, of course, suitable for the wife of a consultant surgeon and at the same time wearable each day in the country. 'Tweeds,' she wrote. 'Suit and a top-coat'—even though spring was well settled in it could be cold on the moor.

One or two pretty dresses, she thought, and undies, shoes—and perhaps she could find a hat which actually did something for her. She would need boots and slippers—and should she look for something to wear in the evenings? Did those people she'd met at the church give parties or rather grand dinners?

She asked Paul at breakfast. He was a great help.

'The dinner parties are usually formal—black tie and so on, short frocks for the ladies. I suppose because we tend to make our own amusements, celebrating birthdays and so on. But more often, as far as I remember, the ladies wear pretty dresses. You'll need a warm wrap of some kind, though, for the evening. It'll stay chilly here for some time yet.' He looked across at her list. 'Don't forget a warm dressing-gown and slippers.'

'I need rather a lot...'

'You have plenty of money coming to you.'

'How much should I spend?'

He named a sum which left her open-mouthed. 'But that's hundreds and hundreds!'

Poker-faced, he observed that good clothes lasted a long time and were more economical in the long run.

'You really don't mind lending me the money?'

'No. I'll come with you and write the cheques. If you out-run the constable, I'll warn you.'

Thus reassured, Emma plunged into her day's shopping. She would have gone to one of the department stores but Paul took her instead to several small, elegant and very expensive boutiques. Even with a pause for coffee, by lunch-time she had acquired a tweed suit, a cashmere top-coat—its price still made her feel a little faint—more skirts, blouses and sweaters, a windproof jacket to go with them, and two fine wool dresses.

When she would have chosen shades which she consid-

ered long-wearing he had suggested something more co-
lourful—plaids, a dress in garnet-red, another in turquoise
and various shades of blue, silk blouses in old rose, blue and
green, and a dress for the dinner parties—a tawny crêpe,
deceptively simple.

He took her to lunch then. Watching her crossing through
her list, he observed, 'A good waterproof, don't you think?
Then I'll collect the parcels and go to the car and leave you
to buy the rest. Will an hour be enough?'

'Yes, oh, yes.' She paused, wondering how she should tell
him that she had barely enough money to buy stockings, let
alone undies and a dressing-gown.

'You'll need some money.' He was casual about it, handing her a roll of notes. 'If it isn't enough we can come again
tomorrow.'

They bought the raincoat, and a hat to go with it, before
he left her at a department store. 'Don't worry about the
time; I'll wait,' he told her, and waited until she was inside.

Before she bought anything she would have to count the
notes he had given her. There was no one else in the Ladies,
and she took the roll out of her handbag. The total shocked
her—she could have lived on it for months. At the same
time it presented the opportunity for her to spend lavishly.

Which she did. Might as well be hung for a sheep as for a
lamb, she reflected, choosing silk and lace undies, a quilted
dressing-gown, and matching up stockings with shoes and
the soft leather boots she had bought. Even so, there was
still money in her purse. Laden with her purchases, she left
the shop and found Paul waiting for her.

He took her packages from her. 'Everything you need for
the time being?' he asked.

'For years,' she corrected him. 'I've had a lovely day, Paul; you have no idea. There's a lot of money left over...'

'Keep it. I'm sure you'll need it.' He glanced sideways at her. 'Before we marry,' he added.

It was at breakfast the next morning that he told her that he would be away for a few days. 'I have an appointment in Edinburgh which I must keep,' he told her. 'If you want to go to Exeter for more shopping ask Truscott at the garage to drive you there and bring you back here. I'll have a word with him before I go.'

'Thank you.' She was very conscious of disappointment but all she said was, 'May I take the dogs out?'

'Of course. I usually walk them to Lustleigh Cleave in the early morning. If it's clear weather you'll enjoy a good walk on the moor.'

'I can christen the new tweeds,' said Emma soberly. He wouldn't be there to see them; she had been looking forward to astonishing him with the difference in her appearance when she was well-dressed. That would have to wait now. 'You're leaving today?'

'In an hour or so. Mrs Parfitt will look after you, Emma, but feel free to do whatever you like; this house will be your home as well as mine.'

He had gone by mid-morning, and when she had had coffee with Mrs Parfitt she went to her room with Queenie and tried on her new clothes.

They certainly made a difference; their colours changed her ordinary features to near prettiness and their cut showed off her neat figure. It was a pity that Paul wasn't there to see the chrysalis changing into a butterfly. She had to make do with Queenie.

She had to admit that by teatime, even though she had filled the rest of the day by taking the dogs for a long walk, she was missing him, which was, of course, exactly what he had intended.

Mrs Parfitt, when Emma asked her the next day, had no idea when he would be back. 'Sir Paul goes off for days at a time,' she explained to Emma. 'He goes to other hospitals, and abroad too. Does a lot of work in London, so I've been told. Got friends there too. I dare say he'll be back in a day or two. Why not put on one of your new skirts and that jacket and go down to the shop for me and fetch up a few groceries?'

So Emma went shopping, exchanging good mornings rather shyly with the various people she met. They were friendly, wanting to know if she liked the village and did she get on with the dogs? She guessed that there were other questions hovering on their tongues but they were too considerate to ask them.

Going back with her shopping, she reflected that, since she had promised to marry Paul, it might be a good thing to do so as soon as possible. He had told her to decide on a date. As soon after the banns had been read as could be arranged—which thought reminded her that she would certainly need something special to wear on her wedding-day.

Very soon, she promised herself, she would get the morning bus to Exeter and go to the boutique Paul had taken her to. She had plenty of money still—her own money too... Well, almost her own, she admitted, once the house was sold and she had paid him back what she owed him.

The time passed pleasantly, her head filled with the delightful problem of what she would wear next, and even the steady rain which began to fall as she walked on the moor with the dogs did nothing to dampen her spirits.

She got up early and took them out for a walk before her breakfast the next day and then, with Mrs Parfitt's anxious tut-tutting because she wouldn't get the taxi from the garage ringing in her ears, she got on the bus.

It was a slow journey to the city, since the bus stopped whenever passengers wished to get on or off, but she hardly noticed, and when it arrived at last she nipped smartly away, intent on her search for the perfect wedding-outfit.

Of course, she had had her dreams of tulle veils and elaborate wedding-dresses, but theirs wasn't going to be that sort of wedding. She should have something suitable but pretty, and, since she had an economical mind, something which could be worn again.

The sales lady in the boutique remembered her and nodded her head in satisfaction at the vast improvement in Emma's appearance now that she was wearing the tweed suit. The little hat she had persuaded her to buy had been just right... She smiled encouragingly. 'If I may say so, madam, that tweed is exactly the right colour for you. How can I help you?'

'I want something to wear at my wedding,' said Emma, and went delightfully pink.

The sales lady concealed a sentimental heart under her severely corseted black satin. She beamed a genuine smile. 'A quiet wedding? In church?'

Emma nodded. 'I thought a dress and jacket and a hat...'

'Exactly right, madam, and I have just the thing, if you will take a seat.'

Emma sat and a young girl came with the first of a selection of outfits. Very pretty, but blue would look cold in the church. And the next one? Pink, and with rather too many buttons and braid for her taste—it was too frivolous. The third one was the one—winter white in a fine soft woollen material, it had a short jacket and a plain white sheath of a dress.

'I'll try that one,' said Emma.

It fitted, but she had known that it would. Now that she was wearing it she knew that it was exactly what she had wanted.

The sales lady circled her knowingly. 'Elegant and feminine. Madam has a very pretty figure.'

'I must find a hat...'

'No problem. These outfits for special occasions I always team up with several hats so that the outfit is complete.' She waved a hand at the girl, who opened drawers and tenderly lifted out a selection and offered them one by one.

Emma, studying her reflection, gave a sigh. 'I'm so plain,' she said in a resigned voice, and removed a confection of silk flowers and ribbon from her head.

The sales lady was good at her job. 'If I may say so, madam, you have fine eyes and a splendid complexion. Perhaps something... Ah, I have it.'

It looked nothing in her hand—white velvet with a pale blue cord twisted round it—but on Emma's head it became at once stylish, its small soft brim framing her face.

'Oh, yes,' said Emma, and then rather anxiously, 'I hope I have enough money with me.'

The older woman waved an airy hand. 'Please do not worry about that, madam. Any money outstanding you can send to me when you return home.'

Emma took off the hat and, while it and the outfit were being packed up, counted the money in her purse. There was more than enough when she was presented with the bill. She paid, feeling guilty at spending such a great deal of money. On the other hand she wanted to look her very best on her wedding-day. They would be happy, she promised herself, and stifled the sadness she felt that her mother wouldn't see her wed.

There were still one or two small items that she needed. She had coffee and then bought them, and by that time she was hungry. She had soup and a roll in a small café tucked away behind the high street and then, since the bus didn't leave for another hour or so, wandered round the shops, admiring the contents of their windows, thinking with astonishment that, if she wanted, she could buy anything she desired, within reason. She would have plenty of money of her own when the house was sold; she would get Paul to invest it in something safe and use the interest. She need never ask him for a penny, she thought, and fell to wondering where he was and what he was doing.

Sir Paul, already on his way back from Edinburgh, had turned off the main road to pay a visit to his mother and father, and, as he always did, gave a smile of content as he took the Rolls between the gateposts and along the short drive which led to their home—an old manor-house built of Cotswold stone, mellow with age and surrounded by a large, rambling garden which even at the bleakest time of year looked charming.

One day it would be his, but not for many years yet he hoped, catching sight of his father pottering in one of the flowerbeds. He drew up before the door, got out and went to meet him and together they walked to the house, going in through the garden door. 'My dirty boots, Paul; your mother will turn on me if I go in through the front door.'

They both laughed. His mother, to the best of his knowledge, had never turned on anyone in her life. She came to meet them now. Of middle height, rather stout and with a sweet face framed by grey hair stylishly dressed, she looked delighted to see him.

'Paul—' she lifted her face for his kiss '—how lovely to see you. Are you back at work again? Going somewhere or coming back?'

'Coming back. I can't stay, my dear, I need to get home—but may I come next weekend and bring the girl I'm going to marry to meet you both?'

'Marry? Paul—is it anyone we know?'

'No, I think not. She has lived at Buckfastleigh all her life except for her time at boarding-school. Her mother died recently. I hope—I think you will like her.'

'Pretty?' asked his mother.

'No—at least, she has a face you can talk to—peaceful—and she listens. Her eyes are lovely and she is also sensible and matter-of-fact.'

He didn't look like a man in love, reflected his mother. On the other hand, he was of an age to lose his heart for the rest of his life and beyond; she only hoped that she was the right girl. He had from time to time over the years brought girls to his parents' home and she hadn't liked any of them. They had all been as pretty as pictures, but he hadn't been in love with any of them.

'This is wonderful news, Paul, and we will make her very welcome. Come for lunch on Saturday. Can you stay until Monday morning?'

'I've a teaching round in the afternoon. If we leave soon after breakfast I can take Emma home first.'

'Emma—that's a pretty and old-fashioned name.'

He smiled. 'She's rather an old-fashioned girl.'

Watching him drive away presently, his mother said, 'Do you suppose it will be all right, Peter?'

'My dear, Paul is forty years old. He hasn't married sooner because he hadn't found the right girl. Now he has.'

Emma got off the bus in the village, walked the short distance to Paul's house, went along the alley and in through the side-door. Mrs Parfitt would be preparing dinner and she didn't want to disturb her. She went through to the hall and opened the drawing-room door, her parcels clamped under one arm.

Sir Paul was sitting by the fire, with the dogs resting their chins on his feet and Queenie on the arm of his chair. Emma gave a squeak of delight, dropped her parcels and hurried across the room.

'Paul! Oh, how lovely; you're home. Don't get up...'

He was already on his feet, his eyes very bright, scanning her happy face. He said lightly, 'Emma, you've been shopping again.' And she pulled up short beside him, conscious that she had been quite prepared to fling herself into his arms. The thought took her breath so that her voice didn't sound quite like hers.

'Well, yes, my wedding-dress.' She added earnestly, 'I couldn't buy it the other day because you mustn't see it until we're in the church.'

'A pleasure I look forward to.' He picked up the box and parcels she had dropped. 'You'd like a cup of tea? I'll tell Mrs Parfitt while you take off your things.'

When she came down the tea-tray was on a little table by the fire—tea in its silver teapot, muffins in their silver dish, tiny cakes.

She was pouring their second cups when he said quietly, 'Next Saturday we are going to my parents' home in the Cotswolds—just for the weekend.'

She almost dropped the pot. 'Oh, well, yes, of course. I—I hope they'll like me.' She put down the teapot carefully. 'I think that perhaps I'm not quite the kind of girl they would expect you to marry, if you see what I mean.'

'On the contrary. You will find that they will welcome you as their daughter.' He spoke kindly but she could sense that it would be of no use arguing about it.

She said merely, 'That's good. I'll look forward to meeting them.'

'If you've finished your tea shall we go along to the vicarage and discuss dates with the vicar? If you're not too tired we can walk.'

The vicarage was on the other side of the church. I suppose I shall walk to my wedding, thought Emma as Paul rang the bell.

The vicar was a man of Paul's age. 'I'll read the first banns this Sunday, tomorrow, which means that you can marry any day after the third Sunday. You've a date in mind?'

They both looked at Emma, who said sensibly, 'Well, it will have to fit in with Paul's work, won't it?' She smiled at him. 'I know I'm supposed to choose, but I think you had better...'

'Will the Tuesday of the following week suit you? I believe I'm more or less free for a few days after that.' He glanced at Emma, who looked back serenely.

'In the morning?' she asked.

'Whenever you like; since I chose the day you must choose the time.'

She realised that she had no idea if there would be anyone else there, and her face betrayed the thought so plainly that Sir Paul said quickly, 'There will be a number of guests at the reception.'

He was rewarded by the look of relief on her face. 'Eleven o'clock,' she said.

The vicar's wife came in then, with a tray of coffee, and they sat for a while and talked and presently walked back to the cottage.

'You said there would be guests,' observed Emma, in a voice which held a hint of coolness.

'It quite slipped my mind,' he told her placidly. 'I'm sorry, Emma. We'll make a list this evening, shall we?' He smiled at her and she forgot about being cool. 'Mrs Parfitt will be in her element.'

The list was more lengthy than she had expected—his parents, his sisters and their husbands, a number of his colleagues from Exeter, friends from London, friends in and around the village, Doreen Hervey and her husband. 'And we must ask Mr Dobbs—I take it there is a Mrs Dobbs?'

'Yes, I think they'd like to come. Shall I write to them?'

'I'll get some cards printed—no time to have them engraved—and I'll phone everyone and tell them the cards will arrive later.' He glanced at his watch. 'I can reach several friends after dinner this evening.'

They told Mrs Parfitt the wedding-date when she came to wish them goodnight. 'The village will turn out to a man,' she told them happily. 'Been wanting to see you wed for a long time, sir. Your ma and pa will be coming, no doubt.'

'Indeed they are, Mrs Parfitt, and we hope you will be our guest too.'

'Well, now—that's a treat I'll enjoy. I'll need a new hat.'

'Then you must go to Exeter and get one. I'll drive you in whenever you wish to go.'

Emma saw very little of Paul until the weekend; he had consulting rooms in Exeter and saw his private patients there, and, in the evenings, although they discussed the wedding from time to time he made no mention of their future. All the guests were coming, he told her, and would she mind very much if he went to Exeter on the day after their wedding? He had promised to read a paper at a seminar; he had hoped to postpone it but it hadn't been possible.

'Well, of course you must go,' said Emma. 'May I come with you? I shan't understand a word but I'd very much like to be there.'

He had agreed very readily, but she wasn't sure if he was pleased about it or not.

They left early on Saturday morning and Emma sat silently beside him, hoping that she had brought the right clothes with her and that his parents would like her. She was then comforted by his quiet, 'Don't worry, Emma, everything will be all right.' And as though Willy and Kate had understood him, they had uttered gentle grumbling barks, and Willy had got down off the back seat and licked the back of her neck.

It was a day when spring had the upper hand and winter had withdrawn to the more remote stretches of the moor, and once they had bypassed Exeter and were racing up the motorway the country showed a great deal of green in the hedges. The car was blissfully warm and smelled of good leather, Paul's aftershave and the faint whiff of dog and, soothed by it, Emma decided in her sensible way that there was no point in worrying about something she knew very little about. So when Paul began a rambling conversation about nothing much she joined in quite cheerfully.

Just past Taunton he stopped for coffee and then turned off the motorway to drive across country—Midsomer Norton, Bath and then onwards towards Cirencester—to turn off presently into a country road which led them deep into the Cotswolds.

'Oh, this is nice,' said Emma. 'I like the houses—all that lovely pale yellow stone. Where are we exactly?'

'Cirencester is to the north-east, Tetbury is away to the right of us—the next village is where we are going.'

When he stopped the car in front of his parents' home, she sat for a moment, peering at it. 'It's beautiful,' she said softly. 'Do you love it very much?'

He said gravely, 'Yes, I do, and I hope that you will love it too. Come inside...' He took her by the elbow and went towards the opening door.

His mother stood there, smiling a welcome. She offered a cheek for his kiss and turned to Emma. 'Emma—such a pretty name—welcome, my dear.' She shook hands and then kissed Emma's cheek and tucked her arm in hers. 'Come and meet my husband.' She paused a moment to look up at her son. 'Paul, you described Emma exactly.'

He smiled but didn't speak, and when they entered the drawing-room and his father came to meet them he shook hands and then drew Emma towards him. 'Father, this is Emma—my father, Emma.'

Mr Wyatt wore his years lightly, and it was obvious where his son had got his good looks. She put out a hand and he took it and then kissed her. 'Welcome, my dear. We are delighted to have you here with us.'

After that everything was perfect. Going to bed that night in the charming bedroom, Emma reflected that she had had no need to worry—Paul's mother and father had been kindness itself, and Paul had taken her round the house and the large garden while Willy and Kate and his father's elderly spaniel trotted to and fro, dashing off following imaginary rabbits and then coming back to trot at their heels.

It had been an hour she didn't think she would forget; they hadn't talked much but somehow there hadn't been the need for that. All the same, when they had gone back into the house for tea, she'd had the strange feeling that she knew Paul better than she had done.

In the evening, after dinner, they had sat talking about the wedding and who would be coming to it and Mrs Wyatt had admired her dress—one of the pretty ones Paul had persuaded her to have. 'You will make a charming bride,' she had told Emma. 'Paul is a lucky man.'

Emma, curling up in the comfortable bed, promised herself that she would make sure that he was. Not loving him didn't seem to matter, somehow, and she supposed that he felt the same about her. They were friends and they liked each other; everything would be all right, and on this cheerful thought she went to sleep.

They all went to church the next morning, and Emma got stared at. Somehow the news had got around that Sir Paul had got himself engaged at last and everyone wanted to see the bride-to-be. Wedged between father and son, Emma did her best not to notice the interested stares, hoping that they wouldn't be disappointed that she wasn't a girl whose good looks would match her bridegroom's. She peeped up at Paul's face and found him looking at her and took heart at his kind smile, knowing that he understood how she felt.

They left early on Monday morning, and his mother kissed her and gave her a little hug. 'My dear, we are so happy for you both. You are exactly right for Paul and we wish you every happiness. We shan't see you before your wedding-day—it's something we both look forward to. You'll meet the rest of the family then—they will love you too.'

Emma got into the car feeling a pleasant glow of content; she had been accepted by Paul's family—something which mattered to her.

They were home by lunchtime but he went back to Exeter directly after, saying that he might be late back and that she wasn't to wait up for him. He didn't say why he was going and she didn't ask, although she longed to. Instead she offered to take the dogs for their walk in the late afternoon.

'Yes, do that. But not after teatime, Emma. I'll give them a good run when I get home.'

He patted her shoulder in what she considered to be a highly unsatisfactory manner and got back into the Rolls and drove away. The day, which had begun so pleasantly, had turned sour, and although she told herself that she had no reason to complain, she felt ill done by. She sat still when he had gone, looking at her ringless hand. Had he forgotten that it was the custom to give one's intended bride a ring? Or perhaps he thought that the unusual circumstances of their marriage didn't merit one.

Moping about and feeling sorry for herself would do no good, she told herself, and, leaving Queenie by the fire, she took Willy and Kate for a long walk.

She was late getting back to the cottage and Mrs Parfitt

said severely, 'Another ten minutes and I'd have been getting worried about you, miss. Sir Paul said most particular
that you weren't to go out after teatime. And quite right too!'

It was a remark which cheered her up a little, and tea
round the fire, with the lamps lighted against the gloomy
day, restored her usual good spirits. She spent a careful half-
hour writing her bread-and-butter letter to Mrs Wyatt, then
stamped it and left it on the hall table. The postman would
take it in the morning.

She lingered over dinner, helped Mrs Parfitt clear the
table and, since there was no sign of Paul, went to bed with
a book. She read for a long time, one ear cocked for the
sound of his footfall, but by midnight she was half-asleep.
She put the book down, telling herself that this was no way
to behave—there would probably be years of similar evenings, and if she lay in bed worrying about him she would
grow old before her time. Queenie, glad at last that the bedside lamp was out, crept up beside her and she fell asleep.

When she went down to breakfast the next morning, Paul
was already at the table. His good morning was cheerful
and friendly. 'You slept well?' he wanted to know.

'Like a top, whatever that means! What a nice morning
it is…'

'Yes, indeed—a pity I have to go back to Exeter this
morning. Unfinished business, I'm afraid.'

'Would you like me to take the dogs out?' She buttered
toast, not looking at him.

'I'll take them before I go; I'm sure you have a lot to do
here.'

What, in heaven's name? Mrs Parfitt got upset if she offered to help in the house, the garden was beautifully kept

by the part-time gardener, but there was a chance that she could go to the village shop for Mrs Parfitt...

'Oh, yes, I've lots to do,' she told him serenely.

'You won't mind if I leave you?' And at her cheerful, 'Of course not,' he got up.

On his way to the door, though, he paused and came back to the table. 'I must beg your forgiveness, Emma.' He took a small box from a pocket. 'I have been carrying this round since we left yesterday and forgot all about it.'

He took a ring out of the box and held it in the palm of his hand—sapphires and diamonds in an old-fashioned setting. 'It has been kept in the safe in father's study, waiting for the next bride in the family. It is very old and is handed down from one generation to the next.' He picked up her hand and slipped the ring on her finger.

'It fits,' said Emma.

'As I knew it would.' He bent and kissed her, a quick kiss which took her by surprise. 'That augers well for our future.'

Emma said, 'Thank you, Paul,' and, while she was still trying to think of something else to add to that, he patted her shoulder and was gone.

Chapter 6

Emma didn't see much of Paul during that week; he took her with him to Exeter one day, so that she might do some last-minute shopping, and once or twice he was home early so that they could walk the dogs together. On the Saturday he drove down to Buckfastleigh.

They had been invited by the Herveys to have drinks and at the same time they called at the house agent's. There were enquiries, they were told; it was certain that the house would sell, especially now that the warmer weather was coming.

'You don't mind waiting for the money?' asked Emma worriedly as they got back into the car.

'No, Emma, there's no hurry for that.' He turned to smile at her. 'There's time for us to get an armful of flowers and visit your mother's grave.'

She hadn't liked to ask but that was exactly what she wanted to do. He bought the flowers she chose—roses and carnations—and they took them to the quiet churchyard. Emma's sadness was mitigated by the feel of Paul's great arm round her shoulder and his unspoken sympathy.

The Herveys were delighted to see them and Emma was borne upstairs to see Bart, asleep in his cot. Emma was relieved to see that Nanny had been replaced by an older woman with a pleasant face and a ready smile.

'He's grown,' said Emma. 'He's perfect...'

'He's rather a duck,' said his mother fondly, 'and Nanny's splendid with him—and I'm getting better, aren't I, Nanny?'

On the way downstairs she took Emma's arm. 'Mike took one look at that other nanny and gave her notice,' she confided. 'Didn't fancy her at all—a regular sargeant major, he said she was. This one's an old dear, and she's taught me a lot—you know, how to hold Bart properly and what to do when he yells. I'm not afraid of him any more.'

She was quite serious; Emma murmured sympathetically, reflecting that it was fortunate that the Herveys could afford a nanny.

They had their drinks then, talking about the wedding and the baby and listening to Mike's amusing account of his trip to America. Then the two men went upstairs to see Bart and Mrs Hervey described in great detail what she intended to wear at the wedding.

Listening to her, Emma thought it likely that she would outshine the bride. Not that she minded—she liked Doreen Hervey; she might be helpless and unable to do much for herself but she was kind and friendly and light-hearted, and she went into raptures over Emma's ring.

'It's a family heirloom, isn't it? You deserve it, Emma, for you're such a nice girl, and Paul's the nicest man I know—excepting Mike, of course. He's frightfully rich, of course, and awfully important—but you'd never know, would you? Never says a word about himself—never told anyone why he was knighted... I don't suppose you would tell me? I'll not breathe a word...'

'Well, no,' said Emma. 'He wants to keep it a private matter.'

So private, she thought, that he had never mentioned it to her. She would ask him...

Which she did as they were driving back to Lustleigh, and was thwarted by his placid, 'Oh, you know how it is—names out of a hat and I happened to be lucky.' Even though he sounded placid there was something in his voice which prevented her from asking any more questions. Perhaps, she thought wistfully, when they had been married for a long time and had got to know each other really well he would tell her.

They went to church in the morning and heard their last banns read, and after the service an endless stream of people stopped to wish them well. They all wanted to know the date of the wedding.

'It will be very quiet—just family and a few close friends,' said Paul and, when pressed, told them the day on which they were to marry, knowing that if he didn't tell them they would find a reason to call at the cottage and ask Mrs Parfitt.

If Emma had hoped to see more of Paul during the next week she was disapointed; even at the weekend he was called away urgently to operate on a road casualty so that her wedding-day loomed without her having had the chance to get to know him better. Indeed, suspicion that he was avoiding her lurked at the back of her head and became so urgent that on the evening before her wedding, left to her own devices while he worked in his study, she put down the book she was reading, thumped on the door and then entered the study before she could change her mind.

He got up as she went in. 'Emma—what's wrong? You look as though...' He paused and asked mildly, 'Something has upset you?'

'Yes—no, I'm not sure.' She gave him a worried look. 'Why don't I see you more often? You're always going somewhere, and even when you're at home you keep out of my way. Don't you want to marry me? It's quite all right if you've changed your mind; it isn't as if... I wouldn't like you to get married to the wrong person and be unhappy.'

He came round the desk and took her hands in his. 'Emma, my dear girl, what can I say to reassure you? Only that I want to marry you and that you are the right person. If you haven't seen much of me it is because I've had a good deal of work, and I'm afraid that is something you will have to learn to live with.' He smiled down at her, a tender smile which set her heart thumping. 'And I haven't changed my mind, nor will that ever happen.'

'I've been silly,' said Emma. 'I'm sorry—and I've interrupted your work.'

He turned her round and put an arm round her shoulders. 'We will sit down and go over the arrangements for tomorrow.' He was propelling her gently out of the study and back into the drawing-room. 'Are you feeling nervous? No need— you know almost everyone who'll be there. The car will fetch you tomorrow morning; I know it's only a few yards to the church but I can't have my bride walking there...'

'The car? But what about you?'

'I'm spending the night at Eastrey Barton—the family are already there. It is considered very bad luck, so I'm told, for the bride and groom to spend the night before their wedding under the same roof. Mrs Parfitt will look after you and I'll phone you in the morning.'

'Oh, I thought we'd just have breakfast together as usual and then walk to church.'

'I have neglected you shamefully, Emma—the truth is...'

'You forgot that you were getting married!' she finished for him, unaware that that hadn't been what he had been going to say.

She spoke matter-of-factly and Sir Paul gave a soundless sigh. Patience, he reminded himself—she wasn't ready to hear his reason for avoiding her company, and, when he was with her, treating her with a casual friendliness.

Dressed for her wedding, Emma took a final look at herself in the pier glass, and even to her critical eye she considered that she didn't look too bad. Not beautiful—brides were supposed to look beautiful—not even pretty, but the outfit suited her and the little hat framed her rather anxious face with its soft velvet brim.

She went downstairs to where Dr Treble, who was to give her away, waited, and was much heartened by his surprised admiration. He and Mrs Parfitt, who was on the point of leaving for the church, chorused their approval in no uncertain terms, so that she got into the car feeling more confident.

Her confidence faltered a little as they started down the aisle and she clutched the small bouquet of pink roses which Paul had given her in a nervous hand; she hadn't expected the church to be full of people—the entire village appeared to be in the pews, nodding and smiling at her as she passed them. When she reached the front pews Paul's mother looked round and smiled and nodded too, but Emma scarcely noticed her; her eyes were on Paul's broad back—if only he would turn round and look at her...

He did, smiling a little, and her heart gave a great jump against her ribs so that she caught her breath. Her thoughts were wild; it was a bit late in the day to fall in love with him, wasn't it? And not at all a good idea either, for now everything was going to be a bit complicated.

She stood beside him and the vicar began to speak the opening words of the service. She did her best to listen but odd thoughts kept popping in and out of her head. She had loved him for quite a while, she thought, only she hadn't known it, and if she had would she have married him?

The solemn words the vicar was speaking cut across her reflections at last and she listened then. Never mind the future. She would make her vows and keep to them; she would be a good wife, and if Paul didn't need her love, only her companionship, then she would do her best to be the kind of person he wanted. When the moment came, she spoke her 'I will' in a clear, steady little voice that everyone could hear, and then took comfort from Paul's deep voice, as assured and certain as hers had been.

They exchanged rings then and went to sign the register, and presently were walking down the aisle and out into the bright morning, but before they could get into the Rolls they were surrounded by guests with cameras poised and had to pass through a barrage of confetti and good wishes.

Paul had been holding her hand, and as they reached the car at last gave it an encouraging squeeze. 'So much for our quiet wedding,' he said. 'I'm enjoying it, aren't you?'

'Oh, yes,' said Emma. 'It's the most wonderful day of my life.' She spoke with such fervour that he looked down at her, but the little hat shaded her face from his as she got into the car.

The rest of the day was like a dream; the cottage was full of people laughing and talking and drinking champagne and eating canapés. Paul had Emma by the hand, and as various friends greeted him he introduced her.

His sisters had been the first to join them after his mother and father—handsome young women who kissed her warmly and listened smilingly as their husbands flattered her gently and congratulated Paul—and after them there were people she realised she would meet again—colleagues from the hospital, several from London, old friends with their wives and of course the Herveys and Mr Dobbs and his wife.

Mr Dobbs had given her a smacking kiss. 'Wait till I tell 'em all about this,' he said. 'I'll make sure that Mrs Smith-Darcy gets the lot. I've taken some photos too.' He transferred his beaming smile to Sir Paul. 'You are a lucky man, and no mistake,' he told him.

Since they weren't going anywhere, the guests lingered, renewing acquaintances, plying Emma and Paul with invitations, and then at last taking their leave. The cake had been cut, the last toast drunk and Emma longed to take off her new shoes. The moment the last guest had gone, she did so. 'You don't mind, do you? Just for a few minutes— they're new...'

'And very pretty. You look charming, Emma, and I do like that hat.' He took her arm as they went indoors to where his mother and father and sisters were waiting. 'We're going out to dinner—just the family—but we can sit around for a while and talk.'

'I'll get Mrs Parfitt to make a pot of tea...'

'A splendid idea, although I suspect she's already got the kettle on.'

As indeed she had, and presently she bustled in with the tea-tray and a plate of cucumber sandwiches. 'After all that cake and bits and pieces,' she explained. 'Not but it wasn't a rare fine party.' Her eyes fell on the dogs, basking in the late afternoon sunshine. 'Queenie's in the kitchen having her tea.'

'And what about you, Mrs Parfitt?' asked Emma. 'You've worked so hard; you must have your tea too...'

'That I shall, ma'am—wetted it not five minutes ago with a nice boiled egg and a bit of toast.'

Emma, in bed that night, thought back over her wedding-day. It had ended on a light-hearted note at Eastrey Barton, where they had all dined splendidly with a great deal of talk and laughter, and she had been happy because Paul had given her a wedding-present—a double row of pearls which she had immediately worn.

When they had returned to the cottage he had kissed her goodnight—a quick, friendly kiss—almost a peck—she thought wistfully, but at least it was a kiss. It had been difficult not to kiss him back, but she hadn't. She would keep to her resolve of being a good companion, however hard it was, and perhaps in time he would come to love her. At least, she told herself stoutly, she had several advantages— she was his wife and she loved him.

The next day he took her to Exeter with him as he had promised, and she sat in the lecture hall and listened to him addressing a large and attentive audience. She understood very little of the lecture—that it was about bones went without saying, and some of it must have been amusing for the audience laughed quite often. When he had sat down they clapped for a long time before someone on the platform got up and made a speech about him in glowing terms.

Emma, sitting at the back of the hall, beamed with pride and Sir Paul, who had seen her the moment he started his lecture, smiled—his dear little Emma...

They had tea with a number of his colleagues—several foreign surgeons and members of the hospital board—and Emma—being Emma—had little to say for herself but listened to the opinions of various learned gentlemen who were quick to observe to Sir Paul that his wife was a charming young lady and a splendid listener. 'Such beautiful eyes,' sighed an Italian surgeon, over in England to exchange ideas with his colleagues. 'I hope we shall meet again.'

Driving back to Lustleigh presently, Paul repeated this. 'How fortunate that I'm not a jealous husband,' he said lightly. 'You were a great success, Emma.'

'Oh, was I? I didn't understand half of what they were talking about but they were all very nice to me.' She turned to look at him. 'Perhaps it was because I'm your wife and they were being polite.'

'No, no. They all fell for you...' He was laughing and that hurt.

'I expect it was my new clothes,' said Emma.

'You enjoyed the lecture?' he asked her.

'Very much, although I didn't understand very much of it. Do you lecture a great deal?'

'From time to time. Sometimes I'm invited to other countries—you shall come with me.'

'Oh, may I? Don't you have a secretary with you?'

'Yes, if it's a long tour, but for the present I shall be in England.'

'Not always at Exeter?'

'No—but I'm usually only away for a day or two—not long.'

At dinner that evening he asked her if she would like to drive to Torquay in the morning. 'It's pleasant at this time of year—not too many people yet, and the dogs love the beach.'

She peeped at him over her glass. He looked tired and preoccupied—a carefree day by the sea would be pleasant. 'I'd love it,' she told him.

They left soon after breakfast, and since it was a clear day, Emma wore a skirt with a cashmere sweater and a velvet beret perched over one eye. 'Very fetching,' said Sir Paul. 'You are sure you'll be warm enough?'

He drove to the A38 and took the fork over Haldon to the coast and, as he had said, Torquay was not too crowded.

'Coffee first or walk the dogs?' he asked her.

'The dogs,' said Emma, conscious of two anxious, whiskery faces turned towards her. So they parked the car and took them down on to the beach and walked arm-in-arm for a mile or more, stopping every now and again to throw sticks for the dogs and look out to sea.

'It looks very cold,' said Emma, and then added, 'I expect you can swim...'

'Yes.' They were standing at the water's edge and he flung an arm around her shoulders. 'You don't?'

'Well, I tried—at school, you know—and once or twice when I went on holiday with Mother and Father. I think I'm a coward.'

His arm tightened. 'Nonsense. You haven't had the chance to learn, that's all. I'll teach you. I've a small yacht which I keep at Salcombe; we'll go there when I'm free.'

'I've never been on a yacht.'

'I shall very much enjoy having you for my crew,' he told her.

He took her to the Imperial Hotel for lunch—lobster bisque and *boeuf en croute*, rounded off by a chocolate soufflé, and washed down by a claret handled by the wine waiter as though it were a precious baby rather than a bottle.

Emma, who knew almost nothing about wines, took a sip, then another. 'It's perfect—I've never tasted anything as heavenly.'

Sir Paul thought it unlikely that she had, but he expressed the view that it was considered a good wine and that he was glad that she enjoyed it.

The day was fine. They walked again after lunch, on the beach once more but this time in the opposite direction, with the dogs rushing about, barking at the water, begging for sticks to be thrown. Presently they turned back and got into the car and began to drive back to Lustleigh, stopping on the way at a tea-room in one of the villages. It was old-fashioned—a front room in a thatched cottage—but they had a splendid tea of muffins, oozing butter, and a large pot of strong tea, while the dogs sat under the table, gobbling the bits of muffin Emma handed them.

'You'll spoil them,' observed Sir Paul.

She said at once, 'Oh, I'm sorry, I shouldn't have done it.'

He frowned, annoyed with himself for sounding as though he was criticising her. She saw the frown and guessed quite wrongly that he was vexed with her so that she became ill at ease.

The day had been heavenly—just being with him had been wonderful—but now, in her efforts to behave as the kind of wife he had wished for, she drew back from the friendly rapport they had had, still making small talk, but keeping him at arm's length while willingly answering him when he spoke.

He, however, was practised in the art of putting patients at their ease, and by the time they reached home she was her usual, friendly self and they dined together in the easy companionship that he was so careful to maintain.

That, she was to discover, was to be the last of their days together for some time, for he left directly after breakfast each morning and was rarely home before seven or eight o'clock in the evening. She hid her disappointment and showed a bright face when he got back—ready to listen about his day, even though she understood very little of what he had been doing. She was also careful not to chat at breakfast while he was glancing through his post. True, they had been out to dine on several evenings, but she saw little of him then, though it was pleasant to meet the people he counted his friends.

She filled her days with walking the dogs, working doggedly at a piece of tapestry she had begun with so much enthusiasm, not realising the amount of work and tiny stitches it required before it was finished. She was happy because she loved Paul, but she found herself counting the hours until he came home each evening.

They had been married for several weeks when he told her at breakfast that someone would deliver a Mini that morning. 'For you, Emma, so you can go wherever you want. I'll be home early today and you can take me for a drive in it.'

She smiled widely at him across the table. 'Paul, thank you—how perfectly splendid.' She added, 'I'll be very careful…'

He smiled. 'Keep to the roads around here until you're quite used to it. I'll be home before five o'clock so be ready for me.'

He dropped a kiss on her head as he went away.

The Mini, a nice shade of blue, arrived at lunchtime, and she got into it at once and drove to Bovey Tracey and back and then waited impatiently for Paul to come home. When he did she drove him to Moretonhampstead, very conscious of him sitting squashed up beside her.

'It's a bit small for you,' she said, driving carefully past the sheep wandering across the road.

'Indeed, but just right for you, I hope, Emma.'

'Yes, oh, yes. It's a wonderful present.'

Back home, as they sat at dinner he asked her, 'Do you find the days long, Emma?'

'Well, yes, a bit. You see, I've had to work all day for quite a time and I'm not really used to having so much leisure.'

'Would you like a little job? Voluntary, of course. There is a nursery at Moretonhampstead. It takes unwanted babies and toddlers—most of them are orphaned or abandoned. Not ill, but neglected and very underfed. Diana Pearson, who is in charge, is an old friend of mine and she tells me that she needs more help urgently. Would you like to go there once or twice a week and give a hand? No nursing, just common sense and a liking for infants.'

He wanted her to say yes, she was sure—perhaps that was why he had given her the car. She didn't hesitate. 'Yes, I'd love to help,' she told him.

'Good. We'll go there on Monday; I'm not operating until the afternoon. Would you ask Mrs Parfitt to have lunch ready for us at one o'clock? I'll bring you back and have lunch here.' He added, 'One or two days a week and not

more than four hours at a time, Emma. It has to be interesting, not tiring and demanding, and never at the weekends.'

The nursery was on the outskirts of the town—a long,
low building, with cheerfully coloured walls and a large
playroom and several nurseries. Sir Paul walked in as
though he knew the place well and went straight to a door
with 'Office' written on it.

The young woman who got up as he went in was tall and
dark with almost black eyes in a lovely face. She was elegantly dressed and she smiled at him in a way which gave
Emma food for thought. Her greeting was casual enough
and when Paul introduced her she shook hands with a pleasant murmur and another smile—quite different from the
first one, though.

It was obvious that she knew all about Emma, for she said
pleasantly, 'We'd love to have you here; we're desperate for
help. Paul said two days in a week and not more than four
hours at a time.' She put a hand on his arm and smiled at
Emma, who smiled back, knowing that she was disliked just
as she disliked the speaker. 'Come and look around—there
are a lot of small babies at the moment. The travellers bring
them in for a week or two's feeding up—the little ones get
cold and quickly ill; it's not really an ideal life for babies,
although the children seem happy enough.'

They went round the place together, and Emma said she
would come each Tuesday and Thursday in the mornings.
'Is nine o'clock too early?'

'We take over from the night staff at eight o'clock, but
that'll be too early for you.' Diana stole a look at Paul. 'Won't
it, Paul?' She smiled as she spoke, and Emma repressed a desire to slap her. If it hadn't been for Paul's obvious wish that

she should have something to occupy her days she would have said there and then that she had changed her mind.

On the way back to the cottage Paul said carefully, 'You'll like Diana—she is a marvellous organiser. She has no need to work and it surprises me that she hasn't married—she's quite lovely, isn't she?'

'She's beautiful,' said Emma. 'Have you been friends for a long time?'

'Two or three years, I suppose. We met at a friend's house and found that we had a good deal in common.'

Emma kept her voice pleasant. 'Instant rapport—that's what it's called, isn't it? You meet someone and feel as though you've known them all your life...' She added before he could reply, 'I'm sure I shall enjoy giving a hand—thank you for thinking of it, Paul.'

'I wondered if you were becoming bored with life—I'm not at home much, am I?'

She said cheerfully, 'Well, I didn't expect you to be—doctors never are, are they?'

That evening he asked her if she would like to spend a weekend with his parents. 'Next weekend I'm free. We could drive up on Saturday afternoon and come back on the Sunday evening.'

'I'd like that.'

But first there was the nursery. She drove there in the Mini and within ten minutes, wrapped in a plastic pinny, she was bathing a very small baby in a room where five other babies were awaiting her attention.

Diana Pearson, elegant and beautiful, sitting behind her desk, had greeted her pleasantly but without warmth. 'Hello, Emma—so you have turned up. So many volunteer ladies change their minds at the last minute. Will you go to the end nursery and start bathings? Someone will be along to give you a hand presently.'

Emma had waited for more information but Diana had smiled vaguely and bent her head over the papers before her. At least she'd been credited with enough good sense to find her own way around, reflected Emma, and anyway she'd met another girl on the way to the nursery, who'd shown her where to find a pinny before hurrying off in the opposite direction.

Emma, not easily flurried, had found the pinny, assembled all that she needed to deal with the babies and picked up the first one...

She had just picked up the second baby, a small, wizened creature, bawling his head off, tiny fists balled in rage, eyes screwed up tightly, when she was joined by a middle-aged woman with a sour expression.

'New, are you?' she wanted to know as she tied her pinny. 'What's yer name?'

Not a local woman, thought Emma, and said pleasantly, 'Emma—Emma Wyatt, and yes, I'm new. I hope you'll tell me when I do something wrong.'

'You bet I will. 'Ere, you that Professor Wyatt's wife?'

'Yes, I am.'

'Well, don't expect me ter call yer 'yer ladyship', 'cos I'm not going to.'

'I'd like it if you'd call me Emma.'

The woman looked surprised. 'OK, I'm Maisie.' She picked up the third baby and began to take off its gown with surprisingly gentle hands. 'He's the worst of the bunch you've got there,' she observed. 'Proper little imp, 'e is—always shouting 'is 'ead off.'

Emma looked down at the scrap on her lap; he had

stopped crying and was glaring at her from bright blue eyes. 'He's rather sweet...'

Maisie gave a cackle of laughter. 'Your first day, isn't it? Wait till you've been 'ere a couple of months—that's if you last as long as that.'

'Why do you say that?'

'You'll find out for yerself—Madam there, sitting in her office, doing nothin'—that is, until someone comes along. Pulls the wool nicely over their eyes, that she does. That 'usband of yours—she's 'ad her sights on 'im this last year or more. 'Ad her nose put out of joint and no mistake.' She was pinning a nappy with an expertise Emma envied. 'Better watch out, you 'ad.'

The baby, freshly bathed and gowned, looked up at Emma with interest; she picked him up and tucked his small head under her chin and cuddled him.

''Ere, there ain't no time for cuddling—leastways not in the mornings—there's the feeds to do next.'

So Emma put him back in his cot and set to work on the fourth baby, a placid girl who blew bubbles and waved her small arms at her. Maisie had finished before her; she was already feeding the first baby by the time Emma had tidied everything away and fetched her three bottles from the little pantry.

When the infants had been fed and lay sleeping it off, she and Maisie had to tidy the nursery, put everything ready for the afternoon and then go and have their coffee. They sat together in the small room set aside for them and Emma listened to Maisie's numerous tips about the work.

'Have you been here long?' she asked.

'Upwards of two years. It's a job, see. Me old man scarpered off and the kids are at school all day—keeps me mind off things.'

She blew on her coffee and took a gulp. 'You going ter stick it out? It's not everyone's cup of tea.'

'Well, I like babies,' said Emma, 'and my husband's away almost all day. He told me that Miss Pearson was short-handed and asked if I'd like to help out, so I'll stay for as long as I'm needed. I only come twice a week.'

Maisie eyed her thoughtfully over her mug. 'Persuaded 'im, she did? Men—blind as bats! Never mind the "lady this" and "lady that"—you're a nice young woman, so keep those eyes of yours peeled.'

'Thank you for your advice. Shall I see you on Thursday?'

'Yep. Me, I come every morning—oftener if it gets really busy. Some of the babies will be going back to their mums tomorrow—bin waiting for an 'ouse or flat or whatever, yer see.'

'I hope the same babies will be here when I come on Thursday.'

'Well, Charlie—that's the little 'owler—e'll be with us for a while yet. 'Is mum's in prison for a couple of months—won't 'ave 'im near 'er.'

'Why ever not?'

'Dunno; bit flighty, I dare say.' She put down her mug. 'We gotta bag the wash before we go.'

Diana came out of the office as Emma took off her pinny. 'Going? See you on Thursday and many thanks. Oh, would you ask Paul to call in some time? I need his advice about one of the toddlers—a congenital dislocation of the hip—I think the splint needs adjusting.'

'I'll tell him,' said Emma. 'I'm sure he'll come when he has the time.'

Diana laughed. 'He usually comes whenever I ask him to, whether he's busy or not—we're old friends.'

Emma dredged up a smile. 'That's nice—I'll see you on Thursday.'

She drove back home, ate the lunch Mrs Parfitt had ready for her and then took the dogs for a long walk. She had a great deal to think about.

'It's a good thing I'm married to him,' she told Willy, who was loitering beside her. 'I mean, it's an advantage, if you see what I mean—and I love him. The point is, does he love her? That's something I have to find out. But if he does why did he marry me?' She stopped and Kate came lumbering back to see why. 'If it was out of pity...?' She sounded so fierce that Willy gave a whimper.

Paul was home for tea, which surprised her. 'How nice,' she said, and beamed at him. 'Have you had a busy day?'

'I've beds at the children's hospital and an out-patients clinic at Honiton; I seem to have spent a lot of my time driving from here to there.' He bit into one of Mrs Parfitt's scones. 'Tell me, did you enjoy your morning?'

'Very much. I bathed three babies and fed them. There was someone else there in the nursery—a nice woman who was very friendly and helpful. Oh, and Diana says could you go and see the baby with the dislocated hip? She thinks the splint needs changing.'

'It'll have to be tomorrow evening. I've a list in the morning and a ward-round in the afternoon and a couple of private patients to see after that.'

'Where do you see them?'

'I've rooms in Southernhay. I'll phone Diana presently and tell her when I'll be free.'

'I'll ask Mrs Parfitt to make dinner a bit later, shall I?'

'Yes, do that if you will. Did you take the dogs out?'

'Yes, it was lovely on the moor. After all it is summer.'

'That doesn't mean to say we shan't get some shockingly bad weather.' He got up. 'I've some phoning to do, then I'll take the dogs for ten minutes.' He smiled at her. 'You must tell me more about the nursery when I get back.'

The following evening he phoned at teatime to say that he would be home later than he had expected and that she wasn't to wait dinner for him. 'I'll get something here,' he told her.

She gave him a cheerful answer and spent the rest of the evening imagining him and Diana dining together at some quiet restaurant. She knew it was silly to do so but she seemed unable to think of anything else.

Perhaps it wasn't so silly either, she told herself, lying in bed later, waiting for the sound of the car and dropping off to sleep at last without having heard it.

He was already at the table when she went down to break-fast. He wished her good morning. 'You don't mind if I get on? I've a busy day ahead.'

'Did you have a busy time last night?' She kept her voice casually interested.

'Yes. I trust I didn't disturb you when I got back?'

'Will you go and see the baby today? Do you want me to give Diana a message?'

He gave her a thoughtful look. 'No need. I saw her yesterday.'

'Oh, good,' said Emma, bashing her boiled egg, wishing it was Diana.

Chapter 7

Diana's greeting when Emma reached the nursery was friendly. It was as though she was trying to erase her rather cool manner towards her; she asked if she was quite happy with the babies, if she would like to alter her hours and expressed the hope that she wasn't too tired at the end of her morning's work. Emma took all this with a pinch of salt, not convinced by all this charm that Diana was going to like her—and, anyway, she didn't like Diana.

It was refreshing, after all that sweetness, to listen to Maisie's down-to-earth talk, which covered everything under the sun—the royal family, the government, the price of fish and chips and the goings-on of the young couple who had rented rooms beneath hers—and all the while she talked she attended to the babies, raising her voice above their small cries.

They had finished the bathing and were feeding them when she said, 'Your old man was 'ere yesterday—late too.'

Emma was feeding Charlie, who was content for once,

sucking at his bottle as though it would be torn from him at any moment. 'Yes, I know,' she said quietly.

Maisie turned her head to look at her. 'You're a quiet one, but I bet me last penny you'll get the better of 'er.'

'Yes, I believe I shall,' said Emma, and smiled down at Charlie's small face. He wasn't a pretty baby—he was too pale and thin for that. It was to be hoped that when his mother claimed him once more—if she ever did—he'd look more like a baby and not a cross old man. She kissed the top of his head and gave him a quick cuddle and then put him over her shoulder so that he could bring up his wind.

It was after they had had dinner together that evening that Paul told her that he was going to Boston in two days' time.

Emma said, 'Boston? You mean Boston, USA?'

'Yes, and then on to New York, Philadelphia and Chicago. I shall be away for ten days, perhaps a little longer.' He said, carefully casual, 'I expect the trip would be a bit boring for you.'

She was quick to decide that he didn't want her with him. 'Yes, I think it might be,' she said. 'Will you be lecturing?'

She looked to see if he was disappointed but his face gave nothing away. 'If you need help of any sort, phone John Taggart, my solicitor; he'll sort things out for you. I've opened an account for you at my bank—I have also arranged for a joint account but I'd like you to have your own money. The house agent phoned to say that he has a possible buyer for your house; send everything to John—he'll deal with it.'

'The dogs will miss you,' said Emma. She would miss him too, but she wasn't going to tell him that. 'There's a card from the Frobishers—they've asked us to dinner. I'll write and explain, shall I?'

'Yes, do that. Suggest we take up their invitation when I get back.'

It was all very business-like and she did her best to match her manner to his. 'Shall I write to your mother and tell her that we shan't be coming for the weekend?'

'I phoned her last night. They are very sorry not to be seeing us.'

'I could drive myself...'

'I'd prefer you not to, Emma.'

The cottage seemed very quiet when he had gone. Emma couldn't bear to be in it and took the dogs for a long walk on the moor; they walked for miles and the austere vastness of it made his absence bearable. 'It's only for just over a week,' she told the dogs. 'But how shall I bear to be away from him for so long?'

A problem solved for her by Diana, who, when Emma went on Tuesday as usual, asked her if she could manage to help out for a third morning.

'We're so short of staff, I don't know which way to turn. I'm so glad that Paul didn't want you to go with him.' She laughed gently. 'Wives can be a bit of an encumbrance sometimes. It was so wise of him to marry someone like you, Emma.'

Emma asked why.

'Well, you're not demanding, are you? You're content to sit at home and wait for him to come back—just what he needed...'

Emma said, 'Yes, I think it is. He leads a busy life.'

Diana laughed again. 'Yes, but he always has time for his friends. He and I have such a lot in common.'

'I expect you have,' said Emma sweetly, 'but not marriage.' Her smile was as sweet as her voice. 'I'll get started on the babies,' she said.

Maisie, already at work with her three, looked up as she went into the nursery. ''Ello, Emma, what's riled you? 'As her 'igh and mightiness been tearing yer off a strip?'

'No—just a slight difference of opinion. I'm going to do an extra morning, Maisie; I hope you'll be here too.'

'Come every day, don't I, love? I'll be here. So'll Charlie there, from wot I 'eard. 'Is mum don't really want 'im, poor little beggar.'

'What will happen to him?' Emma was lifting him from his cot; he was bawling as usual.

'Foster-mum if they can find one, or an orphanage...'

'He's so small...'

'Plenty more like 'im,' said Maisie. 'Maybe there'll be someone who don't mind a bad-tempered kid.'

'Well, I'd be bad-tempered if I were he,' said Emma, smiling down at the cross little face on her lap. 'Who's a lovely boy, then?' she said.

She thought of Paul constantly, and when he phoned from Boston that night she went around in a cloud of content which was, however, quickly dispelled when she went into the nursery the next day.

'Heard from Paul?' asked Diana, with a friendly concern Emma didn't trust.

'Well, yes. He phoned yesterday evening...'

'He always does.' Diana smiled at Emma—a small secret smile, suggesting that words weren't necessary.

She had no right to be jealous, reflected Emma, bathing a belligerent Charlie, for she had no hold on Paul's feelings, had she? He had wanted a companion and the kind of wife to suit his lifestyle. He had never promised love...

That afternoon when she took the dogs on to the moor she saw the clouds piling up over the tors and felt the iciness of the wind. Bad weather was on the way, and even though it was summer the moor could be bleak and cold. She turned for home and was thankful for the bright fire in the drawing-room and the delicious tea Mrs Parfitt had ready for her.

Diana came out of her office as she arrived at the nursery on Thursday. 'Emma, I'm so glad to see you. You know the moor well, don't you? There's a party of travellers camping somewhere near Fernworthy Reservoir—one of them phoned me. We've one of their toddlers here already and he says there are several children sick—not ill enough for the doctor—colds, he thinks, and perhaps flu. He asked me to send someone with blankets, baby food and cough medicine. I wonder if you would go? It's not far but a bit out of the way. Perhaps you can get them to come off the moor until the weather gets warmer again.'

'Yes, of course I'll go. I'll phone Mrs Parfitt, though, so that she can take the dogs out if I'm not back.'

Mrs Parfitt didn't fancy the idea at all. 'Sir Paul would never allow it,' she demurred. 'You going off on your own like that.'

'I'll be gone for an hour or two,' said Emma. 'It's not far away, you know...'

Mrs Parfitt snorted. 'Maybe not, madam, but it's so isolated it could be the North Pole.'

It wasn't quite the North Pole but it was certainly isolated. Emma had a job finding the camp, tucked away from the narrow road which led to nowhere but the reservoir. When she found it eventually it took quite a time to unload the blankets and baby food and hand them over.

There were half a dozen broken-down buses and vans drawn up in a semicircle and their owners clamoured for her attention as she was led from one to another ramshackle vehicle. In one of them she found a sick baby—too ill to cry. 'She's ill,' she told the young woman who was with her. 'She needs medical attention—will you bring her to the nursery? I'll take you now...'

The girl needed a lot of persuading. ''Tis only a cold,' she told Emma. 'There's half a dozen kids as bad. Come in and look if you don't believe me.'

She was right. There were more than half a dozen, though—some of them small babies. Emma, although no nurse, could recognise the signs of whooping cough when she saw it. It would need several ambulances to take them to the nursery. 'Look,' she said to one of the older women, 'I haven't room to take them all, but I'll go back now and send an ambulance for them.'

They gathered round her, all talking at once, but at last she got back into the Mini, with the baby and its mother in the back, and began her journey back to Moretonhampstead. As Diana had said, it wasn't far, but the road was narrow and winding and little used and there were no houses or farms in sight. She was glad when they reached the nursery and she could hand the baby and mother over to Diana.

It was Maisie who led them away while Emma explained to Diana that there were more babies and toddlers needing help. 'An ambulance?' she suggested. 'They are really quite ill and it's so cold for them.'

Diana frowned. 'Wait here. I'll see if I can get help. Go and have a cup of coffee; you must need one.'

When Emma returned Diana shook her head. 'Would you

believe it, there's nothing to be had until tomorrow morning—it's not urgent you see...'

'But they need more baby food and someone to clean them up—nappies and warm clothes.'

Diana appeared to think. 'Look, I wouldn't ask it of everyone but you're so sensible, Emma. If I get more stuff packed up would you take it back? Why not go back to Lustleigh and pack an overnight bag just in case you feel you can't leave them? I'll get a doctor to them as soon as I can and you can go straight home once he's got organised.'

'You're sure there's no one available?'

'Quite sure. There's a flap on with a major road accident—whooping cough just doesn't count.'

Emma was only half listening, which was a pity for then she might have queried that, but she was worried about the babies wheezing and gasping, so far from the care they needed. She said, 'All right, I'll go. I wish Paul were here...'

'Oh, my dear, so do I. He's such a tower of strength—we have been so close.' Diana's voice was soft and sad. 'We still are and I know you won't mind; it isn't as if you love each other.' She turned away and dabbed at a dry eye. 'You see, his work is all-important to him; he cannot afford to be distracted by the all-embracing love I—' She choked and took a long breath. 'Of course, he has explained all that to you—he told me how understanding you were.'

Emma said, 'I'd better be on my way,' and left without another word.

She went over the conversation word for word as she drove back to the cottage, and although she hated Diana she had to admit that it was all probably true. Paul didn't love her; he liked her enough to marry her, though, knowing that she would provide the calm background his arduous work demanded, whereas Diana's flamboyant nature would have distracted him.

It was well into the afternoon by now, and the sky was threatening rain. She hurried into the cottage, explained to Mrs Parfitt that she might not get back that night and ran upstairs to push essentials into a shoulder-bag. Mrs Parfitt came after her. 'You didn't ought to go,' she said worriedly. 'Whatever will Sir Paul say when he hears?'

'Well, he doesn't need to know. I'm only going to the reservoir, and don't worry, Mrs Parfitt, there'll be a doctor there tomorrow and I'll come home.' She turned to look at the faithful creature. 'Think of those babies—they really need some help.'

'Sir Paul wouldn't let you go, ma'am, but since you won't listen to me at least you'll have a bowl of soup and a nice strong cup of tea.'

Emma, who hadn't had her lunch, agreed, wolfed down the soup and some of Mrs Parfitt's home-made bread, drank several cups of tea and got back into the car. It was raining now and the wind had got up. She waved goodbye to Mrs Parfitt and Willy and Kate and drove back to the nursery.

It was amazing how much could be packed into the Mini; it was amazing too how helpful Diana was. 'Don't worry,' she told Emma. 'Someone will be with you just as soon as possible.'

She waved goodbye as Emma drove away, then went into the office and picked up the phone. 'There's no hurry to send anyone out to that camp on the moor. I've sent everything they need and the girl who is taking the stuff is sensible and capable. I'll let you know more in the morning!'

Emma was still a mile or so from the reservoir when she saw the first wisps of mist creeping towards her, and five minutes later she was in the thick of it. It was eddying to and fro so that for a moment she could see ahead and then the next was completely enshrouded.

She had been caught in the moorland mists before now; to a stranger they were frightening but she had learnt to take them in her stride. All the same, she was relieved when she saw the rough track leading to the camp and bumped her way along it until the first of the buses loomed out of the mist. The mist had brought Stygian gloom with it and she was glad to see the lights shining from the open doorways. As she got out several of the campers came to surround her.

They were friendly—happy in the way they lived, making nothing of its drawbacks—but now they were anxious about the babies and Emma, taken to see them, was anxious too. No expert, she could still see that they were as ill as the one she had taken to the nursery. She handed out the blankets, baby food and bags of nappies, drank the mug of strong tea she was offered and prepared to return.

The mist had thickened by now and it was almost dark— to find her way wouldn't be easy or particularly safe; she would have to stay where she was until the morning and, since there were hours to get through, she could curl up in the back of the Mini for the night. She helped with the babies, looking at their small white faces and listening to their harsh breathing and hoping that, despite the awful weather, an ambulance or at least a doctor would come to their aid.

No one came, however, so she shared supper with one of the families and, after a last worried look at the babies, wrapped herself in a blanket and curled up on the Mini's back seat. It was a tight fit and she was cold, and the thin wails of the babies prevented her from sleeping, and when she at last lightly dozed off she was awakened almost immediately by one of the men with a mug of tea.

The mist had lifted. She scrambled up, tidied herself as best she could and got back into the car. If she drove round the reservoir and took the lane on the other side she would reach a hamlet, isolated but surely with a telephone. She explained what she was going to do and set off into the cold, bleak morning.

It was beginning to rain and there was a strong wind blowing; summer, for the moment, was absent. The lane was rutted and thick with mud and there was no question of hurrying. She saw with relief a couple of houses ahead of her and then a good-sized farm.

There was a phone. The farmer, already up, took her into the farmhouse when she explained, and shook his head. 'They'm foolish folk,' he observed. 'Only just there, I reckon. Leastways they weren't there when I was checking the sheep a few days ago.' He was a kindly man. 'Reckon you'd enjoy a cuppa?'

'Oh, I'd love one, but if I might phone first? The babies do need to go into care as quickly as possible.'

A cheerful West Country voice answered her. They'd be there right away, she was told, just let her sit tight till they came. Much relieved, she drank her tea, thanked the farmer and drove back to tell the travellers that help was on the way.

'Likely they'll move us on,' said one woman.

'It's common land, isn't it? I dare say they'll let you stay as long as the babies are taken care of. I expect they'll take them to hospital and transfer them to the nursery until they are well again. You'll be able to see them whenever you all want to. Some of you may want to go with them.' She looked around her. 'I can give three of you lifts, if you like.'

One of the younger women offered to go.

'How ever will you get back?' asked Emma.

'Thumb a lift and walk the last bit—no problem.'

The ambulance came then, and Emma stood aside while the paramedics took over. They lifted the babies into the ambulance presently, offered the young woman who was to have gone with Emma a seat, and drove away. That left her free to go at last. No one wanted a lift—they were content to wait and see what the young woman would tell them when she got back. Emma got into her car and drove home, to be met at the door by an agitated Mrs Parfitt.

'You're fit to drop,' she scolded kindly. 'In you come, madam, and straight into a nice, hot bath while I get your breakfast. Like as not you've caught your death of cold.'

Not quite death, as it turned out, but for the moment she was very tired and shivery. The bath was bliss, and so were breakfast and the warm bed she got into afterwards.

'I must ring the nursery,' she said worriedly, and began to get out of bed again, to Queenie's annoyance.

'I'll do that,' said Mrs Parfitt. 'No good going there for a day or two, and so I'll tell that Miss Pearson.'

'I'm not ill,' said Emma peevishly, and fell asleep.

She woke hours later with a head stuffed with cotton wool and a sore thorat and crept downstairs, to be instantly shooed back to her bed by Mrs Parfitt bearing hot lemon and some paracetamol.

'It's more than my job's worth, Lady Wyatt, to let you get up. Sir Paul would send me packing.'

Emma, aware that Mrs Parfitt only called her Lady Wyatt when she was severely put out, meekly got back into bed.

'Did you phone the nursery?' she croaked.

'I did, and there is no need for you to go in until you

are free of your cold. You'd only give it to the babies.' Mrs Parfitt eyed her anxiously. 'I wonder if I should get the doctor to you, ma'am?'

'No, no—it's only a cold; I'll be fine in a day or two.'

Sir Paul, back from his travels, drove himself straight to the hospital, listened impatiently to his senior registrar's litany of things which had gone wrong during his absence and then, eager to get back home, phoned his secretary, who read out a formidable list of patients waiting for his services.

'Give me a day?' he begged her. 'I've a short list on the day after tomorrow. I'll come to my rooms in the afternoon—I leave it to you...'

He was about to ring off when she stopped him. 'Sir Paul, Miss Pearson phoned several times, and said it was most urgent that she should see you as soon as you got back.'

He frowned. 'Why didn't she speak to my registrar?'

'I don't know, sir; she sounded upset.'

'I'll call in on my way home.'

He was tired; he wanted to go home and see Emma, watch her face light up when she saw him. She might not love him but she was always happy to be with him. He smiled as he got out of the car and went along to Diana's office.

He might be tired but good manners necessitated his cheerful greeting. 'You wanted to see me; is it very urgent? I'm now on my way home.'

'I had to see you first,' said Diana. She was, for her, very quiet and serious. 'It's about Emma. Oh, don't worry, she's not ill, but I'm so upset. You see, she went dashing off; she simply wouldn't listen...'

Sir Paul sat down. 'Start at the beginning,' he said quietly. Which was just what Diana had hoped he would say. She began to tell him her version of what had happened and, because she was a clever young woman, it all sounded true.

Sir Paul let himself into his house quietly, took off his coat and, since there were no lights on in the drawing-room, went to the little sitting-room at the back of the house. Emma was there, with Queenie on her lap and the dogs draped over her feet.

When he walked in she turned round, saw who it was, flew to her feet and ran across to him in a flurry of animals. 'Paul—you're back!' Her voice was still hoarse, and her nose pink from constant blowing, and it was a silly thing to say but she couldn't hide her delight.

He closed the door behind him and stood leaning against it, and it was only then that she realised that he was in a rage. His mouth was a thin hard line and his eyes were cold.

'What possessed you to behave in such a foolish manner?' he wanted to know. 'Why all the melodrama? What are the ambulances for? Or the police, for that matter? What in the name of heaven possessed you, Emma? To go racing off on to the moor in bad weather, sending dramatic messages, spending the night in a God-forsaken camp. Ignoring Diana's pleading to wait and give her time to phone for help. No, you must race away like a heroine in a novel, bent on self-glory.'

Emma said in a shaky voice, 'But Diana—'

'Diana is worth a dozen of you.'

It was a remark which stopped her from uttering another word.

'We'll talk later,' said Sir Paul, and went away to his study and sat down behind his desk, his dogs at his feet. He'd been too hard on her; he tried not to think of her white, puzzled face with its pink nose, but he had been full of rage, thinking of all those things which could have happened to her. 'The little idiot,' he told the dogs. 'I could wring her darling neck.'

Emma gave herself ten minutes to stop shaking, then went in search of Mrs Parfitt. 'Sir Paul's home,' she told her. 'Can we stretch dinner for three?'

Mrs Parfitt gave her a thoughtful look, but all she said was, 'I'll grill some more cutlets and shall I serve a soup first? No doubt he's hungry after that journey.'

'That would be fine, Mrs Parfitt. I dare say he's famished. Could we have dinner quite soon?'

'Half an hour, ma'am—gives him time to have a drink and stretch out in his study.'

Emma went to her room, re-did her face and pinned her hair back rather more severely than usual, and then practised a few expressions in the looking-glass—a look of interest, a cool aloofness—she liked that one best...

Downstairs again, in the drawing-room, she picked up her tapestry work and began poking the needle in and out in a careless fashion, practising cool aloofness. She succeeded so well that when Paul came into the room intent on making his peace with her he changed his mind at once—the look she cast him was as effective as a barbed wire fence.

All the same, after a moment or two he essayed some kind of a conversation while he wondered how best to get back on a friendly footing once more.

Emma, her hurt and anger almost a physical pain, had no intention of allowing him to do that. She sat, mangling her needlework most dreadfully, silent except when it was absolutely necessary to say yes or no.

They had their dinner in silence, and as they got up from the table Paul said, 'I think we should have a talk, Emma.'

She paused on her way to the door. 'No, I have understood you very well, Paul; there is no need to say it all over again.'

'Do I take it that you don't wish to work at the nursery any more?'

Her eyes were very large in her pale face. 'I shall go tomorrow morning as usual. Why not?'

His cold, 'Just as you wish,' was as icy as her own manner.

At breakfast she treated him with a frigid politeness which infuriated him—asking him if he would be late home, reminding him that they were due to attend a dinner party on the following evening and wishing him a cool goodbye as he got up to go.

When he had gone she allowed her rigid mouth to droop. She supposed that in a while they would return to their easy-going relationship, but it wouldn't be the same—he had believed Diana, he had mocked her attempts at helping the travellers and, worst of all, he hadn't asked her if any of the things Diana had told him were true. So, if his opinion of her was so low why had he married her? To provide a screen of respectability so that he and Diana could continue as they were? So why hadn't he married her?

Emma's thoughts swirled around in her tired head and didn't make sense. All she did know was that Diana had lied about her and Paul had listened willingly. She didn't think that Diana would expect her back but she was going. Moreover, she would behave as though nothing unusual had occurred, only now she would be on her guard. It was a pity that she had fallen in love with Paul but, since she had, there was nothing more she could do about it—only make sure that Diana didn't get him.

Her imagination working overtime, Emma took herself off to the clinic.

It was a source of satisfaction actually to see that Diana was actually surprised and a little uncomfortable when she walked in.

'Emma—I didn't expect you. You're sure you feel up to it? I heard that you had a heavy cold.'

'Not as heavy as all that. I'll wear a mask, shall I? Are there any new babies?'

Diana's eyes slid away from hers. 'Three from that camp. They're in isolation—whooping cough. They were in a pretty poor way, you know.' She added casually, 'I hear that Paul is back?'

'Yes, didn't he come to see you? I thought he might have popped in on his way home. He's got a busy day—I dare say he'll do his best to call in this evening. I'd better get on with the bathings or I'll have Maisie on my tail.'

Maisie was already busy with the first of her three babies. She looked up as Emma wrapped her pinny round her and got everything ready before picking up Charlie, who was bawling as he always did.

'I heard a lot,' said Maisie. 'Most of which I don't believe. You look like something the cat's dragged in.'

'As bad as that? And I don't think you need to believe any of it, Maisie.'

'You're a right plucky un coming back 'ere. I couldn't 'elp but 'ear wot madam was saying—being busy outside the office door as it were. And that 'usband of yours coming out like a bullet from a gun, ready to do murder. If 'e'd been a bit calmer I'd 'ave spoke up. But 'e almost knocks me over, sets me back on me feet and all without a word. 'E's got a nasty temper and no mistake.'

They sat in silence for a few minutes, then Maisie asked, 'Going to tell 'er awf, are yer?' She scowled. 'I could tell a few tales about 'er if you don't.'

'No—please, Maisie, don't do that. There's a reason...'

'Oh, yeah? Well, yer knows best, but if yer want any 'elp you just ask old Maisie.'

'I certainly will, and thank you, Maisie. I can't explain but I have to wait and see...'

'You're worth a dozen of 'er,' said Maisie, which brought a great knot of tears into Emma's throat, so that she had to bury her face in the back of Charlie's small neck until she had swallowed them back where they belonged.

Sir Paul came home late that evening and Emma, beyond asking politely if he had had a busy day, forbore from wanting to know where he had been. Anyway, Maisie, who was at the nursery for most of the day, would tell her soon enough if he had been to see Diana.

They exchanged polite remarks during dinner and then he went to his study, only coming to the drawing-room as she was folding away her tapestry. Sir Paul, a man of moral and physical courage, quailed under her stony glance and frosty goodnight.

Where, he asked himself, was his enchanting little Emma, so anxious to please, always so friendly and so unaware of his love? He had behaved badly towards her, but couldn't she understand that it was because he had been so appalled at the idea of her going off on her own like that? Perhaps Diana had exaggerated a little; he would go and see her again.

Emma wasn't going to the nursery the following morning. She took the dogs for a long walk and spent an agreeable half-hour deciding which dress she would wear to the dinner party. It was to be rather a grand affair, at one of the lovely old manor-houses on the outskirts of the village, and she wanted to make a good impression.

She had decided to wear the silver-grey dress with the long sleeves and modest neckline, deceptively simple but making the most of her charming shape. She would wear the pearls too, and do her hair in the coil the hairdresser had shown her how to manage on her own.

She had changed and was waiting rather anxiously for Paul to come home by the time he opened the door. She bade him good evening, warned him that he had less than half an hour in which to shower and change, and offered him tea.

He had taken off his coat and was standing in the doorway. 'Emma—I went to the camp this afternoon—'

She cut him short gently. 'You must tell me about it—but not now, you haven't time…'

He didn't move. 'I went to see Diana too.'

'Well, yes, I quite understand about that, but I don't want to talk about it, if you don't mind.' She added in a wifely voice, 'We're going to be late.'

He turned away and went upstairs and presently came down again, immaculate in his dinner-jacket, his face impassive, and courteously attentive to her needs. They left the cottage, got into the car and drove the few miles to the party.

It was a pleasant evening; Emma knew several of the people there and, seated between two elderly gentlemen bent on flattering her, she began to enjoy herself. Paul, watching her from the other end of the table, thought how pretty she had grown in the last few weeks. When they got home he would ask her about her night in the camp.

The men and women he had talked to there had been loud in her praise.

'Saved the kids lives,' one young man had said. 'Acted prompt, she did—and gave an 'and with cleaning 'em up too. Didn't turn a hair—took our little un and 'er mum back with 'er and then came back in that perishing fog—couldn't see yer 'and in front of yer face. Proper little lady, she were.'

He bent his handsome head to listen to what his dinner partner was talking about—something to do with her sciatica. He assumed his listening face; being a bone man, his knowledge of that illness was rudimentary, but he nodded and looked sympathetic while he wondered once again if Diana had exaggerated and why Emma hadn't told him her side of the story.

He glanced down the table once more and squashed a desire to get out of his chair, pick her up out of hers and carry her off home. The trouble was that they didn't see enough of each other.

Chapter 8

'A very pleasant evening,' observed Sir Paul as they drove home.

'Delightful,' agreed Emma. It was fortunate that it was a short journey for there didn't seem to be anything else to say, and once they were at home she bade him a quiet good-night and took herself off to bed. As she went up the stairs she hoped against hope that he would leap after her, beg her forgiveness... Of course he did no such thing!

In the morning when she went downstairs she found him on the point of leaving. 'I'll have to rearrange my day,' he told her. 'There's a patient—an emergency—for Theatre, so the list will run late. I'll probably be home around six o'clock, perhaps later. Don't forget that we are going to Mother's for the weekend.'

'Shall I take the dogs out?'

He was already through the door. 'I walked them earlier.' He nodded a goodbye and drove away as Mrs Parfitt came out of the kitchen.

'Sir Paul will knock himself out,' she observed, 'tearing

off without a proper breakfast, up half the night working, and down here this morning before six o'clock, walking his legs off with those dogs.' She shook her head. 'I never did.'

Emma said, 'It's an emergency...'

'Maybe it is, but he didn't ought to go gallivanting around before dawn after being up half the night—he's only flesh and blood like the rest of us.' She bent her gaze on Emma. 'Now you come and have your breakfast, ma'am; you look as though you could do with a bit of feeding up.'

When Emma got to the nursery she found Diana waiting for her.

'Emma, did Paul remember to tell you that I am giving a little party next week? Tuesday, I thought—it's one of his less busy days.'

She smiled, and Emma said, 'No, but we were out to dinner until late and he left early for the hospital.'

'Yes, I know,' said Diana, who didn't but somehow she made it sound like the truth. 'He works too hard; he'll overdo things if he's not careful. I'll try and persuade him to ease off a bit.'

'I think you can leave that to me, Diana. You know, you're so—so motherly you should find a husband.' Emma's smile was sweet. 'Well, I'll get started.'

She wished Maisie good morning and Maisie said, 'You're smouldering again. Been 'aving words?'

'I'm afraid so. I'm turning into a very unpleasant person, Maisie.'

'Not you—proper little lady, you are. Don't meet many of 'em these days. Now, that young woman downstairs...' She branched off into an account of the goings-on of the young couple on the landing below her flat and Emma forgot her seething rage and laughed a little.

'Doing anything nice this weekend?' asked Maisie as they sat feeding the babies.

'We're going to spend it with my husband's parents.'

'Like that, will you?'

'Oh, yes, they're such dears, and it's a nice old house with a large garden. What are you going to do, Maisie? It's your weekend off, isn't it?'

'S'right.' Maisie looked coy. 'I got a bloke—'e's the milkman; we get on proper nice. Been courting me for a bit, 'e 'as, and we're thinking of having a go...'

'Oh, Maisie, how lovely. You're going to marry him?'

'I ain't said yes, mind you, but it'll be nice not ter 'ave ter come 'ere day in day out, with Madam looking down her nose at me.'

'You'll be able to stay home—oh, Maisie, I am glad; you must say yes. Does he got on well with your family?'

'They get on a treat. Yer don't think I'm silly?'

'Silly? To marry a man who wants you, who'll give you a home and learn to be a father to the children. Of course it's not silly. It's the nicest thing I've heard for days.'

'Oh, well, p'raps I will. Yer're 'appy, ain't yer?'

Emma was bending over Charlie's cot, tucking him in. 'Yes, Maisie.'

'Me, I'd be scared to be married to Sir Paul, that I would—never know what 'e's thinking. 'E don't show 'is feelings, do 'e?'

'Perhaps not, but they are there all the same.'

'Well, you should know,' said Maisie, and chuckled.

The weather was still bad later on, so Emma walked the dogs briefly and went home to sit by the fire. She had a lot to think about; Diana seemed very confident that Paul was in love with her and he had said nothing to give the lie to that, and there was that one remark that she would never forget—that she was worth twelve of Emma. 'Oh, well,' she told the dogs, 'we'll go to this party and see what happens.'

She was glad that they were going away for the weekend, for two days spent alone with Paul, keeping up a façade of friendliness, was rather more than she felt she could cope with. She packed a pretty dress, got into her skirt and one of her cashmere jumpers, made up her face carefully and declared herself ready to go directly after breakfast on Saturday.

It was easier in the car, for she could admire the scenery and there was no need to talk even though she longed to. She sat watching his hands on the wheel—large, capable hands, well-kept. She loved them; she loved the rest of him too and she wasn't going to sit back tamely and let Diana dazzle him...

His parents welcomed them warmly, sweeping them indoors while the dogs went racing off into the garden. 'And where is Queenie?' asked Mrs Wyatt.

'She's happy with Mrs Parfitt and they're company for each other.'

'Of course. You're quite well again after that cold? We missed seeing you while Paul was away. Such a shame. Never mind, we'll make the most of you while you are here. Let Paul take your coat, my dear, and come and sit down and have some coffee.'

It was Mrs Wyatt who asked her how she had come to catch cold. 'Paul tells me that you work twice a week in a nursery in Moretonhampstead; I dare say you caught it there.'

Emma didn't look at Paul. She murmured something and

waited to see if he would tell them how she had caught a cold. He remained silent. As well he might, she reflected crossly as he stood there looking faintly amused. Really, he was a most tiresome man; if she hadn't loved him so much she would have disliked him intensely.

There might have been an awkward pause if he hadn't, with the ease of good manners, made some trifling remark about the weather. Smooth, thought Emma, and went pink when her mother-in-law said, 'Well, cold or no cold, I must say that marriage suits you, my dear.'

Emma put her coffee-cup down with care and wished that she didn't blush so easily. Blushing, she felt sure, had gone out with the coming of women's lib and feminism, whatever that was exactly. Mrs Wyatt, being of an older generation, wasn't concerned with either and found the blush entirely suitable.

Paul found it enchanting.

The weekend passed too quickly.

No one would ever replace her mother, but Mrs Wyatt helped to fill the emptiness her mother had left, and if she noticed the careful way Emma and Paul avoided any of the usual ways of the newly wed she said nothing.

Paul had never worn his heart on his sleeve but his feelings ran deep and, unless her maternal instinct was at fault, he was deeply in love with Emma. And Emma with him, she was sure of that. They had probably had one of the many little tiffs they would have before they settled down, she decided.

'You must come again soon,' she begged them as they took their leave on Sunday evening.

It was late by the time they reached the cottage, which gave Emma the excuse to go to bed at once. Paul's 'Goodnight, my dear,' was uttered in a placid voice, and he added that there was no need for her to get up for breakfast if she didn't feel like it. 'I shall be away all day,' he said. 'I've several private patients to see after I've finished at the hospital.'

In bed, sitting against the pillows with her knees under her chin, Emma told Queenie, 'This can't go on, you know; something must be done.'

The Fates had come to the same conclusion, it seemed, for as Paul opened the front door the next evening, Emma, coming down the stairs, tripped and fell. He picked her up within seconds, scooping her into his arms, holding her close.

'Emma—are you hurt? Stay still a moment while I look.'

She would have stayed still forever with his arms around her, but she managed a rather shaky, 'I'm fine, really...'

He spoke to the top of her head, which was buried in his waistcoat. 'Emma—you must tell me—this ridiculous business of spending the night at that camp. Why did you refuse to listen to Diana? She is still upset and I cannot understand...'

Emma wrenched herself free. 'You listened to her and you believed her without even asking me. Well, go on believing her; you've known her for years, haven't you? And you've only known me for months; you don't know much about me, do you? But I expect you know Diana very well indeed.'

Paul put his hands in his pockets. 'Yes. Go on, Emma.'

'Well, if I were you, I'd believe her and not me,' she added bitterly. 'After all, she's worth a dozen of me.'

She flew back upstairs and shut her bedroom door with a snap and when Mrs Parfitt came presently to see if she should serve dinner she found Emma lying on her bed.

'I have such a shocking headache,' sighed Emma. 'Would you give Sir Paul his dinner? I couldn't eat anything.'

Indeed she did look poorly. Mrs Parfitt tut-tutted and offered one of her herbal teas. 'You just get into bed, ma'am. I'll tell Sir Paul and I dare say he'll be up to see you.'

'No, no, there's no need. Let him have his dinner first; he's had a busy day and he needs a meal and time to rest. I dare say it will get better in an hour or two.'

The headache had been an excuse, but soon it was real. Emma got herself into bed and eventually fell asleep.

That was how Paul found her when he came to see her. She was curled up, her tear-stained face cushioned on a hand, the other arm round Queenie. He stood studying her for some minutes. Her hair was loose, spread over the pillows, and her mouth was slightly open. Her cheeks were rather blotchy because of the tears but the long, curling brown lashes swept them gently. When he had fallen in love with her he hadn't considered her to be beautiful but now he could see that her ordinary little face held a beauty which had nothing to do with good looks.

He went away presently, reassured Mrs Parfitt and went to his study. There was always work.

Emma went down to breakfast in the morning, exchanged good mornings with Paul, assured him that her headache had quite gone and volunteered the information that she was going to the nursery that morning. 'And I said I would go tomorrow morning as well—they're short-handed for a few days. Will you be home late?'

'No, in time for tea I hope. There's the parish council meeting at eight o'clock this evening.'

'Oh, yes. I am helping with the coffee and biscuits.'

He left then, and very soon after she got into the Mini and drove herself to the nursery.

''Ere,' said Maisie as she sat down and picked up the first baby, 'wot yer been up ter? 'Ad a tiff?'

'No, no, Maisie. I'm fine, really. How's your intended?'

It was a red herring which took them through most of the morning.

It was just as Emma was leaving and passing the office that Diana called to her. 'Emma, don't worry if Paul is late this evening—he's coming to check one of the babies from the camp—a fractured arm as well as whooping cough.'

Emma asked, 'Did he say he'd come? He's got a parish meeting this evening; he won't want to miss it.'

Diana smiled slowly. 'Oh, I'm sure it won't matter if he's not there.' She stared at Emma. 'As a matter of fact, he said he was coming to see me anyway.'

'That's all right, then,' said Emma. She didn't believe Diana.

She had lunch, then took the dogs for a long walk and helped Mrs Parfitt get the tea. Buttered muffins and cucumber sandwiches, she decided, and one of Mrs Parfitt's rich fruit cakes.

Teatime came and went, and there was no Paul. At last she had a cup of tea anyway, and a slice of cake, helped Mrs Parfitt clear away and went upstairs to get ready. She put on a plain jersey dress suitable for a parish council meeting.

When seven o'clock came and went she told Mrs Parfitt to delay her cooking. 'Sir Paul won't have time to eat in comfort before eight o'clock. Perhaps we could have a meal when we get home?'

'No problem,' said Mrs Parfitt. 'The ragout'll only need

warming up and the rest will be ready by the time you've had a drink.'

'You have your supper when you like, Mrs Parfitt.' Emma glanced at the clock; she would have to go to the meeting and make Paul's excuses.

The councillors were friendly and very nice about it. Doctors were never free to choose their comings and goings, observed old Major Pike, but he for one was delighted to see his little wife.

Emma smiled shyly at him—he was a dear old man, very knowledgeable about the moor, born and bred in Lustleigh even though he had spent years away from it. He thoroughly approved of her, for she was a local girl and looked sensible.

The meeting was drawing to a close when the door opened and Paul came in. Emma, sitting quietly at the back of the village hall, watched him as he made his excuses, exchanged a few laughing remarks with the rest of the council and sat down at the table. He hadn't looked at her, but presently he turned his head and gave her a look which shook her.

He was pale and without expression, and she knew that he was very angry. With her? she wondered. Had Diana been making more mischief between them? She hoped he would smile but he turned away and soon it was time for her to go and help the vicar's wife in the kitchen.

They made the coffee and arranged Petit Beurre biscuits on a plate and carried them through just as the chairman closed the meeting. Eventually goodnights were exchanged and everyone started to go home.

Emma, collecting cups and saucers, saw that Paul had stayed. Waiting for her, she supposed, and when she came from the kitchen presently he was still there.

He got up when he saw her, passed a pleasant time of

day with the vicar's wife, helped them on with their coats,
turned out the lights, locked the door and gave the key to
the vicar, who had walked back for his wife. That done, he
turned for home, his hand under Emma's elbow.

She sensed that it was an angry hand and, anxious not to
make things worse than they apparently were, she trotted
briskly beside him, keeping up with his strides.

In the drawing-room she sat down in her usual chair,
but Paul stood by the door, the dogs beside him. Perhaps it
would be best to carry the war into the enemy camp, Emma
decided.

'You were very late; did you have an emergency?'

'No.'

'You went to see Diana...?'

'Indeed I did.'

Emma nodded. 'She told me that you would go and see
her, and that you were going to see her anyway.'

'And you believed her?'

'Well, no, I didn't—but I do now.'

He said softly, 'And why do you suppose that I went to
see her?'

Emma said carefully, 'Shall we not talk about that? Something has made you angry and you must be tired. I'll tell
Mrs Parfitt that we are ready for dinner, shall I? While you
have a drink.'

She was surprised when he laughed.

It was while they were eating that Paul said quietly, 'I do
not wish you to go to the clinic any more, Emma.'

She had a forkful of ragout halfway to her mouth. 'Not
go? Why ever not?'

'Would it do if I just asked you to do as I wish? There
are good reasons.'

Emma allowed her imagination to run riot. Diana would have convinced him in her charming way that she was no good at the nursery, that she was too slow, too independent too. She said slowly, 'Very well, Paul, but I should like to go tomorrow morning to say goodbye to Maisie. I have been working with her and she is getting married—I've a present for her. And I'd like to see Charlie—he's so cross and unloved...'

'Of course you must go. Diana won't be there, but you could leave a note.'

'Very well. I'll think up a good excuse.'

She wrote it later when Paul was in his study. Obviously Paul didn't want her to meet Diana again. Why? she wondered. Perhaps she would never know. It had been silly of her to refuse to talk about it; she hadn't given him a chance to explain why he was angry. She thought that he still was but he had got his rage under control; his manner was imperturbable.

He had looked, she reflected, as though he could have swept the extremely valuable decanter and glasses off the side-table. She sighed—everything had gone wrong. Their marriage had seemed such a splendid idea and she had been sure that it would be a success.

The mousy little woman who deputised for Diana was at the nursery the next day.

'Is Diana ill?' asked Emma, agog for information.

'No, Lady Wyatt. She felt she should have a few days off; she's been working hard just lately. You'll be sorry to have missed her. I hear you're leaving us.'

'Yes, I'm afraid so. I shall miss the babies. May I go and say goodbye to them and Maisie?'

'Of course. I'm sure Diana is grateful for your help while you were with us.'

'I enjoyed it,' said Emma.

Maisie was on her own, and Emma resisted the urge to put on her pinny and give her a hand. 'I'm leaving, Maisie. I didn't want to but Sir Paul asked me to.'

'Did 'e now?' Maisie looked smug. She had been there yesterday evening when Sir Paul had come to see Diana and, although she hadn't been able to hear what was said, she had heard Diana's voice, shrill and then tearful, and Sir Paul's measured rumble. He had come out of the office eventually, and this time Maisie had been brave and stopped him before he got into his car.

'I don't know the ins and outs,' she had told him briskly, 'but it's time you caught on ter that Diana telling great whoppers about that little wife of yours. Little angel, she is, and never said a word, I'll bet. 'Oo pretended there weren't no doctors nor ambulances to go ter the camp? Moonshine. I 'eard 'er with me own ears telling 'em there weren't no need to send anyone. Sent little Emma back into all that mist and dark, she did, and tells everyone she'd done it awf her own bat and against 'er wishes.' Maisie had stuck her chin out. 'Sack me if yer want to. I likes ter see justice done, mister!'

Sir Paul had put out a hand and engulfed hers. 'Maisie—so do I. Thank you for telling me; Emma has a loyal friend in you.'

'Don't you go telling her, now.'

He had kept his word. Emma obviously knew nothing about his visit. Now everything would be all right. 'I'll miss yer, but I dare say you'll 'ave a few of yer own soon enough.'

Emma had picked up Charlie. 'I do hope Charlie will be wanted by someone.'

'Now, as ter that, I've a bit of good news. 'E's ter be adopted by such a nice woman and 'er 'usband—no kids of their own and they want a boy. 'E'll 'ave a good 'ome.'

'Oh, lovely. Maisie, will you write and tell me when you're to be married? And here's a wedding-present.'

Emma dived into her shoulder-bag and handed over a beribboned box.

'Cor, love, yer didn't orter...'

Maisie was already untying the ribbons. Inside was a brown leather handbag and, under that, a pair of matching gloves.

'I'll wear 'em on me wedding-day,' said Maisie, and got up and offered a hand.

Emma took it and then kissed Maisie's cheek. 'I hope you'll be very happy, and please write to me sometimes.'

'I ain't much 'and with a pen, but I'll do me best,' said Maisie.

Back home again, Emma took the dogs for a walk, had her lunch and then went into the garden. She pottered about, weeding here and there, tying things up, examining the rose bushes, anxious to keep busy so that she didn't need to think too much. She supposed that sooner or later she and Paul would have to talk—perhaps it would be best to get it over with. He had said that he would be home for tea. She began to rehearse a casual conversation—anything to prevent them talking about Diana.

The rehearsal wasn't necessary; when Paul got home he treated her with a casual friendliness which quite disarmed her. It was only later that she remembered she had told him that she had no wish to discuss the unfortunate episode at the camp and Diana's accusations. Which, of course, made it impossible for her to mention it now. They spent the evening together, making trivial talk, so that by the time she went to bed she was feeling peevish from her efforts to think up something harmless to say.

Paul got up to open the door for her, and as she went past him with a quick goodnight he observed, 'Difficult, isn't it, Emma?'

She paused to look up at him in surprise.

'Making polite small talk when you're bursting to utter quite different thoughts out loud.' He smiled down at her—a small, mocking smile with a tender edge to it, but she didn't see the tenderness, only the mockery.

For want of anything better, she said, 'I've no idea what you mean.'

Over the next few days they settled down to an uneasy truce—at least, it was uneasy on Emma's part, although Paul behaved as though nothing had occurred to disturb the easy-going relationship between them.

He was due up in Edinburgh at the beginning of the following week, but he didn't suggest that she should go with him. Not that I would have gone, reflected Emma, all the same annoyed that he hadn't asked her.

He would be back in three days he told her. 'Why not call Father to take you up to the Cotswolds, and spend a couple of days with them?'

'Well, Mrs Parfitt did say that she would like a few days to visit her sister at Brixham. I thought I might drive her there and fetch her back. Willy and Kate can sit in the back and I can leave Queenie for most of the day.'

'You would like to do that? Then by all means go. I don't really like your being alone in the house, though, Emma.'

'It won't be the first time, and I have the dogs. I'm not nervous.'

'I'll leave my phone number, of course. Perhaps it would be better if Mrs Parfitt waited until I am back home.'

'No, it wouldn't. There's lots more to do around the house and more cooking when you're home.'

'A nuisance in my own house, Emma?' He sounded amused.

'No—oh, no, of course not. But I know she'd prefer to go away when you're not here.'

'As you wish. In any case, I shall phone each evening.'

Paul left soon after breakfast, so Emma was able to drive Mrs Parfitt to her sister's very shortly after that.

It was a pleasant drive and the morning was fine, and when she reached Brixham she delivered Mrs Parfitt and then drove down to the harbour, where she parked the car and took the dogs for a run. She had coffee in a small café near by and then drove back to Lustleigh. When she reached the cottage and let herself in she realised that she felt lonely, despite the animals' company.

She wandered through the house, picking things up and putting them down again and, since Mrs Parfitt had left everything in apple-pie order, there was nothing for her to do except get the lunch.

A long walk did much to dispel her gloom and took up the time nicely until she could get her tea, and then it was the evening and Paul had said that he would phone...

She wondered how long it would take him to get there; it was a long way and he might be too tired to ring up.

Of course he did, though; she was watching the six o'clock news when the phone rang and she rushed to it, fearful that he might ring off before she reached it.

Yes, his cool voice assured her, he had had a very pleasant drive, not all that tiring, and he had already seen two patients who needed his particular skills. 'I have a clinic tomorrow morning,' he told her, 'and then a lecture before dining with friends. I may phone rather later. You enjoyed your drive to Brixham?'

'Yes. We went for a long walk this afternoon; Willy got a thorn in his paw but I got it out. I'm getting their suppers...'

'In that case, don't let me keep you. Sleep well, Emma.'

He didn't wait for her answer but hung up.

An unsatisfactory conversation, thought Emma, snivelling into the dog food. He hadn't asked her if she was lonely or cautioned her kindly about locking up securely; indeed, he had asked hardly any questions about her at all.

She poked around in the fridge and ate two cold sausages and a carton of yoghurt, then took herself off to bed after letting the dogs out and then bolting and barring all the doors and the windows. She had no reason to feel nervous—it was a pity that she didn't know that the village constable, alerted by Sir Paul, had made it his business to keep an eye on her.

She lay awake for a long time, thinking about Paul. She missed him dreadfully; it was as though only half of her were alive—to have him home was all she wanted, and never mind if they no longer enjoyed their pleasant comradeship. She would have to learn to take second place to Diana and be thankful for that.

'But why he couldn't have married her and been done with it, I don't know,' Emma observed to the sleeping Queenie and, naturally enough, got no answer.

She walked to the village stores after breakfast, took her purchases home and went off for another walk with the dogs. The fine weather held and the sun shone, and out on the moors her worries seemed of no account. They went back home with splendid appetites and, having filled the dogs' bowls and attended to Queenie's more modest needs, Emma had her own lunch. The day was half done, and in the evening Paul would phone again.

She was putting away the last spoons and forks when there was a thump on the door-knocker. She wiped her hands on her apron and went to open it.

Diana stood there, beautifully dressed, exquisitely made-up, and smiling.

'Emma—I've been lunching at Bovey Tracey and I just had to come and see you. I know Paul's in Edinburgh and I thought you might like a visit. I'm surprised he didn't take you with him. It's great for a professor's image to have a wife, you know.'

She had walked past Emma as she held the door open and now stood in the hall, looking round. 'Nothing's changed,' she observed and heaved a sigh. 'I never liked that portrait over the table, but Paul said he was a famous surgeon in his day and he wouldn't move him.'

She smiled at Emma, and Emma smiled back. 'Well, it is Paul's house,' she said pleasantly. 'Would you like a cup of coffee?'

'I'd love one.' Diana had taken off her jacket and thrown it over a chair. 'I had the most ghastly lunch at the Prostle-Hammetts and the coffee was undrinkable.'

It was the kind of remark Diana would make, thought Emma as she led the way into the drawing-room.

'Oh, the dogs,' cried Diana. 'We always had such fun together...'

Neither dog took any notice of her, which cheered Emma enormously—they were on her side.

'Do sit down,' she said. 'I'll fetch the coffee.'

'Can I help? I know my way around, you know.'

'No, no. Sit down here—you look a bit pinched. I expect you're tired.' She saw Diana's frown and the quick peek in the great Chippendale mirror over the fireplace.

In the kitchen she poured the coffee and wondered why Diana had come. To see how she had settled in as Paul's wife? Or just to needle her? Emma told herself stoutly that she wasn't going to believe anything Diana said. After all, so far she had done nothing but hint at her close friendship with Paul; all that nonsense about her love distracting him from his work had been nothing but moonshine. All the same, Diana had played a dirty trick on her when she had been at the nursery and she wasn't to be trusted.

She took the coffee-tray in, offered sugar and cream and sat down opposite her unwelcome guest. She didn't believe that Diana had called out of friendliness—it was probably just out of curiosity.

'Paul has a busy few days in Edinburgh,' said Diana. 'Patients yesterday and today after that long drive, and a clinic tomorrow. What a blessing it is that he has good friends—we always dined there…' She cast a sidelong look at Emma and gave a little laugh. 'Of course, everyone expected us to marry.'

'Then why didn't you?' Emma lifted the coffee-pot. 'More coffee?'

'No, thanks—I have to think of my figure.'

Emma said pertly, 'Well, yes, I suppose you do; we none of us grow any younger do we?'

Diana put her cup and saucer down. 'Look, Emma, you

don't like me and I don't like you, but that doesn't alter the fact that Paul still loves me. He married you for all kinds of worthy reasons: you're an ideal wife for a busy man who is seldom at home; you don't complain; you're not pretty enough to attract other men. I dare say you're a good house-wife and you won't pester him to take you out to enjoy the bright lights. As I said, you're an ideal wife for him. He's fond of you, I suppose—but loving you? I don't sup-pose you know what that means; you're content with a mild affection, aren't you? Whereas he...'

She had contrived to get tears in her eyes and Emma, seeing them, had sudden doubts.

'We love each other,' said Diana quietly. 'He has mar-ried you and he'll be a kind and good husband to you but you must understand that that is all he will ever be. I know you think I'm not worthy of him, and I know I'm not.' She blinked away another tear. 'He's not happy, you know, Emma.'

Emma said, 'You could go away—right away.'

Diana said simply, 'He would come after me—don't you know that? There's nothing I can do—I've talked and talked and he won't listen.' She looked at Emma. 'It is you who must go, Emma.'

Emma, looking at her and not trusting her an inch, found herself half believing her. She detested Diana, but if Paul loved her that didn't matter, did it? However, she didn't quite believe Diana; she would need proof.

Where would she get proof? It would have to be some-thing that would hold water, not vague hints. She said, 'I don't intend to go, Diana.'

She got up to answer the phone and it was Paul. His quiet voice sounded reassuring to her ear. 'It will be late before

I can phone you this evening so it seemed sensible to do so now. Is everything all right at home?'

'Yes, thank you—have you been busy?'

'Yes. I'll be here for another two days. Do you fetch Mrs Parfitt back tomorrow?'

'No, the day after.'

'You're not lonely?'

'No. Diana is here, paying a flying visit.'

She heard the change in his voice. 'I'll speak to her, Emma.'

'It's Paul; he'd like a word with you.' Emma handed the phone to Diana. 'I'll take the coffee out to the kitchen.'

Which she did, but not before she heard Diana's rather loud, 'Darling…'

Chapter 9

Emma hesitated for a moment; to nip back and listen at the door was tempting, but not very practical with the coffee-tray in her hands. She went to the kitchen, letting the door bang behind her, put the tray on the table and then returned noiselessly to the hall. The drawing-room door was ajar; she could hear Diana very clearly.

'I'll be at home until Friday. Goodbye, Paul.'

Emma retreated smartly to the kitchen and rattled a few cups and saucers and then went back to the drawing-room, shutting the baize door to the kitchen with a thump. Diana was putting on her coat.

'My dear, I must go. Thanks for the coffee, and I'm so glad to see that you've altered nothing in the cottage.' She paused, pulling on her gloves. 'Emma, you will think over what I have said, won't you? It sounds cruel but we are all unhappy now, aren't we? If you let Paul go then there would be only one of us unhappy, and since you don't love him you'll get over it quickly enough. He'll treat you well—financially, I mean.'

'I think you'd better go,' said Emma, 'before I throw something at you.' She went ahead of Diana and opened the cottage door. 'You're very vulgar, aren't you?'

She shut the door before Diana could reply.

She went back to the drawing-room and sat down; Queenie got on to her lap while Willy and Kate settled beside her. She didn't want to believe Diana but she had sounded sincere and she had cried. Moreover, she had told Paul that she would be at home until Friday. Why would she do that unless she expected him to go and see her? There was no way of finding out—at least, until Paul came home again.

He phoned the following evening. 'You're all right?' he wanted to know. 'Not lonely?'

'Not in the least,' said Emma airily. 'I had tea with the Postle-Hammets. I like Mrs Postle-Hammet and the children are sweet; I enjoyed myself.'

Largely because Mrs Postle-Hammet had been remarkably frank about her opinion of Diana, she thought. 'Cold as a fish and selfish to the bone and clever enough to hide it,' she had said—hardly information she could pass on to Paul.

'I should be home tomorrow evening, but if I should be delayed will you leave the side-door locked but not bolted? You'll fetch Mrs Parfitt tomorrow?'

'Yes, after lunch.'

'Good. I'll say goodnight, Emma. I've several more phone calls to make.' One of them to Diana? she wondered, and tried not to think about that.

She had an early lunch the next day and drove to Brixham through driving rain to fetch Mrs Parfitt, and then drove home again, listening to that lady's account of her few days' holiday. 'Very nice it was too, ma'am, but my sister isn't a good cook and I missed my kitchen. Still, the sea air was nice and there are some good shops. You've not been too alone, I hope?'

'No, no, Mrs Parfitt. I've been out to tea and Miss Pearson came to see me and Sir Paul has phoned each evening, and of course there were the dogs to take out. I had no time to be lonely—' Emma turned to smile at her companion '—but it's very nice to have you back, Mrs Parfitt. The cottage doesn't seem the same without you. Sir Paul is coming back this evening.'

'He'll need his dinner if he's driving all that way. Did you have anything in mind, ma'am?'

They spent the rest of the journey deciding on a menu to tempt him when he got home. 'Something that won't spoil,' cautioned Emma, 'for I've no idea exactly when he'll be back.'

Mrs Parfitt took off her best hat and her sensible coat and went straight to the kitchen. 'A nice cup of tea,' she observed, 'and while the kettle's boiling I'll pop a few scones in the oven.'

Emma went from room to room, making sure that everything was just so, shaking up cushions, rearranging the flowers, laying the pile of letters on the table by Paul's chair and, since it was going to be a gloomy evening, switching on lamps here and there so that there was a cheerful glow from the windows.

Satisfied that everything was as welcoming as she could make it, she went upstairs and changed into a patterned silk jersey dress, did her face with care and brushed her hair into a knot at the back of her head; it took a long time to get it just so but she was pleased with the result. Then she went downstairs to wait.

At ten o'clock she sent Mrs Parfitt to bed and ate a sketchy meal off a tray in the kitchen. When the long case clock in the hall chimed one o'clock she went to bed herself.

She was still awake when it chimed again, followed by the silvery tinkle of the carriage clock in the drawing-room. She slept after that but woke when it was barely light to creep downstairs to see if Paul was home. If he was, the back door would be bolted. It wasn't!

Emma stared at it for a long moment and then went to the phone and picked it up. The night porter answered it. Yes, Sir Paul had been in the hospital during the late evening and had left again shortly after—he had seen him leave in his car.

He sounded a little surprised at her query and she hastened to say that it was perfectly all right. 'Sir Paul said that he might do that. I'll ring him now. Thank you.'

She went to the kitchen then, and put on the kettle. She spooned tea into the pot, trying not to think about the previous evening, trying not to believe Diana's remarks but quite unable to forget them.

She was making tea when the kitchen door opened and Paul walked in. Emma caught her breath and choked on a surge of strong feelings.

'A fine time to come home,' she snapped, rage for the moment overcoming the delight of seeing him again, and she made unnecessary work of refilling the kettle and putting it back on the Aga.

Sir Paul didn't speak, but stood in the doorway looking at her indignant back, and since the silence was rather long she asked stiffly, 'Would you like a cup of tea?'

'Er—no, thank you, Emma. I'm sorry if you were worried.'

'Worried? Why should I be worried?' said Emma at her haughtiest. 'I phoned the hospital early this morning and I was told that you had been in and gone again late last night.' She drew a long breath. 'So I had no need to worry, had I?'

When he most annoyingly didn't answer, she said, 'I knew where you were...'

'Indeed.'

She had her back to him, busy with mug and sugar and milk and pouring tea. 'Well, Diana came to see me—I told you that—you spoke to her...'

'Ah, Diana—of course. *Latet anguis in herba*!' murmured Sir Paul.

Emma's knowledge of Latin was sketchy and, anyway, what had grass got to do with it? For she had recognised the word *herba*, and if he was trailing a red herring she meant to ignore it. In any case her tongue was running on now, regardless of prudence.

'So of course I knew you'd go to her when you got back. She was very—very frank.' She gave an angry snuffle. 'She was glad I hadn't altered the pictures or anything.' She wouldn't look at him. 'Would you like breakfast?'

'No, Emma, I'll shower and change and go to the hospital.'

'You'll be back later? Teatime?'

'Don't count on that.' He spoke quietly, and something in his voice made her turn to look at him. He looked very tired but he gave her a bland stare from cold eyes. She had no doubt that he was angry. She was angry too, and miserable, and she loved him so much that she felt the ache of it. The urge to tell him so was so great that she started to speak, but she had barely uttered his name when he went away.

He had left the house by the time she had dressed and gone back downstairs to find Mrs Parfitt in the kitchen.

'Gone again,' cried Mrs Parfitt. 'I saw him drive off not ten minutes ago. By the time I'd got downstairs he'd gone. He'll wear himself out, that he will. How about a nice leg of lamb for dinner this evening? He'll need his strength kept up.'

When Emma said that he had come home very early in the morning Mrs. Parfitt commented, 'Must have been an accident. Now you go and eat your breakfast, ma'am, for no doubt you've been worrying half the night. Who'd be a doctor's wife, eh?' She laughed, and Emma echoed it in a hollow way.

She took the dogs for their walk after breakfast while Mrs Parfitt took herself off to the village shop and paid a visit to the butcher. It was while she was drying the dogs in the outhouse by the kitchen that Mrs Parfitt joined her.

'Postie was in the stores—there's been a nasty accident on the M5 where it turns into the A38.' Mrs Parfitt paused for breath, bursting with her news. 'Nine cars, he said, all squashed together, and Sir Paul right behind them on his way back here. Goes back to the hospital and spends the night in the operating theatre, he does. He's back there now, no doubt, working himself to death. He didn't ought to do it. He didn't say nothing to you, ma'am? No—well, of course, he wouldn't; he'd have known how upset you'd have been.'

Emma had gone very pale. 'Not a word. He didn't want tea or his breakfast but he said he had to go back.' The full horror of what she had said to him dawned on her—she had accused him of being with Diana while all the time he had been saving lives. She hadn't even given him the chance to tell her anything. She felt sick at the thought, and Mrs Parfitt took her arm and sat her down by the table.

'There, I shouldn't have come out with it so quick; you're that pale—like a little ghost. You stay there while I fetch you a drop of brandy.'

Emma was only too willing to sit. It was chilly in the little room, and the dogs, released from the tiresome business of being cleaned up before going into the house, had slipped away to lie by the Aga.

Mrs Parfitt came back with the brandy. 'It don't do to give way, ma'am,' she urged Emma. 'He's safe and sound even if he's tired to his bones, but you must show a bright face when he gets home, for that'll be what he needs.'

Emma drank the brandy, although she thought he wouldn't care if her face was bright or not. He would be polite, because he had beautiful manners and they wouldn't allow him to be otherwise, but he would have gone behind the barrier she had always sensed was between them—only now that barrier was twice as high and she doubted if she would ever climb it.

She spent a restless day, dreading his return and yet longing for it, going over and over in her aching head the awful things she had said and rehearsing the humble speech she would offer him when he came home. Which he did just as Mrs Parfitt brought in the tea-tray, following her into the drawing-room.

'There,' said Mrs Parfitt. 'Didn't I bake that fruit cake knowing you'd be here for your tea? I'll fetch another cup and a sandwich or two.'

She trotted off; she firmly believed that the way to a man's heart was through his stomach, and his doubtless needed filling.

He thanked her quickly and stooped to fondle the dogs weaving around his feet. 'Hello, Emma,' he said quietly.

'Paul.' The strength of her feelings was choking her as she got out of her chair, spilling an indignant Queenie on to the carpet. She said stupidly, 'I didn't know...' Her tongue shrivelled under his cold stare; underneath his quietness he was furiously angry, and suddenly she was angry again. 'Why didn't you tell me?'

He sat down in his chair and the dogs curled up beside him. 'I don't believe that I had the opportunity,' he observed mildly.

'You could have—' Emma burst out, only to be interrupted by Mrs Parfitt with fresh tea, cup and saucer and a plate of sandwiches.

'Gentleman's Relish,' she pointed out in a pleased voice. 'Just what you fancy, sir, and cucumber and cress. I shall be serving dinner a bit earlier, ma'am? I dare say the master's peckish.'

Emma glanced at Paul, who said, 'That would be very nice, Mrs Parfitt.' He sounded like any man just home and sitting by his own fireside but Emma, unwittingly catching his eye, blinked at its icy hardness.

After Mrs Parfitt had gone Emma poured the tea, offered sandwiches and strove to think of something to say; she would have to apologise, and she wanted to, but for the moment the right words eluded her. All the same she made a halting start, only to have it swept aside as Paul began a conversation which gave her no chance to utter a word.

It was an undemanding and impersonal stream of small talk, quiet and unhurried. He could have been soothing a scared patient before telling her his diagnosis. Well, she wasn't a patient but she was scared, and the diagnosis, when it came, left her without words.

She was pouring his second cup of tea when he said casually, 'I've been offered a lecture tour in the States...'

He watched her pale face go even paler and saw the shock in it.

'The States? America? For how long?'

'Four months.'

She gulped back a protesting scream. 'That's a long time.'

'Yes. Time enough for us to consider our future, don't you agree?'

If only he wasn't so pleasant about it, Emma thought unhappily, and if only I could think of the right thing to say. After a minute she said, 'I expect you'd like to go?'

He didn't answer that so she tried again, asking a question her tongue uttered before she could stop it. 'Will you go alone?'

'Oh, yes.'

He didn't add to that, and she seized the opportunity and plunged into a muddled apology. None of the things she had meant to say came out properly. 'I'm sorry, Paul, I'm so very sorry; it was terribly stupid of me and unkind...'

He stopped her quite gently. 'Don't say any more, Emma. I thought that when we married...' He paused. 'You must see that if you don't trust me our marriage is going to be unhappy. That is why I shall go on this tour; you will have time to decide what you want to do with your future.'

She gave him a bewildered look. 'You mean, you don't want me to be your wife?'

'I didn't say that...'

'Well, no—but I think you meant that, only you are too polite to say so. I expect it's a good idea.'

At the end of four months, she thought sadly, he would come back, and they would separate without fuss and he would go his way and she would go hers. What about Diana? He hadn't mentioned her, had he? And she didn't dare to ask.

'I've made you very angry.'

'Indeed you have,' he agreed politely.

'I think it would have been better if you had shouted at me...'

'I could never shout at you, Emma.'

He smiled a little, thinking that he wanted to pick her up and shake her and carry her off somewhere and never let her go—his darling Emma.

Perhaps he was too old for her; perhaps she regretted marrying him. Certainly she had been a constantly good companion, and at times he had thought that she might become more than that, but once she had got over the shock she had given no sign that she didn't want him to go away. Indeed, she had taken it for granted that she would stay here.

He got up. 'I've one or two letters to write,' he told her. 'I'll go and do them before dinner—I can take the dogs out later.'

Emma nodded, and when he had gone carried the tray out to the kitchen. She stayed there for ten minutes, getting in Mrs Parfitt's way, and presently went back to the drawing-room and got out her embroidery. She wasn't being very successful with it and spent the next half-hour unpicking the work she had done the previous evening. It left her thoughts free and she allowed them full rein.

Somehow she must find a way to convince Paul that she was truly sorry. If he wanted to be free—perhaps to marry Diana—then the least she could do was to make it easy for him. She owed him so much that she could never repay him.

She must find out when this lecture tour was to start; if she were to go away first, then he wouldn't need to go.

Her head seethed with plans; she could tell everyone that an aunt or uncle needed her urgently. That she had no relations of any kind made no difference—no one was to know that. She would do it in a way that would arouse no suspicions. Diana would guess, of course—she had suggested it in the first place—but she wasn't likely to tell anyone.

She would write a letter to Paul, saying all the things she wanted to say—that she loved him and wanted him to be happy and thanked him for his kindness and generosity. Her mind made up, she attacked her embroidery with vigour and a complete disregard for accuracy.

Out-patients' sister watched Sir Paul's vast back disappear down the corridor. 'Well, what's the matter with him?' she asked her staff nurse. 'I've never known him dash off without his cup of tea, and him so quiet too. Something on his mind, do you suppose? He's got that nice little wife to go home to and you're not telling me that they're not happy together. Mention her and his face lights up—looks ten years younger. Ah, well, he'll go home and spend a lovely evening with her, I dare say.'

Sir Paul drove himself to the nursery, got out of his car and walked into Diana's office. She was getting ready to go home but put her jacket down as he went in. 'Paul, how lovely to see you—it's ages.'

He closed the door behind him—a disappointment to Maisie, who was getting ready to go home too, standing in the cloakroom near enough to the office to hear anything interesting which might be said.

'Perhaps you will spare me ten minutes, Diana?'

He hadn't moved from the door and she sat down slowly. 'All the time in the world for you, Paul.'

'You went to see Emma—why?'

She shrugged her shoulders. 'I thought she might be lonely.'

'The truth, Diana...'

Now Maisie edged nearer the door. She couldn't hear what was being said but she could hear Diana's voice getting more and more agitated, and Sir Paul's voice sounding severe and, presently, angry.

Sir Paul wasn't mincing his words. 'I have never at any time given you reason to believe that I was in love with you.' He added, with brutal frankness, 'Indeed, you are the last woman I would wish to have for a wife.'

Maisie, her ear pressed to the keyhole, just had time to nip back into the cloakroom as he opened the door.

He saw at once on his return home that this was not the right time to talk to Emma. She was being carefully polite and the expression on her face warned him not to be other than that; so the evening was spent in a guarded manner, neither of them saying any of the things they wanted to say, both waiting for some sign...

Emma went to bed rather early, relieved that she was alone and could grizzle and mope and presently go over her plans to leave. Just for a little while that evening, despite their coolness towards each other, she had wondered if she could stay, if they could patch things up between them. But trying to read Paul's thoughts was an impossible task; they were far too well hidden behind his bland face. He wasn't going to reproach her; he wasn't going to say another word about the whole sorry business. Presumably it was to be forgotten and they would go on as before, just good friends and then, when the right moment came, parting.

'I hate Diana,' said Emma, and kicked a cushion across the floor. 'I hope she makes him very unhappy.' It was a palpable lie which did nothing to restore her spirits.

She didn't sleep much—she was too busy making plans. Many were wildly unsuitable to begin with, but by the early morning she had discarded most of them in favour of one which seemed to her to be simple and foolproof.

She would give Mrs Parfitt a day off—it would have to be in two days' time, when Paul had his theatre list and a ward round, which meant he wouldn't be home before about six o'clock. Once Mrs Parfitt was out of the house she would pack a few things in a suitable bag, write a letter to Paul and one to Mrs Parfitt—the illness of a fictitious aunt would do very well—walk to Bovey Tracey, get a bus down to the main road and another bus to Plymouth.

She could lose herself there and get a job in a restaurant or a hotel—surely there would be temporary jobs in the tourist trade. She would have to buy some kind of a bag—a knapsack would do. In the morning she would take her car into Exeter and get one. It was morning already, she reminded herself, and got up and dressed and did the best she could to disguise her sleepless night.

Sir Paul bade her good morning in his usual manner, remarked on the fine day and studied her tired face. She looked excited too, in a secret kind of way, as though she were hatching some plot or other. He decided to come home early but told her smoothly when she asked if he would be home for tea that he thought it unlikely, watching the relief on her face.

It was easy to get Mrs Parfitt to take a day off; Emma

knew that she wanted to go to Exeter and buy a new hat. 'Take the whole day,' she suggested. 'I might go over to Mrs Postle-Hammett's—it's a good walk for the dogs and she's very fond of them. I'm sure Sir Paul will give you a lift tomorrow morning.'

'Well, if you don't mind, ma'am. I must say I'd like a day to shop around.'

'I'm going to Exeter this morning,' said Emma. 'One or two things I want. Do we need anything for the house while I'm there?'

There was nothing needed. She went to her room and got into her jacket, found her car keys and drove herself to Exeter. She soon found exactly what she wanted in a funny little shop at the bottom of the high street, walked back to the car park in Queen Street and on the way came face to face with Maisie.

'Come and have a cup of coffee?' said Emma. She was glad to see her and steered her into a café. 'Aren't you at the nursery any more?'

'Leaving on Saturday,' said Maisie and looked coy. 'Getting married, yer see.'

'On Saturday? Oh, Maisie, I am glad; I hope you'll both be very happy. In church?'

'Baptist. Just the kids and 'is mum and dad.' Maisie sugared her coffee lavishly. 'Saw yer old man at the nursery—leastways, 'eard 'im. In a bit of a rage, it sounded like, and that Diana going 'ammer and tongs. Sounded all tearful she did—kept saying, "Oh, Paul, oh, Paul." Didn't come to work today neither. Nasty piece of work she is; turns on the charm like I switches on the electric.'

'She's very attractive,' said Emma, and felt sick. So, he

was still seeing Diana; it was a good thing she had decided to go...

'Suppose so,' said Maisie. 'Leastways, to men. Good thing you're married to yer old man!'

She chuckled and Emma managed a laugh. 'Yes, isn't it? Tell me what you're going to wear...'

Which filled the next ten minutes very nicely before Maisie declared that she still had some shopping to do.

'We'll 'ave some photos,' she promised. 'I'll send you one.'

'Please do, Maisie, and it was lovely meeting you like that.'

They said goodbye and Emma went back to the car and drove home. The small hopeful doubt she had had about leaving had been doused by Maisie's news. Tomorrow she would go.

She was surprised when Paul came home at teatime, but she greeted him in what she hoped was a normal voice, and, when he asked her, told him that she had been to Exeter— 'One or two things I wanted'—and had met Maisie. Maisie's approaching wedding made a good topic of conversation; Emma wore it threadbare and Paul, listening to her repeating herself, decided that whatever it was she was planning it wouldn't be that evening.

He went to his study presently and spent some time on the phone rearranging the next day's work. When his receptionist complained that he had several patients to see on the following afternoon he told her ruthlessly to change their appointments. 'I must have the whole of tomorrow afternoon and evening free,' he told her, and then spent ten minutes charming Theatre Sister into altering his list.

'I'll start at eight o'clock instead of nine,' he told her, and, since she liked him and admired him, she agreed, aware that it would mean a good deal of rearranging for her to do.

As for his registrar, who admired him too, he agreed cheerfully to take over out-patients once the ward-round was done.

Sir Paul ate his supper, well aware that he had done all he could to avert whatever disaster his Emma was plotting.

The cottage seemed very empty once Paul and Mrs Parfitt had gone the next morning. It was still early; she had all day before her. Emma took the dogs for a long walk, went from room to room tidying up, clearing the breakfast things Mrs Parfitt hadn't had the time to do, and then she sat down to write her letters.

This took her a long time, for it was difficult to write exactly what she wanted to say to Paul. She finished at last, wrote a letter to Mrs Parfitt about the sick aunt and went to pack her knapsack. Only the necessities went into it—her lavish wardrobe she left. She left her lovely sapphire and diamond ring too, putting it in its little velvet box on the tallboy in his dressing-room.

She wasn't hungry but she forced herself to eat some lunch, for she wasn't sure where she would get her supper. She had some money too—not very much but enough to keep her for a week, and as soon as she had a job she would pay it back; she had been careful to put that in her letter.

It was going on for three o'clock by then. She got her jacket, changed into sensible shoes, took the dogs for a quick run and then carefully locked up the house. It only remained for her to take her letter and leave it in Paul's study.

She left the knapsack in the hall with Mrs Parfitt's letter and went to the study. The letter in her hand, she sat for a moment in his chair, imagining him sitting in it presently, reading her letter, and two tears trickled down her cheeks. She wiped them away, got out of the chair and went round the desk and leaned over to prop the letter against the ink-stand.

Sir Paul's hand took it gently from her just as she set it down, and for a moment she didn't move. The sight of the sober grey sleeve, immaculate linen and gold cufflinks, and his large, well-kept hand appearing from nowhere, had taken her breath, but after a moment she turned round to face him. 'Give it to me, please, Paul.' Her voice was a whisper.

'But it is addressed to me, Emma.'

'Yes, yes, I know it is. But you weren't to read it until after...'

'You had gone?' he added gently. 'But I am here, Emma, and I am going to read it.'

The door wasn't very far; she took a step towards it but he put out an arm and swept her close. 'Stay here where you belong,' he said gently and, with one arm holding her tight, he opened the letter.

He read it and then read it again, and Emma tried to wriggle free.

'Well, now you know,' she said in a watery voice. 'What are you going to do about it? I didn't mean to fall in love with you—it—it was an accident; I didn't know it would be so—so... What are you going to do, Paul?'

His other arm was round her now. 'Do? Something I wanted to do when I first saw you.' He bent and kissed her, taking his time about it.

Emma said shakily, 'You mustn't—we mustn't—what about Diana?'

'I can see that we shall have to have a cosy little talk, my darling, but not yet.' He kissed her again. 'I've always loved you. You didn't know that, did you? I didn't tell you, for I hurried you into marriage and you weren't ready for me, were you? So I waited, like a fool, and somehow I didn't know what to do.'

'It was me,' said Emma fiercely into his shoulder. 'I listened to Diana and I don't know why I did. I suppose it was because I love you and I want you to be happy, and I thought it was her and not me.' She gave a great sniff. 'She's so beautiful and clever and the babies were darlings and she told me to go to the travellers' camp...'

Sir Paul, used to the occasional incoherence of his patients, sorted this out. 'Darling heart, you are beautiful and honest and brave, and the only woman I have ever loved or could love.' He gave a rumble of laughter. 'And you shall have a darling baby of your own...'

'Oh, I shall love that—we'll share him. Supposing he's a girl?'

'In that case we must hope that we will be given a second chance.'

His arms tightened round her and she looked up at him, smiling. 'We'll start all over again—being married, I mean.'

He kissed her once more. 'That idea had occurred to me too.'

* * * * *

When Two Paths Meet

Chapter 1

Katherine rolled over in bed and pulled the blankets over her ears; it wasn't time to get up, she was sure of that, and she resented whatever it was that had awakened her. She tucked her cold feet into her nightie and closed her eyes, only to open them immediately at the steady thumping on the front door below her window. The milkman? Unreasonably early. A tramp? A would-be thief? But he wouldn't want to draw attention to himself.

She got out of bed, thrust her feet into slippers and dragged on her dressing-gown. By the light of her bedside lamp the alarm clock showed well past five in the morning. The thump came again, and she went softly along the landing and down the stairs; her brother and his wife, who slept at the back of the house, and very soundly too, wouldn't have heard it—nor, with luck, would the two children in the room next to her own.

It took a few moments to open the door, and she left it prudently on the chain, to peer through the narrow opening at the man on the doorstep. It was the tail end of October, and only just beginning to get light, but she could make out what appeared to be a giant.

He spoke from somewhere above her head. 'Good girl. Let me in quickly.'

He had a deep, unhurried voice which reassured her, nevertheless she asked, 'Why?'

'I have a new-born baby here, likely to die of exposure unless it gets warmed up pretty quickly.'

She undid the chain without wasting words, and he went past her. 'Where's the kitchen, or somewhere warm?'

'The end door.' She waved a hand, and applied herself to locking and bolting the door once more. All at once, she reflected that she could have bolted herself in with an escaped convict, a thief, even a murderer. And it was too late to do anything about it; she hurried him along and opened the kitchen door on to the lingering warmth of the old-fashioned Rayburn. He brushed past her, laid the bundle he was carrying on the kitchen table and unfolded it carefully and, from the depths of his car coat, exposed a very small, very quiet baby. Katherine took one look and went to poke up the fire, quietly, so as not to arouse the household.

When the man said, 'Blankets? Something warm?' she went like a small shadow back upstairs to her room and took the sheet and a blanket off her bed. The linen cupboard was on the landing outside her brother's room, and he or Joyce might hear the door squeaking.

She handed them to the man, who took them without looking at her, only muttering, 'Sensible girl,' and then, 'Warm water?'

There was always a large kettle keeping warm on the Rayburn; she filled a small basin and put it on the table.

'Now, just stay here for a moment, will you? I'll go to the car and get my bag.'

'I've locked the door, and my brother might hear if you go through the back door, it creaks. I'll have to go and unlock...'

He was looking around him; the house was old-fashioned, and the kitchen windows were large and sashed. He crossed the room and silently slid one open, climbed through soundlessly and disappeared, to reappear just as silently very shortly after. He was a very large man indeed, which made his performance all the more impressive. Katherine, who had picked up the blanketed baby and was holding it close, stared at him over the woolly folds.

'You are indeed a sensible girl,' observed the man, and put his bag down on the table. 'This little fellow needs a bit of tidying up...'

It was a relief to Katherine to see a little colour stealing through the scrap on the table. She handed the things he asked for from his bag and whispered, 'Will he be all right?'

'I think so, babies are extremely tough; it rather depends on how long he's been lying on the side of the road.'

'How could anyone...?' She stared across the table at him, seeing him properly for the first time. He was a handsome man, with fair hair and sleepy blue eyes under straight brows, and above a wide, firm mouth his nose was pure aquiline. Katherine was aware of a strange sensation somewhere under her ribs, a kind of delightful breathlessness, a splendid warmth and a tingling. She stayed quite still, a small, rather thin girl, with an ordinary face which was redeemed from plainness by a pair of beautiful grey eyes, heavily fringed with black lashes. Her hair, alas, was a pale, soft brown, straight and long. Wrapped as she was in the useful, dark red dressing-gown Joyce, her sister-in-law, had given her the previous Christmas, she presented a picture of complete mediocrity. Which made it entirely unsuitable that she should have fallen in love with a man who was looking at her kindly enough, but with no hint of interest in her person.

She said in her quiet voice, 'Would you like a cup of tea? And where will you take the baby?'

'To hospital, as quickly as possible...' He paused, looking over her shoulder, and she turned round. Joyce was in the doorway.

She was a handsome young woman, but now her good looks were spoilt by the look of amazed rage on her face.

'Katherine—what on earth is the meaning of this? And who is this man? Have you taken leave of your senses?'

'If I might explain?' The man's voice was quiet, but something in it made Joyce silent. 'I found a new-born child on the roadside—this house was only a few yards away, I knocked for help. This young lady has most kindly and efficiently provided it. May I trespass on your kindness still further, and ask her to come with me to the hospital so that she may hold the baby?'

Joyce had had time to study him, and her manner changed rapidly. She tossed a long curl over her shoulder, and pulled her quilted dressing-gown rather more tightly around her splendid figure. If Katherine had looked ordinary before, she was now completely overshadowed. Joyce ignored her.

'You're a doctor? I must say all this is very unusual. I'll make you a hot drink. You must be so tired.' She smiled charmingly at him and said sharply to Katherine, 'You heard what the doctor said, Katherine. Don't just stand there, go and get dressed.'

And, when she had slipped away without looking at anyone, 'My husband's young sister—she lives with us.' She gave a tinkling little laugh. 'Not ideal, of course, but one has certain responsibilities. Now, what about that drink? I don't know your name...'

'I'll not stop for anything, thank you, Mrs...'

'Marsh—Joyce Marsh.'

He was bending over the baby again. 'I'll see that your sister-in-law gets back safely.' He straightened himself to his full height. 'Please make my apologies to your husband. Ah, here is Miss Marsh.'

Katherine, very neat in slacks and a short jacket, her hair screwed into a bun, came into the room. Without a word, she held out her arms for the baby, waited while the doctor picked up his coat and bag and bade a courteous goodbye to Joyce, and then followed him down the passage, with Joyce trailing behind. She made rather a thing of unbolting the door.

'I'm not very strong,' she murmured. 'So sorry, and having to get out of my bed at such an unearthly hour.' She gave her little tinkling laugh again.

'Wait here,' the doctor bade Katherine. 'I'll get the car.' He went down the short path to the gate.

It was very quiet and his hearing was excellent, so he couldn't fail to hear Joyce's sharp, 'Just you get back here without wasting any time. I'm not seeing to the children; they'll have to stay in bed until you're here to get them up.'

The morning light was strengthening; the car outside the gate looked large. The doctor got out and took the baby from Katherine, bade Joyce a coldly courteous goodbye, and opened the car door. Katherine got in, took the baby on to her lap, and sat without speaking while he got in beside her. She was a little surprised when he picked up the phone and had a brief conversation with someone—the hospital, she supposed. She had heard of phones in cars, but she had never seen one, only on television.

He drove in silence, a little too fast for her liking, along the narrow road which brought them to the main road in Salisbury. The early morning heavy traffic was building up, but he drove steadily and fast, circumventing the city until he reached the roundabout on its outskirts and took the road to the hospital.

They were expected. He drew up smoothly before the accident centre entrance, opened Katherine's door and urged her through into the hospital. The baby was taken from her at once by a tired-looking night sister, and carried away with the doctor, a young houseman in a white coat, and another nurse behind them. Katherine watched them go and, since there was no one to ask where she should go, she sat herself down on one of the benches ranged around the walls. She would have liked a cup of tea, breakfast would have been even better, but she was a sensible girl, there were other more pressing matters to see to. She suspected that she had already been forgotten.

But she hadn't; within ten minutes or so she was approached by a young nurse. 'Dr Fitzroy says you're to have breakfast. I'll take you along to the canteen and you are to wait there when you have had it—he'll join you later.'

'I have to get back home…' began Katherine, her thoughts wincing away from Joyce's wrath if she didn't.

'Dr Fitzroy says he'll take you back, and you are please to do as he asks.'

The nurse so obviously expected her to do so, that Katherine got to her feet, mentally consigning Joyce and the children to a later hour, when she could worry about them at her leisure. For the moment, she was hungry.

The canteen was empty; it was too soon for the night staff going off duty, too early for the day staff, even now getting out of their beds. The nurse sat Katherine down at one of the plastic-covered tables and went over to the counter. She came back with a loaded tray: cornflakes, eggs and bacon, toast, butter and marmalade, and a pot of tea.

'I haven't any money with me,' Katherine pointed out anxiously.

'Dr Fitzroy said you were to have a good breakfast. I don't think he meant you to pay for it.' The nurse smiled and said goodbye and disappeared.

Katherine's small nose sniffed at the fragrant aroma rising from the tray. To have breakfast served to her, and such a breakfast, was a treat not to be missed. And she applied herself to the cornflakes without further ado.

She ate everything, and was emptying the teapot when Dr Fitzroy joined her.

She smiled up at him. 'Thank you for my breakfast,' she said in her quiet, sensible way. 'Is there no way I can get back without you bothering to take me?'

At the sight of him, her heart had started thumping against her ribs, but she looked much as usual—rather a nonentity of a girl, badly dressed and too thin. Dr Fitzroy sat down opposite her; a kind man, he felt sorry for her, although he wasn't sure why. He hadn't been taken in by her sister-in-law's gushing manner. Probably the girl had a dull life, as well as having to live with a woman who obviously didn't like her overmuch.

He said kindly, 'If you're ready, I'll drive you back and

make my excuses to your sister-in-law. They will be wondering where you are.'

Katherine got to her feet at once; the pleasant little adventure was over and she would be made to pay for it, she had no doubt of that. But it would be worth it. Joyce's spite and her brother's indifference wouldn't be able to spoil it. It was ridiculous to fall in love as she had done; she had had no idea that she could feel so deeply about anyone. It would be a dream she would have to keep to herself for the rest of her life; it hadn't the remotest chance of ever being more than that. She buttoned her jacket and went with him through the hospital and out to the forecourt where the car was standing.

'Is the baby all right?' she asked as he drove away.

'Yes, although it's rather early days to know for certain that he's taken no harm. A nice little chap.'

She shivered. 'If you hadn't seen him and stopped...'

'We must try and find the mother.' He glanced sideways at her. 'I hope I haven't disrupted your morning too much.'

She said, 'Oh, no,' much too quickly, so that he looked at her for a second time, but her face was quite calm.

All the same, when they reached the house he said, 'I'll come in with you.'

She had her hand on the car door. 'Oh, really, there's no need, you must be busy...'

He took no notice, but got out of the car and went round to her door. He opened it for her and they walked up the path to the side door. 'We don't use the front door much,' she explained matter-of-factly. 'It makes a lot of extra work.'

She opened the side door on to a flagstoned passage, and prayed silently that he would go before Joyce discovered that she was back home. Prayers aren't always answered—

Joyce's voice, strident with ill temper, came from an open door at the end of the passage.

'So you're back, and high time, too! You can go straight upstairs and see to the children, and if you think you're going to have your breakfast first, you are very much mistaken.' The door flung wide open and Joyce appeared. 'You little...' She stopped short. The change in her manner was ludicrous as she caught sight of the doctor behind Katherine.

'There you are, dear.' She smiled widely as she spoke, 'Do run upstairs and see if the children are ready, will you? I've been so busy.'

Katherine didn't say anything to this, but held out her hand to the doctor. It was engulfed in a firm grasp which was very comforting, and just for a moment she wanted to weep because she wouldn't see him again, only be left with a delightful dream.

'Thank you for bringing me back, and for my breakfast, Dr Fitzroy. I hope the little baby will find someone to love him.'

He looked down at her gravely. 'It is I who thank you, Miss Marsh. Your help undoubtedly helped to save his life. Be sure we shall try and find his mother, and if not, get him adopted.'

She looked up into his face, learning it by heart, for the memory of it was all she would have of him. 'Goodbye,' she said, as she went away, past Joyce, into the hall and up the stairs to where Robin and Sarah could be heard wailing and shouting.

They were unlovable children, largely because their mother had no patience with them, and their father, a schoolmaster, had no time for them. They had been thrust into Katherine's care when she had gone to live with her brother two years ago, after her mother died, with the frequently expressed opinion on his part that, since he was giving her a home, she might as well keep herself occupied by looking after the children. It was something she had been unable to dispute, for she had left school to nurse her mother, and when she died she had been glad to go to her brother's home. She had been nineteen then, with vague ideas about training for a job and being independent, but now, two years later, without money and with very little time to herself, she was no nearer that. She had made several efforts to leave his house, but somehow she never managed it. The children fell ill with measles, or Joyce took to her bed, declaring that she was too ill to be left. On her last attempt, her brother had reminded her in his cold way that she owed everything to him, and the least she could do was to remain with the children until they were old enough to go to school. Almost two years still to go, she reflected, opening the nursery door on to a scene of chaos. The pair of them had got out of their beds, and were running round, flinging anything they could lay their hands on at each other.

Katherine suppressed a sigh. 'Hello, dears. Who's going to get dressed? And what would you like for breakfast?'

They had wet their beds, so she stripped the bedclothes off, caught the children in turn and took off their sopping nightclothes, then bathed and dressed them. Shutting the door on the muddle she would have to sort out presently, she took them down to the kitchen.

Joyce was in the hall, pulling on her gloves. 'I'm going to the hairdressers. If I'm not back, get lunch, will you? Oh, and take them out for a walk.'

The day was like all her other days: Robin and Sarah to feed and care for, unending ironing and the washing machine in everlasting use, beds to make, the nursery to keep tidy. She went steadily ahead with her chores; she was a girl with plenty of common sense, and months earlier she had realised that self-pity got her nowhere. She was fed and clothed, albeit as cheaply as possible, and she had a roof over her head. Unemployment, her brother had reminded her on a number of occasions, was high; she had no chance of getting a job, not even an unskilled one. When she had protested that she could train as a typist, or get a job in some domestic capacity, he had told her that the chance of a job for a newly qualified typist would be slender, and the training a complete waste of money. And, as for domestic work, what was she thinking of? No sister of his was going to be anyone's servant!

'But I would at least get paid,' she had told him with quiet persistence, in consequence of which he hadn't spoken to her for several days.

Apart from her lack of money, and the heavy-handed persuasion of her brother, Katherine couldn't bring herself to leave because of the children. They had no affection for her, nor she for them, but she was sorry for them. Other than herself, no one bothered much about them. Joyce was out a great deal, sitting on a variety of committees in the cause of charity, leaving the running of the house to Katherine and the spasmodic assistance of Mrs Todd from the farm cottages down the road, who came each day to dust and vacuum and, occasionally, when she felt like it, to polish the furniture or wash the flagstone floors in the hall and kitchen. She was a bad-tempered woman, and she disliked the children, so Katherine did her best to keep them out of her way.

In the afternoon, Mrs Todd had signified her intention

of washing the kitchen floor, provided those dratted children were out of the way, so Katherine prudently dressed them warmly and took them for a walk. Sarah was still too small to walk far; it meant taking the pushchair and, since Robin declared that he was tired, she pushed them both back from the village, thankful to find when they got in that Mrs Todd had gone, leaving a tolerably clean kitchen and a terse note, reminding Joyce that she was owed two weeks' wages. Katherine left the note where it was, got the children's tea and, since there was no sign of Joyce, began to make preparations for the evening meal. Joyce came back just as she was finished with cleaning the vegetables, slammed a parcel down on the kitchen table, said, 'Sausages,' and turned to go out of the kitchen again.

'There's a note from Mrs Todd,' Katherine pointed out, 'and it's either sausages or children—which do you want to do?'

Joyce cast her a look of dislike. 'I have never met such an ungrateful, lazy girl—' she began and caught Katherine's mildly surprised eyes. 'Oh, I'll cook the supper, I suppose, since there's no one else. Really, too much is expected of me! Here am I, busy all day with Oxfam and Save the Children and that jumble sale for the primary school, and you've been at home, doing nothing...'

Katherine let that pass; she had heard the same thing on any number of occasions. She collected the children and bore them off to their baths. While she got them ready for their beds, she thought about Dr Fitzroy. He would be married, of course, to a pretty wife, and there would be children, well-behaved, loving children, and they would live in one of those nice old houses close to the cathedral in Salisbury. Pure envy shot through her at the thought, and was instantly stifled.

Robin, being dried, kicked her shins and ran out of the bathroom. Unfortunately, he ran straight into his father's path as he was on his way to his room to freshen up for the evening. The boy was led howling back to the bathroom.

'Really, Katherine, you must control the children! This is surely proof that you are quite unsuitable for any kind of responsible job. I can only hope that you will learn something from us while you are living here.'

She was wrestling a nightie over Sarah's head and didn't look up. 'Don't be pompous,' she begged him, 'and don't talk nonsense. And I've learnt a good deal while I've been living here, you know. How to manage without help from either you or Joyce, how to live without so much as a ten-penny piece to call my own...' She spoke quietly because she was a quiet girl, but inside she was boiling with frustration. She added kindly, 'Don't gobble like that, Henry. It's no good getting in a rage. I do my best, but I'm beginning to wonder why.'

She went past him with a squirming Sarah in her arms, intending to tuck her up in her cot and to go back for Robin, who was bawling his head off.

Supper was by no means a pleasant meal: Joyce, sulking because Henry had been sarcastic about burnt sausages and not quite cooked potatoes, had little to say, while he delivered a few well-chosen words about his day's work, the pursuit of which had left him, he said, drained of energy. From this, he hinted strongly that the effort to keep his household in comfort was almost too much for him.

Here, Joyce interrupted him in a cross voice. Did he forget, she wanted to know, how hard *she* worked, getting to know the right people for his benefit? Did he realise how her day was entirely taken up with meeting boring women on committees?

Katherine, sitting between them, ate her sausages because she was hungry, and said nothing at all. Indeed, she wasn't really listening, she was thinking about Dr Fitzroy, a small luxury she hugged to herself. She had embarked on a pleasant daydream where she fell and sprained an ankle and was taken to hospital, there to find him waiting to treat it while he expressed delight and pleasure at meeting her again…

'Katherine, I wish that you would attend when I speak to you.' Henry's voice snapped the dream in two, and she blinked at him, reluctant to return to her present surroundings.

'I feel that it's time for Robin to start simple lessons. There is no reason why you shouldn't spend an hour with him each morning, teaching him his letters and simple figures.'

'What a good idea,' she agreed cheerfully. 'He's quite out of hand, you know, because he hasn't enough to occupy his brain. What will Sarah do while I'm busy with Robin?'

'Why, she can stay in the room with you.'

'Out of the question.' She was still cheerful. 'He wouldn't listen to a word. Perhaps Joyce could spare an hour?'

Her sister-in-law pushed back her chair. 'Whatever next? Where am I to find an hour, even half an hour? You can argue it out between you.'

'The thing to do,' observed Katherine mildly, 'would be to take him with you when you go to work, and drop him off at that playschool in Wilton. He needs other children, you know. Perhaps Joyce could take her car and collect him at lunch time?' She felt Henry's fulminating eye upon her, and added calmly, 'I'm sure several children from the village go there. I dare say they would give Robin a lift?'

She took no notice of his shocked silence, but began to clear the table. Mrs Todd strongly objected to washing the supper dishes when she arrived in the morning.

The subject of Robin's education didn't crop up again for several days. Indeed, Henry showed his displeasure at Katherine's lack of co-operation by saying as few words to her as possible, something she didn't mind in the least. As for Joyce, they met at meals, but very seldom otherwise. Katherine, her days full of unending chores, had no time to worry about that. In bed, in the peace and quiet of her room, she strengthened her resolve to find a job of some sort. Lack of money was the stumbling point, and she hadn't found a way round that yet, but she would. She promised herself that each night, before allowing her thoughts to dwell on Dr Fitzroy. It was a pity that she was too tired to indulge in this for more than a minute or two.

She was in the kitchen, washing up the supper dishes, more than a week since she had answered the knock on the door which had so changed her feelings, when Henry's voice, loud and demanding, caused her to put down the dishmop and hurry along the passage to the drawing-room. One of the children, she supposed, not bothering to take off her apron; they had been almost unmanageable all day, and were probably wrecking the nursery instead of going to sleep. She opened the door and put her untidy head round it.

'I'm washing up,' she began. 'If it's the children...'

Dr Fitzroy was standing in the middle of the room, while Henry stood with his back to the fireplace, looking uneasy, and Joyce sat at a becoming angle in her chair, showing a good deal of leg.

'Dr Fitzroy wishes to speak to you, Katherine.' Henry was at his most ponderous.

'Hello,' said the doctor, and smiled at her.

Her face lit up with delight. 'Oh, hello,' said Katherine. 'How very nice to see you again!'

She had come into the room, and stood unselfconsciously in front of him. That she was a deplorable sight hadn't entered her head; it was stuffed with bliss at the mere sight of him.

'What about the baby? Is he all right?'

'Splendid. Perhaps we might go somewhere and talk?' He looked at Henry, who went puce with temper.

'Anything you have to say to Katherine can surely be listened to by myself and my wife? I am her brother,' he blustered.

'Yes, I know.' The doctor's voice was silky. He didn't say any more, so Henry was forced to speak.

'There is the dining-room, although I can't imagine what you can have to say to Katherine...'

'No, I don't suppose you can.' Dr Fitzroy's voice was as pleasant as his smile. He held the door open, and Katherine went past him to the dining-room. It was chilly there; she switched on the light and turned to look at him.

Just for a moment he had a pang of doubt. What had made him think that this shabby, small young woman would be just right for the job he had in mind? But, even if he had had second thoughts, the eager face she had turned to him doused them at once. She had shown admirable common sense about the baby; she hadn't bothered him with a lot of questions, nor had she complained once. And, from what he had just seen, life at home was something she wasn't likely to miss.

'Do sit down. I'm sorry it's chilly in here.'

She sat composedly, her hands quiet in her lap, and waited for him to speak.

'I have a job to offer you,' he began without preamble. 'Of course, you may not want one, but I believe that you are exactly right for the kind of work I have in mind.' He paused and studied her face; it had become animated and a little pink, but she didn't speak. 'I have been attending two elderly patients for some years, and they have reached the age when they need someone to look after them. They have help in the house, so there would be no housework...' His eyes dwelt for a moment on her apron. 'They refuse to have a nurse—in fact, they don't really need one. What they do need is someone to fetch and carry, find their spectacles, encourage them to eat their meals, accompany them in the car when they wish to go out, and see them safely to their beds, and, if necessary, go to them during the night. In short, an unobtrusive companion, ready to fall in with their wishes and keep an eye on them. I've painted rather a drab picture, but it has its bright side—the house is pleasant and there is a delightful garden. You will have time for yourself each day and be independent. The salary is forty pounds a week...'

'Forty pounds? A week? I've never had...' She stopped just in time from telling him that she seldom had more than forty pence in her pocket. He wouldn't believe her if she did. She finished rather lamely, 'A job, I'm not trained for anything, Henry says...'

'Perhaps you will allow me to be the judge of that?' he suggested kindly. 'Will it be difficult for you to leave home?'

She thought for a moment. 'Yes, but I'm twenty-one.

Would you mind very much if I told them now, while you are here?'

'Certainly I will stay. Perhaps if there is any difficulty, I may be able to persuade your brother. When could you come with me to see Mr and Mrs Grainger?'

She resisted the wish to shout 'Now!' and said in her matter-of-fact way, 'Whenever you wish, Dr Fitzroy.'

'I'll come for you tomorrow morning, and if you and they like each other, perhaps you could start on the following day?'

Katherine closed her eyes for a moment. There would be angry words and bad temper and endless arguments, but they couldn't last for ever. 'I'd like that.'

She got up, went to the door and found him there, pushing it open for her, something Henry had never done for her; good manners weren't to be wasted on a sister that he didn't particularly like. He was still standing before the fireplace and, from the way that he and Joyce looked at her as she went in, she knew that they had been talking about her. She crossed the room and stood in front of her brother.

'Dr Fitzroy has offered me a job, which I have accepted,' she told him in a voice which she was glad to hear sounded firm.

Henry gobbled, 'A job? What kind of job, pray? And what about the children?'

She said calmly, 'I should think you could get a mother's help—after all, most people do—or Joyce could give up some of her committees.' She sighed because Henry was working himself into a rage, and Joyce, once the doctor had gone, would be even worse.

Dr Fitzroy spoke now in a slow, placid manner which disregarded Henry's red face. 'Your sister is exactly right for an excellent post with two of my elderly patients. I have been searching for someone for some time, and her good sense when I asked for her help the other morning convinced me that she is exactly what Mr and Mrs Grainger need. I shall call for her in the morning so that she may have an interview, and I hope she will be able to go to them on the following day.'

Joyce said shrilly, 'Who are these people? We know nothing about them! Katherine has never been away from home before; she'll miss home life...' She caught the doctor's sardonic eye and paused. 'She can go now, as far as I'm concerned,' she said sulkily.

He ignored her. 'I'll be here at nine o'clock, if that suits you?' He had spoken to Katherine, and then turned to Henry. 'You may have my word that your sister will be happy as companion to the Graingers. There will be no housework, of course, and she will be paid a salary.' He added a very civil goodnight, and Katherine, walking on air, took him to the door.

Before she shut it, he asked, 'You'll be all right?'

She nodded; there would be a good deal of unpleasantness before she could go to her room and start packing and looking out something suitable to wear in the morning, but she felt capable of outfacing the forthcoming recriminations with the promise of such a splendid future before her. And she would see Dr Fitzroy, too, sometimes. She hugged the thought to herself as she went back to the drawing-room.

Chapter 2

It was a good thing that Katherine felt so euphoric about her future, for the next hour tried her sorely. Henry, having recovered from his first surprise, had marshalled a number of forceful arguments, hampered rather than helped by Joyce's ill-natured complaints.

Katherine listened patiently and, when he had quite done, said kindly, 'Well, Henry, I would have thought that you would have been pleased. You don't need to be responsible for me any more, do you?'

Henry was an alarming puce once more. 'Your ingratitude cuts me to the quick,' he told her. 'After all this time, giving you a home and food and clothes...'

She smiled at him and said sensibly, 'And look what you got for that—unpaid housework, someone to look after the children and, because I'm your sister, there was no need to give me an allowance.' She added, 'It will be nice to have some money.' Emboldened by the prospect of a glowing future, she walked to the door, just as Henry got his breath for another speech. 'I'm rather tired,' she said matter-of-factly. 'I think I'll go to bed. I haven't finished the washing up, but there are only the saucepans left to do. Goodnight, Joyce—Henry.'

In her room, she sat down on her bed and cried. She had tried hard to please Henry and Joyce, she had accepted the care of the children and she had done her best to love them, but it was a singularly unloving household. She had never been happy in it and she was glad to leave it. All the same, it would have been nice if Henry and Joyce had uttered just one word of encouragement or thanks.

She got up presently, and crossed the landing to the children's room. They needed tucking up once more, and she did this with her usual care, before going to the boxroom and fetching her two cases. Packing wouldn't take long: her wardrobe was small, and most of it wasn't worth packing. She had a tweed suit, elderly but well cut and good material; she would have to wear that until she had enough money to buy some decent clothes. She hoped that Mr and Mrs Grainger weren't the kind of people to dress for dinner; it seemed unlikely, but she had a plain wool dress, very out-of-date, like the suit, but it had at one time been good, and would pass muster at a pinch.

She felt better now she had started her packing. She got ready for bed, hopped between the chilly sheets, closed her eyes and, very much to her surprise, went to sleep at once.

It was a scramble in the morning. Katherine got up earlier than usual, got into the suit and the sensible, low-heeled shoes which were suitable for everyday wear and country walks with the children. Then she did her face carefully with the sketchy make-up she possessed, tied her hair back with a narrow ribbon and went along to the nursery. For once, good fortune was on her side; the children were quite willing to be washed and dressed and given their breakfast. She took them downstairs and made tea for herself, laid the table for the children and for Henry, who wouldn't be down for half an hour or so, and gave them their breakfast. She was too excited to eat, and she hadn't considered what meals they would have later on. She wasn't even sure when she would be back; what was more, she didn't much care!

She cleared the table, took the children to the playroom and made more tea for Henry, who, on his way downstairs, put his head round the door to wish the children good morning but ignored her. She heard him leave the house presently and Mrs Todd crashing plates and saucepans in the kitchen. She would have to get Joyce out of bed before she went. Dr Fitzroy had said nine o'clock, and it was ten minutes to the hour.

Joyce didn't answer as she went into the bedroom. Katherine drew back the curtains. 'I'm going now,' she said. 'The children have had their breakfast and are in the playroom. I don't know when I'll be back.'

Joyce lifted her head. 'I feel ill,' she said pettishly. 'You simply can't go—you'll have to put this interview off until I'm better.'

Katherine took a look at her sister-in-law. 'I'll tell Mrs Todd. I dare say she'll keep an eye on Sarah and Robin. Henry can always come back here—you could phone him.'

Joyce sat right up. 'I hope these people hate you on sight and you lose the job. It would serve you right! And don't expect to come crawling back here. Job or no job, out you go tomorrow.'

Katherine turned to go, and the children, bored with their own company, came hurtling past her and flung themselves onto their mother's bed.

Katherine closed the door quietly behind her. She didn't like her sister-in-law, but a pang of sympathy shot through her; the children were small tyrants, and Joyce had little patience with them. She would demand a mother's help and Henry would have to agree. Whoever it was would want a salary and days off and weekends and holidays... Katherine had another pang of sympathy for Henry, who hated to spend his money.

Dr Fitzroy was waiting for her when she opened the door and looked out, and she hurried to the car.

'Good morning.' She was a bit breathless with an upsurge of feeling at the sight of him. 'I hope you haven't been waiting.'

'Just got here. Jump in.' He held the door for her, and she settled in the seat beside him. 'Nervous?' he asked. 'You needn't be.'

He gave her a reassuring smile, and thought what a dim little thing she was in her out-of-date suit and sturdy shoes. But sensible and quiet, just what the Graingers needed, and they would hardly notice what she was wearing, only that her voice was pleasant and she was calm in a crisis. He started the car. 'I'll tell you something about Mr and Mrs Grainger. In their seventies, almost eighty, in fact. He has a heart condition and is far too active, can be peppery if he can't have his own way. Mrs Grainger is small and meek and perfectly content to allow him to dictate to her. She has arthritis and suffers a good deal of pain, but never complains. They are devoted to each other. They lost their only son in an accident some years ago, but they have a granddaughter...'

Something in his voice caught Katherine's attention; this granddaughter was someone special to him. She had known from the moment she knew that she had fallen in love with

him that he would never look at her—all the same, it was a
blow. So silly, she told herself silently, he could have been
married already, with a houseful of children. At the back
of her head, a small, defiant voice pointed out that he might
have been heart-whole and single and miraculously bowled
over by her very ordinary person. She became aware that
he had asked her something and she hadn't been heeding.

'So sorry,' she said quickly. 'You asked me something?'

They were at the roundabout on the outskirts of Wilton,
waiting to find a place in the traffic streaming towards Salisbury. He slipped smoothly between two other cars before he
answered. 'You do understand that there will be no regular
hours? You will, of course, have time to yourself each day,
but that time may vary. It would be difficult to arrange to
meet your friends or make dates.'

She said quietly, in a bleak little voice, 'I haven't any
friends, and no one to make a date with.' She added quickly,
in case he thought she was wallowing in self-pity, 'I had
lots of friends when my mother was alive, but there wasn't
much time to spare at my brother's house. I—I like to be
busy, and I shan't mind at all if Mr and Mrs Grainger make
their own arrangements about my free time.'

'That's settled then.' He sounded kind but faintly uninter-
ested. 'But I expect you will want to go shopping.' He was
annoyed that he had said that, for she went pink and turned
to look out of her window, very conscious of her dull appearance. All the same, she agreed cheerfully; in a week or
two she would indeed go shopping. Clothes made the man,
it was said—well, they would make her, too!

She liked Salisbury; the cathedral dominated the city, and
its close was a delightful oasis in the city centre. When the
doctor drove down High Street and through the great gate,

circled the small car park and drew up before one of the charming old houses abutting the close, she declared, 'Oh, is it here? I've always wanted… I came here with Mother…'

'Charming, isn't it? And yes, this is the house.' He got out and went round to open her door. They crossed the pavement together, and he rang the bell beside the pedimented doorway. The door was opened almost at once by a middle-aged woman with a stern face, dressed soberly in black. She gave the doctor a wintry smile and stared at Katherine.

'Ah, Mrs Dowling, I have brought Miss Marsh to meet Mr and Mrs Grainger. They are expecting us.'

She wished him a reluctant good morning and nodded at Katherine, who smiled uncertainly. 'You'd better come up,' she observed dourly.

The house, despite its Georgian façade, was considerably older. A number of passages led off the small, square hall, and half a dozen steps at its end ended in a small gallery with two doors. The housekeeper opened one of them and ushered them inside. The room was large and long, at the back of the house, overlooking a surprisingly large garden.

Its two occupants turned to look at the doctor and Katherine as they went in, and the elderly gentleman said at once, 'Jason, my dear boy—so here you are with the little lady you have found for us.' He peered over his glasses at Katherine. 'Good morning, my dear. You don't find it too irksome to cherish us, I hope?'

'How do you do, Mr Grainger?' said Katherine politely. 'Not in the least, if you would like me to come.'

'Take a look at her, my dear,' begged the old gentleman, addressing himself to the equally elderly lady sitting opposite him.

She was small and frail-looking, but her eyes were bright

and her voice surprisingly strong. She studied Katherine and nodded. 'I believe that she will do very nicely, Albert. A little on the small side, perhaps?'

'I'm very strong,' declared Katherine on a faintly apprehensive note.

'And competent,' put in the doctor in his calm way. 'Besides not being wishful to dash off to the discos with a different young man each evening.'

He had pulled a chair forward, and nodded to her to sit down, and Mrs Grainger asked, 'Have you a young man, my dear?'

'No,' said Katherine, 'and I've never been inside a disco.'

The old couple nodded to each other. 'Most suitable. Will you come at once?'

Katherine looked at the doctor, who said placidly, 'I'll take her back to her brother's house now, and she can pack her things. I dare say, if you wish it, she could be ready to come back here this evening.'

'Oh, yes,' said Katherine, 'there's a bus I could catch...'

'I'll pick you up at six o'clock.' He barely glanced at her. 'Mrs Grainger, you do understand that Miss Marsh has to have an hour or so to herself each day, and at least a half-day off each week? We have already discussed the salary, and she finds it acceptable.' He got up. 'I'm going to have a word with Mrs Dowling, if I may, before I take Miss Marsh back.'

He was gone for ten minutes, during which time Katherine was plied with questions. She answered them readily enough, for she liked her employers.

She was sensible enough to realise that sitting here in this pleasant room wasn't indicative of her day's work; she would probably be on the run for a good part of each day and probably the night, too, but after the cheerless atmosphere of Henry's home this delightful house held warmth, something she had missed since her mother had died.

When Dr Fitzroy returned, she rose, shook hands, declared that she would return that evening, and accompanied the doctor out to his car.

He had little to say as they drove back, only expressed himself satisfied with the interview, warned her to be ready that evening and reminded her that he called to see Mr and Mrs Grainger two days a week, usually on Tuesdays and Fridays, at about eleven o'clock. 'So I should like you to be there when I call.' He shot her a quick glance. 'You will be happy there?'

'Yes, oh, yes!' she assured him. 'I can't believe it! I'm so afraid that I'll wake up and find that it's all been a dream.'

He laughed. 'It's true enough, and I do warn you that you may find the work irksome and sometimes tiring.' He stopped the car outside Henry's gate and got out. 'I'll come in with you and speak to your sister-in-law.'

Joyce was waiting for them in the drawing-room, beautifully turned out and, judging from the din the children were making from the nursery, impervious to their demands.

As Katherine went in with the doctor, she said, 'Katherine, do go upstairs and see to the children. I'm exhausted already—I had to sit down quietly...'

She smiled bewitchingly at the doctor, who didn't smile back. 'Mrs Marsh, Miss Marsh will be taking up her job this evening. I shall be here for her at six o'clock. I'm sure you'll make certain that she has the time to collect her things together before then.' He smiled at Katherine. 'You can be ready by then? I have an appointment in the evening and must go to the hospital this afternoon, otherwise I would come for you after lunch.'

'I'll be ready.' Katherine gave him a beaming smile. 'Thank you for taking me this morning.'

'You'll stay for coffee?' asked Joyce persuasively.

'Thank you, no.' He shook her hand and Katherine took him to the door.

'Scared?' he asked softly. 'Don't worry, if you haven't been given the chance to pack, I'll do it for you when I come.' He patted her briskly on the shoulder. 'I bless the day I knocked on this door; I've been searching for weeks for someone like you.' Her heart leapt at his words, and then plummeted to her toes as he added, 'You're exactly what the Graingers need.'

She stood for a moment or two after he had gone, dismissing sentimental nonsense from her head, preparing herself for the unpleasantness to come. And unpleasant it was, too, for Joyce was at her most vindictive.

Katherine allowed the worst of it to flow over her head and, when Joyce paused for breath, said in her calm way, 'Well, Joyce, Robin and Sarah are your children, after all. If you don't want to look after them, Henry can quite afford to get someone who will.'

She went up to her room and finished her packing which, since she had very few possessions, took no time at all. She was just finishing when Mrs Todd called up the stairs. 'Mrs Marsh 'as gone out, and them dratted kids is all over my kitchen!'

Katherine had changed back into elderly jeans and a sweater. She pulled on her jacket now and went downstairs. The children were running wild, sensing that something was happening and cheerfully adding to the disruption.

'Mrs Todd, help me cut some sandwiches and prepare a thermos—I'll take the children out and we can find somewhere to picnic. I know it's not much of a day, but it'll get them out of the house. Leave the key under the mat if we're not back, will you?'

They set out half an hour later, the children unwilling at first but, once away from the house, walking along the bridle paths, they could race about and shout as much as they wanted to. Katherine suspected that Joyce had taken herself off for the day in the hope that, if she didn't return, Katherine would feel bound to stay, but Henry would be home by five o'clock, and an hour later Dr Fitzroy would come for her.

She found a hollow out of the wind, and they ate their sandwiches there and then started back home. The children were tired now and, once they were back in the empty house, they were willing enough to have their outdoor things taken off and to settle at the kitchen table while Katherine got their tea. They had just finished when their father got home.

Katherine greeted him briskly. 'Joyce isn't back—I don't know where she went. The children have had their tea, and I've put everything ready for them to be put to bed presently.'

'What about my supper?'

'I really wouldn't know, Henry. I'm sure Joyce will have arranged something. Dr Fitzroy is coming for me at six o'clock.'

He looked aghast. 'But you can't leave us like this! Who's going to put the children to bed and get the supper?'

He had treated her as a kind of maid of all work for the last two years, but she could still feel sorry for him. 'Henry, you knew I was taking this job. You need never bother with me again, for you have never liked having me here, have you? Find a nice strong girl to help Joyce with the children, and persuade Joyce to give up some of her committees and spend more time at home.'

'I'll decide what is best, thank you, Katherine.' He was being pompous again and her concern for him faded. 'While you are waiting, you might get the children to bed.'

'They don't go until half-past six,' she pointed out. 'Why not take them to the nursery and read to them? I have a few last-minute things to do…'

She left him looking outraged.

It was five minutes to six when Joyce came home. Katherine heard her voice, loud and complaining. 'Where's Katherine? Why aren't the children with her? What about supper? I'm far too tired to do anything—she'll have to stay until tomorrow, or until someone can be found to help me…'

Leaving her room, her cases in either hand, Katherine heard her brother's voice, raised against the children's shrill voices and then, thankfully, the front door bell.

She hurried downstairs and opened the door and heaved a sigh of relief at the sight of Dr Fitzroy, large and reassuring. 'I haven't said goodbye,' she told him, rather pale at the prospect.

He took her cases from her, put them in the porch and went past her into the hall. 'I'll come with you,' he said and gave an encouraging little smile.

A waste of time as it turned out; Joyce turned her back and Henry glared at her and began a diatribe about ungrateful girls who would get what they deserved, deserting young children at a moment's notice. The doctor cut him short in the politest way. 'Fortunately, they have parents to look after them,' he observed in a bland voice which held a nasty sharp edge. 'We will be on our way.'

Katherine had said goodbye to the children, so she bade

Henry and Joyce goodbye quietly and followed Dr Fitzroy
out of the house, shutting the door carefully behind her. She
got into the car without a word and sat silently as he drove
away. It was silly to cry; she would not be missed, not as a
person who had been loved, but just for a moment she felt
very lonely.

The doctor said cheerfully, without looking at her, 'I often
think that friends are so much better than relations, and I'm
sure you'll quickly make plenty of friends.' And then he
added very kindly, 'Don't cry, Katherine, they aren't worth
it. You are going somewhere where you're wanted and where
you'll be happy.'

She sniffed, blew her ordinary little nose and sat up
straight. 'I'm sorry. You're quite right, of course. It's just
that the last two years have been a complete waste of time...'

'How old are you? Twenty-one, you said? I am thirty-
six, my dear, and I believe I have wasted a good many more
years than two. But they are never quite wasted, you know,
and all the other years make them insignificant.'

She wished with all her heart that she could stay close to
his large, confident person for ever, but at least she would
see him twice a week. She smiled at the thought as he said,
'That's better. Now, listen carefully. I shall only stay a few
minutes at the Graingers; they dine at eight o'clock, that
gives you time to find your way around and to unpack. They
go to bed at ten o'clock, never later. Mrs Dowling likes her
evenings to herself once she has seen to dinner, so you will
get their bedtime drinks and so forth. She takes up their
morning tea at half-past seven, but I don't expect she will
do the same for you. It's quite a large house to run and she
manages very well with two women who come in to help.
Your job will be to leave her free to do that; lately she has

been run off her feet, now that Mr and Mrs Grainger have become more dependent on someone to fetch and carry.'

'Does she mind me coming?'

'No, I think not, but she has been with them for twenty years or more and she is set in her ways.'

'I'll help her all I can, if she will let me. Oh, I do hope I'll make a good job of it.'

'Don't worry, you will.' They had reached Salisbury, and he was driving through the streets, quiet now after the day's traffic. Although the shops in the High Street were still lit, there were few people about, and once through North Gate it was another world, with the cathedral towering over the close and the charming old houses grouped around it at a respectable distance, as was right and proper. The doctor pulled up before the Graingers' house and got out, opened her door and collected her cases from the boot, then rang the doorbell. The door was opened so briskly that Katherine had no time to get nervous, and anyway it was too late to have cold feet. She bade Mrs Dowling a civil good evening, and accompanied the doctor to the drawing-room. Mr and Mrs Grainger were sitting on each side of a briskly burning fire, he reading a newspaper, she knitting a large woolly garment.

'There you are,' declared Mrs Grainger in a pleased voice. 'And I suppose that you must rush away, Jason? But we shall see you tomorrow, of course.' She beamed at him, and then at Katherine. 'Such a relief that you are here, my dear. Now, what shall I call you?'

'By her name, of course,' observed Mr Grainger.

'Katherine,' said Katherine.

'A very good name,' said his wife. 'I had a sister of that name—we called her Katie. She died of the scarlet fever. No one has the scarlet fever nowadays. Are you called Katie, my dear?'

'No, Mrs Grainger, although my mother always called me that.'

The old lady turned to the doctor. 'She seems a very nice girl, Jason. Not pretty, but well spoken and with a pleasant voice. I think we shall get on splendidly together.'

Mr Grainger put down his newspaper. 'Glad to have you here,' he said gruffly. 'Don't see many young faces these days, only Dodie—our granddaughter, and she has got a life of her own, bless her. You're only young once.' He glanced at Dr Fitzroy, standing placidly between them. 'Seen her lately?'

'Yes, and we're dining together this evening.'

'Then you won't want to be hanging around here with us old fogeys.'

The doctor left very shortly, and Mrs Dowling was summoned to take Katherine to her room. She was led silently up the carpeted stairs with shallow treads and along a short passage leading to the back of the house.

'Here you are,' said Mrs Dowling, rather ungraciously. 'The bathroom's beyond.' She opened a door, and Katherine went past her into a fair-sized room, prettily furnished, its window overlooking the large garden. Her cases were already there and Mrs Dowling said, 'Dinner's at eight o'clock, so you'll have time to unpack first. They won't expect you to change this evening. Mrs Grainger asked me to take you round the house. Come downstairs when you are ready and I'll do that, though it's not the easiest of times for me, what with dinner to dish up and all.'

'Would you prefer me to come with you now? I can un-

When Two Paths Meet

pack later when I come to bed, and it won't take me long to tidy myself.'

Mrs Dowling relaxed her stern expression; the girl looked harmless enough and, heaven knew, she had no looks to speak of, not like some of the pert young things these days who thought that because they had pretty faces and smart clothes, they could indulge in bad manners towards their elders and betters. She cast an eye over Katherine's sober appearance.

'Suits me, Miss…'

'Would you mind calling me Katherine?' She smiled at the older woman. 'I haven't had a job before, and Miss Marsh is a bit—well, I *am* going to work here.'

Mrs Dowling folded her arms across her chest. 'Well, I don't know, I'm sure—how would Miss Katherine do?'

'If you prefer that, Mrs Dowling.'

They toured the bedrooms, the bathroom and the small pantry off the front landing, where Katherine would be able to make hot drinks if Mr and Mrs Grainger were wakeful during the night.

'And that's often enough,' observed Mrs Dowling, 'but the doctor will have told you that.' She led the way downstairs. 'Very kind and good he is, too. Of course, him being smitten with Miss Dodie, I dare say he sees more of them than he needs to, though they're not in the best of health.'

She opened a door in the hall, and Katherine saw the dining-room: a rather gloomy apartment, heavily furnished, with a great deal of silver on the sideboard. There was a small study next to it and a charming little room opposite, used as a breakfast-room and sitting-room, its door leading to the drawing-room and with french windows opening out on to the garden at the back of the house.

'You'd best go tidy yourself,' said Mrs Dowling. 'It's almost eight o'clock, and they'll want their drinks poured. There now, you know where the drawing-room is?'

'Yes, thank you, Mrs Dowling. Do you want me to help with dinner? I could carry in the dishes for you.'

'They wouldn't like that, thanks all the same. Besides, you'll be busy enough; they ring the bell half a dozen times in an evening for me...'

'Oh, well,' said Katherine cheerfully, 'they won't need to do that now, will they? You must have been busy.'

Mrs Dowling watched her go back upstairs. Not such a bad young woman, after all, she decided. No looks, but a nice voice, and not in the least bossy.

Mr and Mrs Grainger didn't appear to have moved when Katherine went back into the drawing-room. She poured their sherry, accepted a glass for herself, and made gentle small talk until Mrs Dowling appeared to say that dinner was on the table. And from then on the evening went well. The old people liked to talk; indeed, half the time they talked at the same time, interrupting each other quite ruthlessly.

Katherine fetched their hot milky drinks from the kitchen at ten o'clock and then saw them upstairs, staying with Mrs Grainger until that lady declared that she could very easily manage for herself.

'And if I wake in the night, my dear, there's a bell in my room. Mr Grainger has one, too. I must say it's a comfort to have you here.' She bade Katherine a kind goodnight. 'We'll have a nice little talk in the morning,' she promised.

Katherine unpacked, admired her room, had a leisurely bath and thought how lovely it was to have a bathroom all to herself. She thought, too, fleetingly of Henry and Joyce, and felt guilty because she hadn't missed them or the children. I can't be a very nice person, she reflected as she curled up snugly in her bed. Not that the idea kept her awake; she slept within moments of her head touching the pillow.

Twenty-four hours later, tired though she was, she stayed awake long enough to review her day. Not too bad, she thought sleepily. The highlight of it had been the doctor's visit, although he had been impersonal in his manner towards her; all the same, he had smiled nicely at her when he left, and expressed the view that she was exactly right for the job. The old people were demanding in a nice way, but they seemed to like her, and even Mrs Dowling had unbent a little. She had had no chance to go out, or even take an hour off, but she had hardly expected that for the first day; it had been filled with undertaking the multiple small tasks the Graingers expected of her. Going upstairs to fetch a forgotten book, Katherine found time to sympathise with Mrs Dowling, who must have been dead on her feet by bedtime…

All the same, she had been happy. The house was warm, cheerful and charmingly furnished, she had a delightful room all to herself, the meals were elegantly served and the whole tempo of life slowed down. And, over and above all that, she would be paid. It was a splendid thought on which to close her eyes.

The week wound to a close. By Saturday she had found her feet, and for the last two days she had gone out while Mr and Mrs Grainger snoozed on their beds after lunch. Mrs Dowling, she discovered, liked to put her feet up after tea for an hour or so, and Katherine had offered to do any small chores for her during that time, an offer accepted rather ungraciously by that lady.

Katherine had spent her two brief outings window-shopping. She saw at once that forty pounds would go nowhere; she would have to buy essentials during the first few weeks then save up. All the same, she was willing to wait until she had enough money to buy the kind of clothes she wanted; good clothes, well cut and well made.

On Saturday night she had gone to bed content; she had found her week's wages on the breakfast table, and that afternoon she had gone to Marks and Spencer and spent almost all of it on undies. A methodical girl, she had made a list of the clothes she intended to buy, and crossed out the first line with satisfaction; next week it would almost certainly have to be a dress, Marks and Spencer again, something simple and unobtrusive to tide her over until she could afford something better. And perhaps a nightie? She hated the plain cotton ones she had had for so long.

On Sunday the Graingers went to church. It was a major undertaking, getting them there, for they insisted on walking through the close, a journey which took a considerable time at their leisurely pace. Katherine, between them, her arms supporting them, was thankful that the sun shone and that the early morning frost had dwindled away. And when they reached the cathedral there was still quite a long walk through the vast building to the seats they always occupied. But once settled between them, she was able to flex her tired arms and look around her. It was some years since she had been there, and she looked around her with peaceful content. They were seated near the pulpit, and she had a splendid view of the great building; she would be able to come as often as she liked, she thought with satisfaction, for it was barely five minutes' walk for her. The opening hymn was announced, and she helped her companions to their feet as the choir processed to their stalls.

The congregation was a large one and leaving the cathedral took time. They were outside, beginning their slow progress back home, when Dr Fitzroy joined them. There was a young woman with him, tall and good-looking and beautifully dressed. Dodie, thought Katherine, bristling to instant dislike; and she was right, for the young woman bent to kiss the old lady and then pat her grandfather on his arm with a gentle pressure.

'Darlings!' she declared in a clear, high voice. 'How lovely to see you, and how well you look.'

She had very blue eyes; she turned them on Katherine for an indifferent moment. Her nod, when the doctor introduced Katherine, was perfunctory.

'So clever of you, Jason, to find someone so suitable.'

'I can't take any credit for that,' he said placidly. 'Katherine more or less dropped into my lap—an answer to prayer, shall we say.' He smiled at Katherine, who was vexed to feel her cheeks redden. 'You've settled in? No snags?'

'None, Dr Fitzroy.' She heard her voice, very stiff and wooden and awkward-sounding, but for the life of her she couldn't do anything about it.

Dodie gave a chuckle. 'I should think not indeed! These are the two dearest, sweetest people I know.' She kissed them both, smiled at Katherine quite brilliantly, and took the doctor's arm. 'We shall be late...'

His goodbyes were brief. Katherine, scooping her elderly companions on to each arm, heard Dodie's high, penetrating voice quite clearly as they walked away.

'She will do very well, Jason. Dreadfully dull, poor dear, but I dare say she's very grateful—living in a pleasant house, good food and wages...'

The doctor's reply, *if* he replied, was lost on the wind.

Katherine subdued a violent wish to leave her two companions as from that moment and never see them or the doctor again. As for Dodie…words failed her. Common sense prevailed, of course; it was a good job and she *did* live pleasantly, and it was wonderful to have money to spend. She sighed soundlessly and turned her full attention to Mr Grainger, who was busy pulling the sermon to pieces. She would stay for ever, she mused, while she had the chance of seeing Dr Fitzroy. It was the height of stupidity to love someone who had no interest at all in you. Dodie had said that she was dull, she might as well be stupid, too!

Chapter 3

October had given way to November, and the late autumn sunshine had disappeared behind low banks of cloud, tearing around the sky, pushed to and fro by a ferocious wind. The Graingers didn't venture out; Katherine unpicked knitting, played bezique with Mr Grainger, read the newspapers to him and romantic novels to Mrs Grainger and, in between whiles, gave a hand around the house. The cleaning ladies who came each day were excellent workers, but they did their work and nothing more; Katherine, perceiving how Mrs Dowling's corns hurt, took to carrying the trays to and from the dining-room and, occasionally, when Mrs Dowling was in need of a rest, she dried the dishes and loaded and unloaded the dishwasher. Mrs Dowling always thanked her rather coldly for these small tasks, but her manner had softened considerably; the small, quiet girl was no threat to her authority, and she was proving a dab hand at keeping Mr and Mrs Grainger happy.

During the second week of Katherine's stay she was invited to go down to the kitchen each morning before she dressed and share Mrs Dowling's pot of tea, something she was happy to do, for it made a pleasant start to the day, sitting at the kitchen table, drinking Mrs Dowling's strong tea and listening to that lady's views on life in general and the household where she lived and worked in particular.

Within a very few days it was Katherine who carried the early morning tea trays up to Mr and Mrs Grainger. As she pointed out, she was going upstairs anyway, and it would save Mrs Dowling's corns. But although her days were filled by small chores she had two hours off each afternoon, something she looked forward to; there was so much to do and see. The cathedral was a never-ending source of interest; she pored over the Magna Carta in its library, studied the ancient manuscripts there, and wandered to and fro, examining the tombstones. When she had had her fill, she explored the narrow streets around the close, admiring the houses and wishing that she could live in one of them. The Graingers' house was delightful but, although she lived in it, she was aware that sooner or later they would die and she would be out of a job. She wondered who would have the house; probably Dodie, who certainly wouldn't want to employ her in any capacity.

Katherine paused to admire a particularly fine Georgian house bordering on to the close. Dodie wouldn't want her grandparents' house; she would be married to Dr Fitzroy by then, and he must surely have a house of his own. She had seen him when he visited his patients, of course, but she knew no more about him than the first time they had met.

At the end of her second week she took herself off to Marks and Spencer again, and bought a dress: pale grey with a white collar and a neat belt—unexciting, but she would not get tired of it as quickly as a brighter colour. She bore it back and wore it that evening. Examining herself in the long glass in her bedroom she was pleased with her appearance, for it was a distinct improvement on anything else hanging in her wardrobe.

She went downstairs feeling pleased with herself, and when Mrs Grainger observed, 'You look nice, Katherine,' she beamed with pleasure. A pity that Dr Fitzroy couldn't see her now...

The wish was father to the thought: she was setting Mrs Grainger's knitting to rights when Mrs Dowling opened the door. 'Dr Fitzroy,' she announced as he came into the room.

He had brought a book which Mr Grainger had wished to read, and stayed only briefly, but he paused by the door to ask Katherine, 'Everything is all right?' and when she said 'Yes,' he gave her a vague, kindly look. 'Splendid. You must be looking forward to buying yourself some pretty clothes. I'm sure if you ask her, Dodie will tell you where to go.'

Katherine's calm face gave away nothing of her feelings about this unfortunate remark. Nothing, just nothing would make her buy anything at a shop recommended by Dodie, even if she could afford it, which she couldn't. She said in a wooden voice, 'How kind,' and shot him a look of such rage that he blinked. There was more behind that composed face than he had thought, and he found himself interested to know what it was.

He said pleasantly, 'If you should want to visit your brother, let me know. I could drive you out there.'

'That's very kind of you, but I hadn't planned to—to go back for a little while.' She could hardly tell him that her letters had gone unanswered and a visit from her would be unwelcome. Joyce had said that she didn't care if she never saw her again... 'I'm very happy here,' she told him, and wished him a polite goodnight. Before she undressed that evening, she took a good look at her image in the pier-glass in her room. There was nothing wrong with her new dress; it was suitable, cheap and completely lacking in high fashion, but then, high fashion was something quite useless for someone like herself. It was a very nice dress, she told herself defiantly, and next week she would buy some shoes; high-heeled and elegant. By Christmas she would have an adequate wardrobe; by the time she had bought the basic items, she would be able to save her money and start to pick and choose.

She got into bed, planning what she would buy; clothes which would make Dr Fitzroy look at her twice. She was just dropping off on her hopeful thought when Mr Grainger rang. He couldn't sleep, he complained, and would she get him a drink? Ovaltine or Bengers...

Another week went by, highlighted by the doctor's visits, always brief, during which he took blood pressures, listened carefully to his patients' mild complaints and went away again with barely a word to Katherine. There was a visit from Dodie too, as brief as the doctor's had been. She arrived just as the old couple were preparing to take their afternoon nap, wrapped in a beautifully cut coat and wearing high patent-leather boots. She had been to the hairdressers, she explained and just had to pop in and see how her darlings were getting on, although she cut her grandfather short when he started to describe his bad chest, laughingly telling him to stop worrying.

'You'll live for ever, darling,' she told him and hugged him briefly. 'You know how it depresses me when you talk about being ill.' She perched on the arm of his chair. 'Let me tell you about the party I'm going to this evening…'

'Alone?' asked her grandmother.

'Of course not—Jason will take me. I've told him that he must. He's always at the hospital or seeing patients, such a bore…' She jumped up. 'I must go now—I've promised to meet someone…'

She went in a flurry of haste, leaving behind her a strong scent of Opium and an equally strong feeling in Katherine that she couldn't leave quickly enough.

It was difficult after that to get the Graingers to settle down to their naps, and there was only an hour left of Katherine's free time by the time they had finally dozed off. She got into her elderly raincoat, tied a scarf over her head, and hurried through the North Gate into the heart of the city.

She had a week's wages in her pocket, and this time it was to be a raincoat to replace the deplorable garment she was wearing. Marks and Spencer's was more than her pocket could afford; she plunged into Woolworth's.

There was a surprisingly good selection of clothing; she found what she wanted and put it on, a sensible garment in lovat, but it felt comfortable and fitted well. With the money she still had, she nipped along to a small hat shop on the further side of the High Street and invested in a green felt hat; it was plain with its small brim and plain ribbon, but it suited her and it went well with the raincoat.

She hurried back to the close, stuffed the old raincoat into the dustbin at the back of the house with glee, and went in through the kitchen door. Mrs Dowling was there, getting the tea tray ready. She glanced up and said severely, 'Been spending your money again…burns a hole in your pocket, doesn't it?'

'Well, no, not really.' Katherine went to the kitchen glass and took a satisfied look at the hat. 'You see, I haven't had any new clothes for two years, and I've almost nothing to wear. I don't want Mr and Mrs Grainger to feel ashamed of me.' She added fervently, 'I hope it rains on Sunday so that I can wear this.'

It was several days later, soon after the doctor's usual visit, that Mr Grainger complained of not feeling well. He had just eaten a splendid tea, after an equally special lunch of soup, cheese soufflé and one of Mrs Dowling's egg custards, and Katherine decided that he had probably overeaten. She fetched his indigestion tablets, settled him for another nap and, since Mrs Grainger was disinclined for sleep, found one of the novels that lady delighted in, and sat down to read to her. It was the one time in the day that she should have called her own, but it was raining anyway, and she had no plans of her own. Mr Grainger snored on the other side of the hearth and woke refreshed, so that they presently dispersed to tidy themselves for the evening.

Mrs Dowling was a first-class cook; they sat down to prawn cocktails, minute steaks with a variety of vegetables and one of her delicious trifles. They played three-handed whist afterwards, until Katherine shepherded them to their rooms and went to the kitchen to get their hot drinks.

Mrs Grainger was already in bed, awaiting the ritual of her drink and the arranging of the various objects on her night table which were designed to get her through the night hours. Katherine put everything just so and went along to say goodnight to Mr Grainger. He was sitting up in bed, and she thought uneasily that he looked a bad colour and was puffing a bit.

'Do you feel all right?' she asked him.

'Of course I do.' He sounded so testy that she didn't say any more, but wished him a goodnight and went back to the kitchen to tidy away the cups and saucers before going to bed herself, to lie and dream about Dr Fitzroy. A useless occupation, but one she seemed unable to avoid.

Thinking about it afterwards, she had no idea what had awakened her, but the sense of urgency caused her to put on her dressing-gown and slippers and go soft-footed first to Mrs Grainger's room. That lady was asleep, swathed in shawls, snoring lightly, so Katherine turned her steps towards Mr Grainger's room next door. There was a dim night-light by his bed; he liked to have that and by its faint glimmer she could see that he was sitting up in bed, struggling to breathe.

Dr Fitzroy had told her that the old gentleman had congestive heart failure, a condition he had had for some years, but which had been kept more or less stable. Now, to her frightened eyes, it had erupted with a vengeance. Her first thought was to fly to the telephone and get help, but her good sense sent her to the bedside to reassure the old man and then to open the window so that the over-warm room could cool off.

'You're perfectly all right,' declared Katherine stoutly. 'I know you can't breathe properly, but you'll feel better presently. I'm going to telephone Dr Fitzroy…'

She padded downstairs to the phone and rang the number he had given her. She was answered at once by a brisk, 'Yes, Dr Fitzroy speaking.'

'Oh, it's you,' said Katherine thankfully. 'Please will you come? Mr Grainger isn't well. He can't breathe properly.'

His calm voice sounded almost placid. 'I'll be with you in ten minutes. Leave the front door unlocked. Go back to

Mr Grainger and keep him happy until I get there. Oh, and open a window.'

'I have.'

She heard his grunt of approval as she put the receiver down, glancing at the clock as she did so. Half-past five.

She unbolted the door and flew back upstairs, to find Mr Grainger puffing and panting. If he had had the breath, he would have been snarling with rage, too; he had never been a man to take kindly to illness, and he had no intention of changing his attitude now. He glared at Katherine and began to struggle from his bed. He was old, but he was a big, heavily built man still; she was struggling to keep him quiet against his pillows when Dr Fitzroy came quietly into the room. He didn't speak, only disentangled Katherine and Mr Grainger, laid his patient gently back and set her back on her feet.

'Now, let's see what we can do,' he observed. He could have been making one of his routine calls at a more conventional hour, the only difference being that he was dressed in casual trousers and a thick sweater. He smiled at Katherine and bent over his patient. His vast, calm presence did much to reassure the old gentleman; Mr Grainger still puffed and panted, but his furious panic had been checked. The doctor examined him without haste and then opened his bag. 'You'll do,' he said cheerfully. 'I'm going to give you something to let you sleep, and you'll feel perfectly all right when you wake up.' He drew up an injection and pushed up Mr Grainger's pyjama sleeve, slid in the needle and observed, 'I dare say you had too heavy a meal—I shall talk to Katherine presently and tell her what you can and can't eat, and you'll oblige me by listening to her if she warns you. I'm going to stay here until you drop off—you are quite all right now, so don't worry, and when I'm gone, Katherine will be here.'

He glanced across the bed to where she was standing, wrapped in the same useful garment in which he had first seen her. Her hair hung down her back, and she was a little pale from fright. There was nothing about her to attract his notice, and yet he glanced at her a second time, and this time she looked up and met his eyes. Not a nonentity, he decided then, not with those beautiful grey eyes. He smiled at her. 'We'll have a talk before I go,' he told her.

Mr Grainger's breathing had slowed to a reassuring, gentle snore. After five minutes or so, they left him, and Katherine led the way downstairs. 'I expect you would like a cup of tea? I'm sure Mrs Dowling won't mind if I make one.'

He put his bag on the kitchen table and sat down beside it. 'Have one with me? Now, listen carefully, and I will explain what you may expect from Mr Grainger...'

She made the tea and listened. She would have listened all night if he had chosen to go on talking, but he gave her explicit instructions, drank his tea and explained in simple terms exactly what was the matter with Mr Grainger.

'He is elderly, his heart is tired, and from time to time he overdoes things and nature takes over and stops him. Mrs Grainger worries about him, so skim over the details if you can.' He smiled at her. 'Go back to bed for an hour or so. You'll be busy enough in the morning. I'll call in about lunch time, but telephone me if you're worried. The hospital will know how to find me.'

She didn't know what prompted her to ask, 'Do you live near here, Dr Fitzroy?' but she wished she hadn't spoken, for his, 'Yes, I do,' was uttered in a voice in which coolness and indifference were nicely blended.

It was the indifference which did it; she had spent two years with Henry and Joyce, fighting their intentions to turn her into a willing doormat, but her new-found freedom had made her courageous, and she said haughtily, 'I have no wish to pry, I merely wish to know how long it would take you to get here in an emergency.'

He got up from the table and stood looking at her; it was surprising how she grew on one, he thought, despite the fact that as far as he could see she looked no more glamorous than on the occasion of their first meeting. That terrible dressing-gown, fit for a jumble sale!

He asked, 'Have you been paid?'

'Yes—each week. It's over three weeks...'

He went to the door. 'Oh, good—so you *will* be able to buy yourself some pretty clothes.' He had his hand on the door-handle. 'Don't bother to see me out, I'll shut the door behind me.'

She watched him go, loving him to distraction and seething with bad temper. She washed the mugs and emptied the teapot and calculated how many weeks it would take before she could buy some really decent clothes. Not that he would notice!

In this she was quite correct; he had remarked that she would want to buy some clothes because he guessed that she had been deprived of that pleasure for far too long, but he had meant to be kind. He dismissed her from his thoughts as he drove back to his house.

Katherine didn't go back to bed. It was already half-past six, in half an hour Mrs Dowling would be getting up, and Katherine suspected that Mr Grainger was going to keep her fully occupied during the day. She went to her room and showered and dressed, and went downstairs again just as Mrs Dowling entered the kitchen.

'Well, I never heard a sound,' declared that lady when Katherine explained about the night's events. 'You've had a busy time of it. Sit down for a minute and I'm going to make us a cup of tea.'

After that, there was very little rest for Katherine. Mr Grainger, peevish at having to remain in bed, was prepared to dislike and disagree with everyone, and his wife, convinced that he was dying, spent a good deal of time sitting listlessly in a chair, only brightening when Katherine coaxed her to have something to eat or found time to read aloud one of the romantic novels she loved. Even Dr Fitzroy had difficulty in convincing her that her husband was in no danger. All in all, it was a trying day for everyone, and Katherine, for one, was heartily glad when, her two charges safely in their beds and asleep, she was able to get into her own bed. She wondered, as she closed her eyes, why Dodie hadn't called; another pair of hands would have been welcome, and she professed a deep affection for her grandparents. She was asleep before she could pursue the matter.

The next two days were almost as bad, and on the third morning Dr Fitzroy called, declared that his patient was perfectly fit to get up again, warned him to keep to a light diet for a few days, and took himself off again with no more than a few words to Katherine, and those were concerning Mr and Mrs Grainger.

She showed him to the door, since Mrs Dowling was busy in the kitchen, and he paused on the step, nodded briefly and crossed the pavement to his car. Very touchy, she decided, closing the door after him. Probably, he worked too hard.

Dodie came that very afternoon, just as Katherine had

got Mr Grainger out of bed and into a rather splendid dressing-gown, and helped him downstairs to where his wife was waiting in the sitting-room. Dodie was wearing a scarlet coat and soft leather boots, and swinging a shoulder bag to match them. She was as pretty as a picture, and no wonder the doctor doted on her, thought Katherine, wishing her a polite good afternoon.

'Darlings!' exclaimed Dodie, and swooped upon them both with little cries and hugs. 'I would have come sooner, but I had the teeniest cold and I was so afraid of you getting it.' She pulled up a stool and sat down between them. 'I've come to tea, if you'll have me.' She looked over her shoulder at Katherine. 'You can go out for half an hour, only be back by four o'clock. I suppose Mrs Dowling will get the tea?'

'I'll tell her you are here as I go,' said Katherine. 'That is, if Mr and Mrs Grainger don't mind me going out for a while?'

She was told to go; they would be perfectly all right with their darling Dodie to look after them. The two old people hardly looked up as she slipped out of the room.

It was nice to be outside again, even for half an hour. She walked down High Street and into the shopping arcade, looking in its windows—her next pay would have to go on shoes or boots. Shoes, she decided; the boots she liked were too pricey, but she could get some good shoes... She walked back, happily mulling over her future purchases.

The Bentley was parked outside the house as she reached it. She went upstairs, took off her outdoor things, tidied her hair and went to the sitting-room. Dodie was still there, her hat and coat cast over a chair now, fussing over her grandparents while Dr Fitzroy sat watching her. She looked up as Katherine went in.

'Oh, there you are,' she exclaimed, faintly reproachful. 'I was beginning to think you had forgotten the time. Can we have tea, do you suppose?'

Katherine said, 'Oh, of course,' and went along to the kitchen, swallowing resentment. Perhaps she had been away for too long but, after all, Dodie *had* said half an hour, and she had been exactly twenty-five minutes...

Mrs Dowling was looking impatient. 'Why don't they want their tea?' she wanted to know. 'Miss Dodie told me to wait until you got back, but I can't think why. I always take in the tea, and she's surely able to pour out?'

Katherine thought she knew the answer to that, but she didn't say so. 'I dare say Miss Dodie thinks I take up the tea,' she said peaceably. 'Dr Fitzroy's there...'

She fetched another cup and saucer from the dresser and picked up the tray. 'Do you mind if I take it? Miss Dodie seems to expect it.'

Mrs Dowling nodded rather coldly. 'Better if you do, I suppose, just this once.'

Katherine arranged the tea tray carefully on the round table by the window, and Dodie said carelessly, 'All right, Katherine, you can go back to the kitchen. We'll ring if we want anything.'

She had gone, closing the door quietly behind her, before Dr Fitzroy said quietly, 'I thought Katherine had tea here?'

'Oh, does she?' Dodie sounded vague. 'Well, I dare say she'll be glad of a chat with Mrs Dowling,' she declared, and added, so softly that her grandparents couldn't hear her easily, 'She's been happy enough to do that for the last few days.' She smiled at the doctor. 'I've popped in each afternoon, you know.'

He looked a little surprised. 'Oh, have you? That was thoughtful of you, Dodie.'

She pouted prettily at him. 'Just because I don't go around with my hair scraped back and no make-up doesn't mean to say that I'm not just as capable as any other girl.' She poured the tea, and urged tiny sandwiches and cakes upon the old people, looking the very picture of sweet domesticity.

Presently, on their way out, they met Katherine coming from the kitchen and the doctor stopped. 'I'm glad that you've had a little time to yourself in the afternoons.' he observed. 'Dodie tells me that she's been standing in for you.'

The hall was rather dim, so he missed the fleeting look of astonishment on her face. 'Oh—yes. It—was nice to get out.'

Dodie tugged his arm. 'Darling, do come on, I've a dinner date.' She looked across at him and on to Katherine, and a little smile curled at the corners of her mouth. 'I'll be here at the same time tomorrow, Katherine.'

Katherine shut the door after them; if Dodie came the next day, she was prepared to eat her week's wages!

It was a safe bet, there was no sign of her; but Mrs Dowling rather surprisingly offered to keep an eye on her employers while Katherine had an hour to herself after lunch. The weather had become wintry; Katherine bought a warm and pretty dressing-gown and cosy slippers. She didn't mind getting up in the night to tend her charges, but it was chilly in the small hours.

The shops were beginning to show signs of Christmas; she drooled over the pretty things on display, at the same time determined not to spend any more money until she had at least three weeks' wages, so that she could buy an outfit for Christmas. A coat, it would have to be cloth and plain, and a dress to go under it. Besides, there were presents to buy for Henry and Joyce and the children. They wouldn't want to see her, but all the same she had made up her mind to take her gifts and wish them a happy Christmas. Who knew, they might be glad to see her...

Because she was determined not to buy anything, she took another direction on the following afternoon, past the Graingers' house, circling the close, past the King's House and on towards the Bishop's Palace. The houses here were larger, in a variety of architectural styles, most of it centuries old. Despite the cold wind, she dawdled along, studying them with pleasure, pretending to herself that she had the choice of living in one of them. She found her ideal presently: red-tiled gables, lattice windows and a stout oak door, heavily nailed. Probably a mass of small rooms and narrow passages, a nightmare to keep clean, but all the same a house to love and dream over. There was no one about. She loitered in front of it, trying to picture its interior, momentarily lost to her surroundings, so that when Dr Fitzroy said quietly from behind her, 'Spying out the land, Katherine?' she gave a squeak, and whirled round to face him.

'Exploring,' she said, and beamed up at him. 'I've never been as far as this, only seen it from a distance when I've been to the cathedral.'

'I should have thought that you found the shops more interesting.'

'Oh, I go there too, but I'm saving up, and that's easier to do if I keep away from them.'

He said carelessly, 'Oh, Christmas presents and so on. Will you go to your brother's?'

She nodded. 'I hope they'll be glad to see me—just for an hour or two, I expect...' She paused, aware that, although he was listening, it was with the air of a man who had other things to do but didn't wish to be unkind. She felt the colour rush into her cheeks. 'I must go—I've come too far. Goodbye, Doctor.'

She whisked away, going at a great rate, and he stood and watched her small figure until it had disappeared round a curve in the road before crossing to the house she had been admiring and letting himself in.

It was the following afternoon, on her return from a brisk walk, that she went into the drawing-room and discovered that the Graingers had a visitor.

He was sitting between them before the fire, and it was obvious that they were enjoying his company. He turned to look at Katherine as she paused in the doorway, and then stood up. 'Ah, the estimable Katherine,' he said genially, and she felt a prick of resentment at his use of her name. 'I've been hearing about you and your many kindnesses to my aunt and uncle.'

They shook hands, which gave her the chance to study him, without appearing to do so. He was not young, forty, she judged, perhaps older, with a round, jovial face, pale blue eyes and receding hair, neither grey nor fair. He smiled too much, decided Katherine at once, and his hands were warm and a little damp. She didn't care for him at all, but she had no reason to dislike him and he seemed anxious to be on good terms with her. She replied suitably to his rather banal remarks, and went away to fetch the tea; it was one of those days when Mrs Dowling's corns were playing her up.

'Still there, is he?' asked that lady as Katherine went into the kitchen. 'And likely to stay, as far as I can see.' And, at Katherine's enquiring look, 'He's Mrs Grainger's step-nephew, if you see what I mean—his mother was her step-sister. Lives in Cheltenham—a bachelor—no money to speak of, but likes to spend it whether he's got it or no.'

Katherine received these confidences in prudent silence. No doubt Mrs Dowling would be annoyed with herself for airing them, later on. She picked up the tray and murmured suitably before going back to the drawing-room.

Perhaps she had been a bit hasty in her first opinion of the visitor, she reflected as she collected the tea things and bore them back to the kitchen. Tom Fetter hadn't put a foot wrong during tea. Indeed, he had kept the Graingers amused and interested, and they obviously liked him. It hadn't surprised her when Mrs Grainger had invited him to stay. 'For this is quite a large house and we would love to have you— it would be silly to go to a hotel. Besides, you have so much to tell us.'

The old lady was quite animated, and as for Mr Grainger, Katherine had never seen him so good-natured. She excused herself presently and went away to prepare a room for their unexpected visitor.

She was grateful that he didn't disrupt the mild routine which governed the household. He made no demur when she suggested to the old couple that it was their usual bedtime, and in the morning he arrived punctually at the breakfast table and then took himself off for a walk while Katherine organised the day.

Dr Fitzroy paid his usual visit in the morning, listened good-naturedly to his patients' long-winded account of their guest, pronounced himself satisfied with their health and suggested that Katherine should go with him to his car parked outside to fetch some tablets.

'Well?' he asked, once they were free of the street door.

'What do you think of this nephew? Can you cope with a guest in the house? Mrs Dowling has enough to do...'

For all the world, thought Katherine, as though I sit about all day reading novels... 'Of course I can,' she said rather tartly. 'He's very considerate, and he's someone new for them to talk to. They like having him here.'

'But you don't. And don't frown at me like that, Katherine. Your face is like an open book when it comes to feelings.'

She went pink, and looked at him with such horror that he added, 'Now what have I said? You look as though I've caught you stealing...'

He might say that he could read her thoughts, but he hadn't discovered that she was head over heels in love with him; she thanked heaven fervently for that, managed a smile and decided not to answer him.

Dodie came that afternoon, professed herself delighted to meet a member of the family she had heard of but never seen, and stayed for tea. She and Tom Fetter got on splendidly, and when she got up to go he offered to walk with her.

In the hall, putting on her coat, Dodie asked, 'And how is our little paragon?' She glanced at Katherine and smiled brilliantly. 'Dr Fitzroy seems to think you are the eighth wonder of the world—I can't think why. Do you like him?'

Katherine said calmly, 'Yes, I do, he's been very kind to me and I'm happy here.'

'Just the kind of little willing work-horse he was looking for, and of course you think he is marvellous... You ought to see the nurses at the hospital falling over each other to work for him! He's got charm, all right, and knows how to use it, too. He comes home and tells me of some new conquest and we have a good laugh...' She got out a lipstick and studied her face in the hall mirror. 'Still, you're too sensible to get taken in, aren't you? I mean to say...he can take his pick of pretty girls, and I don't mind, he's not serious with them.' She smiled quite brilliantly again. 'I'm the one who matters.' She nodded. 'I thought I'd let you know that.'

Tom Fetter came into the hall, and she added, 'See you some time, Katherine,' and went away with him, leaving Katherine quite speechless. She had to stay where she was for a few minutes to calm down, for she found that she was shaking with rage. Why had Dodie told her that load of rubbish—for she was sure that that was what it was—unless, horrid thought, she had somehow guessed at Katherine's feelings for Dr Fitzroy? She went hot and cold at the very idea.

It surprised her when Dodie came the following afternoon and stayed to tea, and again Tom Fetter saw her home. The next day, he told Mrs Grainger that he was taking Dodie out to lunch.

'So nice that they are enjoying each other's company,' declared the old lady. 'He is such a splendid companion, isn't he, Katherine? So amusing and thoughtful. I'm sure we haven't enjoyed ourselves so much for a long time.'

And, true enough, he kept them happy, even though Katherine now found it difficult to keep them to the gentle routine Dr Fitzroy had mapped out for them. They wanted to stay up later, change their suitable diets for the more exotic dishes he was always describing to them.

At lunch, Mr Grainger said suddenly, 'I wish Tom lived with us, he's such splendid company. I did hint at it, but he says he has this very pleasant house in Cheltenham—too big for him, it seems, and costs a great deal to maintain...'

Katherine settled them for their afternoon nap, glad that

the house was quiet, and then put on her outdoor things and went into the town. She had intended to save her week's wages, but she had seen, days ago, a winter coat in an unassuming peat-brown cloth, not quite what she had hoped to buy, but the days were becoming cold and a thick coat was a must. She hurried back with it, well pleased with her purchase, despite the fact that she had very little money left in her purse.

She went into the house through the kitchen door, and found Mrs Dowling loading the tea tray. 'I don't know why they're all here,' she complained, 'the doctor and Miss Dodie and that Mr Fetter, all wanting their tea.'

Katherine took off her outdoor things and laid the carrier bag containing the new coat carefully on top of them. 'I'll take the tea in,' she offered. 'They won't want me to stay, I'll come back here, if I may, and have tea with you.'

They all turned to look at her as she went in; the doctor took the tray from her as she murmured a good afternoon to the room in general and added, 'I'll just bring in the cakes and scones. I expect Miss Dodie will pour out.'

She whisked away and returned with a second tray, which she laid on a side table before she made for the door once more.

'You'd better stay,' said the doctor. 'Mr Grainger has something to say to you.'

She turned slowly to face them all, all of a sudden aware that something awful was about to happen, a guess borne out by the sly look of satisfaction on Dodie's face.

Chapter 4

'Let me pour the tea first,' said Dodie gaily. 'And, Katherine, pass the scones round before you sit down.'

Katherine did as she had been asked. Dodie was making it worse, she guessed that, prolonging the moment when she was going to be told something which was going to shatter her newly found independence and contentment. She sat down presently, a cup and saucer in her hand, and took a sip of tea. She was going to need it before they had finished.

It surprised her a little that the doctor had said nothing, merely sat there, looking calmly from one to the other. Dodie went to sit beside him and laughed across at her grandfather. 'Now, darling, do tell Katherine what you've decided.'

She looked around the circle of faces, smiling prettily, quite sure that they were all enjoying themselves as much as she was. 'And I can't take all the credit for it,' she told them. 'Tom shared my idea and made it possible.'

'So, shall we hear what it is?' suggested the doctor. 'I, for one, can't spare more than a few more minutes.'

Old Mr Grainger coughed importantly and glanced across at his wife. 'Well, it's like this,' he began. 'Dodie, bless the darling child, thinks that a change of scene would do us good, and Tom here has invited us to go back with him to Cheltenham—and we've agreed…' He was interrupted by Mrs Dowling coming quietly into the room to whisper into the doctor's ear. He got up at once, excused himself and left the room with her, to return within a few moments. 'I have to go to the hospital—something has come up…' He glanced briefly at Katherine, and then at Mr Grainger. 'Perhaps we can talk about this later?'

He didn't stay for an answer.

A pity he had been called away, reflected Katherine, listening to plans being made—plans in which she was not included. 'We will give you a splendid reference,' Mr Grainger told her, 'and I'm sure you'll find another job at once, Katherine. Why, Dodie tells me that she knows of several people who would love to have you. We can't take you with us, you understand. Tom's house isn't large enough for that, and we plan to stay some months.'

He looked at his wife and went on, 'Mrs Dowling will stay on here, of course, and you are most welcome to remain until you move to another job.'

Katherine found her voice, and marvelled that it sounded just as usual. 'When do you intend to go?'

'Within a few days. There will be a few arrangements to make, and the packing, but, of course, you will be here to do that.'

She agreed calmly, and if her face was pale she didn't allow her dismay to show; she wasn't going to give Dodie the satisfaction of that. She wondered why Dodie hadn't persuaded her grandparents to ask her to go with them—

she would have been out of the way then, and that was obviously what she wanted. So silly, really: Dodie had never been in any danger of losing the doctor to her. Her vague speculations were cleared almost at once.

'I know just the job for you,' declared Dodie. 'A nice old couple who live near Stockbridge—rather rural, but then you like the country, I expect.'

'I'm sure I'll be able to find work, but it's kind of you to bother.' Katherine stood up. 'Shall I clear the tea things? I expect you have a lot to discuss. I'll be in the kitchen.'

She went unhurriedly from the room, her throat so choked by tears that, when she reached the kitchen, she couldn't speak. Mrs Dowling took one look at her, took the tray and asked, 'Bad news? I had a feeling it was. Sit down and I'll make a cup of tea, and you can tell me if you want to.'

Katherine wasn't going to cry, but she couldn't speak either, so she nodded her head and sat down at the table. The tea, a strong brew favoured by the housekeeper, steadied her. She was able to tell Mrs Dowling the plans which had been made, and ended, 'You don't have to worry, you're to stay here while they're gone.'

Mrs Dowling nodded. 'Suits me, but what about you? Turning you off at a moment's notice, I can't understand it! You've been such a help, and they like you.'

'But Mr Fetter amuses them...'

'Don't trust the man, myself,' declared Mrs Dowling.

Katherine was inclined to agree with her when, the following morning, coming downstairs after searching for Mrs Grainger's spectacles, she overheard Mr Grainger's voice, always rather loud. 'You're sure five thousand is enough, Tom? And of course we'll arrange for extra help in the house while we're with you. Just let me have the bills—you'll have a good deal of extra expense...'

It wasn't her business, of course, and Mr Fetter was a kind of relation. But there had been no need for him to invite the Graingers to his house; they had been happy enough. She hoped there would be someone at his home to fetch and carry for the elderly pair. She handed over the spectacles and began to unravel Mrs Grainger's knitting, wondering what Dr Fitzroy would have to say when he was told.

He came half an hour later, gave his brief examinations, asked to sit down for a few moments, then did so.

He heard Mr Grainger's news with no sign of disquiet, and that was something Katherine hadn't expected.

'I see that you are determined to go,' he observed calmly, 'and I imagine that there is nothing I can say which will make you change your mind? I cannot say that I like the idea, though. And whose idea was it?'

Mrs Grainger said excitedly, 'Dodie's, bless her, always thinking of us—and Tom was only too ready to fall in with her plans. She had them all settled for us, too. We shall go in a couple of days' time, Katherine will pack for us...'

'She goes with you?' He didn't look at Katherine as he spoke.

'Oh, no! Dodie says there is no need, Tom will have plenty of help at his home. We shall miss her, of course, but I'm sure she'll find more work easily enough.'

She glanced at Katherine and smiled. 'Dodie knows some people near Stockbridge...'

He said easily, 'I don't think you need to worry about Katherine.' He got up. 'I'll come the day after tomorrow and give you both a check-up and let a colleague of mine in Cheltenham know that you'll be staying there for a time. You're quite sure that you want to go?'

It was Mr Grainger who replied, 'Quite sure, Jason. Of course, you'll keep an eye on us when we get back?'

'Of course.' He bade them a pleasant goodbye, and Katherine went with him to see him out.

At the door he said briskly. 'I shouldn't worry about finding work. Something will turn up.'

She agreed quietly, watching him cross the pavement to his car. He hadn't even offered to give her a reference. A great wash of self-pity threatened to swamp her. If only she hadn't spent almost all her money on a coat! The week's wages she would be paid wouldn't go far. She fought back tears; being sorry for herself was no help at all. She gave a defiant sniff and went up to the attics to fetch the cases needed for packing.

She was kept fully occupied after that, packing and then unpacking again, because Mrs Grainger couldn't make up her mind what she wanted to take with her. Mr Fetter was much in evidence, laughing a great deal, making rather grandiose plans and, when Dodie called, which she did each day, falling in with her own plans to visit them in Cheltenham. It all sounded delightful, but Katherine didn't feel very happy about it. Somehow, Tom Fetter didn't sound quite right, although she didn't know why. Perhaps he laughed too much, and when he wasn't laughing he was smiling, and yet his eyes were restless, as though he expected someone to query his good humour. Not that it concerned her, she reminded herself sternly; on the following day they would all be gone and she would have started looking for work. Mr Grainger had given her an extra week's wages and told her that she might stay at the house until she found something else to do, so that her immediate worries had been quietened. All the same, on the last evening, after she had seen the Graingers safely into their beds, she had gone to her room and packed. Surely she would find work within the next day or two?

It was something of a chaotic morning. Mr and Mrs Grainger took time to prepare themselves for their trip, various comforts for the journey needed to be stowed about their persons, cases—already packed—had to be opened and checked, and a variety of instructions needed to be given to Mrs Dowling. At the last minute, Dr Fitzroy had driven up, got out of his car and strolled over to say a final good-bye. That done, he turned to Tom Fetter, who was fussing round his car.

'I've telephoned Dr Carver, a friend of mine in Cheltenham. He promises that he will attend Mr and Mrs Grainger. You do realise that they need medical supervision regularly?'

'My dear chap,' began Tom Fetter, 'I wasn't born yesterday—you medics aren't the only people with brains. I'll keep a sharp eye on them, never fear.'

Dr Fitzroy nodded. 'As you like—as long as you understand your responsibilities. Dr Carver will keep me informed.'

Tom Fetter laughed uneasily. 'Good lord, you sound as though you don't trust me.'

To this, the doctor made no reply, merely turned on his heel, got into his car and drove away. He had neither looked nor spoken to Katherine, and she watched him go with mixed feelings: bitter regret that she was unlikely to see him again, and a waspish desire to say something really nasty if ever she did. She was discovering it was hard to love someone who completely ignored her.

The house was very quiet once they had all gone; Dodie had been there to see them go, but she hadn't stayed. 'I expected Jason to be here,' she had grumbled. 'I told him to wait for me.' She had flounced off, looking cross.

It was nice to be kept busy for the next hour or two; there was really no need for Katherine to help Mrs Dowling, for the daily cleaner was there and was to stay all day, but it kept her occupied—stripping beds and getting the rooms ready for what Mrs Dowling called a good turn-out. After lunch, Katherine went into the city and sought out the agencies she had looked up in the telephone directory. She visited three, and none of them had anything suitable; she couldn't type, and although she could cook she had no cordon bleu qualifications, nor had she any nursing experience. She was advised to return in a few days; home helps were always in demand, she was told encouragingly, but of course, with Christmas not far off, most people had made their arrangements well ahead. She went back to the house, not exactly worried, but vaguely apprehensive.

She spent the next day round the house, polishing the silver for Mrs Dowling and wrapping it carefully in baize so that it might be taken to the bank for safe-keeping. She was putting on the kettle for tea when Dodie arrived.

'Still here?' She sounded annoyed. 'I'll give you the address of those people at Stockbridge. You can get a bus there tomorrow and be interviewed. They're desperate for someone, so there's no doubt that you'll get the job.'

Katherine thanked her with a calm she didn't feel. Dodie had been the means of her losing her job with the Graingers, and now she was trying to push her into a household she knew nothing about, and buried in the country to boot! She had no intention of going there, but there was no point in annoying Dodie. That young lady departed presently, well pleased with herself, having left exact instructions as to how Katherine was to get to the place. 'I'll phone this evening and let them know you're coming,' she promised.

Mrs Dowling was going to spend the night with her sister who lived on the other side of Salisbury; it was a chance, she explained to Katherine, which she might not get again for a long time, for, once Katherine had gone, she didn't feel she could leave the house empty. 'You don't mind?' she wanted to know. 'You're not nervous?'

'Not a bit,' declared Katherine, and promised to shoot every bolt, double lock the doors and close every window before she went to bed.

All the same, the old house seemed very empty, even with the TV on. She went to bed early, her head full of plans for getting a job as quickly as possible in Salisbury, plans hindered by thoughts which had nothing to do with them and wholly to do with Dr Fitzroy.

She got up early in the dark of the winter morning, made herself tea and set about getting breakfast. Mrs Dowling would be back for lunch, and she would have ample time to go back to the agencies and try her luck once again. She was making toast when the bell rang.

The postman, probably, with Christmas parcels—a bit early, but some people always posted them too soon... She undid the bolts, turned the key in the lock and took down the chain. She found the doctor on the doorstep.

'My goodness, you are up early!' said Katherine. 'Is something wrong?' She ushered him inside, full of delight at the sight of him. 'I've just made breakfast. Would you like a cup of tea?'

'Please. I've been at the hospital since four o'clock. I wanted to see you, and this seemed a good opportunity.'

He followed her through the house, and she sat him down at the kitchen table, poured tea and put a plate and the toast before him. He looked tired and hungry, and she offered him eggs and bacon.

'Oh, splendid, but only if you're cooking for yourself. Where's Mrs Dowling?'

'She's spending the night with her sister. She'll be back by midday.'

'You've been alone in the house?'

Her delight at seeing him again was fading in the remembered disappointment at his lack of interest in her future. Perhaps he thought that, since he had given her a chance to get away from her brother, that was sufficient; and, in all fairness, probably it was.

All the same, she gave him a resentful look, and said with something of a snap, 'Well, of course.'

He was sitting at the table still, finishing off the toast. He said slowly, 'You're angry, aren't you? Left out on a limb—no job, no home, no future. Don't bother to deny it,' he finished blandly, 'I can see it for myself. You've been looking for work?'

She broke eggs with considerable force. 'Yes.'

'Well, don't. There is a job waiting for you at the hospital.' He took another bite of toast. 'They're desperate for nursing aides—you know what they are?'

'Vaguely.' She ignored the sudden leap of hope; she hadn't got the job yet, she might be quite unsuitable. Besides, she didn't know much about nursing.

'Monotonous work, mostly: getting beds made, fetching and carrying for the nurses, feeding patients, carrying bedpans, cleaning up when someone's sick, but, if you're good at these, in time you will get more skilled work. The pay seems quite good...' He mentioned a sum which was a good deal more than the Graingers had been paying her. 'You get cheap meals in the canteen and, if you want to live out, my housekeeper has a sister who lets lodgings.' He sat back in his chair. 'Has it struck you that we tend to meet in the early mornings? Hardly romantic...'

'I don't think I'm a romantic person,' observed Katherine, piling bacon on to a plate and topping it with eggs. 'And you don't need to be...'

'What do you mean?'

'Well, there's Dodie... I mean, well...' She paused, trying to find the right words. 'You've found someone to be romantic about, so you don't need to bother any more.'

He gave a great snort of laughter. 'Remind me some time to put you right about one or two things! I must say you have some strange notions.'

He began his breakfast as she sat down with her own plate. 'Well, what about this job at the hospital? Do you want it?'

She poured him more tea, and said soberly, 'Yes, please. That is, if I'll do.'

'Good, I'll let you have the particulars some time today.'

'Thank you for bothering, Dr Fitzroy.' She was brimming over with relief and excitement, but she spoke with her usual calm.

'Did you think that I'd washed my hands of you? No, don't answer that.' He finished his breakfast and sighed. 'Will you forgive me if I go? I'm due to start work very shortly.'

He got to his feet, and she followed him out of the kitchen. 'Mr and Mrs Grainger—they'll be all right? I'd got rather fond of them. As long as there is someone to look after them...'

'I shall make it my business to check on that. They were fond of you, too. They should never have gone on this visit, but Dodie persuaded them—and this Tom Fetter backed her up.'

She would have liked to have talked about that, but she could see that he wanted to leave. She opened the door and wished him goodbye. She stood at the open door, watching him drive away, thinking it would be wonderful to work near him and see him each day.

There was a phone call from the people at Stockbridge later that morning; a voice wanting to know when she would come. It seemed the owner of the voice was desperate— four children, home for the Christmas holidays, and an old granny to look after. Katherine explained with polite firm-ness that she already had a job, listened patiently to the moaning voice at the other end of the line and rang off. A fine thing, she told herself, if the hospital decided that they didn't want her, after all!

But it seemed that they did; Christmas holidays, 'flu and a sudden influx of patients had made it an urgent matter to enrol more help as quickly as possible. The rather severe voice asked her to go for an interview that afternoon and, if suitable, to be ready to start work a day or so later. It was usual, the voice went on, for several days to elapse while ref-erences were checked, but Dr Fitzroy had vouched for her.

Katherine reviewed her wardrobe, assembled a light lunch for herself and Mrs Dowling, and spent some time before the dressing-table glass, making the best of her appearance.

After a meal with that lady, she put on the brown coat and walked to the hospital.

She had no idea what to expect. She presented herself at the reception desk, and was led by a rather harassed clerk to the back of the hospital, an area of gloomy corridors and massive doors, relieved only by the busts of former consultants, each on his or her plinth. By the time they reached their destination she was beginning to regret ever having come; the place overawed her, and even the atmosphere—composed of a chilly dampness, old age and a faint hint of Jeyes fluid—was off-putting.

But she had no time to change her mind; the clerk tapped on a door, opened it and ushered her briskly inside.

The room was small, dark, and overcrowded by a vast desk bearing a large quantity of papers, two telephones and a tabby cat. Behind the desk sat the lady she had come to see—formidable in appearance, with a vast bosom straining against her severe dress and severe hairstyle, but she had a kind face and she was smiling. Katherine took heart and advanced a step or two.

'Sit down, Miss Marsh. Dr Fitzroy has told me all about you, and I think that the best thing is for you to come here and work for a month and see if you like the job. I must warn you that it's hard work; we're short of staff and you may find the routine boring. Your salary...' She refreshed her memory from the papers before her, then mentioned a sum which seemed magnificent to Katherine. 'Of course, we don't usually take girls like this, but Dr Fitzroy recommends you highly, and we really are desperate.' She bent forward to stroke the cat. 'Do you need time to think it over?'

'No, thank you. I do need work badly, and Dr Fitzroy

seemed to think that I might do. I'll come when you want me to.'

'Good. There will be forms to fill in and so on. Perhaps you could do that on your way out—reception will tell you where to go, and shall we say the day after tomorrow? I will let you know where to report for duty and at what time. You do understand that nothing is binding for the first month? You can leave with a week's notice on either side.' She nodded majestically and Katherine got up, put her chair tidily back against the wall and made her way back to the reception desk. Her head full of directions, she went off again to find the office where she was to fill in the forms; she got lost once or twice, and it was considerably later by the time she was ready to leave. She was making her way rather uncertainly along a narrow passage when she ran full tilt into Dr Fitzroy.

He put out a hand to steady her, remarking, 'Ah, there you are. Everything settled?'

'Yes, thank you. I've just filled in lots of forms...'

He said kindly, 'Splendid! I asked my housekeeper if her sister had any rooms to let. She has; if you'd like to call round there she will fix you up—unless you want to live in the hospital?'

'Oh, I'd love a room of my own.'

'Yes, well, here's the address.' He fished out a pen and a notebook and scribbled in it, tore out the page and gave it to her. 'Say that I sent you. Let me know if you need any help.'

He nodded, and she could see that he was already thinking about something else. She murmured, 'Thank you,' and moved away to be stopped by his, 'How are you off for money? Did the Graingers pay you? Have you enough to see you through until pay day?'

'Yes, thank you.'

His 'Good, good,' was uttered in an absent-minded fashion, and his smile was vague, even though kind. She watched him stride off, vowing to herself that never, never would she ask him for help. He had been kind, and offered practical help when she needed it, but she wasn't going to make a nuisance of herself. She watched lovingly until he had gone, and then took herself out of the hospital and into the streets, intent on finding the address he had given her.

It was a small, neat house, in a row of similar dwellings quite close to the cathedral, although the narrow little street was quiet. She knocked on the door and a cosy, middle-aged woman opened it. Before Katherine could speak, she said, 'You'll be the young lady Dr Fitzroy told me about. Come in out from the cold and I'll show you the room.'

She led the way upstairs, talking over her shoulder as she went. On the landing, she said apologetically, 'It's on the top floor—used to be an attic, but I had it done up a bit, and there's a lovely view...'

It was quite large, with a sloping ceiling and a dormer window overlooking the nearby close. The furniture was simple but comfortable, and the floor was carpeted. There was a washbasin in one corner and a small gas fire, and in the opposite corner an old-fashioned gas cooker with two rings and a grill, and above it shelves neatly stacked with china and a few pots and pans.

'You can have a hot meal downstairs, but get your own breakfast here. Bathroom's downstairs and there's always plenty of hot water.'

She studied Katherine's face. 'Going to work at the hospital, are you, miss? Nursing aide? You'll not be earning all that much, then?' She named the rent and added, 'That'll include a good hot meal, baths and the use of the washing machine once a week. There's an iron when you need it, just as long as you ask first. There's only three others here—two elderly ladies, and a lady clerk from the post office.'

'Oh, I'll take it, Mrs...?'

'Mrs Potts. Mr Potts passed on two years ago.'

'I think it's very nice here, Mrs Potts, and I'd like to rent the room. Do you want a month's rent now?'

'A week only, and a week's notice on either side. When do you want to come?'

'Tomorrow? In the afternoon?' As they went back down-stairs, she said, 'I'm not sure, but I believe I have to do night duty from time to time.'

'I'll give you a key, and you can come and go as you please.' Mrs Potts eyed her severely. 'I only let to the decent sort of person I can trust with the door key.'

Katherine handed over a week's rent, and took herself back to the Graingers' house to take a substantial tea with Mrs Dowling and speculate over her future.

The next day, she bade Mrs Dowling goodbye with some regret; they had become not exactly friends, but at least they respected each other, and Mrs Dowling had been grudgingly grateful for the running to and fro Katherine had done for her. Bidden to have tea with the housekeeper when she was free, Katherine agreed; she had made no friends since she had been in Salisbury, but until now she hadn't had much time for that. Now she felt rather lonely. But not for long, she told herself bracingly, there would be other girls like herself working in the hospital.

It wasn't far to Mrs Potts', but her cases were heavy; she was glad to put them down on the doorstep and ring the bell. Mrs Potts opened the door, helped her upstairs with the cases, told her that there was tea in the pot downstairs, pointed out that a fifty-pence piece would provide her with warmth from the gas fire, and left her to look around her new home.

There had been a letter from the hospital that morning, telling her to report for work at eight o'clock in the morning. She was to go first to the office, where someone would take her to collect her uniform and show her the ward she was to work on. She had gone straight out and bought a cheap alarm clock, and carefully calculated how long it would take her to walk to the hospital. There was a back way through a car park which would save a lot of time. She had bought tea and a loaf and butter, too, and perhaps Mrs Potts could get the milkman to leave her some milk... She tapped on the kitchen door and went in.

Mrs Potts sat her down at the table, poured her a cup of tea and pressed a plate of scones upon her. 'There's supper at eight o'clock,' she explained. 'We have it here. I've put a jug of milk on the side for you. You've got some groceries?'

Katherine said thank you, she had, but she would be glad if she could have milk delivered, and added, 'I have to be at the hospital at eight o'clock tomorrow morning. They didn't say how long I would be working.'

'If you're not back by supper time, which I doubt, I'll keep something hot for you. Now, you go and unpack, and come down sharp at eight o'clock. We sit down punctually.'

Katherine unpacked, set her brushes and comb and modest make-up on the dressing-table under the window, hung her scanty wardrobe in the cupboard at one end of the room, arranged the photos of her parents on the narrow little mantelshelf, and sat down on the bed to survey her surroundings.

With the gas fire lit, it looked quite cosy, and on pay day

she promised herself she would go to Woolworth's and buy a pretty table lamp. She had been lucky, she reflected; she had a job, a room of her own and more money than she had had for some years. Life wasn't going to be quite as comfortable as it had been with the Graingers, but a great deal better than it had been with her brother...

At eight o'clock she went downstairs, where she met her fellow lodgers. The elderly ladies greeted her politely; Miss Fish and Mrs Dunster, they looked rather alike—faded, genteel and faintly suspicious of her. Miss Kendall, on the other hand, shook hands firmly, declared that it would be pleasant to have someone of her own age in the house, and begged Katherine to call her Shirley. She was a big girl, excessively jolly, who had very little to say to her fellow lodgers, just as it was obvious to Katherine that they had very little to say to her. It was Mrs Potts who, as it were, leavened the dough, keeping up a cheerful conversation first with one side and then the other, so that, even though they didn't actually address each other, they appeared to do so. Katherine was seized upon almost at once as a kind of go-between, with the two elderly ladies plying her with guarded questions as to her family and her work, and Shirley drowning their mild remarks with questions of her own, while Mrs Potts filled in the pauses with some prosaic remark about the weather.

The food was excellent; Mrs Potts was a super cook, and her steak and kidney pudding, followed by apple tart and custard, bore witness to that. Katherine hadn't realised that she was so hungry, and sat back with a satisfied sigh as Mrs Potts put the teapot on the table and handed round cups of strong tea. She had just finished hers when Mrs Potts went to answer the doorbell, and came back almost at once.

'For you, Miss Marsh. Dr Fitzroy—I've put him in the front room.'

A forbidding apartment, seldom used except for interviewing lodgers, sitting in on Sunday afternoons and entertaining guests. Katherine went down the narrow hall and opened the door. The doctor was standing before the curtained window, looking very large and excessively tall. He turned round as she went in and his 'Hello, Katherine' was friendly. 'Having suggested that you should come here, I felt it my duty to come and see if you are comfortable,' he explained, and gave her a kindly smile.

She stood just inside the door, her heart beating a great deal too fast, trying to keep her breathing at a normal rate. He might have come from a sense of obligation, but at least he had come. She beamed at him widely.

'That's awfully kind of you, Dr Fitzroy. I'm very happy with everything here. I've a lovely room, and Mrs Potts is so kind and the food is super.'

'Good. You know where you have to go tomorrow?'

'I had a letter from the hospital. I'm—I'm very grateful to you for all you've done. You have no idea how marvellous it is to have a job and so much money, and also somewhere to live...' She added in her quiet voice, 'I'll work hard, I promise you, and not let you down.'

He stared down at her, not smiling. 'I don't imagine you have ever done that, Katherine—let anyone down. I'm glad to hear that you are settled in here; if you need anything or you want help at any time, please come to let me know.' He sighed. 'You deserve better than this.'

She gave him an astonished look. 'But I'm not trained for anything, and if it hadn't been for you I wouldn't have this job. Please don't worry about me; I shall do very well, and I really am happy.'

Well, not happy, she told herself silently; how could one be happy when one loved a man and knew that he would never feel the least urge to love one in return? Their paths through life were widely separated, and she must never forget that.

He made a small gesture, and she felt that he was impatient to be gone. 'It was kind of you to call,' she said briskly, 'and if I need help I'll let you know, but I'm quite sure I'll be all right.'

She held out her hand, and he shook it and went on holding it. 'You're rather small,' he observed.

'But tough.' She pulled her hand gently to free it, and found it clasped more tightly...

When he bent and gently kissed her cheek, she held her breath. Before she could think of anything to say he had gone, his goodbye echoing from the closing door.

She went back to the kitchen presently and drank her cooling tea, helped to clear the table and then went up to her room. He hadn't meant anything by the kiss, she knew that, but it had unsettled her. She undressed, went down to the landing below, had a bath and then climbed into bed. She had a lot to think about, but she went to sleep at once, her head full of Dr Fitzroy.

Chapter 5

The hospital, when Katherine reached it the next morning, was a subdued hive of activity. She was whisked from reception to the office, handed over to a stern-featured lady in a white overall, and fitted out with her uniform: biscuit-coloured stripes, an armful of aprons and several thick paper caps. She was told to change and, while she did so, the stern lady made up a cap for her. The uniform didn't fit very well, there seemed to be a good deal of extra material everywhere. Katherine gathered it into the striped belt and pinned a cap on her head. Her mentor shook her head in a despairing way, and led her up and down a vast number of corridors before pushing open swing doors. 'You're to work here,' she said, and went away.

The doors led to a wide corridor with more swing doors at its end and doors on either side. There wasn't much point in standing there doing nothing, Katherine decided, so she advanced along the corridor, peering in the half open doors as she went. Which brought her to Sister's office.

She knocked on the door and went in, and the woman

at the desk looked up. She had severe features, scraped-back hair and eyes like dark pebbles, and Katherine knew at once that Sister wasn't pleased to see her. All the same, she said politely, 'I was told to come here to work, Sister. Katherine Marsh.'

Sister put down her pen. 'The girl Dr Fitzroy recruited. Why I should have you, I don't know; probably he didn't want to find you under his feet in his own wards. Have you done any nursing?'

'No, Sister. Just looking after Mr and Mrs Grainger, an elderly couple, and before that I looked after children.'

'Well, at least you're a pair of hands. You don't look very strong.'

Katherine didn't answer that, but waited for Sister to speak again. 'You're quite untrained, Staff Nurse will show you how best you can help in the ward. You are here on a week's trial, Miss Marsh. It's up to you to do your best.'

She bent her head over her desk, and Katherine got herself into the corridor again. Find Staff Nurse? Walk on to the ward? Tear off her apron and run like mad? Her problem was solved for her. A girl, dressed in a similar uniform to her, came bouncing out of one of the doors. She stopped when she saw Katherine.

'You're the new auxiliary,' she cried joyfully. 'Am I glad to see you! What's your name?'

'Katherine. I don't know where to go...'

The girl put out an arm and towed her along at a great rate to the doors at the end of the corridor. 'Miranda— everyone calls me Andy.' She beamed widely, and Katherine smiled back. Her companion was a big girl, with a mop of hair upon which her cap perched precariously, and a round, cheerful face. 'You don't need to know about nursing, not to start with, but it helps if you can do two things at once, carry trays, and clear out the sluice room!'

They were through the doors by then, to fetch up beside a small, fairylike creature in a blue dress with a red belt and a silver buckle. She was talking to a nurse, but she paused to say to Andy, 'Mr Sims hasn't had his paper again...' She cast her eyes over Katherine and went on, 'Ah, the new auxiliary. Good. Have you seen Sister?'

She smiled at Katherine in a friendly way, and Katherine, still feeling that she would like to turn and run for it, smiled back.

'Yes, Staff Nurse, she said that you would show me where to work.'

'Never nursed before? Not squeamish? Will you go with Andy and help with the bottle round? Then strip beds with her. When I've got five minutes, I'll give you an idea of the routine. In the meantime, just cling to Andy.'

Katherine had no idea of what a bottle round was; Andy explained rapidly as they went down the ward to the sluice room. It was a large ward, its beds filled, and its occupants, those who felt well enough, called out cheerfully as they went.

Andy threw replies to them in passing, and in the sluice said, 'They like to pass the time of day, but be careful when Sister's on the ward, she's man's natural enemy.' Andy handed Katherine something that looked like a milk bottle container. 'Got a boyfriend?'

'No, I don't know anybody in Salisbury.'

'Dr Fitzroy knows you, doesn't he? Weren't you looking after some private patients of his? He's a dream, isn't he? On the medical side, of course, so we hardly ever see him over here.'

Which perhaps, reflected Katherine soberly, was just as well. The morning was a cataclysm of half-understood work: she made beds, not very well, getting in a fearful muddle with the corners, urged on by the kindly Andy; she helped with the mid-morning drinks, scuttled up and down the ward fetching and carrying various odds and ends for any number of people, had to heave patients out of bed and in again, and always with Andy near at hand to urge her on or breathe encouragement. By lunch time she was tired, but by no means downhearted; if everyone else there could keep on their feet and know what they were about, then so could she. Not that she *was* always sure what she was about!

She was sent to first dinner with Andy, and told by Sister that she was to go off duty at five o'clock. 'You will work for a week with Miss Snell,' said Sister, indicating Andy, 'and after that you will work alternate duties with her. Come to the office when you report off duty, and I will tell you your duties for the week.'

'Do we always work like this?' asked Katherine, trotting along beside Andy on their way to the canteen. 'I mean, on the go the whole time?'

Andy laughed. 'This is a quiet week—next week's take-in. You should just see us then.' She was still explaining take-in when they reached the canteen.

'Take a tray—it's boiled beef and dumplings—I know one of the cooks. Have you got some money?'

Katherine nodded and watched her plate being piled high. Very good value for money, she reflected when she received it.

'Don't bother with a pudding,' advised Andy. 'Get a cup of tea.'

They found places at a table which was already well

filled. Katherine was introduced to the half-dozen girls already there, and smiled a little shyly at them. They were a friendly bunch, full of helpful advice and hospital gossip as they gobbled their meal. 'A pity that you're with that old tyrant,' commented one of them. 'Sister Beecham is a tartar—talk about throwing you in at the deep end...'

There wasn't time to answer all their questions, much less ask any of her own; she found herself setting off again at Andy's heels, back to the ward. Afterwards, Sister went to second dinner and the ward wore a relaxed air in consequence.

Staff Nurse, busy with the medicine round, nodded cheerfully as they reported back on duty. 'There's some tea in the pot if you want a cup,' she told them. 'Only look sharp about it. Andy, take Mr Crouch down to X-ray as soon as you've had it; take Katherine with you so that she'll know where to go, and then make up the two end beds.' She turned back to her trolley and the student nurse with her, and Andy and Katherine hurried out to the kitchen where the teapot stood warming on the stove.

'We don't do this when Sister's on duty,' explained Andy quite unnecessarily.

X-ray was miles away, or so it seemed to Katherine, whose feet were aching madly, but once there she found it quite interesting. The patient was to have an operation for a duodenal ulcer, and needed a barium meal to confirm the surgeon's diagnosis. He was a cross old man, who contradicted everyone and found fault with each of them in turn. Half-way through the examination, Andy was sent for, leaving Katherine to stay with him. Presently, when the business was over, she was told to escort the trolley and porters back to the ward.

They were in the long corridor leading to the lifts when she saw Dr Fitzroy, accompanied by two young doctors in white coats, coming towards her.

He looked different—older and serious, very elegant in his dark, beautifully cut suit, his head slightly bent as he listened to his two companions' earnest talk. But he looked up as Katherine's little procession reached them, and gave her a brief, friendly smile. She wanted to smile too, but she thought she had better not. One of the nurses at dinner had been talking about him—he was important, a senior consultant, and he would be a professor in no time at all. 'And some lucky girl will get him,' the nurse had observed with ill-concealed envy. Katherine hadn't heard the rest of it. Crammed in the lift with the trolley, the patient and the porters, she reflected that the lucky girl was to be Dodie.

Five o'clock came at last, and with feet like hot coals she went to Sister's office. Staff Nurse was there too, and gave her a friendly little nod, but Sister merely looked up, studied Katherine for a moment and said, 'You seem to be a good worker—time will show, however. Now, Miss Marsh, you're off duty…'

They were already near the end of the week, so she wouldn't get any days off until the following week—Thursday and Friday. In the meantime, she would have the same working hours as Andy: two days from noon until eight o'clock, two eight in the morning until five o'clock in the afternoon and, on the day before her days off, from eight o'clock until four in the afternoon. She would be paid on Thursday morning of the following week, and if she wished she could go to the office to collect her wages between the hours of ten and twelve o'clock.

She would get up early, thought Katherine happily, collect all that money and do her household shopping, join the local library, do some window shopping...

'I hope you are attending, Miss Marsh? It may be necessary from time to time to change your duty times. You must be prepared for that.'

Katherine said, 'Yes, Sister,' in her gentle voice, and smiled because she was, for the moment, happy. Sister very nearly smiled back. She stopped herself just in time; really, the girl wasn't at all the usual type—she hoped she would settle down and learn to do her work well.

'You may go, Miss Marsh,' she said austerely.

Katherine let herself in with the key Mrs Potts had given her, and went up to her room, kicked off her shoes, lit the gas fire and, resisting a strong desire to get into bed and sleep for ever, undressed and went down to the bathroom. The water was hot and plentiful; she lay in it blissfully, making mental lists of all the things she would buy. Only the cooling water got her out finally.

At supper, Mrs Potts wanted to know how she had got on.

'I enjoyed it,' said Katherine, and meant it. 'My feet ached, but I'll get used to that in a day or two.' She didn't say more than that, because Miss Fish and Mrs Dunster chorused a genteel objection to the discussion of one's work at the supper table. Shirley Kendall gave a loud laugh at that, and remarked rudely that honest workers had a right to do what they liked in their free time, and if they wanted to talk about their day's work, they should do so. 'At least some of us earn an honest living,' she remarked loudly.

The elderly ladies bridled at that, and Mrs Potts firmly put a stop to what might have been turned into an argument by offering second helpings.

Katherine went back to her room when the meal was finished, eased her feet into slippers and drew the elderly easy chair close to the fire. Half an hour's reading of the newspaper one of the patients had offered her would be very pleasant before bedtime. She yawned widely, and remembered with pleasure that she wasn't on duty until noon the next day. She would go to the shops and add to her small stock of groceries and have a look at the table lamps—not to buy of course, that would have to be the following week. She made another list, this time of things she needed to make her room a home, but she didn't quite finish it because she allowed her thoughts to wander. Where, she wondered wistfully, did Dr Fitzroy live, and in what kind of house? One day, when she knew Mrs Potts better, she would ask. On second thoughts, she decided against this; it was intruding into his private life.

She was up early, tidied her room, ate her frugal breakfast and took herself to the shops. Her few household needs were quickly dealt with; it would have been nice to have had a cup of coffee but, with an eye on her almost empty purse and two days off to allow for, she contented herself with window shopping.

She was peering into Jaeger's shop window, taking in all the stylish details of their winter coats and wondering if she would ever possess one, when she became aware of someone beside her. Dodie, looking as usual like a model in one of the glossier magazines. She also looked extremely cross.

She wasted no words in greeting. 'You ungrateful girl!' she said in an angry whisper. 'The trouble I took to phone those people at Stockbridge, and you didn't even bother to go for an interview.'

'Well, I didn't need to,' Katherine pointed out reasonably. 'I've got a job here. And I did tell you not to bother.'

'What sort of a job? Here? In Salisbury?'

It seemed that Katherine might be wiser not to say. She said calmly, 'Yes, here—looking after people.'

'All you're fit for,' observed Dodie unforgivably.

'Probably that's true,' agreed Katherine equably. 'Have you heard from Mr and Mrs Grainger?'

'Oh, they're all right. They won't stay with Tom, of course.' Her lovely blue eyes narrowed. 'But don't imagine that you'll get back your job with them, I've already arranged for a woman to be their companion when they return.'

'Why did you want me to go?' asked Katherine. She sounded politely interested, although her heart was thumping with rage.

'Jason—Dr Fitzroy was a fool to employ you in the first place—acted on the spur of the moment, out of pity, I suppose. He was only too glad when I fixed things so that you had to leave; saved him the embarrassment of getting rid of you.' She laughed nastily. 'I can't think why I'm bothering to tell you this.'

'Well, you're enjoying it, aren't you?' Katherine turned on her heel and dived into Country Casuals next door; there was a door at the other end of the shop which brought her into a shopping arcade where she could lose herself in the crowds. She didn't believe Dodie's spiteful remarks, but they had left a tiny doubt in her mind, none the less. Dr Fitzroy had made no effort to object when the Graingers had broached their plans, although he *had* found her another job. She looked at a few more shops, but her pleasure had gone; besides, it was time for her to go back to her attic with her shopping.

Whatever he had thought, she consoled herself, he had helped her to get a job and somewhere to live.

The days passed quickly. She had got the hang of the work within the week and, although she found it hard, she enjoyed it. Her feet ached and she was too tired to do much by the time she went off duty, but that was something Andy assured her would improve with time. Her keenly anticipated days off came at last, and with them pay day. She spent a lovely morning choosing a pretty lamp, having coffee and planning her days. She was still rather short of money. She had paid Mrs Potts the rent and laid out a carefully calculated sum on food, a hot-water bottle and dull things like tights; the rest she was going to save for an eiderdown for her bed and a thick sweater and skirt. She had seen exactly what she wanted. She bore the lamp back, made the tea, and opened a tin of beans and had her lunch by the gas fire.

It was a cold day but dry; she put on the new coat presently and went out again. A good walk would be very pleasant, right round the close perhaps, and then back for tea, and tomorrow she would go to the cathedral again and explore the Chapter House thoroughly.

Her way took her past the Graingers' house and along the narrow street towards the King's House.

Dr Fitzroy, standing at the window of his drawing-room, staring into the street, saw her, head down against the wind, her small, lonely figure the only thing moving there. He went to his front door and stood in the porch, and when she was near enough crossed the street.

Katherine stopped short as he fetched up in front of her. She didn't speak, only stared up at him in surprise. He said kindly, 'Hello, Katherine. Enjoying days off?'

A little colour had come into her cheeks. 'Yes.' She would

have to say more than that, she thought. 'It's just the day for a good walk.' Her motherly instinct overcame her awkwardness. 'You ought not to stand here in the cold... You've got no coat on.'

He smiled again then. 'Then I'll go indoors again, but you must come with me—'

Her 'No, thank you, sir,' was rather sharper than she had intended, but he didn't appear to notice that. 'Then I'll come with you, if I may. The dogs need a run.'

He took her arm, went back to the house and ushered her inside. 'Go into the sitting-room,' he suggested, and opened a door in the wide hall. 'I'll only be a moment.' Katherine waited, trying to overcome her surprise at finding he lived in the very house she had always admired.

He was as good as his word. A moment later he was back again, this time in a thick jacket and accompanied by two golden labradors. There hadn't been enough time to examine the room properly, but she had an impression of warmth and comfort and well-polished furniture.

'Charlie—and this is Flo, and if you find their names peculiar I must explain that one of my small nieces named them.' They went into the hall and he opened the street door. 'Which way were you going?' He glanced at her sensible shoes. 'I usually go past the King's House and then cross into the open ground—the dogs like that.'

She hadn't been that way; even on a gloomy winter's afternoon it was a pleasant walk, and the doctor laid himself out to entertain her. Dodie's spiteful words faded before his friendly, casual talk. She found that she was completely at ease with him and, skilfully led on by his careless questions, told him a good deal more about her life with Henry than she realised.

It was already dusk as they turned back, and almost dark when they reached the house. Katherine bent to pat the dogs. 'I enjoyed our walk, Dr Fitzroy.' Some of the ease she had been feeling had gone, and she was bent on going quickly. 'I…'

She wasn't given the chance to go. 'So did I. Will you share my tea?'

He took her arm and marched her into his house, and an elderly woman came from the back of the hall. She was undoubtedly Mrs Potts' sister, but without the briskness.

'There you are, sir. Tea's in the drawing-room. I'll wipe those dirty paws before they muddy my floors.' She beamed at Katherine. 'I'll have that coat, miss. There's a cloakroom here…' She bustled Katherine across the hall and into a small room, fitted, as far as Katherine could see, with everything a woman could possibly want if she needed to improve her appearance.

Which she undoubtedly did; the cold and wind had given her a fine colour now, but her hair was all over the place. She used the comb laid ready there, cast a critical eye over her appearance, and went back to the hall.

'In here,' called the doctor from a half opened door, and as she reached it he opened it wide. The dogs were already there, sitting before a blazing fire and, curled up on a little stool to one side of the fireplace, was a rather battered-looking cat with a torn ear, and fur in a variety of colours.

'Joseph.' The doctor waved a large hand at the animal.

'Oh, of course—his coat.' She bent to stroke the animal, who purred loudly.

'Have this chair.' He pulled forward a small, velvet-covered armchair. 'Mrs Spooner is bringing tea. I seldom have time for it, but it's one of the nicest meals, don't you think?'

She had a momentary vision of tea in her room; the serviceable brown teapot and pleasant, plain china and a plate of buttered toast. She agreed politely as she took in the delights of the tea table between them. A muffin dish, polished silver glinting in the firelight, wedges of buttered toast spread with what looked like anchovy paste, a plate of little cakes, another with a chocolate sponge oozing cream and, on a silver tray, a silver teapot and milk jug, flanked by delicate china cups and saucers. She could remember, years ago, her mother sitting beside a similar tea table.

The doctor, watching her wistful face, said cheerfully, 'Will you pour, Katherine?' When she had done so, and they had their muffins on their plates, he asked, 'Now, tell me, how do you like your new job?'

'Very much. There's another nursing aide on the ward—Andy—she's been so kind and patient. Sister's very stern, but I expect she has to be. Staff Nurse is kind, too—I don't talk to the student nurses much; I don't go to meals with them and there's no time to talk on the ward.'

'Good. You're not too tired at the end of the day?'

'Just my feet, and they'll be all right once they're used to it. I'm really very happy.'

He passed her the plate of toast and then helped himself. 'And Mrs Potts has made you comfortable?'

'Oh, yes.' She painted an exaggerated picture of the comforts of her room, at the same time aware of the subdued splendour of the room they were sitting in. It was low-ceilinged, with panelled walls hung with portraits and furnished with comfortable chairs, and old, beautifully polished furniture. The curtains had been drawn across the lattice windows, and the crimson brocade reflected the soft light from the table lamps scattered around. Well, she wasn't exactly fibbing, she assured herself, and he would never see her attic, anyway...

They were eating chocolate cake and laughing together about Joseph and the dogs when Katherine heard Mrs Spooner's voice in the hall, and a moment later the door opened and Dodie came in.

She stopped short half-way across the room. 'Well, well—what a picture of cosy domestic bliss!' She gave a little trill of laughter, but her voice had a nasty edge to it. She ignored Katherine and went and sat in a chair close to the doctor. 'Is there any tea left in the pot? I had the absurd notion that you might like to have some company for tea, but I see that you've got it already.'

The doctor had stood up as she went in, but now he sat down again, quite unruffled by the look of fury on her face. 'Katherine and I have had a delightful walk with the dogs.' He paused as his housekeeper came in with fresh tea. 'Any news of your grandparents?'

'Not that I know of.' Dodie shrugged her shoulders prettily. 'You know what old people are; I have an idea they'll be back here again before long. I've heard of a marvellous woman who will live with them.' She glanced at Katherine as though she had just remembered that she was there. 'Bad luck on you, but you've got work, haven't you?'

'How fortunate,' observed Dr Fitzroy smoothly, 'that you've got someone lined up, for Katherine is working at the hospital and doing very well...'

Katherine put down her cup and saucer. 'I'm very happy there,' she said to Dodie as she got to her feet. 'I must go now—thank you for my tea.'

Dr Fitzroy had got up, too; he went to the door with her and leaving it open followed her into the hall. 'Did Mrs

Spooner take your coat?' He took it from the housekeeper and helped her on with it. 'A very pleasant afternoon,' he told her in his calm way, 'we must do it again.'

A remark which Katherine put down to a polite piece of nonsense designed to put her at her ease. It had been a lovely few hours—almost, but not quite spoilt by Dodie.

Mrs Potts' kitchen, cosy though it was, seemed something of a let-down after the splendours of the doctor's drawing-room; Katherine joined in the chatter about Christmas while her thoughts were somewhere else. Was Dodie still at his house, she wondered, or were they spending the evening together, dining and dancing? Mrs Potts, repeating her enquiry as to whether Katherine would be working during the Christmas holiday, wondered why she was so dreamy.

'So sorry,' Katherine apologised. 'Yes, I'll be working on Christmas Day and Boxing Day, but I have Christmas Eve off. I don't mind at all, though. It isn't as though I have a family to go to.'

Mrs Potts, who had heard all about Henry from the doctor, said nothing to this; she liked the doctor and she was sorry for Katherine. 'Well, I'll be here,' she said cheerfully. 'Miss Kendall goes home, don't you, dear? But Miss Fish and Mrs Dunster will be here, too. I dare say you'll have a bit of fun at the hospital, Miss Marsh?'

'Oh, I expect so. Mrs Potts, would you mind very much calling me Katherine?'

'Well, now that you ask, I see no reason why I shouldn't. What do they call you at the hospital?'

'Oh, Sister always says Miss Marsh, but everyone else calls me Katherine. Some of the patients call me Katie.'

'Very familiar,' observed Miss Fish severely.

'Not really, they're only being friendly.' Miss Fish looked

about to argue the point, so Katherine changed the conversation smartly. 'We have a kind of bran tub for the staff presents on the ward, we each put in something. Has anyone any suggestions as to what I should get?'

The elder ladies had no hesitation in choosing nice white hankies, and Miss Kendall instantly countered that with lacy tights, while Mrs Potts voted for a nice headscarf.

None of these really appealed to Katherine; she wandered round the shops the next morning looking for something she would like to have herself. She found it; a little china vase, white, with violets painted on it. There was no price, but there would be no harm in asking.

She became aware that there was someone standing beside her. 'Christmas shopping?' asked Dr Fitzroy, and she nodded for, as usual, her breath had become really erratic at the sight of him. 'So am I. This, by the way is a young cousin of mine, Edward.'

She saw that there was someone with him. A much younger man, not much older than herself, with a cheerful face which wasn't quite good-looking, a shock of brown hair and an engaging grin.

'This is Katherine,' explained the doctor. 'She came to my help some weeks ago; she now works at the hospital.'

Edward shook hands. 'Nice to meet you. I'm staying over Christmas, perhaps we shall see something of each other.'

'Well, I don't expect so. I'm working...'

'You can't be working all the time?'

She smiled warmly at him. 'No.'

'Good. So we'll have an evening out and I'll tell you my life story.' He looked at the doctor, standing impassively by. 'Do you see a lot of each other?'

Dr Fitzroy and Katherine exchanged a glance. 'Hardly,'

said the doctor, 'but I'm sure I can manage to convey any message you might wish to send.'

'I could phone,' said Edward airily.

'Oh, no, you couldn't!' The look of horror on Katherine's face brought him up short. 'Sister doesn't allow phone calls.'

'Old dragon, is she? Just goes to show what happens to nurses if they stay long enough in hospital.'

Katherine went pink. 'Oh, but I'm not a nurse. I'm only an aide; that's between a ward maid and a new student nurse who doesn't know anything.'

Edward was unimpressed. 'Oh, good, you'll not get the chance to turn into a dragon.' He caught the doctor's glance and added, 'Oh, all right, Jason, I know you've no time to dally.'

They bade her goodbye, Edward with the declared intention of seeing her again, Dr Fitzroy with grave friendliness.

She stood there, where they had left her, thinking in a muddled way that it was the greatest of pities that Edward seemed to have taken to her at once, and Dr Fitzroy treated her with an impersonal courtesy which she found most unsatisfactory. She quite forgot about the vase, and wandered along, stopping here and there to appraise some particularly eye-catching garment; eye-catching in the sense that it would attract the doctor's eye—a piece of nonsense actually, for it would take several weeks' wages to pay for any one of them.

The spirit of Christmas was beginning to pervade the ward when she went back on duty the next day. Those patients who weren't actually flat on their backs were pressed into making paper flowers, paper chains and coloured crêpe-paper mats for the bed tables and locker tops. They would be the very devil to keep tidy and clean, observed Andy, but Sister, who considered herself artistic, always got carried away at Christmas.

'Had you ever thought of training as a nurse?' Andy asked Katherine as they made up empty beds. 'Me, I'd be no good, haven't even got O-levels, but I bet you've been to a good school.'

Katherine mitred a corner neatly. 'Oh, I don't think I'd do at all. I stayed home with my mother when I left school, and then I went to live with my brother and his wife for two years.'

'What did you do there? General dogsbody?'

'Well, yes, I suppose I was.'

'Then how did you escape, even if it's hardly a bed of roses here?'

Katherine explained, and when she had finished Andy said, 'Lord, what a bit of luck for you! And Dr Fitzroy's such a duck of a man...' She caught sight of Katherine's face and said quickly, 'Have you been to see your brother since you came here?'

'No, but I thought I'd go on my next days off; just to say hello—I wouldn't stay.'

'When Bill's away, you and I will have an afternoon off together if we can fix it.' Bill was her fiancé, a plumber by trade, who occasionally worked away from Salisbury. 'He's home for Christmas, and I've got Boxing Day off, so I'll go to his place and then he will come home with me.'

'That'll be nice.' Katherine sounded cheerful and thanked heaven that she was working over Christmas. On Christmas Eve she would be free to go into the city and mix with the crowds and feel part of them for a while, and she would be able to go to the midnight service. Everyone said that Christmas on the wards was quite fun...

The ward was quite busy: irascible old men with bronchitis and heart failure adding to the hazards of hernia repairs, duodenal ulcers and colostomies, and a sprinkling of younger ones with appendicitis, nasty injuries from their work or a car accident. Whether they liked it or not, Sister had them all working on Christmas decorations, so Katherine and Andy were in constant demand to give a hand, for the student nurses were too busy learning from their seniors, and they in turn were too busy with dressings and medicine rounds and all the complicated paraphernalia Katherine only half understood. The week went by with no sign of Dr Fitzroy; he seldom came on to the surgical side, but usually she caught a glimpse of him as she did errands to the various departments. Her days off came round once more and she decided she would pay her brother a visit; it was, after all, almost Christmas, and a season of good will.

She set off by bus in the afternoon, bearing small gifts and wearing her new coat and a neat corduroy hat to match it. It was a cold day, but the sun shone fitfully, and she was warmed by the knowledge that there was a week's wages in her purse. Even after paying the rent, there was money over—not much, but more than she had had for a long time.

She could hear the children shouting and screaming as she went up the garden path and, as she knocked on the door, Joyce's voice raised in anger. No one came to the door, so she knocked again, and this time Joyce answered it. 'What do you want?' she wanted to know snappily. 'Don't think you're coming back!'

'No. I don't think that. I brought your Christmas presents. May I come in?'

'I suppose so.' Joyce stood aside for her to go into the hall, and it was at once evident that Mrs Todd hadn't felt like doing the floors for some time, let alone a little dusting. The sitting-room was in a like state. Katherine itched to get her hands on the hoover and a couple of dusters, but it wasn't her business any more.

'Well,' said Joyce, 'let's have these presents. I can't stop to entertain you, I'm busy.'

'Could I see the children?'

Joyce shrugged. 'If you want to. A girl comes to look after them in the mornings, but I have to see to them when she goes home.' She shot Katherine a furious look. 'Thanks to you and your ingratitude.'

Katherine ignored that; she hadn't come to quarrel. She said reasonably, 'They're in the nursery? I'll go along...'

'Do. Don't stay long.'

They weren't particularly pleased to see her, but took their presents without thanks and tore off the wrappings. She had been silly to come, reflected Katherine, but all the same she felt sorry for the pair; they looked uncared-for and grubby, although healthy enough. She bade them an unheeded goodbye and went back to Joyce.

'I won't keep you, Katherine, and there's no point in you being here; Henry won't want to see you.' She studied Katherine's clothes. 'Still working, I suppose?'

'Yes.' She didn't tell Joyce that she had left the Graingers; she wouldn't be interested anyway. She had been stupid to come. 'I hope you all have a happy Christmas,' she said politely as Joyce urged her towards the door.

In the brief half-hour she had been indoors, the weather had changed: the sun had gone for good and the wind was biting. There was no bus for an hour and nowhere she could stay. She walked briskly down to the gate, and heard the door slam behind her. She would start walking. Luckily, she was wearing sensible shoes…

It was several miles until the road she was on joined the main road at Wilton; there would be a good chance of picking up a bus there. She quickened her pace; the sky was lowering and dusk wasn't far off. She had gone a mile or more when Dr Fitzroy's Bentley passed her, going the other way. He had been driving quite fast and she didn't think he had seen her. In any case, he was going in the opposite direction. She walked on, thinking about him; indeed, he occupied her thoughts incessantly.

The Bentley drew up beside her almost without a sound. 'Hop in quickly, I'm on the wrong side of the road,' advised the doctor, leaning over to open the door for her. When she was sitting beside him, he asked, 'Did you miss the bus?'

She shook her head; it was absurd that now that she was being driven back in comfort the desire to weep was overwhelming. The doctor cast her a swift glance—two tears were trickling down her cheeks.

He said with brisk friendliness, 'I'm just going home for tea. Do come and keep me company.'

She found her voice. 'You were going the other way.'

'Nothing important.' He went on cheerfully, 'How is the work going? Not too much for you? Edward will be at home, which is a good thing, for he intended coming round to see you this evening.'

Katherine sniffed, blew her prosaic little nose and said, 'How nice…'

'He's a good lad,' observed her companion easily, 'and looking forward to seeing something of you while he's here.'

They were through Wilton and going fast along the road into Salisbury. It was almost dark now, but the first of the

evening traffic had hardly got started. The doctor turned
away from the city centre before they reached it, and took
a series of small roads which brought him very close to his
house. There were lights shining from the ground-floor windows as he stopped the car outside his front door, got out and
opened Katherine's door for her, and by the time they had
crossed the pavement Mrs Spooner was waiting for them.
Katherine let out a little sigh of contentment as she entered
the hall. The house welcomed her, and Edward's cheerful
face peering round the drawing-room door made the welcome even warmer.

Chapter 6

Edward crossed the hall, flatteringly pleased to see her, and she had a moment's regret that he wasn't Dr Fitzroy, but in such thoughts lay an unhappiness she must avoid at all costs. She returned his exuberant greeting with a warm one of her own, while the doctor stood quietly watching them both.

'Let me have your coat,' he said softly. 'Mrs Spooner will bring tea.'

He let Edward do most of the talking as they had their tea, and presently excused himself on the plea of work, and went away to his study, leaving Edward detailing his life at the London hospital where he was a junior houseman.

Katherine listened and laughed and wished that the doctor would return. Perversely, when he did, she declared that she would have to dash, but not before accepting Edward's pressing invitation to have dinner with him on the following evening. What was more, he declared that he would walk back with her to Mrs Potts' house, so they set off presently, seen on their way by a strangely avuncular doctor. It was as though he had raised an invisible barrier between them, thought Katherine, walking briskly through the streets beside Edward. There always had been a barrier, she admitted to herself, but now suddenly he had turned into a much older man, prepared to be amused at their youthful chatter, but not wishing to be part of it. And yet he wasn't old—not even middle-aged...

Her wandering thoughts ceased abruptly when Edward, who had been rambling on about a nurse on night duty who had caught his fancy, said, 'Jason's a splendid chap, isn't he? A pity if he lets that Dodie get her claws into him. She's a smasher, I grant you, but sheer poison to a man like him.'

'Why?'

'My dear girl, all she thinks about is clothes and having a good time and spending money. Can't think what he sees in her...'

Katherine agreed with him, only silently; Dr Fitzroy needed a loving wife, one who would look after him and be his companion and let him get on with his work when he wanted to, but be there when he wanted her. She herself would be exactly right, but there were a number of drawbacks. She was what Joyce called homely; moreover, unlike a girl who had the means, she had none with which to disguise the homeliness. She didn't move in his circle, either, nor did she see any likelihood of ever doing so.

She parted from Edward at Mrs Potts' front door, promising to be ready when he called the following evening at seven o'clock. He gave her a brotherly hug, wished her a cheerful goodnight and strode off. A nice boy, she earnestly reflected, shutting the front door carefully behind her. Such a pity that her brother couldn't have been more like him.

Edward had suggested that they go to the Rose and Crown for dinner, a well-known hotel dating back some few hundred years, where the food was excellent and the service likewise, and where Katherine's one and only wool dress would pass muster. She went to bed well content, if a little wistful at the doctor's impersonal attitude towards her. It was just as well she wasn't at his house to overhear the conversation he had with his cousin.

Dr Fitzroy had listened to Edward's plans for the following evening. 'Nice little thing,' concluded that young man. 'A bit behind the times, though. Led a sheltered life, probably.'

The doctor was pouring drinks. 'Probably,' he agreed casually, 'and not much money to spend, so don't take her anywhere too dressy.'

'Why doesn't she do her training?'

'I think that probably she might do that once she has some self-confidence. She has been living with a rather overbearing brother and his wife.'

'Needs a jolt, does she?'

The doctor shook his head. 'A series of gentle prods, I think.' He went and sat down in his chair by the fire. 'I'm taking Dodie to a carol concert after dinner. Will you be able to amuse yourself?'

Christmas, vaguely distant, was suddenly there; Katherine helped hang chains of bright-coloured paper on the ward, arranged posies of paper flowers at the foot of each patient's bed, and assembled a series of paper hats for everyone to wear. It was hard work, but she enjoyed it; her evening out with Edward had done her a lot of good; it was pleasant to feel that someone liked her enough to take her out to dinner, besides she thought he was an amusing companion and treated her with the ease of a brother. He was full of good advice, too; she should start her training as a nurse, he counselled her, and get herself a secure future.

'I'm sure you'll get married,' he had told her airily, 'but you can't be sure of that, can you?' And, when she agreed, he added, 'Once you're trained, you could afford a small flat of your own, and get out and about a bit. Of course, it would take a few years, but you're still young enough.'

She had laughed then, but afterwards such a prospect looked bleak and lonely. Still, it would be better than being an aide. She had promised him that she would consider it.

Take-in week started a couple of days before Christmas and, as was only to be expected, the ward filled rapidly with victims of road accidents, those who had anticipated the festive season rather too soon and got themselves drunk enough to fall about and cut themselves on broken glass, or knocked themselves out against doors they thought were open and weren't. Over and above these were the normal quota of ulcers and hernias and appendices. Sister, not to be thwarted from her Christmas celebrations, moved the ill patients to one end of the ward, and chivvied the porters to hang holly wherever there was space for it.

Mrs Potts had done her best too, with a tree in the sitting-room window, lit at dusk, and the curtains undrawn so that the passers-by could enjoy it. There were mince pies at supper, too, and the promise of turkey on Christmas Day. Katherine was assured that hers would be kept hot in the oven until such time as she got back from the hospital.

Several of the nurses had Christmas leave, so her days off had been split: Christmas Eve and the day after Boxing Day, an arrangement which suited her very well. It would be cheerful on the ward, and there was the joy of knowing that she would have plenty to do. The prospect of spending Christmas Day in the company of Mrs Dunster and Miss Fish was daunting, and on Boxing Day Mrs Potts was going to spend the morning with her sister, Mrs Spooner.

The weather had turned very cold, with the prospect of snow. Katherine was about early on Christmas Eve, intent on enjoying the bustle in the shops. And since she had some money in her pocket she intended to have her lunch out, and should she see a pretty dress she would buy it. Edward had suggested that they might have another evening out before he left Salisbury...

The streets were already full of shoppers. Recklessly, she treated herself to coffee at Snell's, sitting lonely amid cheerful family parties and well-dressed matrons comparing shopping lists. Presently, she began her round of the shops. It had begun to snow, and the shops had turned on their lights. She went from one window to the other, choosing what she would buy if ever she had enough money. There were several boutiques where she might find a dress; she went to each of them in turn, searching for something she would be able to wear on any of the likely occasions when she might need to dress up a little. There weren't likely to be many of them, but the wool dress was no longer good enough; besides, she was sick to death of it. She finally decided on a fine wool crêpe dress, paisley patterned in several shades of amber and dark green. It was plain, but it fitted her well, and the price was right. Well satisfied with her purchase, she had coffee and a sandwich at a snack bar, and combed the cheaper shops for shoes to go with the dress. She found these too—plain black leather, because she would be able to wear them with the few clothes she had, but they were high-heeled and suited her small feet.

Well pleased with herself, she bought crumpets for her tea and went back through the snow to her room, where she lit the gas fire, drew the curtains and toasted the crumpets. When she had had her tea she tried on the dress and shoes, craning her neck to see as much as possible of herself in the looking-glass, before putting them away and getting into the wool dress again, and going down to supper. Miss Kendall had gone, and Miss Fish and Mrs Dunster were hardly in a festive mood, but Mrs Potts produced boiled ham and parsley sauce, with coffee to follow and, since it was Christmas, mince tarts. After the two elderly ladies had gone back to their rooms, Katherine stayed behind and helped Mrs Potts with the dishes and told her about the new dress over a second cup of coffee.

'A shame you have to work on Christmas Day,' declared Mrs Potts. 'It didn't ought to be allowed. There'll be a drop of hot soup for you on the stove when you get back from the cathedral. And mind you get straight to bed—it'll be late enough.'

Katherine thanked her and agreed meekly, although what she was supposed to do to keep her out of her bed at that hour of night was beyond her. She went back to her room and laid the small gifts she had for Mrs Potts and her fellow lodgers ready on the table, and then sat down by the fire to read until it was time to go to the midnight service. She didn't read for long though. She had barely glimpsed Dr Fitzroy during the previous week, but that didn't stop her thinking about him.

The snow had stopped by the time she left the house, but it lay thick on the pavements and garden walls along the side streets she walked through. The close was a vast white blanket, its paths already filled with those going to the cathedral, which was already almost full. Katherine found a seat to one side, close to the medieval clock, hemmed in by an old gentleman in a hairy tweed suit, with a resounding cough, and a haughty matron who overflowed on to Katherine's chair. Not that she minded; there was a distinct feeling of goodwill and a happy peacefulness all around her, so it was impossible to feel lonely.

It was long past midnight as she made her way through the crowds leaving the cathedral, and she started off briskly along the snowy path towards North Gate, prudently keeping to the main streets. She was almost at the Gate when she was brought to an abrupt halt by Dr Fitzroy's voice.

'I thought I saw you as we left the Cathedral. Come back and have a warm drink before you go to bed?' He had put a hand on her arm, and she saw that Edward was on the other side of her, and Dodie, looking furious, was just behind him.

She stammered a little, her heart thumping with the delight of seeing him. 'Oh—thank you, but I must get back. I'm on duty in the morning…'

She found herself turned round and walked smartly away from the High Street, in the direction of the doctor's house. 'All the more reason why you should enjoy a few minutes of Christmas now. I'll take you back, and at this hour half an hour more or less isn't going to make much difference.'

Edward had taken her other arm and the four of them walked arm-in-arm, the two men talking trivialities, deliberately setting out to make her laugh, while Dodie walked sullenly along. At the house, Mrs Spooner had the door open before they reached it, and in a flurry of good wishes and cheerful talk Katherine was ushered into the drawing-room. There was a roaring fire, with Charlie and Flo and Joseph lying side by side before it, and the table in the window was laden with several covered dishes, a small Christmas tree, bristling with lights and baubles, and a tray of drinks.

The doctor had taken Katherine's coat and urged her to sit down near the fire, and presently Mrs Spooner came in with a steaming jug.

'Hot chocolate,' she declared. 'Just right after that walk

back. And there's sausage rolls and smoked salmon and mince pies on the table.' She looked at the doctor. 'Will you see to the wine, Doctor?'

Edward had sat down beside Katherine and handed her a plate of food; Dodie had flung herself down on one of the sofas, declaring that she couldn't eat a morsel and would someone give her a drink? She didn't speak to Katherine at all, but her silence went almost unnoticed, for Mrs Spooner was handing round cups of chocolate and the doctor was filling glasses, keeping up a flow of small talk.

He brought a glass over to Katherine and said kindly, 'We shall have a party on New Year's Eve. Edward will be here, and he'd like you to come—he's scared to ask you, in case you refuse.'

Katherine bit into a mince pie. 'Why should I do that?' she asked in surprise. 'Oh, you mean if I'm on duty! Well, I'm not and I should love to come, thank you very much.' She added anxiously, 'Will it be a grand affair?'

Dodie answered her. 'You mean black ties? Of course it will. You'll have to mortgage your wages for weeks and buy something presentable—or not come.'

Both men looked at her. 'I say...' began Edward, but the doctor cut in, 'We'll forgive you for that silly joke, Dodie, since it's Christmas. I shouldn't drink any more if I were you.'

He sounded perfectly good-natured, but there was a tinge of ice in his pleasant voice, so that Dodie mumbled, 'Oh, can't anyone take a joke any more?' She got up, and with a defiant look at him, went to the table and refilled her glass.

The doctor took no notice, but sat down on the other side of the hearth and engaged Katherine in a gentle conversation which lasted until she had finished her chocolate, drunk a glass of champagne as a toast to Christmas and suggested quietly and a little hesitantly that she should go back to Mrs Potts. He didn't attempt to dissuade her; she wished Dodie goodnight and the compliments of the season, received a brotherly hug for Christmas from Edward and got into the doctor's car.

It was only a few minutes' drive; he drew up outside Mrs Potts' house and got out with her. 'I have a key,' said Katherine. 'Please don't bother…'

He took the key from her and opened the door, switched on the hall light and stood looking down at her. 'A very pleasant start to Christmas,' he observed, and watched the colour creep into her cheeks. 'And, I hope, a happy one for you, Katherine.' He bent and kissed her cheek, pushed her gently into the hall and closed the door. She stood listening to him driving away, and after a minute or two switched off the light and went upstairs to her room.

Her room was cold; she put the kettle on the gas ring and filled her hot-water bottle, then jumped into bed and with her chilly person curled around its warmth, was asleep before she could put two thoughts together.

It was still pitch dark when the alarm wakened her. She lit the gas fire, crept down to the bathroom and dressed rapidly before sitting by its warmth to eat her breakfast. There had been more snow in the night, bringing with it a stillness made even more apparent by the lack of early morning traffic, and when she let herself quietly out of the house her feet sank into white crispness. It seemed a pity to spoil it with footprints.

The hospital was humming with subdued activity, its windows lit, a kind of background buzz betraying the readying of patients before breakfast, trollies being wheeled round the wards, and the never ending toing and froing of the nurses. Katherine hurried to the changing room and five minutes later made her way to the surgical wing. To save time, she took a short-cut past the theatre block, nipping along smartly, secure in the knowledge that at that early hour there would be no ward sisters to eye her with suspicion or question her speed. She was level with the heavy swing doors which separated the theatres from the main corridors when they were flung open and Dr Fitzroy came out. He was immaculate; she had never seen him otherwise, but he was the last person she expected to see. She came to a slithering halt staring at him.

'Hello again, Katherine.'

He grinned at her from a tired face and she found her voice. 'Haven't you been to bed?' she asked in a shocked voice. 'Have you been here all night?'

'No, to the first question, yes, to the second.' He was standing idly beside her, and for the moment she had forgotten all about going on duty.

She said urgently, 'I hope you're going home now.' Her loving eyes searched his face. 'You're tired. You need a good breakfast and then a nap...'

The slight lift of his eyebrows sent the colour rushing to her face. She stammered, 'I'm late...' and almost ran from him. What a fool he must think her to be! She felt near to tears as she reached the ward, and Staff Nurse, on the point of telling her that she was almost five minutes late on duty, changed her mind; Katherine was a hard worker and didn't watch the clock, and after all it *was* Christmas Day.

Despite Sister's efforts to send home as many people as possible so that they might enjoy the festive season at home with their families, the ward had filled up. The student nurse with whom she was making beds gave her a quick résumé of the admissions during her day off and added, 'There was a bit of a flap on during the night, too—there were three RTAs—we got two of them, the other man died in the theatre. They called in Dr Fitzroy just after two o'clock, but the junior night nurse told me that after five hours they had to admit defeat.'

They smoothed the counterpane of the empty bed and turned to the next one, occupied by a middle-aged man who had had a gastrectomy three days previously, and was beginning to feel himself again. There was no chance to carry on their talk; he wished them a happy Christmas and they made silly little jokes about his diet while they made his bed. After that, Katherine went off to the sluice, and presently to the kitchen to help with the morning drinks.

The ward was in festive mood, even Sister had unbent sufficiently to wish everyone a happy Christmas and take part in the drawing of gifts from the bran tub in her office. Katherine, being the newest member of the staff, and also the most lowly, was last, which meant that there was no choice. She fished around and unearthed a small, flat packet; notelets—so useful, Staff Nurse pointed out kindly, for writing thank-you notes for presents.

Only Katherine hadn't had any presents.

The patients' dinner was the high spot of the day; the consultant surgeon, Mr Bracewaite, arrived with the turkey and, suitably aproned and crowned with a chef's cap, carved with the same precision he exhibited in the theatre. Katherine, trotting to and fro with plates, sitting patients up, cutting up food for those who weren't able to do so for themselves, kept out of his way. He had a reputation for being peppery and ill-tempered, and rarely spoke to anyone less senior than a ward sister, or, if he had to, a staff nurse. He did a hurried round after he had carved the turkey, and then went away to Sister's office to drink a glass of the excellent sherry he gave her each Christmas. With the disappearance of authority, the ward took on a festive air: crackers were pulled, paper hats were donned and the nurses took it in turns to go to the kitchen and pick bits off the turkey carcass. But this pleasant state of affairs didn't last long; Mr Bracewaite went away, and Sister summoned the two staff nurses and the senior of the student nurses into the office to eat their own lunch—sausage rolls and mince pies and a selection of sandwiches with a bottle of plonk. By the time it was Katherine's turn she was famished but, since it was time to settle the patients for their brief afternoon rest, she had to gobble her food and then rush round taking away pillows, filling water jugs and fetching and carrying for Sister and Staff Nurse. She was surprised when Sister told her that she might take an hour off so that she might tour the hospital and visit the other wards. Her companion was the most junior of the student nurses, a pretty girl who, once they were out of the ward, caught Katherine by the hand. 'There's someone I'm going to see,' she told her, her eyes sparkling. 'He's in the residents' wing, and if anyone wants to know, tell them I was with you all the time.'

She dashed away, leaving Katherine open-mouthed. The residents' flats had been pointed out to her when she first arrived; no one went there, she had been told sternly. If they did, the consequences would be dire. She watched the tail end of her companion disappearing along the corridor and then set out on her own.

She went to the medical wards, hopeful that she might see Dr Fitzroy, but he wasn't there. Common sense had told her that he wouldn't be. She went rather shyly round the ward, accepted a glass of something from a friendly nurse, and went along to the orthopaedic wards where she exchanged greetings with the numerous owners of broken limbs, and drank another glass of something in Sister's office. Then she made her way to ENT, where she ate a mince pie, before opening the swing doors into the children's ward.

She had no idea what she had been drinking, but whatever she had been offered mixed into a pleasant glow in her insides, making her feel remarkably carefree. She started down the ward, another mince pie in her hand, stopping to talk to the toddlers in their cots. She was at the end when she saw Dr Fitzroy sitting on one of the small beds, a baby tucked under one arm.

With sorrowful hindsight, much later, Katherine realised that it was the variety of drinks which had loosened her tongue so deplorably, but at that moment she didn't give it much thought. She advanced and said happily, 'Oh, hello, Jason. Shouldn't you be in bed?'

She smiled widely at him and he laughed a little, his eyes gleaming with amusement. 'Oh, but I had to carve the turkey, you know.' He upended the baby so that it faced her. 'See who this is? Our foundling, no less. Growing up into a splendid lad.'

She sat down beside him and took the baby from him. 'He's gorgeous. Has he been christened?'

'Oh, yes—Noel. It couldn't be anything else, could it?'

She tickled the baby under its chin and it smiled widely and windily. 'Did anyone find out who is the mother?'

'No, I'm afraid not.' He took the baby and put him tidily into his cot. 'Are you enjoying your Christmas?'

'Oh, yes, thank you, Dr Fitzroy.'

'You called me Jason. I rather liked that.'

She went very pink. 'Oh, I'm sorry, I can't think why…

that is, I've been given quite a lot to drink…so silly of me.' She stood up quickly and went on breathlessly, 'I hope you have a lovely evening when you get home! I must go, Sister said an hour.'

She went quickly down the ward and out of the doors at the far end, and he watched her small, neat figure dwindling. Almost pretty, he reflected, with those eyes, and now she had filled out with Mrs Potts' wholesome cooking.

It had been a long day, reflected Katherine, going back home through the snow, but she had enjoyed it, all except that last bit when she had met Dr Fitzroy. What a good thing she almost never saw him these days!

Mrs Potts was waiting for her; Miss Fish and Mrs Dunster had retired to their rooms, Christmas or no Christmas, but her landlady had set the table in the kitchen with a holly centrepiece and crackers, and within ten minutes had produced roast turkey and all the trimmings, urged Katherine to sit down and eat it, and sat down opposite to her. 'I reckon you had a busy day,' she invited, and listened while Katherine, between mouthfuls, told of her doings.

'And you're on duty again tomorrow? I call it a shame…'

'I don't mind a bit, Mrs Potts. It isn't as though I have anywhere to go, and the next day I'm free, anyway.'

She started on her pudding, suddenly sleepy, so that she was glad when Mrs Potts offered her a cup of coffee. 'When you've finished, you can have a bath and jump right into bed,' she told her comfortably.

Which was exactly what Katherine did, to fall asleep at once and dreamlessly.

She hadn't expected to get any off duty the next day, so it came as a pleasant surprise when, just after four o'clock, after the last of the visitors who had come for Boxing Day tea on the wards had gone, she was told by Sister that she might go off for the evening. 'You have worked very well,' conceded that lady, 'and it is your day off tomorrow.' She nodded dismissal and Katherine skipped away, intent on getting out of the hospital before some disastrous happening should prevent her leaving.

Usually she came and went through the car park at the back of the hospital and a series of small streets, but there would be little traffic and the main streets were bright with decorations and lights, a small sop to her unconscious wish to be part of the Christmas scene. She pushed the heavy door open and crossed the courtyard, packed with cars, and made for the street, planning her day off as she went. There was no point in getting up too early, so she would enjoy the rare pleasure of breakfast in bed and then go for a walk. She reviewed the areas as far away from Dr Fitzroy's house as possible, and decided that she might walk to Alderbury, three miles away to the south-east of Salisbury, remembering going there years ago when her father was alive. There was an inn there, she would treat herself to a snack lunch and walk back to have her tea by the fire... She hadn't noticed Dr Fitzroy's car creep up beside her and stop.

He wound down the window. 'Off duty? So am I—hop in and come and have some tea.' He looked at her tired face. 'You can curl up by the fire and go to sleep if you want to.' He had leant across and opened the door for her, and with only the faintest of objections she got in beside him. To be with him, even for half an hour, would be heaven, made even more heavenly by the prospect of tea. She said in her calm little voice, 'Do you have to work on Boxing Day, too?'

'Only when I need to—I shall make up for it by having a day off tomorrow. Edward will be leaving in a few days; if the weather's good I think I might drive him over to Stourhead, it should be looking splendid in the snow.'

'Does he plan to stay in London?'

'Only until such time as he needs to get some experience. He wants to be a GP eventually, in this part of the world.'

The doctor drew up in front of his house and got out to help her plough through the snow which the wind had piled into small drifts along the pavement. He unlocked his front door and urged her inside to pleasant warmth and comfort and Edward's pleased welcome, dogs barking and Mrs Spooner coming silently to lead Katherine away to tidy herself.

They had tea round the fire, muffins and rich fruitcake and featherlight scones with butter, while Edward talked. He was a great talker, and an amusing one, too; the doctor sat in his huge chair, the dogs at his feet, and encouraged Edward gently so that presently Katherine was laughing at his outrageous stories and feeling very much at her ease.

A happy state of affairs which wasn't to last. Katherine, invited to go to Stourhead on the following day, had just said a breathless, delighted 'yes' when Dodie joined them.

She made a delightful picture when she paused in the open doorway. 'I crept in without bothering Mrs Spooner—you really should lock your door, Jason…' She paused as her eyes alighted on Katherine. She turned a shoulder to her without speaking, and addressed the doctor.

'I'm sorry, darling, I've been persuaded to go with the Crofts to Winchester for lunch, but will you come and fetch me afterwards? We could go out to dinner…' She smiled beguilingly. 'Naughty me to stand you up—I know I did promise to keep tomorrow free.'

The doctor spoke blandly, without any trace of annoyance. 'Never mind, Dodie, as it happens I'm taking Edward and Katherine over to Stourhead. It's ideal weather for a walk there, and the dogs need a good run.'

Her beautiful eyes narrowed. 'Supposing I had refused the Crofts?'

'Then you could have come, too—a pleasant foursome. You can always change your mind.'

'I can think of nothing more dreary then plodding round Stourhead at this time of the year.' She was in a real temper now, and Katherine looked at the doctor to see what he would do.

Nothing. He looked positively placid, and after a few fuming moments Dodie changed her tactics. 'Well, darling, let's go to town at the weekend and see a show and dance somewhere. I've quite made up my mind—I've got a gorgeous dress I'm simply longing to wear.'

'Can't be done, I'm afraid. I've two consultations on Saturday, and there's a committee meeting on Sunday morning.'

'In that case, there's no point in staying here listening to your excuses. I've no doubt you'll find amusement enough while I'm away.'

Her smouldering eyes turned to Katherine, still sitting there, trying to look as though she was miles away.

'You know, you should do something about your make-up and go to a decent hairdresser. You're a complete nonentity!'

She swept from the room before anyone could speak.

The silence which followed seemed like an eternity to Katherine although it was barely a couple of minutes. 'I'm sorry about that, Katherine,' said the doctor. 'Dodie gets quite worked up, and says things she doesn't mean.'

Edward joined in, anxious to make light of Dodie's rudeness. 'Always was a nasty, rude child,' he observed. 'I suppose I've known her for so long that we don't bother overmuch.'

Katherine looked at their concerned faces. 'It's perfectly all right,' she said to them calmly. 'Dodie was disappointed,

and it made her cross. And I've never had any pretensions
to good looks. She's quite right, I dare say I could do a lot
by way of improvement. It might be a good New Year's
resolution.'

'You're perfectly all right as you are,' declared the doctor,
which perhaps was an unfortunate remark to make.

'Beyond help,' reflected Katherine ruefully. All the same,
it would be rather fun to go to a beauty salon and have a
professional make-up and her hair done elegantly—perhaps tinted...

'What are you brooding about?' Edward wanted to know.

'I was wondering,' she said composedly, 'if it might be a
good idea to have my hair tinted?'

'God forbid!' exploded the doctor, so sharply that she
looked at him in surprise.

'It wouldn't suit you,' he said hastily. He was looking remote and saying little; he probably had plans for his evening
and wanted her gone.

She got to her feet, saying, 'I really must go—thank you
for a lovely tea...'

The two men were standing, one each side of her. 'If you
would stay for dinner, we might have a game of poker,' suggested the doctor to her surprise.

'But I don't know how to play.'

'All the better! Edward and I will enjoy teaching you...'
He didn't wait for her to agree, but reached for the phone.
'I'll let Mrs Potts know.'

Rather high-handed, thought Katherine, agog with delight at the thought of an evening spent in his company, and
Edward's, of course.

Mrs Spooner came to take away the tea things, received
the news that Katherine would be spending the evening, set
a tray of drinks ready and went away again, and the three

of them settled down to the intricacies of poker. Katherine picked it up quickly, and did so well that Edward remarked, 'You wouldn't know to look at her that Katherine was a gambler at heart, would you?'

'Appearances can be deceptive,' agreed the doctor gravely, 'and sometimes a gamble is worth risking.'

They had dinner presently; Mrs Spooner's home-made chicken soup, Dover sole and fluffy baked potatoes swimming in butter, and a trifle the like of which Katherine hadn't seen, let alone eaten, for many years. Edward wanted to play poker again when they had had their coffee, but she had no wish to outstay her welcome. She was driven back by the doctor, who made no effort to keep her. He wished her a brisk goodnight on Mrs Potts' doorstep.

'We'll fetch you about eleven o'clock,' he said as he put her key in the lock. 'Wear sensible shoes.'

All her shoes were sensible, but there was no point in saying so. She wished him goodnight, thanked him for her pleasant evening and went indoors. Mrs Potts was waiting for her.

'Now, what do you think of that?' she wanted to know. 'Having a lovely evening with the doctor and that Mr Edward! You got a bit of Christmas, after all.'

Katherine, a kind girl, could see that Mrs Potts was bored with her own company; she sat down and accepted a cup of tea and gave a blow-by-blow account of her evening. 'And I'm going to Stourhead tomorrow,' she finished as she bade her landlady goodnight and danced up to her attic.

Chapter 7

Katherine woke early, and lay for a while debating with herself what she should wear. She hadn't much choice, but she regretfully ruled out the new dress and her hat; both would look silly at Stourhead. She wished that she had good leather boots, well-cut slacks and a new quilted jacket, but she hadn't. While she ate her breakfast, she puzzled over the problem, counted the money in her purse, tidied her room and went out. Her shoes were low-heeled lace-ups and sensible enough, her slacks were old, but she was a neat girl and they looked well-cared for. Her head buzzing with possibilities, she went to shop. Ten minutes later she came out again, having laid out her money on a woolly cap, gloves and a scarf in holly-berry-red. Her slacks and quilted jacket were in a serviceable dark blue, and she had prudently added thick woollen knee socks to her purchases. She hurried back to try on everything, and the result pleased her well enough; the cap and scarf certainly did a lot to disguise the shabbiness of her slacks and jacket.

She sat down to wait, wondering if they would return before lunch, and decided that it would be more than likely.

An hour's brisk walk round the lake would take them to one o'clock, if you counted in the driving to and fro. She began to plan her afternoon, anxious to make the most of her day off.

She didn't get very far with this, for Mrs Potts called up to say that the doctor was waiting for her. She ran downstairs and felt a faint disappointment that it was Edward standing in the hall and not Jason. And she must stop thinking of him as Jason…

Edward greeted her with a friendly warmth and the remark that he was glad to see that, unlike some girls he knew, she was sensibly dressed for outdoor exercise. They called goodbye to Mrs Potts and went out to the car, to find the doctor sitting behind the wheel, looking placid.

'You'd both better get in the back—that's if you don't mind the dogs!' His eyes swept over Katherine and he added, 'Good—you're sensibly turned out.' This remark did nothing for her ego, although upon reflection she supposed that she might take it as a compliment of a sort.

Edward was in fine form, talking nonsense to make her laugh, while the dogs lolled over their feet; but the doctor had little to say, which wasn't surprising really, since the road, although cleared of snow, was icy. But they could drive the whole way on good roads, only for the last mile or so would the snow still be lying. They stopped at Fovant, a village half-way between Salisbury and Shaftesbury, and had coffee at the pub there, and then they drove on again. The sun had struggled through the clouds, and the snow sparkled around them, deep and untouched on the hills, turning the cottages alongside the road into fairy-tale dwellings.

They went out of Shaftesbury on the Gillingham road, and found that it had been more or less cleared, but when they turned off for Stourhead the country lane was packed with snow and the doctor slowed down, going past the row of cottages at the start of the small village, then down the hill towards the entrance to the park, to turn into the yard of the Spread Eagle Inn. He stopped and turned to look at Edward and Katherine.

'Walk first?' he asked. 'That should bring us nicely to one o'clock or thereabouts; the bar will be open until two, so we have plenty of time.'

They all got out and the dogs were put on their leads. 'See about the tickets, will you, Edward?' The doctor was busy with the dogs. 'We'll follow you.'

He took his time putting the dogs on a double lead, and Edward had gone through the gate to the little rustic kiosk where he could get tickets before they were ready to follow him. 'You like Edward?' The doctor's voice was casual.

'Oh, yes—very much—I wish my brother were half such fun, but of course he's a lot older. Thirty-six.'

'The same as myself,' observed the doctor. Katherine gave an agitated little skip beside him and went the colour of her knitted cap. 'Oh, I didn't mean—that is, you don't seem old at all...'

'But past my first exuberant youth? Edward is a mere twenty-four.'

'Yes, he told me.'

'He will be down again for the odd weekend, so you will be able to see something of each other.'

'That will be nice,' Katherine said politely, and wished they they would talk about someone else—the doctor, for instance. She cast about in her head for the best way of introducing this enthralling subject, but by then they had caught up with Edward.

He tucked an arm into hers. 'I say, this is a super spot! I've not been during the winter, I had no idea that it was so magnificent. We ought to have brought some bread for the ducks.'

'I have—it's in my pocket,' said Katherine, and smiled at the doctor, who gave her a thoughtful look and didn't smile at all.

They ploughed through the snow, exchanging rather smug greetings with the few people they met, and caught brief snatches of, 'A splendid day to be outdoors,' and 'Have you seen the grotto?' or, even more frequently, 'They don't know what they are missing.'

Katherine, walking prudently in the doctor's size twelve footsteps in order to keep her feet as dry as possible, glowed with happiness; never mind tomorrow or the day after, she might not see him for days, even weeks, but just at the moment here he was within inches of her. She listened to Edward's voice, talking of this and that, and answered him light-heartedly and laughed a great deal. By the time they were half-way round the lake, with a brief stop at Diana's Temple, she was as warm as toast; the cold had put colour into her cheeks and her eyes sparkled so that she was almost pretty. The doctor, pausing from time to time, glanced at her, still with a thoughtful look which she didn't notice, and when they got to the winding stone steps leading to the grotto he handed the dogs to Edward. 'You go ahead. I'll give Katherine a hand, it may be slippery.'

As indeed it was. She slithered down with the doctor's hand firm under her elbow, as much agitated by his nearness as the icy steps. At the bottom he released her, and she went to look at Neptune and then the spring of almost freezing water. It was very cold, and the cobbled floor was slippery, but the view from the rough-hewn openings in the grotto's walls was well worth it. They came out into the open air again, and a watery, weak sun shone upon them. Ten min-

utes more and they would be back where they had started
from. Katherine, who would have liked to have gone on
walking for ever with the doctor, sighed gently.

'I've dropped a glove,' said Edward suddenly. 'I took it
off to try the water in the grotto. I'll have to go back.'

'We'll go on—if you don't catch us up before, we'll be
in the bar.'

The path was wide enough for them to walk side by side,
Charlie and Flo trotting at their master's heels while he chat-
ted pleasantly enough about Stourhead. 'Have you been to
the house?' he wanted to know, and when she shook her
head, 'I wouldn't care to live there myself, but the library is
a splendid apartment, with some superb examples of Chippendale's work.' He paused to look down at her eager face
under the holly-berry-red cap. 'Will you marry me, Katie?'

His calm voice hadn't altered in the least.

Here she felt her heart give a great thud, stop for an
amazed second and then begin to beat so fast that she caught
her breath. 'Me?' she squeaked. 'Marry you?' She swallowed. 'Is it a joke or something?'

'Personally, I have never considered a proposal of marriage a joke.'

'Oh, I didn't mean that. I'm sorry, but I...you see, you're
going to marry Dodie.'

She scanned his face, trying to read its expression. It told
her nothing. 'Ah—you have heard that?'

'Well, yes—I mean everyone expects you to. Mr and Mrs
Grainger, Tom Fetter—I heard him say one day that you
had been waiting all these years for her to grow up so that
you could marry her.'

'All these years.' His voice was quiet and without expression. 'Dodie is three years older than you are—twenty-four—I was twelve when she was born. More than a decade.'

She said worriedly, 'But being all that much older doesn't matter a bit. I mean, you don't seem to...that is, it's not even middle-aged.'

He smiled then. 'You reassure me, Katie.'

She said kindly, hiding her hurt, 'I expect you spoke without thinking—I often do. I'll forget it, I promise you. I expect you feel frustrated because Dodie isn't here.'

'So you think that I should marry Dodie as soon as possible?'

She nodded, unaware of the misery in her eyes. 'Oh, yes—she's very pretty.'

'That's a flimsy excuse for marriage. But I promise you I'll give it my earnest consideration.'

She was awash with misery. Here he was, the man she loved more deeply than anything on earth, and she was urging him to marry a girl who would make him unhappy for the rest of his life! She should have accepted him then and there, whatever the consequences. He didn't love her, of course; probably he had been imagining how she would react if he asked her to marry him and he had said it out loud, but she loved him enough for two, and she would be a good wife. Too late now and, even if she had known what to say, Edward was charging along the path towards them.

'Found it!' he bellowed. 'What a bit of luck. I say, I'm famished.'

They ate sausages and chips in the basket, and the men drank beer while Katherine had a pot of coffee and, at the doctor's instigation, a glass of brandy with it. It warmed her nicely, but there was an icy core deep inside her which she knew would only be melted by the doctor's love, and that wasn't going to happen, so she would have to learn to make the best of it.

'A pity the shop is closed, though I don't suppose it would do much business in this sort of weather.' Edward ate the last of his chips and sat back at his ease. 'I might have bought you a souvenir, Katherine.'

'I don't need a souvenir to remind me of such a super morning.'

'Very nicely put. You are no beauty, but you have charm.'

She laughed. 'I shall treasure that compliment.'

'Don't forget that you are coming to Jason's New Year's party.' He grinned. 'You don't need to look at him like that—the invitations are written, you'll get yours tomorrow. So trot out the best bib and tucker, do whatever it is women do to their faces, and present yourself at eight o'clock sharp on Old Year's Night.'

'You will be fetched,' interpolated the doctor. 'There will be quite a few people you already know—from the medical block, Matron, some of the sisters and the consultant and house surgeons from your side.'

'Oh, but I don't know them. At least, it's the other way round, they don't know me. I don't think they know I'm there.'

He smiled a little, remembering his colleague's reference to a pale brown mouse who scuttled into the sluice room as soon as he arrived on the ward.

'All the more reason,' declared Edward cheerfully, 'for you to wear something a bit way out, and take everyone by surprise.'

'I'll do my best.'

Presently, they drove back to Salisbury through the early dusk, the dogs snoring at their feet. Katherine, who had hoped that the doctor might suggest that she sit in front beside him, was disappointed to find herself ushered in with Edward and the dogs. She supposed that she would be dropped off at Mrs Potts' house, and thought up several suitable thank-you speeches. On no account must she outstay her welcome; even if the doctor invited her back for tea it would be because he had nice manners. She could make some excuse if he did.

But at least part of her problem was solved for her. They stopped in Shaftesbury and had teacakes and tea in a well-lit, warm café in the centre of the town, and when the doctor asked her what she was doing with the evening, she crossed her fingers behind her back and said composedly that she was going to the cinema with Miss Kendall, one of her fellow lodgers. That young lady was still away, but it was a small fib and did no one any harm. The doctor concealed a smile, for she was lying so earnestly and making heavy weather of it, too, but all he said was, 'Oh, a pleasant end to your day.'

Which gave her an opportunity to thank him.

They both got out of the car at Mrs Potts'. Edward after a brief hug and a cheery 'see you', got into the front seat, while the doctor unlocked the door for her and waited until she was indoors before closing it behind her with a brief, 'Goodbye, Katherine.'

At Stourhead that afternoon he had called her Katie; no one had called her that since her father and mother had died, and it had warmed her heart to hear him say it, but it seemed she was to be Katherine once more. Which, in the circumstances, was fair enough.

She wasn't on duty until twelve o'clock the next day and, since her invitation to the party had arrived by the morning's post, it seemed a good idea to comb the dress shops for something to wear. The sales were on, and she had enough money, she hoped, to find something suitable. But what *was* suitable? There was a splendid selection, and none of them too highly priced. A pink satin dress with a sequined bodice would certainly draw all eyes, so would a slinky black velvet, although, if Matron was to be there, she might not approve of the bodice, or what there was of it. Finally, she settled on a silver-grey taffeta with a square neckline and elbow-length sleeves; it was a pretty dress in a demure way, and plain enough to go unremembered on future occasions—if there were to be any. It was calf-length, and the skirt was gently gathered into a waistband which showed off her slim waist to perfection. Her shoes wouldn't do; she searched in all the cheaper shops without success, and then found exactly what she wanted, grey velvet court shoes going cheap because the bead work on the toe had become a little tarnished.

There was barely time to make a cup of tea and gobble down a sandwich when she got back to her room, but the morning had been a success, and she hadn't spent quite all of her money.

She went on duty in excellent spirits, which was just as well, for Sister was at her most martial and Andy was in a bad temper because she had quarrelled with her boyfriend. The patients were pernickety, too, suffering from too much Christmas fare and reaction after the excitement of the last few days. No one asked her if she had enjoyed her Christmas, although Staff Nurse observed that she was glad to see her back after her day off.

She was tired when she got back to her room later that evening; she ate the supper Mrs Potts had saved for her, helped to tidy away the meal when she had finished, and then went up to bed. Even the sight of her new dress failed to lift her spirits, and the very idea of going to the doctor's party filled her with doubts.

They were still there as she dressed on Old Year's Night. Perhaps no one would come to fetch her; perhaps no one there would bother to speak to her; probably her dress was all wrong... She had no jewellery save a good gold locket on an old-fashioned chain which had belonged to her grandmother; she put it on, powdered her nose once more, patted her already neat head into even more neatness, picked up her coat and went downstairs to the kitchen.

At least her fellow lodgers and Mrs Potts admired the dress; she was putting on her coat when Mrs Potts went to answer the door and came back with Edward. He breezed in, planted a kiss on her cheek, shook everyone else by the hand, gave Mrs Potts a box of chocolates and urged Katherine to get a move on. 'Jason's up to his eyeballs in half of Salisbury—you ought to see some of the girls' outfits!' He tucked her into the car and got in beside her. 'What's under the coat?'

'A dress,' said Katherine calmly. 'And don't expect anything breathtaking, because it's not.'

'I'll let you know when I see it.'

They arrived at the house, lights streaming from its windows and cars parked half-way down the street. Edward bustled her inside. The door was opened by a solemn, middle-aged man who wished her a good evening, and observed sternly, 'You were quick, Mr Edward.'

'Like the light, Coker.' Edward touched her arm. 'Katherine, this is Coker, Jason's right arm. Been with him man and boy, haven't you, Coker? You've not seen him before because he's been in hospital.' He handed his coat to him. 'It hasn't been the same without you, although Mrs Spooner did her valiant best.'

'Thank you, Mr Edward. If the young lady will go upstairs and leave her coat?'

He led the way up the graceful curved staircase, and opened a door on the landing above. There were coats everywhere; she added hers to the pile of furs and velvets on the bed, cast a quick look at herself in the pier-glass and followed Coker downstairs again. Edward was waiting for her, and she was pleased to see that he approved of her dress.

'Clever girl! You'll stand out like a nun at a circus.' Upon which heartening speech he swept her into the drawing-room.

There were a great many people there; she would never have dared go in on her own. She caught his sleeve and said urgently, 'Don't leave me alone for a bit, will you, Edward?'

He patted her hand. 'Count on me. Jason's seen us.'

The doctor was making his way towards them, pausing here and there to exchange a word. When he reached them he said, 'Thanks, Edward, I'll take Katherine to meet a few people. There's a smashing blonde by the fireplace, waiting for someone to rescue her...'

'Give a yell if you want me.' Edward gave her a wide grin and edged his way towards the other end of the room.

'I do like that dress.' The doctor smiled down at her, his eyes twinkling.

'Thank you.' She wasn't sure why she added, 'I almost didn't come...'

'I thought you might have doubts, but there has to be a beginning—the first step, as it were.'

She stared at him. He was elegant in his dinner-jacket,

his face pleasantly calm but, she thought, tired. 'Towards what?' she wanted to know.

'Why, love, marriage, children—a lifetime of happiness.'

'You really believe that?'

'Yes—do you not?'

She nodded gravely. 'Oh, yes, but sometimes it's best not to take the step.'

He smiled suddenly. 'Am I being warned off?' And before she could say anything, he went on, 'Come and meet one or two people I think you might like.'

People who, strangely enough, had known her parents and who in turn introduced her to other younger men and women. Presently she found herself quite at ease and enjoying herself. True, there was a sprinkling of guests who ignored her completely, and she quickly discovered that they were friends of Dodie's. That young lady, holding court in the centre of the room, joined the small circle of people Katherine was with and brought their casual talk to an abrupt halt.

'Hello, Katherine!' She smiled brilliantly at her. 'So you managed to save enough wages to get a dress. In the sales? What a bit of luck for you, but an evening out like this is well worth going without your dinner to pay for it...'

She slid away before anyone could speak, until one of the girls said loudly, 'She's been drinking too much—she always does. Katherine, your dress is charming, we've all been admiring it. Tell me, what is your uniform like? I'd love to work in a hospital, but I'd be no good at it—only as a kitchen maid, and I can't even cook.'

The talk turned to cooking and food, and the unpleasant little incident was papered over by her companions' good manners. Katherine was glad that she had been too surprised to utter a word; to have made a scene at Jason's party would have been unforgivable, but perhaps that was what Dodie had hoped for. Edward took her to supper presently, a cold buffet laid out in the dining-room, presided over by Mrs Spooner and Coker and two girls wearing black dresses and white aprons. Edward nodded towards them. 'Sheila and Daphne—they help Mrs Spooner in the house—come each day.' He waved his fork at them and they smiled broadly at him.

'When do you go back to London?' asked Katherine, popping a tasty morsel of something cheesy into her mouth.

'Ah! In despair at the thought of me leaving you? In a couple of days, my dear. Jason's going to drive me up in the evening and stay for a short while—he hasn't had a break for months. I suppose Dodie will come with us, though it hasn't been mentioned. Have you seen her? I mean, to speak to?'

'Well, she spoke to me, but she'd gone again before I had a chance to say anything.'

Something in her voice made him look at her. 'Like that, was it? I shall miss you—I should have liked a sister like you...'

'Oh, Edward, what a nice thing to say! Thank you. I already have one brother, did you know?'

He nodded, and she went on: 'But he's a good deal older than I am—and he's rather serious. I'll gladly be a sister to you, Edward.'

'Exactly what I would wish to hear,' said the doctor's voice behind her. 'Are you enjoying yourself, Katherine? When are you on duty tomorrow?'

'At twelve o'clock.'

'Good. Wait behind until everyone has gone, and I'll take you back.'

'Oh, but I could...'

'Don't argue, Katherine.' He smiled briefly, and went to join some of his guests at another table.

There was champagne at midnight to celebrate the New Year, and within the hour the guests left. The last of them had been seen on their way by one o'clock, all save Dodie and a good-looking man in his thirties. His eyes were too close together, Katherine decided, and his dress too flamboyant. He lolled back in a chair while Dodie talked to the doctor. Katherine wasn't near enough to hear what she was saying, but the doctor's reply annoyed her, for she hunched her shoulders and turned away from him and ran across the room to throw her arms round the other man's neck.

'Well, if you won't take me, Nigel will.'

The doctor's voice was placid. 'My dear Dodie, I have a clinic in the morning at half-past eight—by all means let Nigel take you, if he will.'

'You cross old darling,' declared Dodie and shot a quick look at Katherine. 'Take me out to dinner in the evening and I'll let you announce our engagement.'

The doctor laughed. 'I'll take you out to dinner, but I'll not promise more than that.' He nodded at Nigel. 'Enjoy yourselves—Dodie, I'll give you a ring some time during the day.'

After they had gone, Coker appeared with a tray of coffee. 'I know you need to go to bed,' said the doctor, 'but this will warm you, and I promise you I'll have you back at Mrs Potts' within twenty minutes.'

Which he did, rather to Katherine's regret; a short night of sleeping was a small price to pay for his company. As he opened Mrs Potts' door and held it for her to go in, she paused to thank him. 'It was a lovely party,' she assured him, 'I met several people who knew my parents. It was like it used to be...'

'Will you marry me, Katie?'

She was so taken by surprise that she stammered a little. 'No—no, of course not!' She added, with something of a snap, 'You're taking Dodie out to dinner...'

'Ah, yes, but one must keep one's hand in!' He bent and kissed her swiftly. 'Goodnight, Katie.'

He pushed her into the narrow hall and closed the door, leaving her standing there, a prey to a variety of feelings, which were so strong that she cried while she undressed and got into bed. Tears were still trickling down her cheeks as, from sheer weariness, she slept at last.

Morning came much too soon; she got her breakfast, washed her smalls and, because Mrs Potts said she didn't feel very well, did her shopping for her before going on duty. Almost everyone on the ward was in a bad temper, due to not enough sleep on the previous night. Sister, castigating her for spilling water on the ward floor, gave it as her opinion that Katherine would never make a nurse, even if she ever applied to train as one.

'But I don't intend to,' objected Katherine politely, to be told sharply not to answer back.

'And what were you doing at Dr Fitzroy's party?' finished Sister darkly.

'I know his cousin, Edward,' said Katherine in a matter-of-fact voice.

Sister could do nothing more than utter, 'Oh, really?' Obviously, she hadn't expected such a simple explanation.

Mrs Potts looked ill when Katherine got back from the hospital. 'I've caught a cold,' she explained, 'and what can you expect in this weather? I'll be all right in the morning.'

Katherine left just before eight o'clock in the morning; it was one of her long days of duty, and she saw no one as she left the house. Mrs Potts, she suspected, was still in bed, nursing her cold.

The ward was busy, for it was take-in week again. Katherine trotted to and fro about her mundane tasks, thinking about Jason, wondering if he had enjoyed his evening with Dodie, and whether she had coaxed him at last into asking her to marry him. Katherine was very afraid that she might. He was far too good for her and inclined to laugh tolerantly at her tantrums. Perhaps they had known each other for such a long time that he no longer noticed them. But would Dodie make him happy? Tantrums in a pretty girl one took out to dinner and allowed the freedom of your home might not be so amusing in a wife. She frowned so heavily at the thought that the patient whose water jug she was filling asked her if she felt ill.

She was a little late going off duty, and the house, when she reached it, seemed very quiet. No one home, she decided, and stood in the hall, reading a hand-delivered letter from Edward on the eve of going back to London and, according to him, reluctant to go. He bade her a regretful goodbye, with the promise that he would be down to see her again as soon as he could get a weekend. 'Jason always puts me up,' he had told her. 'My people live in Cumbria, too far for a few days' leave.' She would miss him once he had gone back up to London, and it was nice of him to write. He missed her already, he wrote, and went on at some length to describe the nurse who had taken his fancy. Katherine laughed as she went upstairs, eager to get to her room and make a pot of tea.

She was on the first landing when she heard a noise which made her pause. A small wheezing sound, and then a dry, difficult cough. It was coming from Mrs Potts' room. Katherine was aware that her landlady didn't encourage any intrusion into her private life; she looked after her lodgers very well, presided over her table in a friendly fashion, but no one, according to Miss Kendall, had ever been invited to have a chat in her room. Miss Kendall was still away, but surely Mrs Dunster or Miss Fish had noticed that their land-lady wasn't in the kitchen or sitting-room downstairs? There was no point in hesitating. Katherine knocked and went in.

It was dark already, but the curtains hadn't been drawn and there was no light. She advanced a few steps into the room and said softly, 'Mrs Potts? I'm sorry to intrude. I heard you coughing and I wondered if you were ill? Perhaps there is something I can do? A hot drink?'

Mrs Potts' voice—a croak, unlike her usual, brisk tones—came from the bed. 'The lamp on the table—by my bed.'

Katherine went cautiously forward to where the darker outline of a bed was visible. She found the lamp, switched it on and looked at Mrs Potts, lying there with a flushed face, wheezing and coughing her little dry cough.

'I feel ill,' she whispered unnecessarily.

Katherine felt for her pulse and put a hand on her hot forehead. 'Has anyone been in to see you? Have you had a drink?'

'No, love. Mrs Dunster and Miss Fish went downstairs a while ago, but I don't think they heard me call. They came back up to their rooms.'

'Look, if you don't mind, I'll get your doctor—I think you may have 'flu. But first I'll shake up your pillows and get you a drink.'

She sat Mrs Potts up and found another pillow, wiped her face with a wet cloth and combed back her hair, and then hurried down to the kitchen.

While the kettle boiled, she found a bottle of orange squash and made a jugful, then made tea and carried the tray upstairs. 'Drink this first,' she advised, proffering the cold drink. 'I'm going to telephone the doctor and then I'll come back and pour your tea. I'll leave the door open.'

Half-way to the door she paused. 'Who is your doctor, Mrs Potts?'

'Why, Dr Fitzroy, my dear.'

She had to look up his number, and it was Coker who answered. She explained in her quiet voice, and added, 'I think Mrs Potts is quite ill.'

'I'll fetch the doctor, miss,' said Coker, and a moment later Jason's voice, unhurried and calm, sounded in her ear.

He listened while she gave him the few details she had. 'I'll be round in about five minutes.' He rang off and she went back upstairs, meeting Miss Fish on the way.

'Why is no one in the kitchen getting our supper?' She gave Katherine an accusing stare.

'Mrs Potts isn't well—she's in bed. She's been there all day. Didn't you notice she wasn't around the house, Miss Fish?'

'It isn't my business to wonder about my landlady's absence.'

'Well, I'm afraid you'll have to get your own suppers this evening.'

Katherine turned and ran downstairs again as the doorbell rang.

Dr Fitzroy came in, dwarfing his surroundings, exuding confidence and a soothing calm. 'In her room?' he asked and went upstairs, wishing Miss Fish a civil good evening as he passed her.

He took off his car coat and gave it to Katherine, and walked over to the bed. Mrs Potts peered up at him, coughed and said in a wheezy voice, 'I'm sorry to bother you, Doctor—it's only a cold, but I do feel poorly.'

He sat down beside the bed, took her pulse and asked a few questions in his calm way. And then he said, 'If Katherine will help you, I should like to examine your chest, Mrs Potts.'

He got up and walked to the window when he had finished, and stood looking out into the street below until Katherine had Mrs Potts tidily arranged against her pillows once more. 'I should like you to come into hospital for a few days, Mrs Potts. You have 'flu and a touch of pneumonia. We can have you back on your feet again in no time at all with antibiotics, but you will have to stay in bed and be nursed, so that's the best place for you.'

'Who is to look after the house and my lodgers?' whispered Mrs Potts. 'I can't leave them...'

'I shall ask Mrs Spooner to come and stay—we can manage without her for a few days. Now, Katherine will wrap you up warm, and I'll take you back with me and then fetch Mrs Spooner...'

'They'll be wanting their supper...'

'I'll see to that, Mrs Potts,' said Katherine, her head in the wardrobe, looking for woollies and a dressing-gown, 'and I'm not on duty until noon tomorrow, so I can cast an eye over the house in the morning.'

It took time and patience to get Mrs Potts swathed in a variety of woollies and blankets; the doctor carried her downstairs and Katherine went ahead to open the door and then the car door. 'Can you manage?' she wanted to know. 'Shall I telephone the hospital and let them know you're coming?'

He had the car phone in his hand. 'I'll do that now. Get inside before you catch your death of cold. I'll bring Mrs Spooner along as soon as I can.'

'No need to hurry. I'll get supper and make up Mrs Potts' bed ready for her.' She poked her head into the back of the car. 'I'll come and see you tomorrow. Be good, Mrs Potts, and don't worry about a thing—just get well.'

'Miss Fish, Mrs Dun—' began Mrs Potts.

'I'll keep an eye on them.' She bent and kissed Mrs Potts' hot forehead, because she looked so ill and forlorn, and then closed the door and found the doctor right behind her. He said impatiently, 'I said, go indoors.'

She went without a backward glance, feeling put out. He could have said thank you, instead he had sounded annoyed. Perhaps he had planned to spend the evening with Dodie.

She went straight to the kitchen and opened a can of soup, inspected the fridge and decided on omelettes and tinned peas, and the remains of a treacle tart. While she was laying the table, her fellow lodgers joined her.

'Supper is late,' complained Mrs Dunster, and sat down at the table, presumably expecting it to be set before her.

Katherine explained, and was met by a disapproving sniff. 'How very inconvenient,' observed Mrs Dunster. When Miss Fish joined her, she relayed the news with a few embellishments of her own. The two ladies grumbled genteelly together while Katherine got their supper and, having eaten it, rose from the table and went up to their rooms, leaving the remains of their meal for her to clear away. But first she would have to get a room ready for Mrs Spooner. Finding clean bedlinen took a few minutes, but she had become quite expert at making up beds since she had been at the hospital. She had the room to rights in no time at all, and sped to her room to hang up her things. It was icy-cold there, and she was tempted to light the gas fire, but there was still the best part of an hour's work in the kitchen. She nipped downstairs once more and contemplated the mess there.

The front door bell went just as she had tied herself into

one of Mrs Potts' aprons; it was Mrs Spooner, with the doctor looming behind her.

Katherine bade them come in, and Mrs Spooner gave her a worried smile. 'Poor Emily,' she said, 'alone all day. Well, as good as alone, with those two old women not even noticing that she wasn't there.'

She sniffed, and Katherine made haste to say, 'Well, I think they spend a lot of time in their rooms, but it must have been most unpleasant for Mrs Potts.'

They had all gone into the kitchen, and Mrs Spooner eyed the mess in a severe way, so that Katherine felt constrained to tell her that she had been on the point of washing up and tidying everything away. 'But we've had supper,' she added quickly. 'Not quite what Mrs Potts would have given us...'

'Bless you, miss, and you with a day's work behind you. I'll have Emily's room, shall I? I'll just make up the bed.'

'I've done that—that's why the kitchen's untidy.' Katherine sounded apologetic, and the doctor, standing silently, allowed a small sound to escape his lips.

'Perhaps if you'd like to go upstairs with Mrs Spooner, I might make a start on this?'

Both ladies looked at him with horror. Mrs Spooner's outraged 'sir' was a fraction ahead of Katherine's, 'You can't wash up, you don't know how!'

He was taking off his coat. 'I never could resist a challenge,' he told her blandly. 'Off you go and count the sheets or whatever you need to do, and we'll have a pot of tea when you come down.'

In Mrs Potts' bedroom, her sister sat down on the basket-work chair by the window, and Katherine perched on the bed. Mrs Spooner had everything nicely planned; for the greater part of the day she would be there, and when

Katherine got back from work perhaps she wouldn't mind keeping an eye on things while she went back to the doctor's house and made sure that Coker and the girls were managing. Her tone implied that they would make a mess of things without her. 'And then I could pop in and see Emily on the way back.'

Katherine explained her off-duty hours. 'And of course I'll do all I can to help. I hope it won't be for too long. It must be awkward for you.'

'She'd do the same for me,' observed Mrs Spooner, 'and I must say you are very kind, miss. We'd better go down and see how the doctor's getting on.'

He was getting on very nicely; in his shirtsleeves now, with a pipe in his mouth. Miss Fish and Mrs Dunster would smell smoke in the morning and complain, but that didn't matter.

Mrs Spooner took the tea towel from him and said firmly, 'Now, sir, sit down, do. We've got everything nicely fixed up, and you must be wanting to go home...'

'Not before a cup of tea.'

They drank it sitting round the kitchen table, and presently he got up and put on his jacket and coat, then went to the door. 'Come and lock up behind me, Katherine.' His voice was mild enough, but she found herself following him into the hall.

They stood together, of necessity rather squashed in the narrow space. 'Not quite the evening I had planned, but most satisfactory.' He opened the door with one hand, and caught her close with his other arm and kissed her hard. 'Thank you, Katie. Our paths cross so often, they are bound to converge one day.'

Chapter 8

Katherine floated back into the kitchen on a cloud of enchanted rapture, to come back to earth with a terrific thump when Mrs Spooner observed, 'He'll be late for their evening out, and Miss Dodie does hate to be kept waiting—she'll have gone off in a huff, more like.' Mrs Spooner's sniff expressed her opinion better than any words. 'Never one to shirk his duty is the doctor—loves his work and hasn't much time for parties and so on—of course, he's a lot older than Miss Dodie—I dare say she'll settle down once she's married.' She glanced at Katherine. 'You look tired, miss—you go off to bed or you won't be fit for work tomorrow. On in the afternoon, the doctor said.'

'Yes, that's right, Mrs Spooner. Would you like to go and see Mrs Potts before lunch? I don't leave here until just before noon. I could do any shopping you want when I go out in the morning—you'd have time to go to the doctor's house, too.'

'Well, that's a nice idea—you wouldn't mind?'

'Not a bit, only I do have to go before lunch, but I expect

you've got a key? If you would make a list of shopping, I'll leave it on the table here.'

'That would suit me. And since you're being so kind you'll take your breakfast here—that way you'll get a bit of a lie-in.'

'Oh, but won't that be extra work for you?'

'Bless you, no, miss. You come down around eight o'clock and I'll have it ready for you.' She nodded in a satisfied way. 'It's a good thing that the doctor and Mr Edward are going up to London tomorrow evening—they'll go to the doctor's flat. He won't be back for a day or two. All the same, I'd like to pop in each day...'

'Yes, of course. You'll let me know if there is anything I can do to help?'

She wished Mrs Spooner goodnight, and went to her room to make a pot of tea and allow common sense to take over from the romantic dreams of her heart. The doctor had meant nothing by his kiss, and his remark about their paths made no sense at all. She got into bed and lay thinking about it and presently went to sleep—for, however deeply in love she might be, she was dog-tired.

A week went busily by; the ward was still full, and winter colds and 'flu were taking their toll of staff. Besides, there was Mrs Spooner to give a helping hand to, and Mrs Potts to visit each day—something Katherine looked forward to in the hope that she would see Jason. He was away for two days but he still did his usual mid-week round because Andy, who knew everyone and got all the news, had told her so. But Katherine never managed to be on the ward when he was there, nor did she see him around the hospital, despite the fact that she took long and devious ways in which to come and go. On her days off, too, she was unlucky, and on the last day of the week Mrs Potts was to return home.

Mrs Spooner and Katherine, making up the bed ready for her and putting flowers in a vase, discussed the next week or two's plans. Mrs Spooner was to return to the doctor's house that evening and one of the young women who came each day to help in his house would come to Mrs Potts instead. And, as soon as she was well enough, she was to have a short holiday. 'The doctor has a cottage at Bucklers Hard, a nice, quiet place at this time of year, and as cosy a little house as you could wish for. Just the thing for a few days' rest,' explained Mrs Spooner.

Katherine agreed, wishing for an impossible miracle which would make it possible for her to go there too, as Mrs Potts' companion. On the other hand, it would mean that she would have no chance of seeing the doctor at all, whereas now, each day brought the possibility of seeing him.

She was on duty when Mrs Potts returned, to be told on her return that Dr Fitzroy had driven her back himself with one of his daily maids; he had stayed and had a cup of tea, Shirley Kendall told her when she got back from the hospital, and then gone up to Mrs Potts' room to make sure that she was all right.

'I could go for him in a big way,' declared Shirley. 'Ever so polite, he is; makes you feel you're important, if you know what I mean.' She gave Katherine an envious glance. 'I expect you see a lot of him at the hospital.'

'Almost never. I'm on the surgical side and Dr Fitzroy's a consultant on the medical wards. Consultants don't hobnob with nursing auxiliaries.'

'Bit of a snob, is he?'

'Heavens, no! We just don't meet. Did you have a nice holiday?'

'You bet—there was this man…' Shirley embarked on a long and involved account of someone's cousin who had turned up unexpectedly. 'He's coming to take me out next weekend…he's got a Ford Escort…'

Katherine was to have days off on the following weekend. She had put in a good deal of overtime since Christmas, filling gaps where the staff had been ill and, very much to her surprise, Sister had told her that she might have what amounted to a long weekend: Friday from one o'clock until Monday noon.

Katherine spent the week trying to decide what to do with this unexpected treat; she had a little money by now, and she might employ Saturday browsing round the sales, for her wardrobe was still woefully scanty. She might have a meal out and perhaps go to the theatre. It was a pity that Shirley had a date with the man she had met at Christmas, and that Andy would be on duty over the weekend. She would certainly go to the library and get something to read, and there was the cathedral on Sunday—she occupied herself in filling her days; weekends didn't often come her way.

It was on Friday morning that she received a summons to go to Sister's office; she had been making beds with one of the student nurses, now she muttered an apology and hurried down the ward—one didn't keep Sister waiting—wondering what she had done wrong. Or perhaps her weekend off had been quashed…

Sister was looking severe, sitting with a poker-straight back behind her desk, and lounging against the radiator was Dr Fitzroy.

He stood up as Katherine went in, and Sister said, 'Katherine, Dr Fitzroy has a favour to ask of you.'

Miracles weren't always impossible, she thought bemusedly, listening to him suggesting in a cool, impersonal manner that he would be vastly obliged if she would accompany Mrs Potts down to Bucklers Hard. 'Just to see her safely in. Someone will go down on Monday morning to stay with her, but it would oblige me if you could see your way to staying until then. I understand that it is your weekend off, but perhaps you have other plans?'

'No, I haven't,' said Katherine joyfully, and beamed at him. 'I'll be glad to go.'

He studied her thoughtfully. 'Yes, good. You and Mrs Potts will be fetched from her house after lunch today, and transport will be arranged for your return on Monday morning. Thank you, Katherine.'

It was cool dismissal. She said 'Thank you, sir' and looked at Sister. 'You may go, Katherine.' She was dismissed again, and got herself out of the office, not looking at the doctor at all, and went back to making beds. It was lovely to have her weekend so splendidly filled, but need he have been quite so remote in his manner? It was no good worrying about it; she fell to deciding what to wear...

The snow had turned to rain and there was a cold wind with it; she got away from the hospital punctually, and hurried back to her room, ate a quick meal of beans on toast and the inevitable pot of tea, and packed her night things. She got into the wool dress once more, and went to see how Mrs Potts was faring. She was dressed, ready to go, and Katherine helped her downstairs to sit in the kitchen, in the warm, while she fetched their cases. They didn't have to wait long;

Katherine went to open the door when the bell rang, and found the doctor on the doorstep.

His eyes swept over her neat person. 'Ready? And Mrs Potts?'

When she nodded, he went into the kitchen and led Mrs Potts out to the car, stowing her into the back seat with the two dogs. The cases he put in the boot, then he urged Katherine to get in beside him and drove off without further ado.

He took the main road out of the city, but at Downton he turned off towards Cadnam and once there took the main road again to Brockenhurst. He had little to say as he drove and Katherine, happy just to be beside him, kept quiet. They were through Brockenhurst on the way to Beaulieu and Bucklers Hard before he remarked, 'You'll doubtless find the cottage well-stocked with food. There's central heating, and fires, and someone will have been in to keep it tidy and make up the beds and so on. I don't expect you to be with Mrs Potts every minute of the day—take time off for a walk—you look as though you could do with some fresh sea air. There's a nice little pub close by, and the cottage is the end one in a row, so you don't need to be lonely. Don't let Mrs Potts go out in this weather, but I'd like her to potter around the house a bit. By the end of the week she should be pretty fit.'

She said meekly, 'Yes, sir,' and gave a surprised start when he growled, 'Don't call me sir, Katie.' Then, in a quite different voice, he asked, 'Have you given any more thought to marrying me?'

She had to admit silently that one way or another she had thought of exceedingly little else, but all she said, in a collected voice, was, 'I do wonder why you keep on about it.'

'Ah, that is at least a step in the right direction. What a

pity that we have no more time in which to discuss the matter thoroughly.'

He had turned into the broad roadway leading to the quay and Beaulieu river. There were cottages on either side of it, and a hotel at the very end. He stopped at the last cottage on the opposite side and said, 'Stay there a moment while I open up,' and got out of the car to cross the narrow strip of grass and unlock the door. There was no garden at the front, but the cottage was solidly built of red brick, its paintwork fresh and its small windows gleaming. Even in the dull light of a January afternoon it looked inviting. Katherine jumped out when he opened her door, possessed herself of Mrs Potts' various scarves, rugs and handbag, and followed the doctor and her landlady into the cottage.

The doctor switched on a light once they were inside, revealing a small, square hallway with a door on either side and a staircase facing them. The doctor opened a door and ushered them into a low-ceilinged room with windows at either end. There was a bright fire burning in the small grate, and the furniture was exactly right: comfortable chairs and small, antique pieces arranged on a dark red carpet, matching the red and cream chintz curtains. 'I'll get your cases,' he said. 'We might have tea before I go back; the kitchen is through the door.' He nodded towards a small door at the far end of the room, and Katherine, taking the hint for the wish, sat Mrs Potts down and went to investigate. There was a tray already set for tea, with a large cake beside it and a dish of scones as well. There was cream too, and a pot of jam, so it only remained to put the kettle on. She went back to Mrs Potts, helped that lady to remove her coat and wraps, and then fetched the tray and set it on the round table in one corner of the room. She just had time to take off her own outdoor things before the doctor, with the dogs at his heels, came back with their cases. He went straight upstairs with them, which gave her time to light the gas under the kettle and find a bowl for the dogs to have a drink. He tossed his coat on to a chair and followed her into the kitchen.

'There's no back door,' he told her. 'I'll make sure that the heating is OK before I go. There should be plenty of hot water, and the bedrooms are warm. If you get into any difficulties, go across to the hotel and ask for the landlord.'

He watched her warm the pot and then spoon in the tea. 'You look just right here—I thought you would.' Before she could think of an answer to that, he had gone back into the sitting-room, and when she went in he was sitting by Mrs Potts, giving her last-minute instructions as to what she might and might not do.

Tea was a pleasant meal; the doctor showed no signs of hurry on his part, and it was well past five o'clock when he got up to go. Katherine went with him to the door, reluctant to see the last of him.

'It's getting dark, so drive carefully,' she cautioned him.

'You sound exactly like a wife,' he observed, 'so I feel quite justified in behaving like a husband.' He swooped down, scooped her into his arms and kissed her once, very hard. 'I'll see you on Monday morning.'

He got into the car and drove off. Although she was in the doorway watching, he didn't look round or wave. She went back indoors and cleared away the tea things, and then she accompanied Mrs Potts upstairs.

There were three bedrooms, two in the front of the house, which she and Mrs Potts were to occupy and a third beside a splendidly fitted bathroom across the landing. Katherine unpacked for them both, turned down the beds and drew the curtains and, with Mrs Potts in tow, went downstairs again.

Mrs Potts was tired, and Katherine suggested an early supper. 'You sit down for a while and I'll see what there is in the fridge,' she suggested, and went back into the kitchen.

Someone had catered very nicely for their needs; there was a casserole to be warmed up, potatoes already peeled and fruit and custard in a bowl. Katherine found a cloth and cutlery, and arranged the table; while the food cooked, she went to look at the room on the other side of the hall. The dining-room—with a mahogany table at its centre, with four chairs and a small side table. There was a long case clock in one corner, and some charming watercolours on the striped wallpaper. It really was a dear little house, she decided; just the place to come for a quiet weekend. And in the summer one could sail...

'Does the doctor come here often?' she asked.

'Quite a bit, my sister says; likes to get away when he's been busy at the hospital—he's got a boat too. Likes to sail for as much of the year as possible. Of course, Miss Dodie can't bear it here, says it's too quiet for her. Thinks she can twist him round her little finger, but she's wrong there.' She cast a quick look at Katherine. 'He's a good man, too good for her, though I say it as shouldn't.'

Katherine agreed quietly; he was a good man and a splendid doctor—also, he knew how to kiss a girl! Still glowing from it, she reflected that on no account must he do it again, it was too unsettling. Even if she hadn't been in love with him, it would have shaken her; as it was, she wasn't sure if she was on her head or her heels!

There was no point in dwelling upon that; she settled Mrs Potts by the fire with a glass of the port the doctor had said

she must have each evening, and went to the kitchen to cast
an eye over the casserole.

They went to bed really early, for Mrs Potts was tired out
and, although there was television to watch, Katherine felt
lonely sitting by herself. Saturday passed quietly, and Katherine didn't like to leave Mrs Potts alone. But by Sunday,
she had regained some of her energy. The rain had ceased
in the morning, and the wind had died down. Katherine tidied the little cottage, took Mrs Potts her breakfast in bed
and, later, once she had helped her downstairs to sit by the
fire, she got into her coat and headscarf and went for a brisk
walk before lunch.

The fridge was still well stocked; she popped a small
chicken into the oven, peeled potatoes and cleaned sprouts,
and then went to keep Mrs Potts company.

'Ever so awkward, it's been,' averred Mrs Potts, 'me
being ill like this. And everyone's been so kind, I'm that
grateful.' She sounded almost tearful, so Katherine was
constrained to nip across the street and buy a Sunday paper.
They shared it between them while the chicken roasted, and
presently, when they had eaten it, she tucked Mrs Potts up
in her bed for a nap and went to sit by the fire and dream.
A useless occupation, she reminded herself as the afternoon dimmed into a rainy evening, and she washed up the
dinner things, then made tea and went to fetch a much refreshed Mrs Potts.

They watched television in the evening, and after supper Mrs Potts went to bed. 'A whole week of this,' she commented blissfully. 'I feel better already. I'm ever so grateful
to you, my dear, putting yourself out like this.'

'I've not been put out at all,' protested Katherine, 'I'm
enjoying it just as much as you are. This is a super little cot-

tage.' She tucked Mrs Potts into her bed. 'I'll bring you a cup of tea in the morning, but if you need anything in the night, just give me a call.'

The rain had stopped in the morning, leaving a pale, washed-out sky, and sunshine which held no warmth, although it turned the river and the fields into delicate pastel tints. It was cold, too. Katherine cleared away the ashes in the sitting-room, lit another fire, tidied the cottage, and, since she didn't know exactly when she was to be fetched, put a coffee tray ready. She made sure that Mrs Potts was cosily settled by the hearth, and then went briskly down to the river for a last look. She didn't stay long, there was still lunch to prepare for whoever was coming to take her place. The lunch was well in hand when the cottage door opened and the doctor came in, followed by Daphne—whom Katherine had first met at his house, helping with the supper, on New Year's Eve.

If Katherine had been hoping for a leisurely hour drinking coffee and chatting with him, she was disappointed; he drank his coffee, certainly, but beyond examining Mrs Potts and declaring that she was looking better already, and asking in a brisk manner if there were any problems with the running of the cottage, he had almost nothing to say beyond begging Katherine to be as quick as possible since he had an appointment at noon.

A remark which sent her, with a scalded tongue from the coffee, running upstairs to get her case. When she got downstairs again, rather pink in the face, he observed belatedly, 'I'm sorry to hurry you, Katherine.'

She eyed him coldly. 'Think nothing of it Dr Fitzroy. Hurrying from here to there is becoming second nature to me.' And, at his raised eyebrows, 'On the ward, you know.'

In the car, going smoothly along the narrow road to Beaulieu, the doctor said with deceptive blandness, 'You're annoyed?'

'Annoyed? Me?' She ignored her companion's gentle cor-
rection to 'I'. 'Why should I be?'

'I'm treating you like a hired help…?' the doctor said, as
they picked up speed, for the road had widened once they
had passed the park gates.

'But I *am* a hired help,' Katherine pointed out. Usually
a mild-tempered and reasonable girl, she felt decidedly
snappy.

'But not quite in the mood to consider a proposal of marriage?'

'Certainly not.' She wasn't sure whether to burst out
laughing or crying.

'Ah, well, another time.' He sounded positively placid.

'I'm getting tired…' began Katherine crossly.

'Indeed? And so am I, but tiredness was never a good
reason for giving up, you know.'

He was deliberately misunderstanding her; she stared out
at the busy main street of Brockenhurst and said nothing.

When he spoke again, it was to comment lightly about
the weather—the chance of more snow, the prospect of an
early spring. She answered him at random, only half listening, her thoughts in a fine muddle.

He left her at Mrs Potts' front door and drove off at once
with the briefest of goodbyes. She went to her room to eat
a hasty snack lunch before going to the hospital.

It was nice to find that Sister had a day off, and that Andy
was on duty, too. Katherine was immediately immersed in
her mundane duties, which, without Sister breathing down
her neck, she found pleasant enough. The patients, aware

that there was a certain relaxed air on the ward, called across to each other's beds and joked with the nurses, offering sweets and, when it was time to go off duty, proffering their newspapers.

Katherine, back at Mrs Potts', ate the supper waiting for her and repaired to her room to undress, scamper down to the bathroom and then get into bed with a mug of tea and the selection of papers thrust upon her when she had left the ward. She read them from cover to cover, not taking in a word, while she speculated as to what the doctor might be doing. Being very much in love, and having a lively imagination, she pictured him in some softly lit restaurant, dining with Dodie. Or perhaps the girl was at his house, sitting by his fireside, looking prettier than ever in the firelight.

She was not to know that he was still in the hospital, using all his skill to keep alive a young man who had had a massive coronary.

He certainly wasn't thinking of Dodie, nor for that matter of Katherine. Only when he got home at last, and he had eaten the solitary meal waiting for him, did he sit down beside his fire, the dogs at his feet, and allow his thoughts to wander. And they were all of Katherine.

Katherine didn't see him for some days, and then only at a distance, going in or out of the hospital or on the stairs or going along a corridor. And each time she took good care to avoid coming face to face with him.

She had been working when he had brought Mrs Potts back, and she returned one evening to find that lady installed in her kitchen once more, almost as good as new, and anxious to take up the reins of the household again. The talk, naturally enough, was of her week at Bucklers Hard, the comfort of the cottage and the kindness of the doctor, and she constantly referred to Katherine for confirmation of this. 'Kindness itself, wasn't he, Katherine? Driving us there and then fetching you back again, and then coming for me himself, and him such a busy man.'

To all of which Katherine agreed in her quiet voice; he was everything Mrs Potts declared him to be, and he was as distant from her as the stars.

She was on duty at twelve o'clock the following day, and she was met by an intrigued Andy. 'I say,' she began the moment Katherine was on the ward, 'what luck Sister's off duty! You've had a phone call—can you beat it? He was very disappointed that he couldn't speak to you, but he gave me a message. Would you meet him at Snell's for coffee in the morning at half-past ten? He asked when you were off duty, and so I told him. Hope that was OK?'

Edward, back for a few days' leave, thought Katherine; he had promised to let her know when he was back in Salisbury. 'Thanks, Andy, but I must tell him not to phone the ward. What a blessing Sister wasn't here!'

They giggled about it together as they made beds ready for the evening and then went to collect the tea trays. It would be nice to see him again, reflected Katherine. He was good-natured and cheerful and easy-going.

She got to Snell's punctually, her shopping basket over her arm, having prudently done her errands on the way to the café; Edward was a great talker, and she would have to hurry back to get her lunch before going on duty.

Snell's was full, she stood in the doorway, scanning the tables, and presently saw her caller, only it wasn't Edward, whom she'd expected to see, it was her brother, standing up and beckoning her to join him.

She calmed her breath and sat down opposite him. 'Did

you telephone the hospital?' she asked. There was no point in greeting him, for he showed no sign of pleasure at seeing her.

'I did. And if you want to know how I discovered where you were hiding, Mrs Todd saw you a couple of days ago when she visited her daughter.'

'I wasn't hiding...'

'Well, now we know where you are. You must come back, Katherine. Joyce isn't at all well, and the children are too much for her. The least you can do is show some gratitude and repay our kindness.'

She stared at him; he was, if that were possible, more pompous than ever, and his voice was louder and more hectoring.

She said quietly, 'Sorry, Henry, but I'm not coming back. I owe you nothing, and if Joyce isn't well you can afford to get proper help. I have a good job, I'm paid for it and I like my work.' She broke off as a waitress enquired if they would like coffee, and Henry gave a grudging order.

He goggled at her. 'Do you mean to say that you refuse to help your own flesh and blood?'

'That's right, Henry.' She sipped her coffee and he fell silent, bereft of words. 'Is that your last word?'

'Yes, Henry.' She sat composedly watching him and finishing her coffee.

He got up abruptly. 'Then there is no more to be said. Joyce will be bitterly disappointed...'

'So I should imagine.' She put out a hand and caught his coat by the sleeve. 'Henry, you are forgetting—the bill...'

His glare should have annihilated her, but quite failed to do so. He took the bill from the waitress and stalked off to pay it.

Reaction set in when he had gone; Katherine found herself shaking with rage. Her new-found freedom had been, for the moment at least, shattered. There was nothing more he could do, but it had left an unpleasant blot on her day. She had another cup of coffee and pulled herself together, then went back to her room to get her lunch.

It was very nearly time for her to go off duty that evening when she ran full-tilt into the doctor as she was on her way to the ward with some X-rays. She had expected that he would pass her with a brief nod, or even no greeting at all, but he stopped beside her.

'Katherine!' His voice was sharp. 'Why are you looking like that? What's worrying you?'

Naturally she said 'nothing', which was a waste of time, for he gave an impatient grunt and said, 'Don't waste time. I'm busy and so are you.'

She saw at once that she wasn't going to get away without answering him. 'My brother—he found out that I was here—I saw him this morning, he wants me to go back because Joyce isn't well. I said I wouldn't—and he was annoyed.'

His blue eyes studied her worried face. 'There's not much he can do then, is there? You're not afraid of him?'

She gave a surprised look. 'Heavens, no! But he upsets me.'

'A pity I have an engagement this evening. We might have discussed the matter.' He went on smoothly, watching her face. 'I have a date with Dodie.'

She had to say *something*, even if it was inane, 'Well, yes, I expect you have. I won't keep you, she hates to be kept waiting.'

'Yes, she does. Now, *I* could wait for ever for something

or someone I wanted.' Without altering his voice in any way, he added, 'Is *this* the right moment for a proposal, Katie?'

She gave him a startled look and, quite bewildered by his serious face, flew away from him, not slowing her pace until she had put a corner of the corridor between them.

When her days off came, she spent them pottering around the shops, giving Mrs Potts a helping hand from time to time and walking in the cathedral grounds. She had managed to dispel the unwelcome meeting with Henry from her mind; Jason had said that there was nothing her brother could do, and she accepted that with relief. She did her best not to think about Jason, although she wasn't very successful. On the whole, she was glad to go back to work in the morning.

She had just finished bed-bathing a testy old gentleman with a badly injured arm and a nasty temper when Andy came bounding up the ward.

'Matron says you are to go to her office at once,' she breathed. 'Have you done something awful?'

Katherine eased her patient into his pyjama jacket and buttoned it up. 'Me? No.'

'Perhaps she's going to ask you if you would like to do your training?'

'Well, I wouldn't have thought so. Am I tidy?'

'Good enough. Your nose is shining, but Matron approves of that, anyway.'

Katherine made her way down to the office, knocked on the door and was bidden to enter.

Matron sat at her desk, severe, outsized authority, but with no sign of annoyance upon her regular features. 'Ah, Miss Marsh…' She paused at the look on Katherine's face as she saw Henry standing away from the desk, watching her. 'As you see, your brother is here to beg me to release you from your duties, so that you may return with him to look after his wife. I understand that she is gravely ill with anaemia.'

Clever Henry! He had her in a tight corner, but Katherine did her best.

'I think that my brother would do better to get a nurse to look after my sister-in-law. We don't get on very well, and a stranger is often more suitable. Or what about getting her into hospital if she is so ill?'

Matron looked shocked. 'There is, of course, that alternative, but I should have thought that a member of the family, very able to undertake nursing duties, would have been an ideal arrangement.' She paused and, since Katherine said nothing, added, 'Well, might it be a good idea if you were to go with your brother for a day or so and see how things are? If Mrs Marsh is seriously ill, I have no doubt she will be admitted as a patient, and you will be free to return to your duties here.'

'No, I won't,' Katherine said desperately. 'I shall be expected to stay and look after the two children and run the house.'

Matron cast a glance at Henry, standing silent with a resigned look upon his face. Katherine looked at him, too; the two-faced villain!

'I can't force you,' he uttered in a sad voice, and he smiled wistfully.

'I really think that you should go, Miss Marsh. Change into your own clothes and go straight back with your brother. No doubt you can collect a few necessities later on from your lodgings. At least go and see if you are needed.'

Of course she would be needed, thought Katherine furiously. There would be the washing and the ironing and cooking and the children, as well as Joyce. Perhaps she really was ill, though. She would have to go, even if it was only for a day or so, while Henry made other arrangements.

She said, 'Very well, Matron,' and, to Henry, 'I'll be outside in ten minutes.'

'God bless you, my dear,' said Henry. He sounded thankful, but she could see the small, self-satisfied smirk on his face.

She went back to the ward, and found Andy in the sluice. 'I have to go back with my brother; he says his wife is very ill. I don't want to go, Andy, but I can't get out of it. If anyone wants to know where I am, will you tell them? And could you please phone Mrs Potts and tell her I'll be back as soon as I can. I'll explain later.'

She went to the office and reported to Sister, who said crossly, 'I find it very annoying that my staff should be taken from me in this arbitrary manner. Kindly return as quickly as possible, Miss Marsh.'

Katherine got into her clothes, hung her uniform neatly in her locker and went the long way round to the entrance in the hope of seeing Jason. But she didn't see him, although he saw her, standing at a ward window looking out on to the forecourt. Now why, he reflected, should Katie be getting into a car and leaving the hospital when she was supposed to be on duty? He went back to his round, setting aside his thoughts of her until he had finished it, had coffee with the ward sister, given a multitude of instructions to his registrar and gone to the consultants' room, where he sat down and pondered about what he had seen. Presently, he went over to the telephone and rang Mrs Potts, and got scant satisfaction there. After a moment, he got up and went to the surgical block. On the men's ward, his polite request to have a few words with the nursing auxiliary known as Andy met with Sister's lifted eyebrows and a cold assent. He ignored both, and strolled down the ward to where Andy was taking round the dinner trays.

'A word with you, if you please.'

His quiet voice caused her to rattle the knives and forks in her hands. 'Me? You want to talk to me, sir?'

'Indeed I do. I hope you may be able to help me—er—Andy. Why has Katherine left the hospital?'

'She didn't say much, there wasn't time, but she asked me to tell anyone who asked that she had had to go to her brother because his wife was very ill. I suppose it would be to his house, but I don't know. She didn't want to go. Matron sent for her.'

Dr Fitzroy leaned his length against the end of an empty bed. 'Ah—you have been most helpful, Andy. I am indebted to you.'

He gave her a charming smile and left her with a head swarming with any number of exciting thoughts.

Dr Fitzroy went back to the consultants' room and picked up the telephone once more, dialled a number and, when someone answered, said, 'Dick, you have almost everyone along the Wylye Valley, haven't you? Would you check on one of your patients for me?'

He listened without interrupting, uttered his thanks and put down the receiver, glanced at his watch and sighed. He had two new patients to see on women's medical, and then an out-patient clinic starting at one o'clock. He stood thinking for a long minute, and then picked up the telephone and dialled once more. 'Mrs Spooner? Can you contrive a meal which can be dished up at any moment this evening? And I shall have a guest.'

He listened to his housekeeper patiently while she rearranged his dinner out loud. 'That sounds splendid, Mrs Spooner.' He rang off and made his way, placidly, unhurriedly, to the medical wing.

'What exactly is wrong with Joyce?' asked Katherine as Henry drove out of the hospital forecourt.

Henry chuckled. 'You heard what I described to Matron.'

'Yes. Is she in bed? And if she's so ill, why isn't she in hospital having treatment? And if she's at home, why haven't you got any help? You can afford it, Henry.'

He blustered a little. 'Why should I pay a woman to do the work you can do? You are my sister, you owe me something. Besides, Joyce is delicate.'

'What?' Katherine was trying to keep calm, and finding it very difficult. 'Joyce—delicate? What utter rubbish, Henry! She's always been lazy, and so have you.' She heard Henry gobbling with rage beside her, but her new-found independence had given her the courage to voice her opinion. 'It seems that I have no option but to come with you, but I warn you that I don't intend to stay. If Joyce is as ill as you made her out to be, then the best thing you can do is to get her to hospital and get some help in the house. And if she isn't ill, then I shall go straight back to work.'

He said sulkily, 'Well, you can find out for yourself.'

A remark which left her in sudden doubt; perhaps Joyce was really ill, in which case common humanity would force her to stay. Her spirits sank as they stopped outside the gate.

Joyce was in the sitting-room, standing before the nice mirror over the fireplace, putting on lipstick with care. She turned around as Katherine went in. 'Oh, good—it worked. Clever Henry! I'm off to the pub to have drinks with a few friends. You'll find food for the children in the fridge.'

'You're not ill,' said Katherine slowly.

Her sister-in-law turned on her in sudden fury. 'Of course I'm not—just bored to tears with nothing but the house and children and Mrs Todd away. Why shouldn't you have your share of cooking and cleaning?'

Katherine held on to her temper with an effort. 'I had my share,' she said quietly, 'and now I'm going straight back to my job.' But as she said it she heard the car door bang and Henry driving away. She said steadily, 'There is a bus in the late afternoon. I shall go back on that, and don't try and stop me, Joyce. Where are the children?'

Joyce shrugged. 'Upstairs, I suppose. Thank God they'll be going back to school in a few days—there has been 'flu or something, and they've had an extra week. I'm off.'

'You weren't going to leave the children on their own, were you?' asked Katherine.

'Of course not. Knew you'd come, you're a gullible little fool.' She laughed. 'What's known as a soft touch. And don't tell me you're going back now. Your pious conscience wouldn't allow you to do that, would it?'

Katherine turned on her heel and went upstairs. If she had stayed a moment longer, she would have thrown something at Joyce. She had no choice but to stay until she could get the bus just after five o'clock; she must make the best of it.

The children were strangely quiet in a nursery which sadly needed a good clean. She got them to wash their hands and faces, made their beds and tidied the room before going downstairs with them. Joyce had gone, and the kitchen bore evidence of her neglect. The breakfast things were still on the table, and the stove was a clutter of pots and pans.

'Hungry?' asked Katherine, and saw the children's faces light up. She gave them biscuits while she did a lightning clean up, opened cans and made toast and fed them, then settled them to play at the table. There was no sign of Joyce, so she loaded the washing machine and set it going, and then laid one end of the table for the children's tea. The afternoon was waning, and she saw with something like despair the clock hands creeping round to five. There was still no Joyce when she heard the bus go lumbering past.

It was almost an hour later, as the children were finishing their tea, that Joyce came back. She stood in the doorway, laughing. 'Missed the bus?' she wanted to know. 'Now you'll have to stay the night, won't you? And don't expect Henry to drive you back, he's going to some meeting or other, and won't be back until late.' She came further into the kitchen. 'The children have had their tea? Good. I'm very tired, perhaps you'll see them into their beds.' She yawned. 'I think I'll have a really early night myself. Get yourself some supper, and you might bring me up something later on.'

'I'll do no such thing. The children can't cook for themselves, but you can, Joyce.' Katherine turned her back and started to clear the table, and after a moment Joyce went away.

Katherine started to wash the dishes. She longed to drop everything, but how could she? The children were tiresome, ill-behaved and ungrateful, but they were children and needed looking after. She sniffed away threatening tears and stacked the plates with unnecessary violence and a good deal of noise. Which was why she didn't hear the front door bell, nor the voices in the hall. When the kitchen door opened and she turned round to see what Joyce wanted, she saw Jason standing there.

She flung the dishmop into the sink and flew across the kitchen.

'Jason! Oh, Jason, please take me away!' She caught at his coat sleeves with soapy hands, and snivelled into his rock-solid chest. 'The bus went, and I thought I'd have to stay here for ever, and Joyce isn't ill at all—and Henry went away again before I could stop him.' She lifted her head to look at him. 'So sorry,' she said politely, and sniffed mournfully. She would have taken her hands away, but he caught and held them.

'I thought you might be here,' he said calmly. 'Get your coat, Katie.'

Joyce was standing in the doorway, watching them. Katherine brushed past her, put on her coat and found her handbag. 'There's a load of washing in the machine,' she said and added, 'Goodbye, children.'

They scarcely looked up, and Joyce said shrilly, 'You can't go! I'm ill...' But she didn't say any more, for the doctor was looking at her with a detached interest which made nonsense of the words.

He wished her goodnight civilly, nodded to the children and ushered Katherine into the hall and out of the door. As they went down the path, he said casually, 'Sorry I couldn't come sooner. I had out-patients.'

He didn't say any more, and Katherine, unable to think of anything in reply, didn't answer.

Chapter 9

Jason didn't speak again, and it wasn't until he had left Wilton behind and was driving slowly through the outskirts of Salisbury that Katherine said hesitantly, 'If you would put me down by the station, I can walk through to Mrs Potts... and thank you very much for coming for me. How did you know?'

'Your friend Andy.'

'Oh!' She said worriedly, 'Perhaps I shouldn't have left the children—perhaps Joyce *is* ill and didn't want to say so...'

He gave a crack of laughter. 'There's nothing wrong with your sister-in-law, take my word for it. She is perfectly able to look after her own children.'

'Here's the station...'

'So it is.' He swept past it. 'I dare say you had no lunch worth speaking of. I didn't either. We'll see what Mrs Spooner has for us.'

She murmured half-heartedly, and he took not the least bit of notice, but drove through the city until they reached the close and his house. 'I don't think…' began Katherine, making no attempt to get out of the car.

For answer, he undid her seat-belt, got out of the car and came round to open her door. When she got out, very reluctantly, he marched her into the house, all without saying a word.

Once inside, he said, 'Let me have your coat. Ah, here is Mrs Spooner. I expect you want to do your hair, or something of the sort. I'll be in the sitting-room.' He walked away with the dogs crowding round him, and she followed Mrs Spooner to the cloakroom. Once ushered inside, she did her best with her hair and face. She saw her reflection with horror in the looking-glass; it was pale and tear-stained and faintly grubby, and her hair was a mess. She looked a little better when she had finished, but not much, and a faint colour washed over her cheeks as she entered the sitting-room and encountered the doctor's thoughtful stare.

'Come and sit down. There will be a meal presently. In the meanwhile, have a glass of sherry and tell me exactly how your brother managed to get you away from your work.'

She explained in her sensible way, keeping strictly to the facts of it and making no bid for his sympathy. 'I'm sorry I behaved so stupidly when you came,' she finished. 'I was so very glad to see you.'

He said lightly, 'Well, you know the hospital isn't so well staffed that we can afford to lose even one nursing aide.'

A remark which reminded her who he was and who she was too, and uttered in so friendly a voice that she was unable to take umbrage, although it hurt. She said woodenly, 'Well, I'm on duty tomorrow, and I was only away for a few hours. Should I go and see Matron in the morning?'

'I think it might be the right thing to do.' He got up as

Mrs Spooner came to say that the soup was on the table. As they sat down, he said easily, 'Edward is coming next weekend. I dare say he will want to see something of you.'

'Well, I'm supposed to be working long days on Saturday and on Sunday, so I don't think that will be possible.'

'A pity. He likes you. Do you like him, Katie?'

She spooned the last of her soup. 'Oh, yes! He'd be a marvellous brother—but you know that, I can remember telling you.'

'I have a shocking memory,' observed the doctor mendaciously. 'I have to recommend this sole. Have some, will you? Mrs Spooner is a marvellous cook.'

The sole was followed by apple pie and cream. Katherine, who had been quite famished, had a second helping at the doctor's gentle insistence before they went back to the sitting-room for their coffee.

She sighed with pleasure as she poured it; the gadrooned silver coffee-pot, the delicate china cups, set out exactly so on the snowy lace-edged cloth, the little dish of chocolate mints, all added up to an understated elegance which reminded her of her parents' home, a life-style seeming to her to be part of another world, never to be repeated.

She passed Jason his cup and saucer and, since the silence had gone on too long, said, 'You've been very kind, I really am most grateful.'

He smiled a little and sat back in his chair, drinking his coffee, while she sought anxiously for something to say. It was of no use; all she could think of was the fact that she was hopelessly in love with him. She put down her cup, annoyed that her hand shook so that it rattled in the saucer. 'If you don't mind,' she said with a kind of polite desperation, 'I think I had better go.'

The doctor made no move. 'Running away, Katie?' he asked blandly.

It was really too much. 'Yes, if you must know, I am.'

'Am I to know why?'

She studied his face. He knew; she felt cold at the thought, and then went very red. 'You know already.' She got up and started towards the door, but he was there before her, his arms holding her close. She stared up into his face; he wasn't smiling, indeed, he looked almost stern.

'Will you marry me, Katie? This isn't the first time I've asked this question, is it, and you've never quite believed me, have you? But you can't deny your love for ever.'

She said steadily, 'No—but there's Dodie...'

'Shall we forget about Dodie? I have asked you to marry me, Katie. I believe that you love me, perhaps not very much as yet, but love grows if you let it.'

She wanted to tell him that she already loved him so much that it had engulfed her whole life, but she stopped herself in time. She said soberly, 'Well, yes, I think I do love you, Jason, but I don't know you very well, if you see what I mean.'

He laughed a little. 'We'll have to remedy that. I'll not hurry you, my dear. Just get used to the idea of marrying me in the not too distant future.' He bent his head and kissed her gently. 'Now I'm going to take you back to Mrs Potts.'

During the short drive he talked trivialities, opened the door for her, kissed her again, just as gently, and waited while she went indoors. Standing in the little hall, she reflected that he had said nothing about seeing her again, and took comfort from the fact that he wasn't given to unnecessary talk. Of course he would see her again.

She bade Mrs Potts goodnight without going into the

kitchen, and went upstairs to her room, where she sat down on the bed and collected her excited thoughts. It was all her dreams come true, and so—she sought for the word—quietly. She had always imagined that a proposal would be thrilling and exciting, but she hadn't felt either thrilled or excited, only wonderment that it had happened to her, and a great wave of happiness. She went over the whole thing, every word he had uttered, her own words, too. It was while she was undressing that the thought struck her that he hadn't said that he loved her. She worried around the thought for some time, to come to the conclusion that since he wanted to marry her he must naturally love her, too. She got into bed and lay imagining a blissful future until she slept.

It was a dark, wet morning when she got up, but she didn't care about that. Nothing could damp the happiness. She dressed, breakfasted and went out into the miserable morning. The hospital was already in the throes of early-morning busyness, with breakfast trolleys being wheeled through the wards, night staff going off duty and day staff picking up the reins of the ward routine, curtains round the beds of those for operation that morning, and Andy, already there, making up a bed for an emergency admission. She greeted Katherine with her usual good nature, declared that she was delighted to see her back so quickly, and wanted to know what had come over her. 'You look as though you'd won the pools or got yourself a millionaire.'

Katherine smiled widely, but before she could reply one of the senior student nurses came bustling along to tell them importantly to start making beds as soon as possible. 'All right, love,' said the irrepressible Andy, 'keep your hair on! We're women, not machines.'

They began making beds, starting on the other side of

the ward, where most of the patients were in a state to help themselves a little, well enough to read the papers and joke with their neighbours and the nurses. It was while they were making their third bed that the occupant, an elderly man who had lived in Salisbury all his life and professed to knowing everyone and everything there, remarked that there would be a grand wedding before long.

'How come?' asked Andy. 'Anyone we know?'

He took the local paper off his locker and opened it and handed it to her. 'Miss Dodie Grainger,' he told them importantly, 'well-known local upper-crust beauty, as you might say, got herself engaged to Sir Gerald Wilden—he's got a big estate between here and Chippenham—pots of money, too. Done well for herself, she has. I bet she broke a few hearts, too.'

Andy was reading the paper, and when she'd finished she offered it to Katherine, but the sight of Katherine's pale face made her put the paper down. 'I say, love, what's up? Do you feel sick? You look awful. You're not going to faint?'

Katherine forced a voice from a throat gone suddenly dry... 'No, I'm quite all right. It's just that it's warm in here, and it was so cold coming to work, and I didn't have much time for breakfast.' She managed a smile. 'I feel better already.' She smoothed the counterpane, a small, wan ghost of her usual self.

They went steadily down the row of beds, and she listened to Andy's cheerful chatter and answered it mechanically while her unhappy thoughts raced to and fro inside her head. At least she had told no one. Thank heaven for that! She had been a fool, blinded by love, willing to be bamboozled into declaring it, too. Jason had known that; she had been so easily convinced because she had wanted to be. It was as plain as the nose on her face now; Dodie had rejected him for another man, and he wanted to show her that he did not care, even though it must have been a cruel blow to him. What better than to find another girl to marry; show Dodie that he could be happy without her. Only, of course, he *wouldn't* be happy.

She went steadily about her work, only half aware of what she was doing. It was a mercy she was off duty earlier than usual, she would go to her room and get it sorted out for, of course, something would have to be done. She would have to see Jason and tell him that in no way would she consider marrying him. Only not today, she prayed silently. And had her prayers answered when she overheard Sister telling the house physician that it would be no good referring one of the patients to Dr Fitzroy's clinic, because he had gone to Southampton for several days.

The news brought Katherine a respite; at least there was no danger of her meeting him in the hospital, and by the time he returned she would be able to present a cool, level-headed front. Suddenly unwilling to be on her own in her room, she had a coffee at the hospital, and walked home through the main streets, stopping to look at the shop windows without really seeing anything in them.

When she at length got to Mrs Potts' house, she lingered in the kitchen, talking to that lady, to regret it before long when Mrs Potts remarked, 'I see our Miss Dodie has got herself engaged. I always thought she'd set her cap at Dr Fitzroy. I'm sure it was expected, not that he ever did say anything, although she was always hinting.'

Katherine mumbled, 'Oh, really? Well, I must get my letters written...'

'You look tired, love. There's a nice steak and kidney

pudding for supper. Mind you come down for it, it'll put a bit of colour in your cheeks.'

Katherine made tea and then sat by the gas fire, drinking it, but it didn't warm the icy coldness lying like a lump in her chest. She would have to pull herself together. There was bound to be talk about the engagement at supper; after all, Dodie, although not known personally, was known to Mrs Potts through the titbits of gossip she had from Mrs Spooner. When Mrs Potts rang the bell for supper, she went downstairs, nicely in command of herself. It was most fortunate that Miss Fish had witnessed a small street accident that afternoon and insisted on recounting it in much detail, so that most of the meal was eaten to her recital; they were eating their pudding before Mrs Potts mentioned Dodie's engagement, and Katherine was able to utter suitable exclamations to the various opinions of the subject. She was even able to agree that Dodie was a remarkably pretty young woman and would be a beautiful bride.

'All the same,' observed Mrs Potts as they prepared to leave the table, 'I quite thought she'd have Dr Fitzroy.'

'Perhaps he didn't ask her,' said Miss Fish in her dry, elderly voice.

'Why, he's been taking her around for I don't know how long,' protested Mrs Potts, 'and she so free and easy with him, so my sister told me.'

Back in her room, Katherine got out the sweater she was knitting and went doggedly to work on its complicated pattern. Of course, since she wasn't concentrating, the pattern became a nightmare; she was unpicking it when there was a knock on the door. It was probably Shirley, come to borrow tea or sugar, for she never seemed to have any of her own. Katherine called 'come in,' and looked up to see Jason standing in the doorway.

'You're in Southampton!' she gasped, and then, 'Oh, Jason, go away.'

He stayed where he was, eyeing her narrowly. 'I've only just got here,' he pointed out reasonably. 'What's wrong, Katie?'

Despite her best efforts, her voice was shrill. 'Wrong? Everything is.' Her feelings were rapidly getting the better of her. 'Did you know that Dodie was going to get married?'

'Of course.'

'So, to get even because she wouldn't marry you, you wanted to show her that it didn't matter, by marrying someone yourself—me, and what could be easier?' She had stood up, and now she stamped her foot with rage. 'I could die of shame telling you that I loved you…'

He said quietly, 'Will you sit down so that we can talk sensibly?'

'No, I will not. I'm not in the mood to be sensible…'

His face was as calm as it always was, but she sensed anger behind the calm. 'No, I can see that. I'll go, and when you have simmered down and rid yourself of all this nonsense you can come and tell me.'

The anger showed now, although it was tightly controlled. He hadn't moved an inch, but she took a step backwards, something which made him give a short laugh. 'I came racing back from Southampton to be with you, and what do I find? A termagant with her head full of rubbishy fancies.'

'I'm not a ter—termagant…' She wasn't exactly sure what that was, but it sounded unpleasant.

He enlightened her: 'A vixen, a virago, a battle-axe.' He

paused, smiling in a manner to chill her heart. 'No, not a battle-axe, you haven't the shape.'

Katherine drew an indignant breath. 'Go away! I never want to see you again.' And then, because she loved him so much, 'I'm sorry if Dodie has broken your heart, but you need not have broken mine, too.'

He looked at her without expression. 'You know where I am when you want me, Katie.' He had gone, leaving her with her mouth open, ready to deny that she would ever need to speak to him again.

She had a good cry after that, and then sat, her face blotched and her eyelids swollen, and reviewed his visit. Perhaps she should have allowed him to talk as he had wanted to, but she had been upset and very angry. She still was, but the light of reason was creeping in, and she had to admit that perhaps she had been over-hasty, and certainly undignified. She should have been sweetly reasonable, allowed him to make his excuses and then quietly pointed out that she had no wish to marry him. She supposed that only heroines in novels ever did this, but she wasn't in a book, she was flesh and blood and hurt and humiliated, and very much in love, even though she no longer *liked* Jason. She amended this: she didn't like him at the moment.

She got up and made a pot of tea and got ready for bed. There was no point in reiterating her sad thoughts. She got into bed and closed her eyes, but stayed awake until it was almost time to get up.

She was getting ready to go out and shop when Mrs Potts called up the stairs to say that there was a telephone call for her. Her heart leapt; Jason wanted to see her again, despite his unkind remarks about her going to see him. She raced down to the hall and lifted the receiver.

It was Mrs Grainger. 'We're back for a time, dear,' explained the old lady. 'We've been very happy with Tom, but we wanted to come home and see all our friends again. Dodie has found us a very pleasant companion. We would like to see you—could you come to tea one day soon? Tomorrow, perhaps?'

Katherine had no reason not to go, so she agreed to call in on her way home the following afternoon and said goodbye. It was only after she had rung off that she wondered how Mrs Grainger had known where she was. She dismissed the thought, and went back upstairs to get her small shopping list and her purse.

She didn't see Jason that day, but she hadn't expected to, for he had returned to Southampton; she overheard Sister telling the house surgeon that he wouldn't be back until the end of the week. Longing to see him, but determined not to, Katherine went about her work and, when she got back to Mrs Potts' that evening, had her supper and went straight to bed with the plea of a headache.

She had her lunch at the hospital the next day, after she had been on duty for a half-day, so it was well after two o'clock by the time she reached the Graingers' house. Mrs Dowling opened the door to her.

'Well, now, it's a treat to see you again,' she declared, relaxing her stern features into a smile. 'You've filled out nicely, too, though you're a bit pale. Hard work, I've no doubt! Come on in, they're waiting for you. I'll be bringing in the tea a bit early. That new companion's got the afternoon off...' And, at Katherine's enquiring look, 'She's all right, but she doesn't give a hand like you used to.'

Katherine was led through the familiar hall and ushered

into the drawing-room, where Mr and Mrs Grainger were sitting in their usual places on each side of the fire.

They greeted her warmly, and Mrs Grainger launched at once into a rather muddled account of their stay with Tom Fetter. It had been very pleasant, she conceded, but it seemed that his household was a very expensive one to maintain. 'For, of course, Mr Grainger considered it necessary to share any expenses while we were there. But, really, it seemed prudent to return here, for we live very simply ourselves at very much less cost.'

Katherine murmured sympathetically; the Graingers were obviously not lacking in the world's goods, and Mrs Grainger's ideas of living simply were hardly hers; Tom had very likely been getting money from them on one pretext or another, and old Mr Grainger was no fool.

Mrs Grainger, having exhausted Tom Fetter and his house as a topic of conversation, started off again.

'You will have heard about our dear Dodie; the dear girl… done very well for herself, too. She will have a splendid wedding, of course. We always thought that she would marry Dr Fitzroy, but strangely enough he never fell in love with her, although all the other young men did.'

Mrs Grainger turned her gentle face towards Katherine. 'He was always so kind, too, taking her here and there, putting up with her little tantrums, but he treated her like a young sister.' She laughed a little. 'It annoyed Dodie, of course, she liked to think that she could twist any man she knew round her little finger. He's away, you know, but we hope to see him when he gets back. I dare say you see something of him at the hospital?'

Katherine said in a careful, matter-of-fact voice, 'Well, no, very seldom. He is a consultant physician and I'm just a nursing aide on the surgical ward. How did you know where I was, Mrs Grainger?'

It was Mr Grainger who answered her. 'Mrs Dowling told us, and it wasn't all that hard to get hold of you, my dear. You're happy at the hospital?'

'Very happy, and I have a most comfortable room...'

She cast about for something to talk about, and was about to fall back on the weather when Mrs Dowling came in with the tea things, and the little flurry of pouring out, passing cups and offering cakes, made it unnecessary to do more than talk trivialities. Which was a good thing, for she was mulling over what Mrs Grainger had said about Jason and Dodie. If it were true, and there was no reason to believe that Mrs Grainger would tell fibs, then she would have to seek out Jason and apologise. The idea appalled her, and she was thankful that for the next few days he would be away; by the time he returned, she would have decided on what to say, and, what was more important, where. Somewhere she could escape from quickly. She had days off at the end of the week, and the best thing to do would be to go to his house as she came off duty the evening before and then go away for her days off. She had been saving her wages for a jersey suit, and there was enough money to pay for bed and breakfast in some small hotel. Even if he wanted to see her, and she very much doubted that, he would give up after two days, and at the end of that time, she thought hopefully, she would be able to face him if she had to.

She collected her wandering thoughts and made a vague reply to Mr Grainger's enquiries as to her work. Presently, with the promise that she would come again, she took herself off.

She spent a wretched night, reminding herself of all the

things she had said to Jason. She had told him to go away and, what was more, he had done just that, without a backward glance. She burst into tears at the thought. Well, he would see now how little it mattered to her; she would leave the hospital and go miles away and be very successful at something or other—she had no idea what at the moment. She sat up in bed, sniffing and snivelling at the very idea, trying to bring some sense to her unhappy thoughts.

The week went by. If Jason was back, she saw nothing of him and, by the time she was ready to go off duty before her days off, she had convinced herself that he hadn't yet returned. So much the better, she told herself, the longer the time before they must inevitably meet, the better.

'I am, in fact, a coward,' she muttered, changing into her outdoor clothes in the cold cloakroom. He was still away, but she couldn't wait to scurry back to Mrs Potts', pack a case, and take herself off in the early morning, ostensibly to stay with an aunt, but in actual fact to spend her days off in Winchester. Shirley had mentioned casually that there was a small cheap hotel close to the bus station there, and she could spend her days at museums and the cathedral and go window shopping. At least she wouldn't see Jason.

She raced through the hospital, a bundle of nerves, and made for the main doors, to dart through them, straight into Jason's outstretched arms.

'Oh, dear!' said Katherine, aware as she said it that it was a silly, meaningless thing to say. Dodie would have had some witty quip ready on her tongue. She stood, held tight by his arms, staring speechlessly into his face. It told her nothing. She had never known a man, she reflected crossly, who could look so bland. 'I'm going away,' she said rather breathlessly. 'Days off, you know…'

'Yes, I know.' He smiled faintly. 'I thought you might like to know that I'm back—just in case you might have something to say to me.'

'No—yes—no, I haven't.'

'Undecided? A little peace and quiet while you think it over?' He whisked her across the forecourt and into the Bentley, and was beside her, driving away, before she could utter a word.

'I should like to go home.'

'Well, I thought you might.' He was driving round the close, within moments they would be at his own front door.

'I shan't get out,' she spoke very loudly, to convince herself as well as him.

He drew up and turned to look at her. 'Listen to your heart, Katie, my darling girl, and listen to me telling you that I love you.'

'You're not fair!' She sucked in her breath like a child.

'No, I know that, but then, you're such a very stubborn girl. If you had listened to your heart in the first place, and not rushed helter-skelter into a whole maze of silly imaginings...'

'I'm not silly,' said Katherine peevishly.

'Yes, you are, but don't worry, I love you when you're silly, just as much as I love you when you're being fiercely practical.'

He got out, walked round to her side, opened the door and scooped her out. Standing on the pavement before his house, she found her voice.

'It's no use, I won't go in. I'm going away for my days off.' She added, 'But I intended coming to see you after that. I thought I'd be quite—quite sensible by then, you see. You said I'd know where to find you, and I'd have to see you again so that I could apologise—I didn't give you a chance to speak...'

Jason sorted out this speech apparently to his satisfaction. 'Well, since you're here, you might as well come inside and apologise handsomely.'

'No,' said Katherine. It cost quite a lot to say it.

'Well, my darling girl, if you prefer to stand out here in this biting wind, by all means do so. That is, if you don't mind going to the altar with a streaming cold.'

'The altar?'

'I've always fancied the idea of a really quiet wedding, just us and one or two friends. I'll get a licence tomorrow.'

She was conscious of two great arms enfolding her. They felt heavenly, but she said firmly, 'Dodie?'

'My dearest heart, neither Dodie nor any other woman who may have taken my passing fancy means anything to me. But you—the moment I saw you standing there in that old dressing-gown, looking like an earnest mouse with the most beautiful eyes in the world—I lost my heart, Katie, and you have held it in your hand ever since. I never knew that falling in love could be such a devastatingly sudden thing, or so fragile... I hardly dared breathe for fear you might take fright and scamper off.'

'Well, I had thought about doing that. You see, I thought that you and Dodie...'

'Plague take the girl! I love you, Katie, my darling. Will you marry me?'

She said dreamily, 'I fell in love with you in the canteen at the hospital. You'd told them to give me a good breakfast.'

His vast chest heaved with laughter. 'Oh, my darling girl!' He freed an arm and opened his door. 'Come home, my love.'

She held back for a moment. 'You really love me—want to marry me? It's not just a dream?'

'If you come inside, I'll do my best to convince you on both counts,' said Jason, and bent to kiss her.

* * * * *

Keep reading for an excerpt of
The Playboy Doctor's Marriage Proposal
by Fiona Lowe.
Find it in the
Outback Nurse: Anniversary Collection anthology,
out now!

CHAPTER ONE

THE MED STUDENT GAGGED.

'Out!' Linton Gregory, emergency care specialist, vigorously thrust his left arm toward the door, his frustration rising. Using his right hand, he staunched the flow of blood pouring from the deep gash on his patient's scalp. 'And take deep breaths,' he added as an afterthought, softening his terse tone. The last thing he needed today on top of everything else was a fainting student.

Where was everyone? 'Karen,' he called out, breaking his own enforced rule of no yelling in A and E. 'Room two, please, now!' He ripped open a gauze pack. 'Johnno, stick your hand here.' He lifted his patient's hand to his head. 'Press hard.'

'Right-o, Doc, I know the drill.' Johnno gave a grimace.

Linton shone his penlight into the man's eyes, checking his pupils for reaction to light. The black discs contracted at the bright beam and enlarged when the light source was moved away. 'They look OK. Did you black out?'

'Don't remember.'

Linton sighed and started a head-injury chart. 'This is the fourth Saturday in two months you've been in here. It's time to think about hanging up your rugby boots.'

Johnno cleared his throat. 'Doc, now you're starting to sound like the wife.'

He shot the man an understanding look as the familiar ripple of relief trickled through him that he wasn't tied down, that he was blessedly single again. And he intended to stay that way. He raised his brows. 'And yet this time I agree with Donna. Your scalp is starting to look like a patchwork quilt.' He lifted the gauze gingerly, examining the ragged skin edges. 'You're going to need more stitches.'

'Linton?' A nurse popped her head around the half-open door.

'Karen.' He smiled his winning smile. 'Stellar nurse that you are, can you please organise a suture pack and ring X-Ray? Johnno's got another deep scalp laceration. Oh, and check up on the student—he left looking pretty green.'

Her brows drew together in consternation. 'I'd love to, Linton, but the ambulance service just radioed and they're bringing in a crushed arm, ETA five minutes. I've set up the resus room and now I'm chasing nursing staff. The roster is short and half the town is out at Bungarra Station for Debbie and Cameron's inaugural dune-buggy race.'

He swallowed the curse that rose to his lips. 'Keep pressing on that gauze, Johnno, and I'll send Donna in to sit with you until someone can stitch your head.' Three weeks ago his department had been like a slick, well-oiled machine. Now his charge nurse was on unexpected adoption leave and her second-in-charge was on her honeymoon with *his* registrar. Marriage was a lousy idea, even when it didn't actually involve him.

He stripped off his gloves. 'Ring Maternity, they're quiet, and get a nurse down from there to help us.'

'But we're still short—'

'We've got two medical students. Let's see if they've got what it takes.' He strode into the resus room as the screaming wail of an ambulance siren broke the languid peace of a Warragurra winter's Saturday afternoon, the volume quickly increasing, bringing their patient ever closer.

Linton flicked on the monitors and took a brief moment to savour the quiet of the room. In about thirty seconds organised chaos would explode when their patient arrived.

Anticipatory acid fizzed in his stomach. Emergency medicine meant total patient unpredictability and he usually thrived on every stimulating moment. But today he didn't have his reliable team and the random grouping of today's staff worried him.

Andrew, the senior paramedic, walked quickly into the room, ahead of the stretcher, his mouth a flat, grim line. 'Hey, Linton. If Jeremy Fallon is at the game, you'd better page him now.'

Linton nodded on hearing the orthopaedic surgeon's name. 'We've done that already.' He inclined his head. 'Anyone we know?'

Andrew nodded as a voice sounded behind him.

'Can we triage and talk at the same time? His pressure is lousy.'

A flash of colour accompanied the words and suddenly a petite woman with bright pink hair appeared behind the stretcher, her friendly smile for her colleagues struggling with concern for her patient. 'We need Haemaccel, his BP's seventy on not much.'

'Emily?' Delighted surprise thundered through Linton, unexpectedly warming a usually cold place under his ribs.

She grinned. 'I know, I belong in a Flying Doctors' plane rather than an ambulance, although today I don't belong in either.'

'Ben's lucky Emily was driving into town on her day off.' Andrew's voice wavered before he cleared his throat and spoke in his usual professional tones. 'Ben McCreedy, age twenty-one, right arm crushed by a truck. Analgesia administered in the field, patient conscious but drowsy.'

Linton sucked in his breath as he swung his stethoscope from around his neck and into his ears, checking his patient's heartbeat. Ben McCreedy was Warragurra's rugby union hero. He'd just been accepted into the national league and today was to have been his last local game.

The young man lay pallid and still on the stretcher, his legs and torso covered in a blanket. His right arm lay at a weird angle with a large tourniquet strapped high and close to his right shoulder.

'He's tachycardic. What's his estimated blood loss?' Linton snapped out the words, trying for professional detachment, something he found increasingly difficult the longer he worked in Warragurra.

'Too much.' Emily's almost whispered words held an unjust truth as she assisted Andrew with moving Ben from the stretcher onto the hospital trolley.

Two medical students sidled into the room. 'Um, Dr Gregory, is this where we should be?'

Linton rolled his eyes. *Give me strength.* 'Attach the patient to the cardiac monitor and start a fluid balance chart. Where's Sister Haigh?'

Jason, the student who'd almost fainted, looked nervously around him. 'She said to tell you that Maternity now has, um, three labouring women.'

'And?' Linton's hands tensed as he tried to keep his voice calm against a rising tide of apprehension.

'And...' He stared at his feet for a moment before raising his eyes. 'And she said I wasn't to stuff up because she had a croupy baby to deal with before she could get here.'

Linton suppressed the urge to throttle him. How was he supposed to run an emergency with two wet-behind-the-ears students?

He swung his head around to meet a questioning pair of grey eyes with strands of silver shimmering in their depths. Eyes that remained fixed on him while the rest of her body moved, including her hands which deftly readjusted the female student's misapplied cardiac-monitor dots.

He recognised that look. That 'no nonsense, you've got to be kidding me' look. Twice a year he spent a fortnight with the Flying Doctors, strengthening ties between that organisation and the Warragurra Base Hospital. Both times Emily had been his assigned flight nurse.

'Emily.' The young man on the stretcher lifted his head, his voice wobbly and anxious. 'Can you stay?'

Ben's words rocked through Linton. *What a brilliant idea.* Emily was just who he needed in this emergency. He turned on the full wattage of his trade-mark smile—the smile that melted the resolve of even the most hard-nosed women of the world. 'Emily, can you stay? It would help Ben and it would really help me.'

The faintest tinge of pink started to spread across her cheeks and she quickly ducked her head until she was level with her patient. 'I'm right here, Ben. I'm not going anywhere.'

Then she stood up, squared her shoulders and was instantly all business. 'Catheter to measure urine output and then set up for a central line?'

He grinned at her, nodding his agreement as relief rolled through him. For the first time today he had someone who knew what she was doing. He swung into action and organised the medical students. 'Patti, you take a set of base-line obs, Jason you'll be the runner.'

Andrew's pager sounded. 'I have to go.' He gave Ben's leg a squeeze, an unusual display of emotion from the experienced paramedic. 'You're in good hands, mate. Catch you later.'

The drowsy man didn't respond.

Linton rolled the blanket off Ben. 'Emily, any other injuries besides the arm?'

'Amazingly enough, I don't think so. I did a quick in-the-field check and his pelvis and chest seem to be fine.'

'We'll get him X-rayed just to confirm that. Now, let's see what we're dealing with here.' He removed the gauze from Ben's arm. Despite all his experience in trauma medicine, he involuntarily flinched and his gut recoiled. The young man's arm hung by a thread at mid upper arm. His shoulder was completely intact as was his hand but everything in between was a crushed and mangled mess.

'Exactly what happened here?' Linton forced his voice to sound matter-of-fact.

Ben shuddered. 'I was driving to the game down Ferguson Street.' His voice trailed off.

Emily finished his sentence. 'Ben had the window down and his elbow resting on the car door. A truck tried to squeeze between his car and a parked car.' Her luminous eyes shone with compassion.

'You *have* to save my arm, Linton.' The words flowed out as a desperate plea. 'I need two arms to play rugby.'

I can't save your arm. Linton caught Emily's concerned gaze as her pearly white teeth tugged anxiously at her bottom lip. Concern for Ben—she knew it looked impossible.

Concern for Linton—somehow she knew how tough he found it to end a young man's dream with five small words.

'BP sixty-five on forty, respirations twenty-eight and pulse one hundred and thirty.' Patti's voice interrupted, calling out the worrying numbers.

'The blood bank's sending up three units of packed cells and X-Ray is on its way.' Emily spoke and immediately snapped back to the brisk, in-control nurse she was known to be. 'Jason, go and get more ice so we can repack the arm.'

Linton knew Ben's body had been compensating for half an hour, pumping his limited blood supply to his vital organs. Now they were entering a real danger zone. 'What's his urine output like?'

Emily checked the collection bag that she'd attached to the catheter. 'Extremely low.' Her words held no comfort and were code for 'major risk of kidney failure'.

He immediately prioritised. 'Increase his oxygen. Emily, you take the blood gases and I'll insert a central line.' He flicked the Haemaccel onto full bore, the straw-coloured liquid yellow against the clear plastic tubing. 'Patti, ring the blood bank and tell them to hurry up.'

His pager beeped and he read the message. 'Jeremy's arrived in Theatre so as soon as the central line's in place, we'll transfer Ben upstairs.'

Emily ripped open a syringe and quickly attached the needle. The sharp, clean odour of the alcohol swab dominated the room as she prepared to insert the needle into Ben's groin and his femoral artery. 'Ben, mate, I just have to—'

Suddenly Ben's eyes rolled back in his head and the monitor started blaring.

'He's arrested.' Emily grabbed the bag and mask and thrust them at Patti. 'Hold his chin up and start bagging. I'll do compressions.' She scrambled up onto the trolley, her small hands compressing the broad chest of a man in his athletic prime. A man whose heart quivered, desperate for blood to pump.

'I'm in.' Linton checked the position in the jugular vein with the portable ultrasound then skilfully connected the central line to another bag of plasma expander. 'Now he's getting some circulating volume, let's hope his heart is happier. Stand clear.'

Emily jumped down off the trolley.

The moment her feet hit the floor and her hands went up in the air showing a space between her and the trolley, he pressed the button on the emergency defibrillator. A power surge discharged into Ben's body, along with a surge of hope. It was tragic enough, Ben losing an arm. He didn't need to lose his life as well.

Four sets of eyes fixed on the monitor, intently watching the green flat line slowly start to morph into a wobbly rhythm.

'Adrenaline?' Emily pulled open the drug drawer of the crash cart.

'Draw it up in case we need it but he's in sinus rhythm for the moment. Patti, put the oxygen mask back on. We're moving him up to Theatre *now*. That tourniquet is doing its job but there's a bleeder in there that needs to be tied off.' Linton flicked up the locks on the trolley wheels.

'I've got the ice and the blood.' Jason rushed back into the room.

'Take it with you and summon the lift to Theatre. We're right behind you.' He turned to Emily to give her instructions, but they died on his lips.

She'd already placed the portable defibrillator on the trolley and positioned herself behind Ben's head, the emergency mask and bag in her hand. Small furrows of concentration formed a line of mini-Vs on the bridge on her nose as she caught his gaze. 'Ready?'

It was uncanny how she could pre-empt him. She was on his wavelength every step of the way. 'Ready.'

As they rounded the corner he heard the lift ping. Jason held the doors open as they pushed the trolley inside. The silver-coloured doors slid closed, sealing them into a type of no-man's-land.

Heavy silence pervaded the lift. The medical students watched everything in wide-eyed awe. Emily's gaze stayed welded to the monitor as her fine fingers caressed Ben's hair in an almost unconscious manner.

A stab of something indefinable caught Linton in the solar plexus. He shifted his weight and breathed in deeply. Emily Tippett, with hair that changed colour weekly, her button nose with its smattering of freckles that some might describe as cute, her baggy clothing, which he assumed hid a nondescript figure, and her diminutive height, was so far removed from his image of an ideal woman that it would be almost laughable to find her attractive. He exhaled the unwelcome feeling.

But she's a damn good nurse. The doctor in him could only applaud that attribute.

The lift doors slid open. 'Let's roll.' Linton manoeuvred the stretcher out into the corridor. He spoke to the drowsy Ben, not totally sure the young man could hear him. 'Ben, you're going into Theatre now, mate, and Jeremy Fallon's going to do his best for you. You're in good hands.'

The young man nodded. His expression was hidden behind the oxygen mask but his eyes glowed with fear.

Emily squeezed Ben's left hand and then stepped back from the trolley as the theatre staff took over. A minute later the theatre doors slid shut, locking them on the outside.

'What do you think will happen?' Jason spoke the words no one had been prepared to voice in front of Ben.

'High upper arm amputation.'

They spoke at the same time, Emily's words rolling over his, her voice husky and soft.

An image of a late-night, smoky bar with a curvaceous singer draped in a long, silk dress, its folds clinging to every delicious curve, suddenly branded itself to his brain. He'd never noticed what an incredibly sexy voice she had. It was at odds with the rest of her.

He shook his head, removing the image, and focused squarely on his medical student. Warragurra was a teaching hospital and he had teaching responsibilities. 'The X-ray will determine if the arm can be reattached but due to the violence of the impact it's very unlikely. The humerus, radius and ulna will be pulp rather than bone.'

'So what's next?' For the very first time Jason showed some enthusiasm.

'Cleaning up.' Emily turned and pressed the lift call button.

'Cleaning up?' Jason sounded horrified. 'Don't the nurses do that?'

Linton suppressed a smile and silently counted down from five, anticipating the explosion. Every medical student made the same gaffe, the sensible ones only once.

Emily whirled around so fast she was a blur of pink. 'Actually, it's the nurses who supervise the *medical students* doing the cleaning. How else do you learn what is required in a resus room? How else do you learn where everything is kept so you can find it in an emergency?' She folded her arms. 'And if you're really lucky, if you manage to clean and tidy in a timely manner, you might just be allowed near a patient and graduate from running boy.'

Jason's pale face flushed bright red to the tips of his ears as his mulish expression battled with embarrassment.

Linton started to laugh. A great rolling laugh he couldn't hold in. His eyes watered and his body ached. Emily was fantastic. Just the sort of nurse he'd welcome with open arms on his staff. *Just the sort of nurse you need.*

He ushered everyone into the lift and this time the silence was contemplative rather than anxiety charged. If Emily came to work in A and E, so many of his problems would be solved. He could go back to worrying about medicine rather than staff politics because she'd organise everyone and everything. She'd always done that during his rotations with the Flying Doctors. With the resident he'd arranged arriving soon, and with Emily on board, he might even get some time away from work. His fifty-two-year-old father, who had just jetted out after one of his unexpected visits, had accused him of being boring!

Yes, this plan would free him up so he could retrieve his badly missed social life.

Emily in charge would make life very easy.

He started to hum. For the first time in two tension-filled weeks he felt almost carefree. *She might say no.*

He instantly dismissed the traitorous thought. When it came to getting what he wanted he usually achieved it with a smile and some charm. The doors opened onto the ground floor. 'Right, you two,' he spoke to the medical students. 'You make a start clearing up the resus room.'

Emily started to follow them.

'Em, got a minute?' His hand automatically reached out to detain her, his fingers suddenly feeling hot as they brushed the surprisingly soft skin close to her elbow.

She spun round, breaking the contact, her expression questioning as she glanced at her watch. 'About one minute. Why?'

He leaned against the wall. 'Still the same Em, always in a hurry.' He smiled. 'I just wanted to say thank you.'

She twisted a strand of hair around her finger in an almost embarrassed action before flicking her gaze straight at him with her friendly smile. 'Hey, no problem. It was a fun way to spend my day off.' She gave a self-deprecating laugh and shrugged. 'I could hardly walk away and leave you with Jason and Patti, now, could I?'

He spoke sincerely. 'I would have been in deep trouble if you had. You headed off a potential nightmare.'

'Thanks.' He caught a ripple of tiny movement as her shoulders rolled back slightly and her chin tilted a fraction higher as she absorbed his praise.

He flashed her a wide, cheeky smile. 'You said you had fun and we make a great team so how about you come and do it again, say, five days a week?'

The constant motion he associated with Emily suddenly stalled. For one brief and disconcerting moment, every part of her stilled.

Then she laughed, her eyes darkening to the colour of polished iron ore. 'You're such a tease, Linton. Back in February, you spent two weeks bragging to me about your "fabulous team". Where are they now?'

He sighed. 'Love, marriage, babies—the full catastrophe.' The words were supposed to have come out light and ironic. Instead, bitterness cloaked them.

Emily rolled back and forth on the heels of her tan cowboy boots, her brow creased in thought. 'So you're serious?'

He caught the interest reflected in her eyes. He almost had her. 'Absolutely. I'm offering you a twelve-month position of Unit Manager, aka Charge Nurse of A and E.'

Lacing her fingers, she breathed in deeply, her baggy rugby top catching against her breasts.

His gaze overrode his brain, taking control of its focus and sliding from her face to the stripes that hinted at breasts he'd never noticed before. Quickly realising what he was doing, he zoomed his vision back to her face.

Tilting her head to the side, she gave him a long, penetrating look, her eyes a study of diffuse emotion. 'It's an interesting offer.'

Yes! She was tempted to take it on. Life was good. He rubbed his hands together. 'Fantastic. I'll get HR to write up the contract and—'

'I don't think so, Linton.'

Her firm words sliced through his euphoria. 'But—'

'Thanks anyway for the thought.' She rolled her lips inwards and nodded her head slightly. 'So, I guess I'll see you around.' She turned and walked away.

The retreating sound of her cowboy boots on the linoleum vibrated through him. He wasn't used to 'no'. He didn't like 'no' at all.